THOROUGHLY PUCKED

LAUREN BLAKELY

This book is dedicated to Lo and Rae, who knew what I meant to do and made sure I did it.

COPYRIGHT

ABOUT THE BOOK

Picture this. I'm about to walk down the aisle when the groom decides to drop this news on me – he wants to dial it down to just f-buddies.

That's when my brother's **two** pro-hockey playing buddies sneak me out of the church seconds before the wedding march begins. They whisk me away in a convertible and we hit the open road.

But what's a runaway bride to do with a broken heart and a non-refundable honeymoon? Book an extra ticket and take a double honeymoon with two off-limits, totally charming, absolutely gorgeous star athletes who want to lift my spirits.

When we arrive there's only bed in the hotel room.

And it happens to fit three. The goalie, the forward and me.

Looks like I'm about to get thoroughly pucked on my double honeymoon. Talk about lifting my spirits...

DID YOU KNOW?

To be the first to find out when all of my upcoming books go live click here!

PRO TIP: Add lauren@laurenblakely.com to your contacts before signing up to make sure the emails go to your inbox!

Did you know this book is also available in audio and paperback on all major retailers? Go to my website for links!

For content warnings for this title, go to my site.

AUTHOR'S NOTE

Dear Readers,

Since this is a runaway bride storyline, the action MUST take place before the start of the season. While both heroes play pro hockey and talk about it quite a bit throughout the story, the on-ice action does not begin until much later in the storyline, due to the timing of the trip. Rest assured, you'll see hockey scenes...eventually. Until then, enjoy the hockey hotties!

Also, McDoodle Island is a fictional island in Washington State's Puget Sound. It's a mix of Whidbey Island and Vashon Island, both of which are beautiful, outdoorsy, and a little bit whimsical.

xoxo
   Lauren

1

KEEPING IT TIGHT

Aubrey

They say every girl dreams about her wedding day, but who are *they*, and how do *they* know? Did they interview every girl? Also, screw that lie.

I never dreamed of this.

I'm in the musty, wood-paneled bridal room at the non-denominational neighborhood church where my parents were hitched and where my mom still serves as chorus director. I peer down at the lace and tulle dress that feels too long as it grazes my ankles, the diamond solitaire on my ring finger that's a touch too loose, then the princess-cut lace bodice that's too pretty for my taste.

This is someone else's dream for me.

I smooth a shaky hand over my dress, then spin around and meet the gazes of my two bridesmaids—my bookish longtime bestie, Trina, and my feisty and fabulous friend, Ivy.

I put all my energy on them and their unmatching black dresses—I let them pick their outfits because... have you seen bridesmaid's dresses? "You both look amazing," I say, since why focus on me when I can focus on others?

Trina turns it right back on me though, saying, "*You* look beautiful, Aubs."

"It's your day and you're gorgeous," Ivy adds.

I give a big, playful shoulder shrug and pluck at my dress. "This thing? I just grabbed it from a hanger in the closet." I'm the fun one, the loud one, the friendly one. So that's who I'll be right now, dammit.

Trina holds up a hand. "Stop for just a second and listen...You do look beautiful."

It's all too much—these compliments, this dress, this day, these last few minutes before I say *I do*. "Thanks," I say, fidgeting with my ring.

Sensing trouble, Trina steps closer, saying with concern, "You don't seem like yourself, Aubs."

"If you need anything, just say the word," Ivy puts in, then points to the door. "Ride or die."

That offer is far too tempting, but I really shouldn't go there, even in my head.

Aiden's the guy for me. He has been since we went to prom together ten years ago. Since we dated again when he returned to Duck Falls briefly after college. And since my wise old dad with the soft, squishy heart told my mom he thought Aiden would be the perfect husband.

"I'm all good," I say, managing to sound peppy for my friends. I jerk my gaze to the window, staring longingly through the freshly cleaned glass at the parking lot and the white, electric convertible my brother rented for us.

But what if friendly, outgoing Aiden Peters, who returned to town last year to run his family's pie shop, isn't the guy I should marry? My gut churns. I hate making a scene, but surely, Trina and Ivy will have the answer. "Girls, I'm not sure if I—"

The door swings open with a loud *thunk*, the wood slapping the wall behind it.

Ivy flinches. Trina snaps her gaze to the slim guy in jeans and a polo, a smattering of freckles across his fair complexion, his blond hair incongruously messy for today. Aiden's here and he's not wearing his tux.

Ivy whips out an arm, pointing to the door. "Rules, Aiden! You can't see Aubrey."

"And hello? Put your freaking tux on," Trina jumps in, like she can't believe sweet, teddy-bear Aiden forgot to don his duds. "You're getting married in ten minutes."

Aiden plucks at his lavender pastel shirt, like *this thing?* "Actually, I think I look pretty good for today."

I startle, his odd comment and odd demeanor knocking me further off my game. "W-what do you mean?" I stammer, but there's a weirdly shameful hope rising inside me.

"Yeah. What do you mean?" Trina demands.

With his best customer-service-in-a-small-town smile, Aiden grabs the door handle, then shows them the way out. "I promise I'll be quick, ladies. I just need a teeny second with the bride."

Not my bride. *The* bride. That hope rises a little higher.

Trina arches a brow. Ivy practically growls at him, then snaps her gaze back to me. "What were you going to say?"

"I'll tell you later," I say to my friends, reassuring them. Truth is, I'm dying to know why Aiden's here dressed like that. *Dear god, please say he cheated on me. Stole from me. Fell in mad love with the wedding planner and is running away with her.*

They shut the door and it's just us and my big, inappropriate hope. "So listen," he begins, and a few bubbles flow through my veins.

For the record, *listen* is when you know a dude is about to say something dastardly. Why does this fill me with a strange sort of giddy relief?

"I'm listening," I say, crossing my fingers behind my back.

"You're a great girl and all," he says.

There it is. The line that precedes the dump. My heart beats faster. *Bring it on. Tell me you've been making lattes after dark with the coffee shop owner down the block so I can throw things at you indignantly, like that candle on the coffee table or the songbook.* "And you're seriously hot," he says.

Wait. He's supposed to feel guilty as he admits he cheated like a selfish jackass. "You're complimenting me before you—"

"—Yes, I am," he says, so matter-of-factly, and a

little out of character, too, as he steps closer, grips my shoulders, and looks me up and down salaciously. With a long, lingering rumble in his throat, he adds, "We had some good sex, didn't we?"

I blink. Where is his *I'm banging the barista* confession? The *I'm eloping with the wedding planner* proclamation? The *I drained your bank account* blurt-out?

"Okay?" I ask, because did we even have good sex? It seemed middling to me, but what do I know? I'm just a girl with a big vibrator collection.

"And last night when I was out at the piano bar in the city with the guys, all I could think about was you. And how I just couldn't wait for our wedding night. How great the sex would be. How often we'd do it. How much I just, well, let me be blunt," he says, like he's been anything but ultra-blunt in the last three minutes, but he takes a deep breath, then finishes his deep thought. "How much I like sex."

He grabs my bare arm, maybe needing to hold on through his ode to nookie. "But also how little I had of it in high school. *None* is more accurate." He shakes his head over that awful memory. "Same for college. None there too." Another sorrowful shake before he recovers from the hell of his, evidently, barren past. "But now? I can have so much sex now that I'm in my late twenties."

And I'm beginning to see the dots connecting. I wriggle away from the hold Aiden has on my arm so I can get some distance while my erstwhile groom gazes happily out the window. "There's so much sex to be had." He tilts his head as he meets my eyes again. There's a warm kind of seriousness in his expression.

He's buying this bill of goods he's selling. Really buying it. "I think we're both better off exploring that great world out there, right?"

This is how he calls it off? With his explorer dick as his new compass? And me as his...first mate? "You're canceling the wedding so you can have more sex with more women?" I ask with staccato breaths. I need to make sure I'm one hundred percent clear on what he's saying.

Aiden gestures grandly to me, a show of his magnanimity. "And you can have sex too." Tapping his sternum, he adds, "Whatever or whoever floats your boat."

"How generous."

He must miss my sarcasm since he rocks back and forth on his heels and says earnestly, "Thanks." He pauses, like he's gearing up to make a big request. "And maybe *we* can."

What? "W-we? What are you talking about?"

He blows out an appreciative breath. "Well, you know how to keep it tight, after all."

I squeeze my eyes shut, trying to pull myself out of this nightmare.

I'm supposed to be the problem. But I didn't imagine he'd back out so he could *just* fuck me—AND EVERYONE ELSE—instead.

He's definitely the problem now.

When I open my eyes, I try to catch my breath as I collect my thoughts. "Let me get this straight. You don't want to marry me. But you still want to screw me?"

He points finger guns at me. *Bang, bang.* "Tonight even?" Aiden asks, hopeful as he checks his watch. "I decided I'm going to move to Miami. Good thing I didn't move in with you yet, right?"

I have to agree with him there. "Yes," I bite out.

"I was never cut out for this small-town life anyway, so hear me out. What if...we hook up? I've got some neckties from my Catholic school uniform back in the day. You want to be tied to the bedposts, I bet?" He steps closer, gathers some of the tulle near my thigh, fingers it. "I could fuck my former bride tonight. While you're still in this wedding dress. How hot would that be?"

My shock—and my shameful hope—is replaced by red-hot rage. A plume of anger licks my veins. "You actually think I want to be fuck buddies with you?"

His smile is hopeful, a kid asking *please*. "I do."

That is not the *I do* I'd expected. I'm swaying. I'm dizzy. How did this moment go from me imagining him dumping me for another woman, stealing my money, or, I don't know, burning down my house, to him dumping me so he could enter his making-up-for-lost-time era?

He hooks his thumbs into the pockets of his jeans, rocks back on his sneakers. "What do you say?"

Is he for real? But one long glance at his too wide smile, and the genuine anticipation in his eyes, and I have my answer. He means every leading-with-his-dick word. I point to the door, the hundreds of guests beyond. "What do *you* plan to say to all those people in the church? Your parents? How do you think they'll take this? Or my mom? Do you really want to go out there and tell them you're working on your bedroom moves? You're dialing it down? You're breaking out your neckties for a new use?"

Aiden taps his chin, hesitating. "Fair point. Know what? All that time doing hair, you can talk to anyone. You can smooth anything over. I'm gonna pass this one off to you, sweetie pie," he says, then leans in and drops an ambush of a scratchy kiss to my cheek, leaving behind a whiff of wilted lettuce on his breath. He didn't even brush his teeth before he dumped me on our wedding day? Then, just in case this day couldn't get worse, he presses a key card into my hand. "Meet me tonight at eight. Room 131 at the Airport Inn before my flight tomorrow morning."

My head explodes as I throw the card back at him. "You booked an airline ticket out of town *before* you broke it off?"

With zero remorse, he says, "There was only one super-saver flight left when I checked this morning, so I grabbed it. Airlines," he says with a *you get it* shake of his head.

The plume turns into a wildfire, eating all the acreage inside me as I whirl around, grab the song-book, and cock it at his head.

But on his invitation to bone, he's already yanked open the door, and is sauntering out.

A free man.

I can't move. I can't breathe. I can't think. I'm standing in the bridal room, gripping a freaking song-book aimed at his disappearing frame. Out there, a million of my family's friends, including my very eager big sister and my even more eager mother, are waiting for me to walk down the aisle, waiting for my brother to give me away to a getaway groom who's ghosted me.

My brother! That's it.

Garrett's the calm one. Garrett's the cool one. He always knows what to do. I gather my skirt and race across the bridal room, hunting down my clutch purse on an ottoman in the corner, snapping it open with shaky fingers, and fishing out my phone.

As I text him, tears I didn't expect rain down. Hot, heavy, sorrowful tears.

But why the hell am I so sad when *this* is what I actually dreamed of last night?

2

OBJECTION

Dev

Generally speaking, I possess pretty impressive reaction times. Being a goalie and all, it's kind of our thing. But instead of dealing with the nagging voice that's not even in the back of my head—it's at the motherfucking front—I'm standing stupidly in a suit, hanging in the foyer of the church as part of my usher duties, peeking around the doorway at the rows of endless guests, wondering if anyone objects at weddings anymore.

I'd like to object on account of the groom being a douchebag, as I learned last night.

Why am I holding my peace then? At the bachelor party, he sang along with "Single Ladies" like it was his personal anthem then hit on the waitress with a *Hey, babe, give me one last kiss before I get hitched.*

Even though the waitress laughed him off and then he laughed it off, that comment isn't sitting right with me today. Bet it wouldn't sit right with Garrett if he'd been at the table when it'd happened. He was outside the bar, saying goodnight to his twins at the time.

Jaw ticking, I drag a hand through my getting-longer-by-the-day hair, working through the best way to tell Garrett how I feel in, oh, say, the next ten minutes before the wedding march starts, when my buddy Ledger clears his throat from behind me. "I know it's hard to count that high, but by my estimates there are about ten more guests coming. One hundred ninety plus ten still equals two hundred."

Rolling my eyes, I turn his way, meeting his steely blue gaze. "Thanks. I was confused by how math works."

"Happy to help." He hooks his thumb toward the double front doors. "Let's go wait outside to round up the last of the stragglers. Fucking hate tardiness."

"You hate everything."

"Well, I wouldn't have to if most things didn't suck," he says evenly, like that's just the way of the world.

"It's hard being a millionaire athlete, isn't it," I retort, pulling my focus away from how-to-handle-a-dickhead-groom etiquette to rib my buddy. Ledger McBride's a forward for the San Francisco Sea Dogs; I'm the goalie for the recently renamed Golden State Foxes. Technically, that makes us rivals since we play in the same city, but we're friends not enemies.

"Pot. Kettle," Ledger says.

"That's me," I say with more bravado than I feel. My ex liked to say it was hard dating a pro athlete, it was hard being in the limelight, it was hard with me being on the road. Yes, everything about seeing me was *too hard* for her. But that's why Eva's the ex.

Maybe I'm just sour on romance and seeing Aiden through the black-colored glasses I've been wearing lately. I really need to find those rose-colored ones again.

I smooth a hand down my suit jacket, nodding to the front door.

Ledger leads the way. "Let's do this."

Those three words echo loudly. Should Aubrey really do this? Should I say something? I heave a deep sigh as we go, still lost in my head.

"Save the thinking for another time. We need to help G," Ledger says. Garrett asked the two guys he trusts most in the world to be ushers. To handle anything he needed on this important day.

Helping him would also include telling him the truth about the guy his little sister's about to marry, right?

Except something keeps stopping me, a deep-seated worry I barely want to admit. Is Aiden's behavior last night gnawing at me because it was a real problem? Or because I've never thought he was good enough for Aubrey? But I've never thought anyone was good enough for her.

I huff out an annoyed breath. It's time to call in rein-forcements.

I take my post by the door, then say to my friend, "Ledge, what do you think of Aiden? Like, really think of him?"

My longtime hockey friend meets my gaze with an intensely serious one. "You're asking now?"

"Yeah. I'm asking now. Did you see him last night at the bar?"

Ledger scratches his jaw, like that will help him recall the party. "Aiden got shitfaced, but that's what *some* dudes do." His derision makes it clear he's not one of those *some*.

"You were a choir boy at your bachelor party?" I ask the recently divorced guy.

He sneers. "No, I didn't have one. Bachelor parties are dumb. Guys who want bachelor parties shouldn't get married in the first place."

He's...not wrong.

Sure, I like grabbing a pizza and beer with the guys, but I get more than enough of that on the road with the team. Well, low-fat, cauliflower crust pizza since I want to play hockey forever, so I need to treat my body like a high-performance sports car. But last night wasn't a hang-with-the-bros night out. It felt more like a how-to-cheat-on-my-new-wife tutorial.

"But what's really bugging you? Aiden getting wasted before his wedding? Or something else?" Ledger asks, cutting to the chase.

Outside the church entrance, on a perfect summer day in California, as the last few cars pull into the lot, I weigh the cost of telling...anyone. I don't want to come across like I've been thinking too hard about Aubrey, or like I've ever looked at her as more than my best bud's sister. Garrett's my agent, too, and crushing on his sister is just asking for trouble. I don't need to make my neat, orderly, firing-on-all-cylinders hockey life messy in any way whatsoever.

But that guy Aubrey's marrying makes my skin crawl, and he has since I met him last year. He reeked of *too friendly* then too. "He was hitting on the waitress last night," I hiss.

His lips twist in a cruel frown. "Guys like him…"

I scrub a hand across my beard. "But is it my place to say something to G or to Aubs?"

Ledger's older and wiser, a mentor to both Garrett and me, a role he's played since his dad coached all of us back when we were younger. He pinches the bridge of his nose, quiet for a stretch, mulling this over. "Probably should," he finally says with authority, but before I can hunt down Garrett, the side door to the church swings open, and a blur of lavender and denim sprints down the steps.

I squint. "Wait. Is that…?" The dude races across the parking lot to a little pink truck with polka dots and the words *Peter's Pies* stenciled on the side. In no time, he's backing up and peeling out of the lot. "What the hell is the groom doing taking off less than five minutes before the wedding?"

"I don't think he's delivering a last-minute pie order," he says heavily.

Seconds later, the distinctive sound of footsteps slapping on tile grows louder, and Garrett comes racing out that same side door, swinging his gaze from left to right, then landing on us. He runs over, determination etched on his face.

Pointing at the building behind him, he speaks in

his low, always-in-control, I'm-your-agent-and-this-is-what-you-must-do voice. "You need to get my sister out of there, stat. That asshole just left her at the altar, and I have to handle the guests. You guys take care of Aubrey."

And sometimes, fate steps in for you and you don't have to say *I object*.

When Garrett hands me the key fob to the convertible, I don't think. I *do*. As he trots back around to the front of the church, I spin to face Ledger, tossing him the key. "Drive," I tell Ledger, pointing to the *just married* convertible. "I'll get the bride."

With a crisp nod, he palms the keys.

Powered by this new game plan, I hightail it to the side of the church, rush down the hall, and push open the door to the bridal room. Aubrey's standing by the window in the corner, staring out the glass. She turns in slow-motion, her hand clutching a tissue and a tiny purse. Big, soft red curls frame her face, which is ashen with shock and maybe even shame. Her mascara's a little smudged, her cheeks a little red. But there's something like a gleam in her big brown eyes. Something I can't quite read. Now's not the time to figure it out though.

"Hey," I say softly. She's got to be hurting. "We're here to help."

"He just wants to be...*buddies*," she says, east of deadpan, just south of dry, as she sketches air quotes.

Ah, fuck.

"He never deserved you." I should have said something last night. She's still in shock, but I do something now. I scoop her into my arms, stealing her out of the church in time to spare her all the embarrassment, racing to the waiting convertible where Ledger has his foot on the gas.

"We've got you," I tell the bride as I set her down in the passenger seat. I hand her my own sunglasses from inside my jacket pocket and jump into the back seat.

"Step on it," I tell Ledger.

"Done." He floors the accelerator and the car races off.

We're out of there.

3

HER GREAT ESCAPE

Ledger

Driving is easy.

Figuring out what to say to someone whose fiancé left her at the altar? Now that's rocket science.

Seeing as my top two skill sets involve shooting pucks when the opponent least expects it and never overwatering my plants, I keep my mouth shut as I cruise along the winding country road away from the church.

As I maneuver this sweet ride onto the main drag in Duck Falls, there's really no need for words either, since Aubrey's staring at the side of the road, her gaze behind Dev's aviator shades locked squarely on the sights whipping by—the signs for nearby vineyards, the busy shops, the bustling sidewalk. As the wind rustles her veil, she's looking more pensive than I'd have expected.

But what did I expect?

I've never given any thought to how a jilted bride would behave post-jilt. Now that it's top of my mind, my gut says tears streaming down her face, makeup ruined, and shoulders convulsing would be on the menu. Sure, her cheeks seem a little splotchy, like maybe she's just cried, but there are no waterworks coming from the passenger next to me right now.

Just a stark sort of silence.

It's eerie.

What the hell do I do with a broken-hearted bride's silence? I barely knew how to handle the divorce papers Marla served me more than a year ago, along with a cup of her tears, lamenting how we'd grown apart, and how she needed to find someone *more available*.

I'd hated her crying too, so I'd shut up and signed the papers. Only to find out later they were crocodile tears.

Dev doesn't break the silence either. That's odd, since he's a chatty one. But maybe he knows how to handle runaway brides and silence is the way? Wouldn't be surprised if he read an article on it recently. Something his parents sent to him in one of their daily emails.

Mine don't send me shit like that, so I keep my eyes on the road and my hands on the wheel, stealing occasional glances at Aubrey.

She's still unreadable, but she's got to be seconds away from another round of tears. Doesn't matter that she's been tough when I've seen her at family events, like Garrett's barbecues, where she was always asking if anyone needed another drink or scoop of potato salad, or a fresh set of bags for a round of cornhole. Or at the arena with him, when she'd taunt the opponents on the ice. Heckle queen, we'd called her.

But that toughness doesn't matter now. Nobody wants to be dumped on their wedding day.

I focus on the mission Garrett gave me. *Get her far away from that prick.* I owe him the world, and helping his sister is the least I can do to help the guy who makes my career possible. I flash back to last night, wishing I'd seen the signs at the party. Only I was too caught up in the same swirl of thoughts that have been chasing me all summer—this fucking knee.

At least Aubrey learned the truth of Aiden's cheating ways before she said *I do.*

As I slow at a light near the highway entrance, the electric motor in the car lulling to a space-age hum, the quiet still hangs over us, and really, it's only polite to ask what's next. I turn to Aubrey, a little wary of how she'll take any kind of convo right now. But I've got to ask. "North or south?"

The question feels weighty too. More important than a simple "which way do I go" ought to feel. North means we're cruising farther away from home. It means we're spending the rest of the day together and I'll need to take good care of her for several hours. South means returning her to the city, forty-five minutes from here. Both have their pros and cons. Especially since I have no clue if Aubrey wants me to be more emotionally available or less emotionally available, or something else entirely. I don't fucking know at all, but one thing

I'm certain of—given my history, I'm no good at relationship advice, so I sure hope there won't be too much advice I need to dole out if Aubrey chooses door number one.

Bracing myself for her answer, I snag the chance to study the woman in the passenger seat, all lace and tulle, and teeth worrying away at the corner of her lips.

But hold the hell on. Is that worry or something else? Something like...restrained delight as she draws a contemplative breath?

She turns to me in slow-mo, and there's not a shred of pain in her brown eyes. With an impish shrug, she declares, "North."

"What the lady wants." When the light changes, I gun the engine.

As we cruise along the highway, the corners of her lips curve into a bigger grin. "Maybe a little faster," she says.

"You an adrenaline junkie?"

"Considering it," she says, smiling more.

"Okaaay," I say, still treading lightly. Maybe she's in shock and it'll all hit her later.

Dev chuckles in the back seat. "You heard the woman."

"Yeah. Step on it, Ledger," she says, sounding downright giddy now.

That's surprising, but maybe it's a sign? Perhaps this escape isn't such a bad thing for her? Or maybe she's laughing before she cries?

No clue.

In a heartbeat, I'm speeding past seventy, barreling

toward Wine Country. As much as I'm down with silence, I'd still like to know what the hell is going on in the head of our guest of honor. A little intel would be nice so I can do my job today. "You in the mood for a wine tasting, Aubrey?" I shout against the wind. Maybe I can gage how she's doing that way.

She snort-laughs, but she doesn't answer the question. Instead, she asks one. "Can you ride a roller coaster?"

That's random. "Yes. I'm tall enough."

She turns back to me, rolling her eyes as the wind whips past us, kicking up the ends of her veil, so it flits around her jaw. "I meant are you guys allowed to? With your contract?"

"It's not skiing, hang-gliding, skydiving, or moped riding, so yeah." Dev rattles off some of the hockey contract no-can-dos.

"My dad was obsessed with amusement parks," Aubrey says, gazing into the distance again and seeing something, maybe the memory of her father. My heart squeezes. Garrett misses the guy too. "He used to take us when we were kids. Since I'm the youngest, he let me pick the order. We rode everything. Every single ride."

"Sounds nice," I say. My life as a kid was all hockey, all the time. My path has been crystal clear from the moment my dad took me skating when I was four. If there's any truth to his story, I was a natural. Soon, though, my path's going to become all kinds of blurry.

My jaw clenches. Don't want to think about the season coming up, or the way my knee barked when I went for a run the other day.

Aubrey goes quiet again. Dev's surprisingly quiet too. When I peek in the rearview mirror, his head is down, bent over his phone.

I want to smack him for scrolling mindlessly at a time like this. But I don't want to make this moment about digital etiquette, so I ignore his distracted ass, mentally cycling through options for the rest of the day. Maybe there's an amusement park we could take her to. But before I can even suggest it, Dev shouts victoriously, "The Ultra Blast Amusement Park is two miles away. Want to go?"

Aubrey thrusts an arm in the air, like a rocker salute. "Let's do it!" Then she shakes her head, like she's forgotten something. "If you guys want to, that is? Are you up for it?"

She's seriously asking *us* what we want to do on her worst day?

"Anything you want," I answer, then Dev leans forward to add, "I'm all in, Aubrey."

"Good," she says, then lets out a strangely contented sigh, her shoulders relaxing as she leans back into the seat, settling in.

Huh.

Maybe Aiden Peters' exodus in his pie truck wasn't entirely the worst fate for the bride today. Don't know if that's because of her ex's behavior last night or some other reason entirely.

I don't really know Aubrey well. For more than a decade, I've kept my distance from the little sister of my best friend who also happens to be my agent. I've got enough trouble in my life. Don't need to invite more in the form of a dangerously pretty redhead with a smart mouth, a passion for sports, and a fiancé.

Make that…a former fiancé.

I'd like to punch that asshole. I'd like to tell him he'll regret the day he ever hurt Aubrey Emerson.

But as I steal a glance at her, I can't help wondering —did he hurt her? Or…help her?

I noodle on that for another mile or so, until I see the sign for Ultra Blast and turn off the highway, slowing my speed on the street. But the wind whips up Aubrey's hair again and blows her veil right across her face, lacy fabric smacking her cheeks, sticking to her lips. She bats at it.

"Let me help—" I say when lace flies past my face. Out of the corner of my eye, I see the fabric skitter across the sidewalk, then divebomb over a railing and tumble into a stream below. I grip the wheel harder.

"My veil!"

The urgent cry is the first sign of devastation from the jilted bride today. Also, it's one-hundred percent real. Nothing fake in her reaction and no crocodile tears there.

I do what any problem solver would do—yank the car into the parking lot of a nearby 7-Eleven.

Barely pausing to turn off the motor, I fling open the door and tear down the hill.

4

DO THEY HAVE FLIP-FLOPS AT 7-ELEVEN?

Aubrey

Don't cry over a veil. Don't cry over a veil. Don't cry over a veil.

I gather up the fabric of the skirt of my dress, repeating the words as I rush down the hill. But it's no use—the tears are freaking waterfalls down my cheeks, and I can't stop chanting *my veil, my veil, my veil.*

I have to get it. I can't let it drift away downstream. It was my grandma's, and it was my mom's, and it was my sister Claire's, and Claire gave it to me a month ago, all reverent and serious as she said, "Dad asked me to set this aside for you a while ago. He knew it'd make Mom happy to see you in it."

I took it then, even as the knot twisted in my throat, even when I had to look away from her earnest eyes.

I can't lose the family veil. My heart slams against my rib cage as I grip the tulle in the skirt, tug it higher, then take a few more steps down the hill. Ledger's hell-bent on saving the veil too. He's a tall blur of black suit and determination as he races down the grassy hill, dodging small shrubs with pink and white flowers on his path to the water.

Through my annoying torrent of tears, I can just make out a flash of white lace slipping amongst the wet stones in the stream, bobbing on the surface, about to be sucked under.

"Oh god," I moan, and it sounds like a cry ripping from my soul.

I have to get it. I swallow my stupid sobs, buckling down as I reach for my even stupider satin pumps and sling them off, tossing them I don't even know where. I pop back up, ready to fly down the grass the rest of the way, when I spot the tall, strapping man wading into the water.

Holy shit.

Ledger's taking big, hearty steps in the stream, pushing against the current, hunting that mother-fucking veil like it's a puck he intends to own. In three seconds, he reaches it, bends, and plucks it from the watery depths.

Behind me, Dev applauds. "Dude! If you were that fast in the morning, I'd never pass you when we go out for a run."

He jogs down the hill, stopping next to me, while in the middle of the creek, Ledger flashes Dev a fuck-off grin and flips him the bird with his free hand. "I *let* you pass me so I can run alone."

"Whatever you tell yourself to sleep at night. Also,

fuck yes. Well done," Dev says, his jeers turning fully to cheers.

I should cheer too.

But I can't stop crying. I'm a hot, sobbing, frustrating stew of ridiculous emotions as I sink down onto the grass right in front of one of those pretty shrubs. Ledger strides out of the water in his black suit, looking a little Colin Firth-y in *Pride & Prejudice*.

Too bad Ledger's white shirt isn't sticking to his chest.

Wait.

Why the hell am I thinking about Ledger's chest while I'm trying to dry up my tears? I'm supposed to be sad.

I *am* sad, dammit.

When Ledger flops down beside me, handing me the waterlogged veil, it's not sadness I feel. It's relief I didn't lose something important. I clutch the wet veil to my chest, not caring that my dress is a mess. My shoulders are heaving with the remnants of my Tear Extravaganza Brought To You By A Totally Fucked Up Wedding Day. Dev sits on my other side, offering me a tissue.

Does he carry tissues all the time? Or did he pack it especially given the circumstances?

"Thanks." I take it gratefully and wipe my eyes under the shades, then my cheeks. After a few deep breaths, I mutter, "I'm sorry, guys. Sorry for crying like this. Normally, I'm more fun. I swear."

Ledger shoots me a look like I'm nuts. "You're allowed to be sad today," he says gruffly.

"Yeah. You're allowed to feel anything. Say anything," Dev seconds with genuine sympathy.

Right.

Of course.

They think I'm sad my ex ditched me minutes before I promised to love him forever. They don't know I'm *mostly* secretly glad Aiden walked out. They have no clue about the playdough mix of emotions inside me. They don't know I'm dancing a jig while also feeling ridiculously stupid, while battling all this guilt, while wanting to kick Aiden in the balls for being a total fuckcake and booking a flight hours before he ditched me.

All they know is I'm hysterical over something as inconsequential as a piece of lace. I cradle the veil tighter and take off my shades, setting them in my lap. "It's a family heirloom," I explain, my voice still heavy with emotion. I don't say anything more. I don't want to admit how I really feel about today. "Thanks for getting it," I say to Ledger.

His blue eyes, normally steely, soften the slightest bit as he squints against the sun, then gives a crisp nod. "No problem."

I turn to the guy who carried me out of the church in his arms. "And thanks for rescuing me."

"Happy to do it," Dev says, then gestures to the water streaming by. "And I'm happy Ledger hustled like I've never seen before."

"She needed the veil. I got the veil. Case closed."

My gaze strays to Ledger's wingtips. My breath stops. "Your shoes are sopping wet. They're ruined. I ruined them. God, I'm a mess," I say, then I drop my head in my hands, and for a hot, awful second, tears sting the backs of my eyes.

But they don't come.

Instead, something ignites in my chest, then glows brighter, bolder, and sparks into a loud, joyful laugh.

Soon, I'm cracking up on the side of a road, gripping my veil while I'm parked on my ass in a white wedding gown covered with grass stains. Flopping down on my back, I stretch out in my dress and stockinged feet, right next to my older brother's two best friends. I stare up at the wide-open sky and all its endless blue, enjoying the view immensely, feeling lighter at last.

I can't believe I was about to walk down the aisle.

I can't believe Aiden left me so he could screw other people.

Mostly, though, I can't believe I broke down over a piece of fabric. "Did I really make you chase after a veil?" I ask in between more laughs over my own ludicrousness.

Ledger tilts his head at me, quirking one eyebrow, his gaze full of intrigue. "Honey, you didn't make me do anything. I chose to chase a veil," he says, all gravelly and matter of fact.

But it's the *honey* that stops my pulse. Did he just give me an affectionate nickname?

Yes, yes, he did.

I sit up. The tightness in my chest has vanished. I look down at my wedding dress with its messy hem, the skirt streaked with dirt and dusted with little twigs. My tiny ankle tattoo of a bird is visible through the white sheer stockings. If only I had my lace-up black boots on. They're in the trunk though. I'd asked Garrett to put them there for the reception at a nearby restaurant because I hate dancing in heels.

The reception. I groan silently. I don't want to mention yet another problem to my two knights. But what am I going to do with hundreds of plates of chicken and rice? With all that cake? With the wedding singer? With my mother and her wishes for today? My stomach dips, but I don't want to think about any of it right now. "Well, thank you. I appreciate it. And I will get you some new shoes," I say, apologetically.

He waves a dismissive hand. "Nope. I knew what I was getting into." He gestures to the stream. "Water."

I glance around at the hillside. "And looks like I watered this bush here with my tears, so maybe I helped the earth today," I say, trying to make light of things.

Ledger tips his chin to the white and pink flowers. "Oleander doesn't really need water. That's why they plant it on highways and the sides of roads."

With an aggrieved groan, Dev cuts in. "What he means to say is *thanks for thinking of the plants*."

Ledger stretches, reaching for the ends of his pants to roll up the water-soaked cuffs. He doesn't thank me for thinking of the plants, and that's A-OK. Instead, he says, "They're also poisonous so don't eat them."

"Useful intel if we were on the run from all of humanity," Dev replies.

"Don't knock zombie apocalypse prep, Dev," I say,

and I'm tempted to nudge him in solidarity for teasing the man I'd long ago nicknamed Stern Brunch Daddy. Just the right amount of disciplinarian when you want him to be.

But I'm not sure we're at that level yet, even when Dev says, "You're right. Ledger will be helpful as our amateur botanist when we run from the brain-eaters."

With a sigh, Ledger adds, "If we're going to get to the amusement park, I better buy a new pair of flip-flops now." He points to the 7-Eleven one hundred feet away.

"Do they have flip-flops at 7-Eleven?" Dev asks.

Ledger shrugs, like *fuck if I know.* "Guess we'll find out."

"Sounds like an adventure," Dev says to me. "You like adventure?"

I haven't been on an adventure in ages, it seems. Aiden never wanted to have an adventure. "Love it," I say.

Ledger rises to his feet, making quite a sight in black wingtips, socks with illustrations of mushrooms under the words *Don't Shiitake On Me*, and his soggy pants rolled up to just under his knees.

It's weirdly sexy. Because of *why* they're rolled up.

For me.

Dev stands next, offering me a hand. As I take it, the ring on my finger catches my attention again. I'll need to deal with that soon. There's a long list of things to deal with—the collateral damage to the lives Aiden and I were about to mingle.

Shoving those thoughts away, I let Dev pull me up

so I'm between them, the ushers who ushered me out. I can't even imagine what's happening at the church, or how many texts are blowing up my phone inside my purse on the floor of the car—calls from my mother every two minutes, messages from my friends checking on me. My stomach somersaults at the thought of the explanations I owe my guests and my family.

Including the ones I owe these guys.

As the water gurgles nearby, the afternoon sun shining brightly behind us, I'm tempted to tell them the truth—that I'm not entirely a jilted bride.

But I could barely tell Trina and Ivy all my what-ifs less than an hour ago. I shouldn't blurt out to my brother's two best friends *and* top clients that I didn't have the guts to even be a runaway bride.

I just...got lucky. Or as lucky as one can be when being left by a guy who's angling for more nookie.

And I'm not going to ruin our adventure with a big old truth bomb. As I head up the hill, I grab my discarded heels and slide them on, then head to the store, but along the way, Dev whispers, "You might want to..." He draws an air circle around my face.

For some reason—maybe that he noticed, or maybe because I didn't even like the wedding makeup—his observation loosens something else inside me. Unlocks another layer of freedom.

"Then I better go wash off my makeup while my getaway driver hunts for new shoes," I say, and it feels like the three of us are in cahoots today, especially when Dev flashes me a smile, then says, "Slurpees on me."

5

TRASH THE DRESS

Aubrey

Fifteen minutes later, I leave 7-Eleven with my face scrubbed free of makeup, carrying a pound of Twizzlers, a cherry Slurpee, my veil, and a Sharpie in a bag.

Ledger is wearing Crocs with his rolled-up suit pants and popping gummi bears into his mouth. The other guy is noshing on baked chickpeas, his suit jacket slung over his arm, the sleeves of his dress shirt rolled up, revealing seriously strong forearms.

I'd be lying if I said I didn't check out Dev's arms as we walk back to the car. Or Ledger's hands as he reaches into a bag, tosses a red bear into the air, and catches it frog-style on his tongue. An arrow tattoo curves across the light skin of his wrist. I bet that hurt when he got it. I bet he didn't even flinch under the needle.

But I should stop checking them out. I definitely

should stop. The last thing I should be thinking on my former wedding day is that my brother's best friends are hot. About the hotness of any guys, for that matter.

"I guess we have our answer. They sell Crocs," I say, then hold up my Slurpee. "And this is better than champagne."

Ledger proffers an orange gummi, lifting it high in the air. "And this is better than wedding cake."

"I don't know. The cake is pineapple-flavored," I say.

"Who gets pineapple wedding cake?" Dev asks with a snort.

"There was a mix-up with the caterer," I say. "So I said I'd settle for pineapple wedding cake."

Dev stops a few feet from the car, meeting my gaze with intensity in his green eyes. They're flecked with gold—sometimes they look green, sometimes hazel. Mercurial eyes. "Don't settle when it comes to cake or men. You hear me, Aubs?"

My chest warms. "I hear you."

"But is pineapple cake settling?" Ledger muses. "It sounds kind of good to me."

Dev tilts his head, seeming to consider the proposal for a beat, then agreeing. "You know, it kind of does. But it's not on my diet." He fishes into the chickpea bag and munches on one, and as we reach the car I'm struck by the *Just Married* sign dangling from the trunk.

Well, that won't do.

"Allow me to handle this," I say, then uncap the marker I just bought, kneel, and fix the sign.

I cross out *Just Married* and instead I write... *Runaway Bride!*

It's not entirely true, but it feels true enough.

The trouble is a runaway bride can't exactly ride a roller coaster in a wedding dress. "I can't wear something this long to the amusement park."

Dev crinkles his nose. "Do you want to go...shopping?" It sounds like he's gargling dishwasher detergent.

I can't resist teasing him. "The outlet mall is a couple miles away. You guys want to go?"

"Sure," Ledger says, like, if there's a fate worse than wearing Crocs, he's found it in shopping.

Dev winces then pastes on a fake smile. "Whatever you need."

Ha! I've found Dev's kryptonite. He dreads commerce. But he loves helping more.

I have another plan though. But first, I need better shoes. "Can you pop the trunk?" I ask Ledger.

Fishing out the key fob from his pants, he complies. I root around inside my bag and grab my black lace-up boots my brother left for me. I'm going to owe him a lifetime of babysitting his twins for saving me today.

Hopping on one foot in the parking lot, I yank off a satin pump and toss it in the trunk. Then I tug on a boot and tie it up. I flamingo my way through the next one, then chuck the other white heel in the trunk too.

After slamming it closed, I clomp over to the passenger side, grabbing my purse from the floor of the car. "I'll be right back," I tell the guys.

I march into the store and grab what I need, paying with my phone and ignoring the messages that have lit up the screen like a Vegas slot machine.

I leave the store and find both men standing on the sidewalk, looking a little perplexed, until I wield a pair of scissors. I park my butt on the hot concrete. "Sometimes, you just need a new style."

Concern flashes in Dev's eyes. Ledger's too. Maybe they're worried I freaked out over a veil but am somehow willing to murder all this lace. "I bought the dress myself. This isn't an heirloom," I explain.

Dev's expression flashes with understanding. "You're gonna trash the dress."

I'm impressed he knows what that means. "Yup."

Ledger shoots him a curious look. "What is that? Is that a thing?"

"It was this whole trend for a while," Dev explains as I gather up the material. "The bride ruins the dress on purpose after the wedding while a photographer snaps pictures. The bride and groom run through the ocean, or get covered in paint. Or they stand under a waterfall with her in the dress. Or she's caked in mud in her dress on the side of the road, and he kisses her."

While I snip the first chunk out of the dress, Ledger asks Dev, "How do you know that? You keep up on wedding news?"

"It's not wedding news. It's just news. And yes, I keep up on it. Try reading a paper once in a while."

"A paper? How old are you?"

With the scissors, I bite off another satisfying heap of lace and tulle.

"Dude," Dev says. "I'm five years younger than you! And they have papers online. There's this thing called the Internet."

"And here I thought the Internet was a portal to doomscrolling hell," Ledger says, then they go silent.

For several seconds, I hack up the dress, only stopping when I realize they're staring at me. I look up.

"Whoa," Dev says, a little astonished.

"Holy shit," Ledger seconds, sounding impressed.

Pride radiates through my chest, down my arms to my fingertips. I might not know how to pick men, but give me a pair of scissors? Your girl is a gold medalist. I'm feeling pretty damn good about my handiwork so far. "Not too bad?"

Dev's eyes are wide, his lips parted. "You're a scissor virtuoso."

That gives me an idea. Who doesn't find ripping a sheet in half satisfying? This hits a similar nerve. I waggle the scissors at them. "Want to help?"

Dev raises a finger. "Would you want a pic of you trashing the dress?"

I want nothing more. "Yes!"

Dev dips into his pocket and grabs his phone while I offer the scissors to Ledger. "Want to slice some more off?"

With a *when in Rome* shrug, Ledger kneels in front of me, taking the tool, then wincing for a quick second. Maybe he knelt on a rock? But that flash of pain is gone almost as soon as it appeared. I gather up some of the material from the back of the dress, then twist it around to the front. "Start here."

"Got it," he says, studying the fabric for a beat before he takes the hunk of material, grazing my thigh. A little charge of electricity shoots up my leg.

That's nice.

But he flinches, then freezes. Great. Just great. He's weirded out by touching me. That would be my luck today.

Ledger doesn't even raise his face. He's frozen in place, staring down at my thighs while I look at his short, dark hair. It's different from Dev's. Different from Aiden's. A clean, neat look.

I like it, but that doesn't matter. I don't want him to be uncomfortable. "You don't have to."

He swallows noticeably, maybe sorting out his thoughts. "I just didn't realize you were wearing stockings," he rasps out, his gaze still locked on the sheer white thigh-highs, only a few shades lighter than my can-never-hold-a-tan legs.

"I like stockings. Tights. Thigh-high socks," I say breezily.

He swallows again. Rougher this time. Then, like he's collecting himself, he gives a soldier's nod. "Okay then."

His voice makes it sound almost like he's...aroused?

Oh.

Oh, my.

Is that why he's acting odd? What a wild thought. "Don't cut the stockings though. I like them."

As he snips, he mutters, "Me too."

He diligently works the scissors across the rest of the dress, leaving a jagged edge in his wake. I glance up at Dev, who's snapping photos of the moment.

I could see it on a postcard sold at a roadside gas-and-go. A woman with red hair, beach curls, a face scrubbed free of makeup, and a guy in Crocs and rolled up suit pants slicing up her wedding dress outside a 7-Eleven under the sun.

Congratu-fucking-lations on your un-wedding day.

That's what the postcard would say. When Ledger is nearly done, he stops, lifting the scissors and waving them at Dev. "Want a turn?"

Dev lowers the phone. A flirty grin spreads across his handsome face as he meets my gaze. "I sure do."

Ledger rises, gives the scissors to Dev, then takes his phone. Trading places, Dev kneels in front of me, while Ledger takes a pic of us. I focus on the beautiful damage Dev is doing to the tulle as he finishes with a "Done."

It's now a minidress.

I stand, a pair of scissors in one hand, and a huge swath of dirty, destroyed dress in the other. Yes, the dress finally feels like it fits. There's just one thing left to do. I tug off my engagement ring, then reach behind my neck to undo the simple silver chain I'm wearing with a sparkly star on it—my eighteenth birthday gift from my grandma before she passed. *"Always be sparkly, Aubrey,"* she'd said.

But it's hard to unclasp the chain with this ring in my hand.

Reading the situation, Dev offers an, "I'll do it."

A little shiver shimmies through me. "Thanks," I say, then he moves behind me as I brush my hair to the side, giving him room to see my neck. His fingers skim my nape, and the breath nearly whooshes from me, but I purse my lips in time. Aiden hardly ever touched my neck, but I think I'd love some neck attention. Only, it doesn't last long, since Dev has the chain unclasped in seconds. As Ledger watches the whole scene, I drop the ring on the chain, then Dev clasps it back on me once more. This time, there's a hitch in *his* breath. "There you go."

I drop my hair, and he moves around me.

I strike a pose for them. "What do you guys think?"

They both stare at me for longer than I'd have expected with something like heat in their gazes. Or perhaps that's just admiration? I'm not sure I should be trying to assess the motivation of men today, or any day.

"You look..." Dev begins, but his voice is gravelly. "Great," he manages to say.

Ledger nods a few times. "Nice new style."

I don't know what it says about me that their compliments make me feel better than any I ever got from Aiden.

6

A HARD TIME

Dev

I'm still holding the hammer as the bell rings loud, shrill and damn satisfying.

"Now that's just showing off," Aubrey says as she points to the top of the high striker game, where I've hit the puck and sent it to the top fucking level. I mean, what else was I going to do? *Not* hit it hard?

"Sorry, not sorry," I say. "I'm also not sorry I beat Ledger."

From his place next to the guy operating the game, Ledger rolls his eyes. "Yeah, those are the stats that matter. The pucks I hit in carnival games."

"A puck's a puck," I say.

When Aubrey said she wanted to do everything, she meant everything. We've ridden the roller coaster, the swings, the Tilt-A-Whirl. We've thrown darts, played Skee-Ball, and now, swung mallets.

I place the hammer down and quickly fire off a text to Garrett, letting him know Aubrey's doing okay—or as okay as can be expected on a day like this.

It's her turn, and she's assessing the mallet and the lever. Since I'm unable to resist a challenge, I step closer. "Want a tip?"

"Like, develop sick lats and big biceps in the next five seconds?"

I smile. "That, or focus on technique. Start with the hammer high above your head, let gravity pull it down, then use your hips and thighs as you lower yourself into the shot."

She blinks. "Piece of cake," she deadpans.

"Or I can show you," I offer.

Ledger chuckles under his breath. "Of course you can."

"Mock me for being helpful," I say, then wait for her answer.

"Sure. Show me," Aubrey says with a gamer spirit.

I move behind her, reach around her waist, and lift the hammer with her...but should I really be this close to Garrett's little sister? I'm here to help her forget about her shitty ass ex, not to flirt.

I move back a few inches.

Aubrey turns her neck to look at me. "Dev, you can press your body against mine. I'm not going to get ideas. Don't worry about that."

She's direct. More than I'd expected, but I appreciate the permission. "Okay." I wrap my arms around her more fully, and...damn. She's not supposed to feel this good in my arms.

Everything aligns. Her neck near my lips, her hair close to my nose, her lithe back pressed to my chest. I steal a sniff of her nape. Her perfume is fading, but the faint remnants of something sweet linger, like a summer fruit.

Don't do it. Don't ask her what her perfume is, man. Just don't. "Just don't hold it so tight," I bite out, then slide our joined hands down a tiny bit. "You need to relax a little more."

Or maybe I do.

She loosens her hold slightly.

"Perfect," I say, and since my work here is done, I jump away, giving my dick some breathing room. "Then you bring that hammer down like it's headed for Aiden's face."

She tosses her head back, laughing in utter delight. "Well, why didn't you just say that?"

Aubrey lifts the mallet, takes aim, and slams the hammer hard, letting out a loud *oomph*. She doesn't ring the bell, but she lights up the lever to the halfway point and shouts out a *yes*.

After she thanks the striker operator, she throws her arms around me. I learned my lesson from the lesson, though, so I give her a good, friendly hug. When I break it, she closes the distance between herself and Ledger. She high-fives him, then her brow knits. Like she's unsure if she should hug him too. He doesn't initiate it. But she must think *fuck it*, since she wraps her arms around him as well. "Thank you."

"I didn't do anything," he grumbles.

She lets go and smiles at him, then me. "You both

did." She takes a beat, exhales. "You both did *a lot* today."

Ah, hell. Taking care of her today was a gift. "I'm so glad Garrett called on us," I say, holding her gaze. Her eyes shine.

After a beat, Ledger grunts out, "We're here for you. Whatever you need."

Her smile turns more emotional. She bites the corner of her lips. And oh, shit. Is she going to cry again? Well, I wouldn't be surprised. She draws a deep breath, then parts her lips like she wants to say something, an admission of some sort. Instead, she says, "Up for more?"

"Always." I gesture to the rest of the amusement park. "Carnival shooting range? Roaring rapids? Ferris wheel?"

Ledger shudders at the last one.

Aubrey cocks her head, looking his way. "You hate Ferris wheels?"

"You mean death wheels," he corrects.

"That's a yes then," she says, then studies him. "You're not afraid to play a dangerous game for a living, where you could get body checked, hit by a stick, a puck, or a bear of a man, but Ferris wheels are terrifying?"

"Sounds about right," Ledger says.

Aubrey whips her gaze to me. "Are you afraid of Ferris wheels?"

I shake my head. "Since it's not a snake, nope." I have plenty of other fears too, like, say, what if I could never play hockey again? But no need to discuss those now.

"Snakes and Ferris wheels," Aubrey says, tapping her temple. "Got it. So when I plan a perfect day for both of you to say thanks for whisking me away, I'll just make sure it doesn't involve snakes or Ferris wheels."

The fact that she wants to say thanks makes me feel better than it should. So I shift gears. "Hey! How about bumper cars?"

"Perfect," she says, then she hightails it ahead of us, a woman who knows what she wants. I stare at her as she walks, enjoying the view far too much.

For far too long.

Till I realize Ledger's staring at her too.

The same damn way.

I suppose that shouldn't come as a surprise. This isn't the first time we've had the exact same interest in a woman.

7

A LUCKY SHOT

Aubrey

In the Spin Zone, I barrel toward Ledger, hell-bent on banging my red-and-white car into his orange one. I slam him, shouting a victorious, "Take that!"

"Not so fast," he retorts, then blasts his machine into reverse, shrewd eyes lasered right at me as he jerks it around and hunts me down, ready to hurl into me again. His blue eyes are cold and menacing. Ledger doesn't mess around as he aims, but right before he can ram me, I'm ambushed from behind, another car sending mine right into his bumper car once more.

I bounce forward, a laugh bursting from me.

I'm a bumper car sandwich, and the front of my car lights up, flashing in time to the electronic beat playing overhead while the car spins around. Whenever a car is hit, it spins. Hence, the Spin Zone.

"No fair," I shout, but it's a joyful protest, and with

each hit, I feel another brick come loose inside me, crumbling away.

I steer away from them, weaving through other cars before I jerk my car around, then ram into the side of Dev's lean green machine. His smile is electric, his hair a wild mess around his face, his eyes full of wicked glee.

"Got you," I call out as his car whirls in a circle, beeping loudly like a Vegas slot machine.

I hit him again. Again, his car spins. While he's doing a one-eighty, Ledger hits me from the side with a loud crash.

More bricks crumble inside me, toppling down.

From speeding down the country road, to chasing the veil, to cutting the dress then hitting the hammer, the entire afternoon of my un-wedding day has felt like a necessary explosion of pent-up, complicated, messy emotions leading to this moment—when I'm blowing off steam on an amusement park ride.

But there's one big problem.

My day is a lie.

Dev and Ledger think they've saved me from embarrassment. They think my heart is breaking. They think I'm hurt and they're just applying the Band-Aid of fun for a few hours and now I go home and tend my wounds for months.

Yes, I'm embarrassed. Yes, I'm hurt.

But not for the reasons they think. I can't keep the truth in much longer. It feels so wrong to lead them on. Just like everything felt wrong inside me earlier today when I hadn't told my besties the secret of my doubtful, worried heart.

Look where that silence got me.

Oof.

My torso slams forward, but I jerk my gaze back at a woman with a septum piercing, jet black hair, and a wicked smile. In her electric blue bumper car, her face says *gotcha* before she moves on from me and slams into a guy with a crooked nose and chunky silver rings on all his fingers.

"Babe!" he shouts. "How could you do that?"

"Love you," she says, then slams into him once more.

She's having such a good time. She's here on a date with her honey. And I'm Ledger's and Dev's...pity date.

All the adrenaline burns off.

I can barely move my car. When Dev and Ledger hurtle toward me, I don't jerk the wheel away or race off. Instead, I let them hurl into me.

When my car stops spinning, I'm facing down both men in their bumper cars. "I didn't want to marry Aiden anyway," I say, finally admitting it.

I slump back into the seat as they stare, wide-eyed, at me.

As the sun dips toward the horizon, the unlit vintage sign above the diner beckons, the orange script-y letters for Beverly's visible from the highway exit. We pull off the ramp, then turn into the lot around six.

With its brushed metal exterior, a mint green door, and a poster in the window of a stack of pancakes happily drowning in syrup, this diner might be one of the stars in a road-trip movie.

Today, it's about to become the setting for *Aubrey's big reveal*.

The walk up the steps feels ominous. The whole drive felt that way after my bumper car blurt-out. But the convertible wasn't the place to chat about it further. Besides, on the ride down here I needed to deal with my cell phone. It was like an overstuffed suitcase, bursting at the seams with text messages. I messaged my mom and told her that I was doing okay and I'd talk to her tomorrow. I checked in with Garrett and he said not to worry about a thing. I texted my bridesmaids, telling them to please, pretty please, go dance in their sexy black dresses with their men because I am going to be fine, fine, fine.

And I will be.

We reach the door, and Dev holds it open for me. Once inside, Ledger gives a chin nod and a "How are you doing?" to the woman working behind the counter.

"Doing well. What can I do you for?"

"Table for three, please."

Decked out in a vintage 50s pink waitress dress, she has a short, tight afro and slick red lipstick, and she's topping off the coffee of a guy in a mesh ball cap. He's got a beard, tattoos snaking along his pale arms, and the tired slump of a trucker. "Have yourself a seat anywhere," she says like she's sure glad to see us. "I'll be right with you."

Elvis isn't playing on the sound system. It's Taylor Swift, and that seems fitting. The queen of heartbreak.

Ledger leads the way past a rack of postcards and T-shirts, then a family in a booth arguing over ordering sundaes, and another foursome zoned out, each pair of eyes on their own screen.

Ledger stops by a circular booth in the back. "Ladies first."

I slide in, taking the middle. He moves next to me, Dev on my other side.

"Hungry?" Dev asks, grabbing the menus from the table and distributing them before I can even answer.

I flip open the floppy, red menu, its plastic covering curling at the edges. But the menu is perfunctory. I know this kind of place like I know what colors to mix for a client's balayage.

When the waitress swings by with a pot of coffee, she holds it up like it's the holy grail. "Need a little pick me-up? We make some fine coffee here if I do say so myself."

Dev smiles, then scans her name tag. "It looks good, Beverly." Ah, she's the owner too. "But I'm guessing we're gonna need a chocolate milkshake, a plate of fries, and some burgers."

She shoots me a sympathetic smile, perhaps reading the situation too well, or just putting it together from the context clues of my outfit. "So that's how it's gonna be," Beverly says to me, not at all unkindly.

While I appreciate her sympathy, I don't deserve any more of it today. And I don't want to food-wallow. "Actually, I'd love a veggie burger and a side salad, hold the tomatoes," I say.

"That works too," Beverly says, then writes down

Dev's chicken sandwich order—hold the bread—and Ledger's omelet with spinach and mushrooms.

When she leaves, it's clear there's no more stalling. I hope they don't think I've misled them. I hope they aren't pissed. "Look, Aiden did say he wanted to just be friends. When I told you that in the bridal room," I tell Dev, cycling back to my confession earlier, when he rescued me from the church, "that was true. But..."

The words lodge like marbles in my throat. They're all mixed up with my dad's wishes and my mom's words and my parents' hope for me. *Your dad would be so happy for you. He always hoped you'd get back together with the one who got away.*

The longer I dwell on the reasons I stuck around too long, the harder it'll be to tell Dev and Ledger *some* of the truth. "The truth is...I was actually relieved when he broke it off," I admit. My voice is shaky. "Right up until then, I'd been trying to find the guts to tell Ivy and Trina that something felt off all morning. I kept wondering if it was normal to feel so nervous. Like my dress didn't fit. Like my clothes were all wrong." Dev nods, a gentle sign to keep going.

"And when Aiden showed up ten minutes before..." I picture the groom opening the door, and relief washes over me all over again. I breathe a deep sigh, then look from one guy to the other, and say the words that have been stuck inside me all morning, all afternoon, and perhaps for a lot longer too. "I was grateful he was the one to do it. Because I wasn't all in," I say, my voice still unsteady as I confess it all. "You're the first people I've told."

"Yeah?" Ledger asks, not like he doubts me. More like he's just shocked.

"I'm sorry," I add as the awfulness crawls up inside me. "I didn't say anything because I was just so shocked by the way Aiden left me. He said he wanted to fuck other people," I say, bitter and hurt at the same time. "He said he didn't want to marry me, but he still wanted to sleep with me. And he bought a plane ticket this morning to Miami, so he could move there and have sex with lots of people, apparently. He's catching a flight tomorrow." I hate how my voice threatens to break. I feel so stupid all over again. Which makes no sense since I was ready to tell my best friends my fears seconds before Aiden burst through the door. Still, I didn't. I wince as I look at Dev, then Ledger. "And I let you just amuse me all day. You probably think I'm a—"

I hate saying the word. My parents raised me to be honest.

But Dev sets a hand on mine. "No." His tone is strong, serious.

Ledger growls like a dog. "You're not the villain in this story."

"Aiden is," Dev bites out. "Your fiancé bought a plane ticket this morning." He sounds beyond incredulous. "Then he sat on that news for hours. He's a bag of dicks."

"I'm so fucking glad you didn't marry him," Ledger says, his jaw ticking with irritation, but his tone full of gratitude too.

I set my free hand on my chest, my shoulders relaxing. I was so terrified they'd be pissed. Or think I'd abused their trust. But I still feel bad. "I should have said something sooner. To you guys. To him."

"Timing is everything," Ledger says, like he's been there himself. Dev shoots him a sympathetic look. Despite the way they tease each other relentlessly, I get the sense they look out for each other in a found family kind of way. Makes sense, since they've been friends forever, but it's still nice to see. It does something to my heart—makes it feel kind of warm and fond for them.

"Yeah, I think I learned that today," I say. "About timing."

"Just be glad you found out before you said *I do*," Ledger adds.

I look in his eyes, trying to find the subtext of what he's saying. Maybe an observation about his own brief marriage ending? But I don't know why he and his wife split, and he leaves his comment for me to take at face value.

Dev jumps in to say, "Don't beat yourself up, Aubs. You said you were about to tell your friends. Your gut was telling you something and you listened to it."

"I got lucky," I say, guilt still pricking at me.

Dev laughs. "I can't tell you how many times luck saves my ass in a hockey game."

Ledger gives a soft smile. "Same here. Maybe this was your lucky shot."

Maybe they're right. I had no way of knowing Aiden was heading down the *gimme all the sex* path until he confessed that he wanted to bang anyone and everyone. Perhaps my gut was warning me.

I smile past the guilt and shame, through the relief and the levity. "I guess I'll take luck."

Dev squeezes my hand. "Even if you wanted to end things with him before you walked down the aisle, and even if you were seconds away from telling your friends, that doesn't mean it hurts less when someone says shitty things to you," he says, his green eyes flashing with vulnerability. They look darker now, bordering on hazel. "When someone treats you like you were nothing. Like the time you spent with them was absolutely unimportant."

That sounds like it's spoken from his experience.

"Don't you dare think Aiden's anything but a total flaming jackass," Ledger adds, patting my arm a little awkwardly.

I picture Aiden earlier leaving me to clean up his dirty work. Peeling out of the lot. He didn't even have the guts to face the guests. Garrett had to handle all that. Oh. Wait. "I nearly forgot. This is the cherry on the jackass sundae. He asked me to fuck him *tonight*," I add, with a *can you believe his nerve* smile, "before he leaves town."

Dev sputters.

Ledger's eyes turn into livid slits. "No, he did not," he hisses.

"Yes. He did," I say, and I tell them the rest of Aiden's sex invite.

"He left the room number?" Ledger asks.

"And he thinks you're going to meet him there?" Dev asks.

"I never RSVP'd. I was a little too shocked."

Dev's grin turns dastardly. "Did you know I'm the king of dares and pranks?"

Actually, yes. "Seeing as you dared Ivy and Hayes to get married, I did know that," I answer, flashing back to Ivy's tale of her Vegas wedding to Hayes last season, when this handsome goalie right here dared her and the new guy to get hitched, claiming it was a team tradition. She Vegas-married Hayes but went back to her hotel room with both him *and* the team captain, Stefan. Thus began her very own throupling, and she's happily married to both men now.

Dev lets go of my hand. "And I'd really like to let Aiden know he fucked with the wrong girl."

I'm a little giddy at the prospect of his pranks. "What do you want to do?" I ask. Make that *a lot* giddy.

Dev licks his lips. His eyes flicker with sweet revenge. "Would you be willing to tell him you'll be there at eight and he should answer the door in his boxers?"

Oh, this just keeps getting better. "I absolutely would."

Dev's got his phone out and is studiously tapping away on it. A minute later, he swivels it around to a site that ships...dicks. "They have an express one-hour service. A giant cardboard dick will be standing outside his room at eight. Say the word, Aubs."

I guess they aren't mad at me at all. "I would love to get a picture of his reaction, though," I say.

Ledger clears his throat. "Hold on."

Uh-oh. "Is Stern Brunch Daddy going to be the voice of reason?"

Ledger gives me a long, curious look. "That's what you call me?"

"That's what you are. You're a good amount of strict."

Dev chuckles while Ledger fixes me with another look—a darker one. "Do you want me to be Stern Brunch Daddy right now?"

A shiver runs down my spine. "Yes," I whisper.

"Then what I was going to say is this," Ledger says, leaning a little closer, looking to Dev, then me. "We'll personally deliver that cardboard dick."

It's like I've drunk a glass of champagne. I've scored two front-row tickets to Amelia Stone. I've won the Best Balayage in the City award. "Yes. Please. Now!"

Dev types for a few more seconds, then hits a button on his phone. "We'll meet them in the parking lot to get the dick."

I feverishly tap out a text to my former groom telling him I'll be there at eight to bang. "Done."

Ledger tips his chin toward Beverly, balancing plates as she makes her way to us. "Eat fast, then. We've got to get this show on the road."

I spread my napkin on my lap at lightning speed.

* * *

On the way out, Ledger and Dev argue about who's paying. Ledger wins. Dev harrumphs, then grabs a couple T-shirts from the display, scanning the sizes. Satisfied, he whips out some bills from his wallet, likely way more than needed, then slaps them on the counter.

He adds a diner postcard. It's a retro-style shot with the name lit up in neon. "Keep the change, Beverly," he says.

With the quickness of a woman who can figure out fifteen percent of anything in less than a second, she takes the bills and gives a very approving nod. "Thanks, kid."

I suspect he gave her way more than the recommended tip.

He slips the postcard into his back pocket. On the way out, I pat his arm. "You're swee—"

I swallow the end of the word as Dev makes quick work of the buttons on his dress shirt. In no time, they're undone and he's tugging the material out of the waistband of his slacks, then shedding it, and...where is my jaw?

Dev's abs have abs. His pecs are stacked. And the smattering of golden brown chest hair covering those muscles? It goes down, down, down into a tempting happy trail that teases me as it disappears into his pants.

It's Christmas morning and my birthday all rolled into one. As I walk to the car, I don't know where to furtively look—at his broad chest, or the ladder of his abs, or the way they taper into a tight, trim V at his hips. I choose...everywhere. Up, down, all around, I gawk at his glorious muscles and miles of skin, a little more golden than I'd expect for a guy with a fair complexion. He must like to take his shirt off in the summer. I hope summer never ever ends.

A throat clears. "Aubrey, do you want me to pick up your chin from the ground?"

I startle at Ledger's dry words and try, I swear I try, to collect my thoughts.

"Why...?" It's all I can manage.

With a smug smile, Dev tugs the T-shirt on. "It was hot in that dress shirt all day." With his grin widening, he tips his chin toward me, then his buddy. "Besides, you two are sporting new threads. Seems only fair I got in on the action," he says, tugging the new shirt down the rest of the way as we reach the car.

Bye-bye, shirtlessness. Hello...Try My Pancake Special?

I didn't realize that was what the shirt said. "I guess we'll know what to order when we return," I say.

"It's a deal." Dev tosses me a shirt, and I catch it, faintly hoping we get to try the pancakes someday.

He slings the other one to Ledger, who grabs it one-handed. I hold mine close, liking the gift more than a casserole dish, a cake stand, and a mandolin. All the things Aiden chose. I'll have to deal with the stupid registry soon enough.

Dev wiggles his fingers at Ledger. "My turn. I want to drive this sweet ride," he says.

With zero protest, Ledger hands him the key fob. "You'll love how she handles."

8

LESSONS FROM A CARDBOARD DICK

Ledger

Room 131 is nearly in my crosshairs.

When I get there, I'm raring to bang on the door with the kind of ferocity seen when the muscle shows up in a movie. Hell, when Aiden opens it, I'm going to have to refrain from slamming a fist into that coward's piehole.

I'm clenching and unclenching my fists as we march through the lobby of the Airport Inn like a *Reservoir Dogs* posse, long strides eating up the carpet, Aubrey keeping pace with us, powered by her thirst for romance vengeance.

We must look like a gang of misfits, her in her hacked-up dress, stockings and boots, Dev sporting his new pancake special shirt, and me in my Crocs that squeak as we head down the hallway, a giant cardboard schlong under my arm.

I can't wait to deliver it.

When I turn the corner, I scan the digits on the doors. Almost there. A few more rooms.

Number 131 looms, but before we reach it, I stick out my arm, stopping Aubrey. Dev stops too.

"What is it?" she whispers.

"You still good with this?"

"Yes. Are you having second thoughts?"

I scoff. "Nope. I just want to make sure you're all in."

She gives a soft smile. "Love that you asked, but the answer is yes. Go get 'em...*tiger*."

Mmm...that word. That nickname. Not that I don't like Stern Brunch Daddy—I like it too much. Just like I'm enjoying her saying *tiger* with a little throaty purr to her pretty voice. Just like I'm enjoying everything about her more than I should.

But now's not the time to go soft.

It's not the time to be a dick either. Just to deliver one.

I release my clenched fist and try to loosen the valve on some of my anger. We cover the final feet to the room, set up the life-size dong, and then Aubrey raps twice on the door.

"Hey, babe," she says, but her lips twist in disgust at the end, and I can tell it cost her something to even say those two words.

Seconds later, the door creaks open, and some sort of shtupping music floats out. The chorus of Ginuwine's "Pony." I roll my eyes, muttering, "Jesus."

That's on every sex playlist. It requires zero imagination.

Dev shoots me a *shut the fuck up* look.

My derision got the better of my discretion. I mime zipping my lips as Aiden asks from behind the door, "Sweetie pie? Is that you or is that room service?"

Fuck. I hope I didn't ruin our plan.

Aubrey straightens her spine, plastering on a faux sexy grin even though he can't see her yet. "Hey, babe. It's me. In my bridal dress. And yes, I have room service," she says, in an over-the-top throaty voice that she follows with a mimed gag, just for us.

With a relieved sigh, Aiden tugs the door all the way open, voila style, showing off his...are you kidding me? He's wearing wrinkled boxers?

I loathe him.

His eyes widen to saucers, flashing from Dev to me and back, confusion in those irises. "You brought...your brother's friends, babe?"

"She sure did," I say.

Aiden holds up his hands apologetically, waving us off with a chuckle. "Look, I had a blast at the party last night. And, seriously, guys, I appreciate the compliment big time. But," he says, taking his time to sigh regretfully, "I'm not into dudes."

Of course Mister Horny McFuckerson thinks we're all here for the bang date. Of course he can't conceive we'd be here for any other reason. Like, he's a prick.

"We're not here for that. We're here with a delivery," Dev says as he shoves the cardboard at Aiden.

I pat the head of the cutout. "Yes, Mister Cardboard Dick is here to teach you a few lessons," I singsong as I turn to the standing dick balanced on its formidable cardboard balls. "Because he has more balls than you. Want to know why?"

Oops. That came off angrier than I'd expected. Guess I didn't cool off. Aiden's grin burns off. Cockiness is replaced with worry. "W-why?" he stammers.

I stare down the gutless wonder. "Because you don't get a fucking plane ticket *before* you call off a wedding. You don't run the fuck away and make the bride and her brother tell all the guests," I spit out, fueled by the red-hot flames licking my veins. Possibly I've got some of my own kindling from the charred remains of my failed marriage stoking the fire. I've just had enough of chameleon exes who hide their true natures then kick you out with the trash. Mine and Aubrey's now too.

"And you don't do it ten minutes before the ceremony," Dev adds, stepping closer to the doorway and using his size to overpower Aiden. Not a bad idea.

I crowd him, too, while Aubrey wedges herself next to Dev, watching the scene with wild delight in her eyes.

Dev's not done. He lifts a finger, pokes Aiden's sternum. The one-time groom quakes. What a beautiful sight. "Here's a lesson too. Don't hit on the goddamn waitress at your bachelor party," Dev says, low and menacing.

"I wasn't hit—"

"—You were, man. You fucking were. And here's another lesson." Dev lets go and cracks his knuckles instead. He takes his sweet time making sure the sound snaps, crackles, pops to the sex beat floating from Aiden's room. "When you ask a woman to marry you—

hell, when you ask her to be yours, you don't flirt, sext, kiss, or fuck anyone else. Even Mister Cardboard Dick knows that."

Aiden gulps, holds up his hands in surrender. "I was just messing around."

I mime slamming a buzzer. "Wrong. You mess around with a pie. With bubble wrap. With a video game. You don't mess around with someone's heart."

Dev shoves the dick at him. "Man the fuck up and grow some balls," he says as Aiden stumbles, grabbing onto the cardboard phallus then batting it away from him. It tumbles to the stained carpet of the hotel room.

I turn to Aubrey, gritting my teeth, rage storming through me. It requires all my restraint not to pummel him. I can't believe Aubrey let herself think she lied. I can't stand that she was embarrassed over how he treated her. I hate that she spent the whole day worrying what we'd think because of this jackass.

"Do you have anything you want to add?" I ask.

Aubrey draws a deep breath, then taps her chin. "I think that covers it. Except...there is one little thing." She steps forward into the room, appraises her ex up and down, then says, "You said earlier we had some good sex. But, in the immortal words of Inigo Montoya, *I do not think that word means what you think it means.*" Then she leans closer and stage-whispers, "Good luck learning the mandolin."

She turns on her booted heel and struts down the hall. I can't do a thing but watch her walk off, all badass and bold as she gets the last word in.

What a glorious sight. I watch her till she turns

the corner, and when she does, my anger has vanished. It's replaced by white-hot admiration for the woman.

When I turn around, I just smile and shake my head. "Man, you were *this* close to having her. You really fucked up," I say.

Dev chuckles, curling a hand around Aiden's bare shoulder. "It's all downhill from here, bro." He takes a pause, then lifts his brow. "Also, a mandolin?"

"They sound cool. Women love them," Aiden says, and who's embarrassed now?

Dev laughs harder. "No, man. No one does."

We turn to go, leaving a giant dick with a giant dick.

Outside the hotel entrance, Aubrey's pacing. Her cheeks are glowing, her eyes are sparkling. When we push open the brass-paneled door, she rushes over, grabs my shoulders, and says, "You're my hero."

She dusts a quick, thank you kiss on my cheek. It knocks the breath from my lungs.

"Oh," I say, startled and aroused.

I've leveled up in today's game—my attraction to Aubrey is officially unlocked.

Her lips are so damn soft. When she breaks the kiss, Dev's watching us, his assessing eyes missing nothing. He's a goalie, so his job is to be a hawk. To read all the action on the ice. Pretty sure he's reading me loud and clear right now, just like he read me when we met Zahra in Los Angeles several years ago, and Dev knew before I did that we both wanted her.

He's too fucking astute.

She spins around, grabs his shoulders, and stares at

him, beaming. "You're my hero too," she says, then brushes a kiss onto his bearded jaw.

He has the benefit of seeing it coming, so he lifts a hand in record time and covers her palm on his shoulder, buying himself a few extra seconds.

When she ends it, she draws the biggest breath in the world. "Thank you. I feel like I can face my family now. I need to talk to my mom before—"

But then her smile disappears. The sparkles in her eyes flicker off. She winces, then slumps against the brick hotel wall, dragging a hand through her gorgeous red locks.

"What is it?" I ask, worried.

"Are you okay?" Dev seconds.

Her brow is furrowed, her lips twisted.

"Tomorrow," she gasps like she's short on air. "I'm supposed to leave for my honeymoon *tomorrow*. We have non-refundable tickets."

9

THE JILTED BRIDE REFUND

Aubrey

The lights of a plane high above us wink on and off against the night sky. "So, yeah. That was the plan for our honeymoon," I say as I lie on the hood of the car, staring at the jets taking off at the nearby airport. I don't want to move. Partly because I just can't even with this day. Partly because Dev's lying on one side of me, Ledger on the other, and it's comfy with them. Cozy in its own way. They're just listening, like they've done all day. "I wanted more of an adventure. Spend the day outside exploring, go to a ghost town, and see new things I never expected to see. But he wanted to do touristy things and wine tastings. I mean, I like wine, but I'm more of a stomp-on-the-grapes girl than a swirl-a-glass-and-talk-about-the-oak-and-berry-and-bacon-leather-taste one."

"Bacon leather?" Dev asks.

Ledger shifts his gaze toward me. "What kind of wine have you been drinking, Aubrey?"

"It all kind of tastes like that, though," I say. "Don't you think?"

"Red wine, sure. Now that you say it," Dev says.

"And our flight leaves tomorrow afternoon," I say with another heavy sigh. "I saved up for months for the week-long trip. Well, we both did. But I was making more, so I paid more." And now I'm annoyed that I'm stuck with two tickets, and a room at the inn Aiden wanted to stay at because McDoodle Island has two pie shops, including one that had become an Instagram sensation. Yeah, that was a fun reason to pick a honeymoon destination. To scout its work potential. "Maybe I can call the airline and see if they have a jilted bride refund?"

Both men are quiet for several seconds. No jokes. No teasing. Dev sits up and shoots Ledger a stare I can't read.

Ledger pushes up too, his blue eyes directing question marks to his friend.

Ugh. I hate silence. It reminds me too much of nights at the dinner table when I was younger. When Claire and Garrett were busy with their friends, and I was the only kid there, tasked with single-handedly keeping the conversation alive during the years when my parents barely spoke to each other. "Airlines really should have one if you think about it," I say, all cheery.

When in doubt, make a joke at your own expense.

"Excuse me for a sec, Aubs," Dev says, not taking the bait at all as he swings his legs off the hood of the car, jerking his gaze to Ledger then the parking lot in a *walk with me* gesture.

I sit up.

Worries swim inside me as Ledger hops off the hood and strides into the warm summer night with Dev, the sound of their footsteps fading. Maybe I should just shut up and stop telling them every detail of my failed wedding. They are my brother's besties, after all, but I've been treating them like mine. I have my own besties to share my innermost thoughts with.

But before I can stew in my head much longer, the duet of Crocs and wingtips on pavement grows louder as my escorts return. They stop in front of me, twin gazes a little devilish.

"What if instead of a jilted bride refund," Dev begins, his lips curving into a satisfied grin.

"We take the trip with you," Ledger finishes.

I freeze.

Did they really say that? Tilting my head, I study Dev's green eyes, playful, but hopeful too. Then Ledger's blue ones. Serious. Direct.

They mean this. "A honeymoon for three?" I ask.

Dev gives a casual shrug. "I'm pretty fucking fun."

"Stern Brunch Daddy knows how to have a good time too," Ledger adds. As if he has to sell himself as well when I'm beyond sold. I want to shout *yes, yes, yes* right now. But there's that little matter of my brother. "What about Garrett?"

I've barely mentioned him all day. There's been no need. But I don't want to upset him by monopolizing time with his clients who are also his friends. "Will he mind?"

Dev scratches his bearded jaw, seeming to consider it for a beat. "He did send us to take care of you today. I've been keeping him in the loop over text. He asked us to look out for you."

My heart sags a little. I don't want to be a pity plus-one. But before I can ask if that's the only reason they're suggesting this, Ledger clears his throat and says with authority, "But you're our friend now too. We want to do this. He'll be chill."

And, really, what's not to be chill about? I'm not involved with either guy. And they do feel like friends. "Did we just become best friends?" I say, borrowing the movie line from *Step Brothers*.

"Damn straight we did," Ledger says.

I smile, relieved. But I want to be one hundred percent certain. "You guys don't have stuff to do?"

"Training camp doesn't start for another week," Ledger says.

"Who else can take time off at the drop of a hat?" Dev adds, then steps closer, swiping a strand of hair off my cheek, and tucking it gently behind my ear, making my pulse skip a beat. "My schedule is clear."

When the shiver fades into a warm glow, I shift to Ledger, hunting for any sign he's not on board. "You really want—"

"Yes," Ledger growls, and my damn pulse skitters again. That was a firm, sexy declaration. "Are you in or out?"

I stop thinking. I start planning. "Yes. I'm in. But

what about the airfare? We had two seats, and even though Aiden doesn't need his, I don't think you can just change names on tickets. Plus we'd need one more." I bet Aiden canceled his ticket this morning. Maybe no one scooped up his empty seat yet. I hope there's another one.

I grab my phone from my purse. An email from the airline blinks in the notifications.

"Yep," I say sarcastically, waving the phone around. "He canceled his ticket. So thoughtful. Since he only canceled *his*. Didn't even bother to see if I still wanted to go or not."

"That guy," Ledger grumbles, taking a step toward the hotel. "I should pay him another visit."

In no time, Dev's hand curls around Ledger's shoulder. "He's history, man. Let him be. Let's do this and help Aubs."

Help. Yes, that's what this is. A friendly, helpful gesture from my new best friends.

"Fine. You're right," Ledger admits. "Let's see if there are seats."

In seconds, they break out their phones. We search for tickets, plugging in permutations. Dev shows me flights to Seattle tomorrow, checking them against mine. Ledger tests other options, and my heart races, but reality is making one thing clear.

This is just a pipe dream.

The flights are full. Tonight, tomorrow, and the next day.

All the air leaks out of me in a sigh, but I shrug like it's truly no big deal, even though I wanted it badly for a few minutes there. "It was a fun idea, guys," I say, then lift my chin. I'm not going to run off with my tail between my legs. "But I'll go alone. I don't want to waste the money, and I think it'd be good to get out of town for a little while."

I suck down my disappointment. I've had a good day, all things considered. I blew off steam at an amusement park and got some revenge thanks to my brother's two sexy, charming, protective best friends.

My friends now too. That's enough of a win.

"It'll be fine. I'll be fine," I add, but Dev isn't paying attention. He's tapping away on his phone.

He hits a button and brings the device to his ear. "Hey, Spencer. I need a favor."

There's a pause, then he chuckles.

"You guessed it, buddy."

Another beat.

I turn to Ledger, asking with my eyes if he knows what Dev's up to. Ledger shrugs a *no idea*.

"Can you swing it?" Dev asks.

Another pause.

"Excellent. Gimme one sec to make sure this works for my friends." He covers the phone. "Can you meet at the airfield in Novato at two p.m. tomorrow? Guy I know charters private jets, and he's got a bird available then. He'll put it on my tab."

I blink. Several times. "You're booking us a private plane?"

"You have a tab? Like, an account?" Ledger seconds, rubbing his ear like he's heard wrong.

"Obviously," Dev says with a scoff. "When I moved

my parents here from St. Paul a few years ago—they'd gone back there while I was in college—I booked them a private jet to fly with their rescue Chihuahuas. There's no way Mom was letting Lulu and Virgil fly commercial. They're assholes, those little mutts. Cute, adorable assholes, but assholes, nonetheless. Does two p.m. work for you guys?"

I want to thrust my arms in the air. Dance on the hood of the car. Shout to the sky. Instead, I simply nod, like I fly private every day. "Well, if it's good enough for Lulu and Virgil, it's good enough for me. What about you, Ledger?"

He scratches his jaw, all nonchalant. "I can probably make that time work."

Dev returns to his call. "Book it."

10

JUST LIKE SOUP

Dev

Words to live by—when you realize you and your buddy are both into the same woman, you need to talk to him. Especially when you've just volunteered as tribute in that woman's substitute honeymoon.

We've got to get some things clear first though. We drop off Aubrey at her apartment in the Mission District. It feels weird, leaving her alone, but she insists she's fine and I'm not going to press her. She's a grown woman who doesn't need a babysitter.

When the door to her building shuts, I check my texts from Garrett for the rental car info. We clearly have other things to discuss with our agent aside from car details, but that's an in-person convo, so we make plans with him for tomorrow morning.

With that done, I get to the critical stuff. "Want to grab a drink after we return the car?"

"Yeah. I do." Code for he knows we need to chat too. Just like we did when we met Zahra at a gym in Santa Monica that summer. The second she went into the spin class, I pulled him aside and said, "Let's talk."

When the errand is done, we head over to Sticks and Stones, a bar my buddy runs in the city.

Well, Gage is *everyone's* buddy. Ledger included. Gage is a former Major League pitcher, who had to retire early when he blew out his elbow. Now, he owns and runs this bar and raises his daughter solo.

As we stride to the bustling counter, Gage gives us a curious once-over. "Okaaay?"

Oh, right. Our clothes.

"Well, it's kind of a funny story," I say, plucking at my pancake T-shirt, then glancing down at Ledger's shoes.

"Yeah, that can't be anything but a story," Gage says, then sets down coasters on the beer-soaked wood. "And stories need beer."

They do. Just like trips need rules.

I'd be nowhere without rules. As an athlete, I'm big on following them. As a human, I'm fond of bending them. But as someone who's had his heart smashed, I sure as shit know the value of setting them in advance.

After Gage serves up an Imperial IPA for Ledger and a blackberry lime seltzer water for me, I'm grateful our bartender friend needs to tend to another customer.

I turn to Ledger. "About this trip..." But I don't know what to say, and the rest of the sentence dies on my tongue.

Fortunately, Ledger is sometimes a mind reader. "I know, I know. *We need to talk*. Your favorite thing."

Yes. That. Talking. Which I need to do. "Yeah, and I know *you're* into her."

Ledger stares pointedly at me. "Yes, Dev. I'm the *only* one into her."

Why am I hiding my brewing attraction? I'm the guy who faces feelings. Who talks through issues. What the fuck is up with me? "Fine, fine," I grumble, shoulders tight, body jumpy. "I know we *both* are."

Ledger pats my shoulder. "There, there. Was that so hard? Want to hug it out now too? We can journal about it later if you'd like."

"Fuck you," I mutter, then drown my annoyance—at myself—in a thirsty gulp of the bubbly water. I really should be able to talk about this stuff. Hell, I thought it'd be easy a few minutes ago. I don't keep shit bottled up inside. But ever since Eva blindsided me with a breakup I never saw coming...after *openly* discussing rings, and homes, and plans, talking is a little harder. That's got to be the reason I'm tripping on words.

But he's right. I need to *actually* deal with these feelings head-on. Because this situation isn't about my ex. It's about the fact that we're both attracted to the woman we're about to spend a week with. "This can't be another Zahra," I say.

Four years ago, Zahra was an off-season fling when the sophisticated, devotedly single, thirty-something British-Lebanese attorney spent a summer in Los Angeles working for a sustainable energy client before returning to Beirut. We were both drawn to her. She was drawn to us. Even better—she liked it when two men shared her, so she made a deal to teach us "how to make a woman feel like a queen in bed."

I should seriously send Zahra a thank you gift for all her fantastic lessons.

But even though Ledger and I are both clearly into Aubrey in the same way, the situations couldn't be more different.

"She's Garrett's little sister, but that's not even the main issue. The main issue is Aubrey almost got married today," I say, emphatic, my voice rising as I stab my finger against the wood grain of the bar.

Ledger tilts his head. "Do you think I missed that?"

I hold up my hands in surrender. "Just want to be sure we're both going into this trip with a similar mind-set. We're her friends," I say. The more I say it, the more I'll drill it in. It'll become muscle memory.

"Like we said in the parking lot when we talked. Like we said to her," Ledger seconds. He lifts his glass but doesn't drink, just stares at the chalkboard menu behind the bar listing the craft beers. "What do I know about women anyway?"

Truth. I lift my glass in anti-relationship solidarity. "What do either of us know about women?"

Ledger clinks, then sets down his glass. He seems to give the question some real thought before he smirks. "Well, I do know a thing or two about how to make a woman very, *very* happy in bed."

"Who's the cocky fucker now?"

"It's not cocky if it's true."

"Really? *Really?* Is that the definition of cocky? It's a lie, not the truth?"

Ledger stares at me like *c'mon*. "Semantics are not the point."

"Then what is the point?"

He scrubs a hand across his chin and lets out a lingering sigh, his tone flat. "It'd be a bad idea."

"Yeah, it would. Aubrey's not the kind of woman we could keep it casual with."

I think it over, trying, *really trying*, not to think about how good casual with Aubrey would be.

When Gage finishes with another customer, he heads our way again, giving each of us appraising looks with wise green eyes. "Let me guess. You two are debating the meaning of the universe, the existential nature of hockey itself, or whether you eat or drink soup?"

Like I'm answering on a game show, I bark out "eat" right as Ledger scoffs out "drink."

"I knew you two wouldn't agree." With a tip of his chin, Gage asks, "So, what's the story tonight?"

Right. The clothes. My pancake shirt and Ledger's shoes. I'm not sure I want to go into too many details about the story behind the attire. But Gage is good people, and it's clear something went down. I give him the briefest synopsis about a wedding that didn't happen.

"Damn," he says with a whistle. "That can't be easy."

"Definitely not. And now we're just sorting through

some things...with women," I admit, opening up a smidge.

Gage wiggles his fingers. "Serve it up. I've been waiting."

"We're making sure we both see eye to eye about *a woman*," Ledger adds.

"Good. I don't want to see you getting your hearts broken." Gage points from Ledger to me. "You hear me?"

Ledger lifts his glass high. "Loud and clear."

Gage stares my way, waiting for my agreement. Even if relationships aren't at the top of my mind, he's not wrong. I lift my glass too. "Same."

"Good. A ticker can only take so much." On that stark truth, Gage pats the bar, then wheels around to handle another customer.

After a long pull, Ledger sets his glass down then deals me a dubious stare. "You drink soup, buddy. It's liquid."

I snort. "Things in a bowl are eaten. Case closed. Just like the case of the honeymoon trip."

"Yeah, Aubrey's just like...soup."

I just hope I have it in me to keep thinking of her like food or a friend—instead of a woman I want.

* * *

Garrett swings his hips, lifts his five-iron, and strikes. He's a cobra on the golf course, hitting his target with a venomous precision.

The little white ball has no chance against him as it

arcs against the blue sky of the early Sunday morning, soaring till it makes landfall maybe twenty feet from the hole.

"And that's how you do it," I say, resting my club against my hip so I can clap. I am impressed, but I also want him to stay in a good mood.

"Why are you not mastering the Masters?" Ledger asks—a legit question, the way our agent plays.

Garrett gives an appreciative nod. "Because as good as I am at golf, I'm even better at negotiating."

"Truth." He's a legend with contracts. Sponsorship deals too. My bank account will give him a recommendation letter anytime.

Garrett lets out a deep breath and takes off his shades, hooking them on the neck of his pastel yellow polo. "So, you're leaving this afternoon," he says, returning to the topic of our abbreviated morning round of golf—on the first few holes we debriefed him on the plans for the trip. "And you're sure she's up for it?"

Even though the jet is booked, I feel a little like a kid asking his dad's permission to go away with friends for a few days. "She is," I say with confidence that I hope masks how awkward I feel talking to him about honeymooning with his sister.

I shouldn't feel weird telling him. Yet I do. I still feel tense, too, even after Ledger and I talked last night. I hate feeling unsure of anything. I like knowing what I'm doing on the ice, in the net, in my life. I like things to...work out.

Ledger rests his golf club on his shoulder. "She

wants to go. She put a lot of effort into planning her honey—*trip*," Ledger says, quickly changing his word choice. "Said she'd saved up for it for a while before the *fuckcake* took off."

Garrett lifts a brow, a small smile tipping his lips. "You're using Aubrey's favorite insult?"

Ledger gives a small smile. "Seems I am. Because he is. We paid him a visit last night."

Immediately, Garrett's grin vanishes. His lips are a ruler. He raises both hands, the gloved one still holding his club. "Do not tell me two of my clients got into a scuffle. Do not even tell me there will be video surfacing of you guys roughing him up. I don't need you behaving like assholes." His voice doesn't rise. It deepens. And I know this guy. He's the picture of unruffled chill no matter what, where, or when. But when he uses *that* voice, he means business. He whips his gaze from me to Ledger. "What have I told you? There are cameras everywhere. Also, no. Just no."

These are the roles we've played our whole life. Garrett is the straightlaced man. I'm the troublemaker. "Dude. We only roughed him up a little bit outside an ice cream shop. Relax. I don't think anyone was watching. Ledge, did anyone see?"

"Not that I saw," Ledger says, selling it perfectly.

Unflappable, unbreakable Garrett draws a deep breath. "No big deal. I'll call the agency's PR team. We'll sort this out. It was a misunderstanding," he says to himself, already planning the spin.

I put Garrett out of his misery. "Seriously? I save all my fight for the ice. We brought him a cardboard dick."

Garrett jerks his gaze my way. "What?"

I give him a brief rundown of events, and pretty soon, Garrett's cracking up on the course. When he recovers, he grabs his golf bag, drops his club into it, then slings the bag over his shoulder. He doesn't like to use a golf cart; his life's mantra is *why take the elevator when there are stairs.*

Mine too.

"I appreciate you guys giving him a talking to," Garrett says, shaking his head in obvious disgust as we grab our bags, too, and walk up a small hill with him. "The amount of cleanup I had to do yesterday was insane."

"How did it all go?" Ledger asks.

"Let's just say it's a damn good thing Aiden's leaving town. He'll never be able to show his face at his dad's pie shop again. And listen, thanks for looking out for Aubrey. She's gotta be hurting right now. It'll be good for her to get away. I'd go with Sophie and the girls but..."

"Lina and Rory are starting preschool this week," Ledger supplies. "How are my godchildren doing?"

Garrett smiles proudly. "The best."

I clear my throat. "Ahem. Lina is yours. Rory is mine."

As we walk under a giant willow tree, Ledger stage whispers, "Right, right. You're totally not a figurehead godfather when I'm the real one."

"Now, now, kids, there's enough of me for both of you," Garrett says as we near the next hole. But he goes quiet, his brow creasing as if he's considering a problem. "There's something I've been meaning to ask you guys."

"Sure. Hit me up," I say, eager to please after he gave us his blessing.

Garrett turns to us when we reach the tee. "If I left CMT to do my own thing, would you guys follow me?"

His tone is stripped of his usual cool control. There's real vulnerability there.

"I'd follow you anywhere. You know that." I mean it from the bottom of my heart. "You're the man."

"Thanks," he says, clapping my shoulder. "And you know I'm always looking out for you. We're going to get you the best deal possible at the best team this year. I promise."

I believe him with my whole heart. I've had a good run with the Golden State Foxes, and I intend to keep having one. Besides, hockey *is* my whole heart.

Ledger clears his throat, his tone a little gruff. "You know you're stuck with me," he says, then casts his gaze down toward his knee before he meets Garrett's gaze again.

"Ditto," Garett says, then pulls him in for a quick bro hug.

When they separate, both guys smooth their hands over their shirts, like affection is too hard for them.

"Seriously? You two should have been raised by shrinks. Bring it in," I say, spreading my arms, waggling my fingers. "C'mon. Group hug. You can do it. Show your feelings."

Garrett snorts a no.

Ledger steps away. No, he jumps.

I mime hugging one, then the other. "There. I did it for us."

"Thanks," Ledger mutters.

"And thanks again for taking care of Aubrey," Garrett says sincerely.

"Of course," I say, studying the ball as I set it up. Not sure I want him to see my face. Not as I fight to keep my mind on this moment. I don't dare let my thoughts stray backward to the high striker game yesterday.

I keep them fixed on our promise to her last night in the parking lot outside an airport hotel: *You're our friend now too.*

And I keep them on the promise Ledger and I made last night at the bar. We're not going to act on our attraction. She's not a fling who'll happily wave goodbye to her two hockey hunks before she boards a jet back to Beirut at the end of the summer. "We think of Aubrey like a good friend," I add as I eye the ball, then my club, then the guy I'm traveling with. "Don't we, Ledger?"

"Sure do," he says, then swallows and looks away. Bet he's still thinking of that kiss she dropped on his cheek yesterday. How good it felt. What it'd be like if he'd just turned into it.

Like I'm thinking, even in spite of that damn promise we made.

"That's great," Garrett says. "If anyone sees you two taking her on a honeymoon, it's a damn good thing you're all friends."

Yup. We are definitely friends.

Later, when the short round of golf ends, Ledger

pulls me aside. "I had this idea. Something we could get Aubrey for the flight."

I jump all over that. "Tell me."

He gives me the details of the *little something*, as he calls it, and it sure sounds like he's as eager to get this show on the road as I am.

"I'll be in Sausalito. I'll pick it up," I offer.

"Perfect. We'll look for the right moment to give it to her."

"It's a plan."

"It's a nice, friendly thing to do," he says. "And we're going to make sure she has the honeymoon she deserves."

"Right. A nice, fun, friendly honeymoon." Those are the rules and we've set them.

Too bad I still feel tense all over. And I'd really like this feeling to go the fuck away.

11

WELL, SHE IS SINGLE NOW

Dev

After I pack—which takes all of five minutes since I am the king of the fast pack—I've only got a few more hours before it's wheels up. I leave my place on California Street, hop into my car that still has that fantastic new car smell a year later since I take care of this baby, and cruise over across the bridge to Sausalito. With my shades on and a new podcast blasting called News That Doesn't Suck, I take the curves, loving the feel of this ride. I had it outfitted at a custom car place, and it's a sleek matte-black battery-operated vehicle built from the ground up.

It's a dream car, and ever since I was a kid, I've wanted a ride like this. Now that I'm a big boy, I've got one.

Once I'm on the main drag, I stop at a tourist shop that carries specialty chocolates and grab a box of

Aubrey's favorites. Feeling pleased with this small gift —a show of friendship, that is all—I head up into the hills till I pull into the driveway of a two-story home overlooking Richardson Bay, its glass walls giving it an expansive view of the deep blue quiet water, then the majestic Golden Gate Bridge beyond.

It's a good view for my parents' therapy practice patients, too, and that's why I bought it for them. Also, they'd never have bought it themselves, and they deserve it.

I turn off the car and get out, bringing the chocolate with me so it doesn't melt, then gently rap my knuckles against the sign that reads Ryland and Ryland Counseling Services. Their practice is downstairs, and their home upstairs. It's a Sunday, though, so the shop is closed today. Dad's out with his kayak club. I don't have much time before I need to head to the airfield, but I was compelled to stop by. Some kind of antsy feeling was driving me on.

I bound up the steps to the home level, where a cacophony of barks greets my knock. It's like dogageddon in there, and the familiar sound is the first thing to truly soothe some of the knots I've been carrying in my shoulders.

"Coming, coming," my mom shouts over the noise inside. When she opens the door a few inches, I glimpse her directing stern words over her shoulder. "Lulu, be quiet. It's your brother."

A different dog yaps.

"You too, Virgil. Yes, I know he's your little brother. Now, both of you be quiet."

I smile in amused admiration when they shut up. Mom swings open the door the rest of the way. The little assholes are sitting primly at her feet like they weren't losing their Chihuahua minds a moment ago. Lulu's tail is a blur. Virgil's thumps hard.

My mom's hair is slicked back in a long ponytail. She wears glasses and trendy-looking dark blue yoga gear.

"Say hi to Devon now," she tells the pups.

Lulu hops up and down, whimpering in excitement. After I set the chocolate down on a high table, I bend and scoop up the little brown and tan critter. She licks my face. I breathe easily. Maybe this is what I needed?

"She missed you," Mom says, then urges me inside, shutting the door.

The black-and-white boy circles me, yapping again.

"Give some attention to your big brother," Mom chides.

"Mom, I am older than the dog." I pick him up, too, scratching his head.

"You were once, and then you weren't. It happens, sweetheart. It's called dog years," she says.

After I give them their necessary affection, I set each pup down, then head into the kitchen, passing the big-screen TV on the wall. It's paused on a yoga video. Mom gets to work making tea because it's always teatime for her. "Want some?"

"Nope. I just wanted to say hi before I head out of town." Yeah, I'm twenty-nine and still tell my parents when I leave for a trip. I'm that guy. But I—*gasp!*—like my parents. They're cool people.

She tilts her head as she scoops tea leaves into a pot. "Yes. Details. I've been dying to know since yesterday. Where are you going?"

As I stand at the counter, I give her the short version of what went down after we left the church.

Her jaw is agape. "Wow. All Garrett said was that the groom had taken off, but he was grateful to everyone for coming. Aiden's an even bigger asshole than I'd thought," she says as she hits stop on the kettle.

"Mom, I hope you don't use that language with your clients," I chide.

"Nope. Just my children," she says, then pours the hot water over the tea.

I drum my fingers on the counter, energy coursing through me, but a dose of tension too. "Anyway, so we're taking off. Just wanted you to know in case you can't reach me for, I dunno, a few hours."

"Devon, you say that like I'm not used to you being unreachable during eighty-two hockey games a year."

"You know what I mean."

Her gentle smile says she does. We like to keep in touch. Always have. I still have a group chat with my mom, dad, and big sister, who lives in London with her husband. But Lucy sends us pictures of her meals every day. Earlier today, she had falafels for lunch in Chelsea before shopping for a new tofu press.

"Yes, send me your GPS location," Mom jokes. Then her mood shifts and she sighs thoughtfully, drumming her fingers on the counter. "So...Aubrey?"

"Mom," I chide.

She stares at me over the top of her rose-gold frames. "Well, she is single now."

Like I'm not already thinking of Aubrey in that dangerous way. "Stop, Mom. Just stop." I don't need her fanning the flames. I can do that just fine on my own.

Mom lifts a steaming mug. "She's feisty, outgoing, funny. Sounds like someone I know. Someone I raised."

"She was literally about to walk down the aisle yesterday."

"And now she's literally about to take a trip with you and Ledger," she points out.

"Don't go there." I can't, just can't, linger in that space, for all the reasons Ledger and I laid out last night, starting and ending with the fact that she nearly got married yesterday. The timing is more than wrong.

But that doesn't explain why these feelings are still dogging me.

"I like her," Mom says. "Don't you?"

I say nothing while words tumble in my mind, my muscles tense as sentences start and stop on my tongue. I roll my shoulders, trying to let go of...whatever this is. I think back to the times I've chatted with Aubrey over the years. To the hockey games where I've seen her and the family events we've attended—like Garrett's Christmas party a few years ago, right before I met Eva. I swear there was a moment at that party, while Aubrey drank champagne and we cast guests we didn't know as characters from Christmas movies—*she's the sassy town baker; he's the hard-nosed lawyer with a secret heart of gold*—when I thought about what-ifs.

Then I remembered it's a bad idea to crush on a

friend's sister. Garrett's not the "don't touch my sister" kind of guy, and I'm not the kind of guy a dude needs to keep away from his family.

But I do like things to work out. I like life to go smoothly. I want parents who get along, a career that fulfills me, a body that performs at the highest level. What if I messed around with Garrett's sister and it didn't work out? Would she think I was a prick? I don't like rocking the boat. It might rock back. It probably *would* rock back.

Still, I should have objected to the wedding the night before the ceremony.

Better to speak up now even if these feelings go nowhere. "You know what?"

Mom freezes, mug halfway to her lips, eyes alert. "What is it?"

"I think you're right. I do have a thing for Aubrey, and that thing grew a little stronger after spending the whole day with her yesterday."

She struggles to hold back her smile but fails. Instead, she tries to hide it behind her mug, taking a sip of tea then setting it down. "And?" she asks.

I shrug. "Doesn't really matter if I have a thing for her. Now's just not the right time."

Holy shit. I don't struggle over the words, and I don't feel as tangled up as I did at the bar. Clearly, I needed to get that admission off my chest. Now I can just move forward with the trip, leaving these feelings behind.

"Things don't always happen at the right time," Mom says with a wisdom I'll never possess. "And yet they can still work out."

"Romance has a way of not working out in my life lately," I say. "Do I need to remind you about last Christmas?"

I legit thought I'd propose to Eva on Christmas. Instead, she surprised the hell out of me by breaking it off after we went ring shopping. Said I was too focused on my other love—hockey.

Well, hockey doesn't break my heart, so it's good that I'm not going to do a damn thing about this attraction.

Mom takes a drink of her tea, giving me a thoughtful look. "But that's always how it goes, sweetheart. It doesn't work out until it works out," she says.

Suddenly, her TV unfreezes and an upbeat feminine voice booms from the TV. "Are you ready for a morning Badass Yoga workout?"

I turn toward the big screen. Mom scurries across the room to grab her remote, the little dogs following at her feet like rats after the pied piper. The freckled blonde on the screen gives a confident, California-girl smile and says, "That's what I thought."

"You take Briar's classes," I point out. "That's cool..."

Mom hits pause and whispers conspiratorially. "She's so...motivating."

"She was great when she worked with us." The team hired her to teach some yoga classes last season. She was funny and calm at the same time while giving personalized tips for each athlete who needed them.

"I have a girl crush. Don't tell your father," my mom says, finger over her lips.

"I'll keep your secret."

"And I'll keep yours about your crush on Garrett's sister."

I shake my head at the Chihuahuas at my feet. "Why is she like this?"

But Lulu and Virgil don't have an answer.

12

HONEYMOON PRESENT

Aubrey

"I'm fine. I swear," I tell my mother for the ten millionth time. It's Sunday, a few hours before I'm due at the airfield.

Airfield! I'm still pinching myself.

"Are you sure?" My mom wrings her hands. Her kitchen table teems with boxes wrapped in silver and white foil, satiny ribbons curling over the sides. A pile of pristine envelopes sits next to the boxes. I suspect those envelopes hold gift cards and best wishes.

The sight of them brings a fresh wave of guilt. I hate that I inconvenienced so many people, but Mom is diligent. She'll make sure everyone gets their money and gifts back.

For now, I dry her dishes as I keep reassuring her, just as I've been doing since I arrived.

"I promise," I say. This is familiar choreography.

She frowns. "Really?"

"I swear."

Propping her up is second nature. I don't mind being her shoulder to lean on. That's what I was when my father died three years ago, and of course I'll be her shoulder now. I'm responsible for her woes, anyway.

"There has to be something I can do." She gestures to the fridge, eyes flickering with hope. "Can I pack something for your flight? A lunch? I have crackers and grapes, and I can whip up a sandwich like that." She snaps her fingers to punctuate her offer.

I'd sound like an asshole if I said what I was thinking. *I bet they have amazing snacks on a private jet, like chocolate-covered strawberries.*

I really should save my appetite.

I fight off a smile, not sure I want her to see exactly how excited I am to check out a plane. "Thanks, Mom. But I'm not hungry."

She waggles some freshly washed grapes in front of me. "Grapes are so good."

"I'm okay," I say as I finish drying the last dish and hang the towel on a hook by the sink.

She's quiet for a moment. "I'm sorry, sweetheart," she says softly, her voice quaking, then strengthening. "I should have known better. I should have seen it coming. I hate that he did this."

And her emotion escalated quickly from sorrow to anger.

"Me, too, but I swear I'll be okay. Apparently, he was flirting with the waitress at his bachelor party, so it's all for the best." I resist adding anything more. I'm not sure

I want to tell her I was having doubts myself. Nascent, unformed ones, but doubts, nonetheless. If I confess to second thoughts, she'll ask why, and then she'll dig, and I might say, "I wanted to make Dad happy."

Then she'd be sad all over again.

Best just to let her think I'm the tough, brave girl she's always seen in me.

"I brought the veil back," I say, carefully chipper. I gesture to the front of the house where I left the bag holding the veil. I hand-washed it last night, and it's safe and sound with her. The ring is back at my apartment in the Mission, the tiny one-bedroom I leased a few months ago since it's close to my Hayes Valley salon. Aiden was going to move in once we were married. He honestly never got around to it beforehand. Too busy with the pie shop an hour away, he said. In retrospect, maybe it was a subconscious choice we both made to *not* merge our lives.

I guess hindsight really is twenty-twenty.

"I'm glad it's back where it belongs," I say, chipper, just like I was when she and Dad gave each other the silent treatment during those years when their marriage was on the rocks.

"You can wear it when you m—" She breaks off, catching herself before she starts planning my *next* wedding, and shakes her head. "Well, you have fun. I'm glad those boys are going with you. I always liked them. Let me know if you need anything." She runs a hand down my hair. "Not that I can give you beauty tips anymore. In a few short years, you're better than I ever was."

"Oh, stop. You're an amazing stylist too." I give her a final goodbye, and after thirty minutes that felt like forever, I peel away from her and head out to my car.

Relieved to have that uncomfortable conversation behind me, I take a moment before I start the car to finish a bunch of emails I wrote last week to clients. I send each one a personalized happy birthday email, making sure to check in on life details they shared while I did their hair—the new TV show they started binging, their aunt's hip surgery, their boyfriend's new job.

With that done, I head to Doctor Insomnia's near Novato to meet Ivy and Trina. They texted to tell me they had a honeymoon present for me, and when I reach the coffee shop, they're already at a table outside with their goodest boys and girls. Trina's three-legged rescue pup Nacho sits dutifully at her feet, checking out the dogs walking by. Ivy's tiny senior girl, Roxy, is staring longingly at the vanilla latte Ivy's drinking.

"Hey, bestie," Trina says, thrusting a cup at me when I sit in the empty chair. It's my fave—a mango smoothie.

I take a fueling drink, then I don't waste a second. They get to know the full truth. "I didn't want to marry him in the first place. I was having mega doubts for the last few weeks. They were so strong I was literally about to tell you before he burst into the bridal room, and maybe he kinda did me a favor? But I'm sorry I didn't say anything sooner. Forgive me?"

Trina's smile disappears. "Seriously?"

Shit. She's mad? "You're annoyed?"

"No! You seriously think I'd be mad?" She thumps me playfully on the temple. "I think it's great. Sometimes the universe does you a favor, and your dog barfs up a pair of panties." That's how she learned her ex was cheating—the thong in question wasn't hers. "You're the best snitch," she tells the panty-loving pup, stroking his head.

Ivy sets her chin in her hand. "Or your boss posts a photo of herself, your ex-boyfriend, and a fake blow job."

I laugh, feeling guilt-free at last. "Or your almost groom says he wants to be your fuck buddy."

We lift our drinks to toast. When Trina sets down her ceramic mug, her green eyes are sparkling. "And you know what you do next?"

I shake my head. I know what *she* did next—had a VIP experience with two hot hockey stars.

So, correction: I shake my head *vehemently*. "That is not happening. We are not having a threesome."

Ivy chuckles. "Bet it happens before Trina and I even go to the Amelia Stone concert," she adds, gesturing to Trina and asking with her eyes *am I right*?

Trina nods. "Definitely."

"You're placing bets already?" But of course they are. Funny, I'm not jealous that I'll miss that concert because of my honeymoon. I was a little jealous before.

"Well, it's not like you're going to last till Thursday," Trina says, matter-of-factly. "That's my bang prediction."

I double-thump her head now. "I will last the whole trip. I will last forever."

My friends give exaggerated nods, and Trina adds, "But just in case, I got you a gift." She reaches into a canvas bag and hands me...a bottle of cherry-flavored lube. "It's a double honeymoon present."

I roll my eyes, but I take it since she's insisting. And I get where she's coming from. I gave her one when she moved in with her two hockey heroes for a week that turned into forever. "I won't use it."

"Want to bet on it?" Trina counters.

Ivy smiles slyly. I'm pretty sure Roxy does, too, as Ivy says, "I'll double down on that bet."

"There will be no doubling down," I insist.

Trina and Ivy just look at each other, with the smugness of two happily married and well-fucked babes. "Famous last words," they say in unison.

13

I'M CATNIP

Ledger

My cousin gently fingers the sticky flower on my back deck. "Don't deny it. You totally got this plant for the name," Hollis says, calling me out.

I cross my arms. "I did not."

Scoffing, he lets go of the plant that's hanging on the patio of my San Francisco home. His pointed look says he thinks I'm a big liar. "You did. Just admit it. Sticky monkey flower?" He gestures to the plant's friend, a Lamium, bursting with pink flowers in its pot in the corner. "Bet you're going to tell me the next one is a Leopard Racer. And then, I'm sure you've got a Banana Cat too."

I drag a hand down my face, fighting the laughter that always bubbles up when I'm with this guy. I can't give an inch, though, or he'll take a mile and, I dunno, test out his new sketch comedy on me when I'm eager as hell to get out of town. "Actually, there is a plant called the Dog Banana," I say evenly.

Hollis holds his arms out wide, like he owns the world. "It's official. I can be a plant namer in my next life."

"Or this life. You'll need a post-hockey career, after all." I instantly regret the doom warning. He doesn't need to hear that from me, and I'm the one who needs a career after hockey. My cousin is in the prime of his career, having recently joined Dev's team, the Golden State Foxes.

I wave, dismissing the topic, so we can just move on. "But thanks for taking care of the plants. Normally, my neighbor Shanti handles it, but she's in Houston for the week. One of her matchmaking clients is tying the knot."

His eyes sparkle. "Oh, I've been thinking about using a matchmaker someday."

Arching a brow, I shoot him a dubious look. "She specializes in Indian marriages in the U.S. Not white guys who play pro hockey for a living."

"Fine, fine, piss on my romance dreams. Anyway, stop stalling. And tell me more about the..." He waves a hand toward the Lamium. "I'm sure you're going to tell me it's a Pussycat Fruit."

I don't stifle my laugh this time, but I center myself quickly. I show him the rest of the plants on the patio, then head inside to my friends on the windowsill, giving him the lowdown on the care they need.

When we're finishing by the Calathea on the plant table, a sleek black cat materializes in the living room, slinking past us, stopping to rub against Hollis's leg. What the hell? Is there a blue moon?

"Jack. How's it going, bro?" Hollis says to the cat.

"Jack never comes out. He hates strangers. He hates people. He hates me," I say, incredulous at the unexpected feline appearance.

"Hate to break it to you, but I'm pretty much catnip." Hollis bends and offers a hand to Jack for sniffing.

The cat rubs his head against my cousin's palm. Yeah, Hollis is catnip all right. I glance at the sea-blue clock on the living room wall, made of recycled ocean plastic. My mind races a few hours ahead to the airfield, but I force my focus back to Hollis, who's squinting at the cat.

"He has one eye. Cool. I like that."

"I'm sure he did it for you."

Hollis scratches the traitorous beast's chin. "Jack, we're going to have a good time taking care of the monkey flowers."

A gentle rumble fills the air.

"Is he—" I can't bring myself to say it.

Hollis flashes me an easy grin. "Yes, he's purring. What can I say? Cats like me, dogs like me, people like me. I'm just that kind of guy. Plus, I've been watching this vet show, and I learned a ton of cool shit. Like, do you brush your cat's teeth?"

"No. I don't have a death wish."

"Cool. I'm gonna make it my mission then. I've seen every single one of Doctor Lennox's vids, so I'm pretty sure I can do it just as well as a vet."

I stifle a groan. It's evidently my fate to be surrounded by cocky fuckers. I don't bother to point out that the good doctor, known for his *The Hot Vet* series, *might* have some tricks up his DVM sleeve. "Good luck, buddy. If you freshen Jack's breath...free beer for life."

"It is on," Hollis says. I show him the cat food tin and the litter, giving him the rest of the details as Jack the Traitor follows my cousin everywhere.

When we're done, Hollis reaches into his back pocket and produces a string with a feather at the end.

"Where did you find that?"

Hollis dangles it in front of the cat, who bats it, then pins it to the reclaimed wood floor. "I brought it," Hollis says. "You said you wanted me to take care of the cat, so I figured I'd be the cool cat uncle."

I give him a genuine smile. "Appreciate it. I really do."

"Anytime," he says. "Well, not while I'm at an away game."

"I hear ya."

On the way to the door, Hollis asks with natural curiosity, "Where did you say you're going?"

I pause, unsure if I want to say much about my trip, but I should give him a little. He is helping out after all. "Washington State. Cute little island off a ferry." I leave off who I'm going with. It's not a secret, but it feels private. Especially since it involved a promise made last night at a bar, sealed with a brew and a bubbly water.

"That sounds nice," he says. "Have fun, and don't do anything I wouldn't do."

"That doesn't leave much, does it?"

"Fact," he agrees. "So good luck." With that, he takes off into the city on a Sunday morning.

I shut the door, a pop of adrenaline rushing through me, the kind you feel when you're going away with someone you want to be more than friends with.

Too bad I have no business feeling this way. I can't act on this desire, no matter how much I want to turn the tables on Aubrey and surprise her with one hell of a knee-weakening, toe-curling kiss.

* * *

Two hours later, I roll up to the airfield in Novato, jittery like I've drunk too much coffee when I've had none.

But when I head into the tiny terminal and see Aubrey sitting next to Dev, showing him something on her phone, that jittery feeling morphs into something else.

Something I haven't felt around a woman, or around the game of hockey in a while.

Excitement.

It's both welcome and entirely dangerous.

14

MELTS IN YOUR MOUTH

Aubrey

I've seen enough TV to imagine what flying private looks like. Cushy leather seats, immaculate service, the royal treatment. Reality is even better.

Thirty minutes into a smooth flight up the coast, I run a palm along the buttery material of my chair. There are four spacious seats on this Embraer Phenom jet, one on each side of the aisle, so every seat has a window, and we face each other.

"It's official," I say, meeting the gaze of the guys across from me. "I'm addicted."

Dev smiles in agreement. "It's hard to go back to commercial."

"Especially since you always need the tenth row," Ledger says to Dev.

I swivel my gaze to Dev. "Superstitious?"

"It works. I'm telling you, it works," Dev says, clearly

a believer.

Ledger cups the side of his mouth. "And, he laces his skates up right skate first."

"Because I'm right-handed, man," Dev says.

"Sure," Ledger says.

"Not everything I do is a superstition."

"But most things are," Ledger counters with his eyes on me, and I can tell he's ribbing him for my benefit. Well, ribbing appreciated.

"Can we make always flying private your new superstition?" I tease.

Dev smiles knowingly. "See? They're a good thing. I'm glad you like the service, Aubs."

There's also a flight attendant on the plane. I don't even know why we have one, but Dev said the service came with the plane. Since Sterling has already brought us prosecco, I can't complain. I swirl the crystal flute I'm holding, having too much fun. "Yes, please book me a private flight every time, Fitzgibbons," I say in a snooty British voice.

"Is Fitzgibbons your butler or your personal secretary?" Ledger asks, amused.

"Don't you know? All good hair stylists need personal secretaries." I take a drink of the delicious bubbly and a very obvious idea hits me. "This isn't the same as a private jet or anything, but if either of you ever need a haircut, it's on the house." Already, I know they'll try to pay me, so I preemptively put my foot down. "And if you ever go to another stylist I'll be devastated for life, so consider that before you get your locks trimmed elsewhere."

Dev rakes his fingers through his messy hair. It's light brown, wavy, a little on the long side. More shaggy than anything though. "Aubs, is that your subtle way of saying I need a haircut?"

"No. Your locks are lovely," I say to Dev.

He winks, and then I look at Ledger as I finish off my glass of champagne. "Yours are too."

"Glad you think so," Dev says, tugging at his own hair. "Because while I might not tie up my shoes in a set order due to superstition, *Ledger*"—he drops the name like it's an insult—"I do always save my off-season haircut and get it chopped right before the first game."

In seconds, Sterling materializes at my side. "Would you like some more, ma'am?"

Damn, that is some kind of service. Sterling's older than I am by a couple decades, so I hardly feel like a ma'am but still, I tell the silver-haired, barrel-chested man in the black pants and white dress shirt that I'd love another glass.

"As you wish," he says, then takes the flute to fill it.

He retreats to the galley and Ledger arches a brow at me. "Question for you."

"Hit me up."

"Do you cut your own hair? I've always been curious."

"I can. But I don't." I cross my legs and kick my foot back and forth, the pink knee-high boot like a metronome, keeping the tempo of the conversation.

"Why not?"

"A haircut is one of life's great pleasures. Why deny myself?"

Ledger nods a few times, seemingly liking that answer. "Then who does it for you?"

"My mom," I reply easily. "She says it makes her happy."

The flight attendant returns with another glass. "Here you go, ma'am."

"Thank you so much, Sterling. This is amazing," I say to the helpful man. Maybe he'll use my name now. I've told him to call me Aubrey.

"You're welcome, ma'am." And no such luck. "Is there anything else I can get for you?"

A Jet Ski? A koala? An omelet? "Chocolate with caramel?" I ask, not seriously expecting a yes. Or for Dev to laugh instantly. Ledger chuckles too.

"Of course," Sterling says.

I blink, straightening. The attendant disappears and I stare, slack-jawed, at Dev then whisper, "Is he really getting chocolate with caramel?"

Something passes between the guys—there's a spark in their eyes. Then, Ledger answers, "I told Dev you liked that kind of chocolate. He picked some up for you this morning."

I am floored by his unexpected thoughtfulness. "But I should be giving you guys a gift." I sweep out an arm, indicating the plush travel. "For this. For hanging out with me."

Dev's lips curve into a sexy grin, the kind a man gives before he leans in and kisses a woman possessively. But then, his smile shifts, turns broader. Friendlier. "Like I said, you're our friend now too."

Still, this is above and beyond friendship. "Well, I

like it. And don't think you can escape from my friendship clutches now, or my hairstylist ones. I fully expect you to show up for those cuts on the house," I say, then swivel my gaze to Ledger. "How did you know I liked that chocolate?"

Ledger glances out the window, then back at me, his expression is sheepish. "I just remembered it from one of Garrett's parties."

I smile, a rush of warmth sliding over my skin like last night. Or maybe...I feel even warmer. "I do like chocolate with caramel. *A lot*. My favorite chocolate shop in the city is Elodie's. I go there far too often. They know my name. They say *Hi, Aubrey* when the bell chimes and I go in. They give me this tray with a couple of my favorite chocolates with caramel and I swear they melt in my mouth."

Ledger's blue eyes sparkle as he holds my gaze. "Sounds delicious."

"Bet they taste...incredible," Dev adds, not looking away from me either.

I feel both their eyes on me. That warmth rolls down my chest, heading toward my belly. They're looking at me like they're enjoying those images a lot. Like they're imagining the taste of the chocolate...on my lips.

And I'm picturing...my hands in their hair.

Impulsively, I undo my seatbelt, then scoot next to Ledger, wedging myself by his side in his comfy seat, hip to hip. The press of his strong body is a little distracting. So is his scent, like nighttime and the starlit ocean. But I'm a hairstylist on a mission. I take a fortifying sip of my bubbly, then set the glass in his hand.

He takes it, giving me a quizzical look.

"Just hold it. I have an idea for your hair," I explain, staring at his dark locks, slicked back and neatly combed. I'm pretty sure there's just enough length for my plans. My fingers tingle with excitement. I can't wait to see if this works. "Can I?"

Ledger huffs out a breath, then nods a little unsteadily. "Yes." It sounds like a grunt.

I set one hand on his left shoulder, angling him near to me. There are only inches between us, but I'm used to being close to people. It's part of my job.

I run my fingers through the front of his hair, tousling it, and he tenses, drawing a sharp inhale.

"Is this okay?" I ask, concerned.

He doesn't answer with words. Just a curt nod that's a clear *yes*. I keep going, running my fingers a little more roughly through his locks, mussing them up on top. Just as I suspected. He *does* have enough length to give him some height and volume. With some product I could really do something trendy. But I can still make a difference with my fingers. I play with his hair. A minute later, I lean back, appraising his new style.

Ledger meets my gaze with expectant eyes. "How is it?"

I'm motionless for a few seconds as wild ideas flash through my mind. Of Dev telling me to touch Ledger then asking how it is. Then of Ledger demanding I kiss Dev.

Do they like that? Watching a woman be kissed? Seeing a woman get turned on?

I gulp, trying to cover up my sudden breathlessness at touching my travel companion and thinking about him in new ways.

Wait. Make that *both* of them.

My brain flips faster through those images now, picturing Ledger pulling me all the way onto his lap, then sliding those big hands down my arms. To Dev getting in on the act, coasting a hand over my leg. One man dusting his lips on this side of my neck, the other man kissing the other side of me.

A double kiss. I shudder.

Snap out of it.

Clearly, I have too many besties banging two dudes. Just because it happened to them doesn't mean it'll happen to me.

I'm saved by the bell when Sterling arrives holding a gleaming silver tray. Four pieces of mouth-watering chocolate adorn a plate, next to a stack of fresh linen napkins. "From my favorite place," I say, amazed as I recognize the chocolates.

"Good," Ledger says.

"Enjoy," Dev adds.

The craving in me intensifies. I return to my seat, where Sterling places the tray on a side table.

I don't need two men. I don't even need one. I have chocolate.

When I pop one into my mouth, I feel both men watching me as I eat it.

15

DOUBLE BOOKED

Aubrey

I have to stop thinking about them touching me.

Like, is there a brain eraser somewhere at the rental car counter at the tiny airport? Some potion I can take?

I can't spend the whole trip picturing them pleasuring me.

Just focus on the day, the trip, the agenda.

That's what I tell myself as we head to the SUV. I canceled the compact car I'd reserved at the city's major airport, and Dev rented this one instead.

Dev holds open the passenger door.

We get inside and I yank on my seatbelt as Dev plugs the directions in his phone. We need to catch the early evening ferry to McDoodle Island.

But before he turns on the car, he toggles over to his music app. "First, we need a song to set the mood."

"Another superstition?" I ask.

With a confident nod, he says, "Yup. You pick."

"DJ privileges. Excellent," I say, and this is good. This is trip stuff. It's not dirty stuff.

Though, as I scroll through Dev's music app, I'm not so sure anymore. The man likes seriously sexy music. Two Feet, The Weeknd, Sam Smith, Leon Bridges.

Not helpful, Dev.

Maybe I can find, I dunno, "Over the Rainbow" or "On the Good Ship Lollipop." I pick Sam Smith and hope my hormones don't go into overdrive. Though, doubtful.

I try to ignore the lyrics and the feel as best as I can as we cruise away from the municipal airport in Renton, heading toward the ferry that'll take us across Puget Sound, whisking us to the edge of the state. As we wind through the emerald city, towering evergreens hugging the road, I focus on the trip only. I'm going to be the best travel companion ever. "So what do you guys want to do first? I have a list of all sorts of fun possibilities. We can hike. Or go to Deception Pass," I say, picturing the landmark of the region, a gorgeous bridge connecting two islands.

"Sounds good," Dev says.

"And the grape stomping. We can do that too."

"Cool," Ledger says from the back seat.

I don't stop. I want them to know I've planned a damn good time for us. "There's an old logging town that's supposedly like a ghost town now. I love ghost towns, and—"

"Aubs." Dev's voice is like a warning as he flicks the turn signal at a sign for the ferry terminal.

Shoot. Is he mad at me? For what?

"Yes?"

"I'm good with anything. We're good with anything. You don't have to be a tour guide. We're gonna have fun," he says, and there he goes again, reading me. Figuring me out.

I close my eyes for a second, feeling foolish for having tried so hard. But, in my defense, my libido's been stealing the stage.

"We will," I say.

Once we turn into the ferry lot, Dev heads down a lane for boarding and pays for the ride. "It's all good. We can play it by ear, or we can take turns planning each day," he says, and dammit. With those words—*take turns*—my mind's off to the races again, picturing them taking turns with me as Sam Smith plays in the dimly lit hotel room.

We make small talk as we line up to drive onto the ferry, then as we hang out on the main deck overlooking the bright blue water of the sound. But I'm taking in Dev, his messy hair, his bright eyes, his trim beard, his teal polo shirt. Ledger, with his inked forearm, his trim haircut, his black shirt.

"That's a nice shirt. You look good in black," I say to Ledger, like I'm just giving friendly fashion advice.

He doesn't answer right away. Just lets a slow, almost seductive smile form on his lush lips. "Good. Because my whole wardrobe is black," he says.

"It is?"

"All my shirts are black. Different shades of black," he says.

That's kind of hot in a way I didn't expect. Maybe because he's a man who's decided this is who I am. This is what I wear. That's sexy, knowing yourself.

Just as Dev is sexy with his music playlist, his superstitions, and his big, open heart.

They're different in ways that intrigue me and similar in ways that interest me. As the horn blasts, signaling the ferry's pulling away, I'm struck with a crystal-clear realization.

I'm wildly attracted to both of them. Just like my friends predicted.

If anyone asked me what I talked about on the drive to the inn, I'd be hard-pressed to answer in any kind of intelligent detail.

My head is clogged with one potent thought—I almost got married yesterday and today I'm lusting wickedly after the two men I'm double honeymooning with.

Did I know they were attractive when I planned this trip with them late last night? Of course. But I didn't expect to feel this shivery sensation that's been wreaking havoc with my senses. Only, my lust is growing stronger, beating louder, spreading through my whole damn body.

When we pull up to the inn, it's like I'm floating on a cloud of delectable cologne. Cedar and soft suede, the scent of Dev. Nighttime and the ocean, signaling Ledger.

As we get out of the car, I draw a big inhale of the faint sea breeze air, hoping it recalibrates me.

Once I get to the suite, I'll go to my room with its own en-suite bathroom. I'll get my bearings. I'll take a shower. Wash the dirty thoughts out of my head. Deal with the trip and shelve this lust.

With my suitcase and resolve in hand, I go inside with my brother's best friends.

Blackberry Inn isn't a tiny B and B. It has maybe fifty to seventy-five rooms and it's spread out over a cliff, overlooking the water. I home in on the details in the lobby. The walls are painted a rich orange, contrasting with the wooden beams on the ceiling. Vintage maps line the walls, nestled alongside sea glass artwork. It's rustic meets modern.

At the front desk, a man with ginger hair, freckles sprinkled across his pale skin, and small brown eyes greets us. "Good afternoon. Are you checking into the Blackberry Inn?"

His accent is British, which is unusual in the Pacific Northwest.

"Yes, we are...Harry..." Ledger says, reading the name tag indicating he's the general manager, but then Ledger stops short at the last name. Titterington. That's, um, a mouthful. Clearing his throat, Ledger starts again. "Aubrey Emerson. We called last night to change it from the honeymoon suite to a three-room suite."

Harry flashes a professional ready-to-help smile. "Ah yes, the family suite. Very popular." Harry scans the computer. Squints. "When did you say you called?"

"Last night," Ledger adds. He's calm, but my pulse speeds up. Harry's question concerns me.

"Yes, last night," I repeat, like that'll help Harry find it faster.

"Right. I see a note about the request," he says.

"Oh, good. I thought it was missing," I say, relieved since I don't want anything going wrong on this trip. Not after the fiasco of my whole damn wedding.

The manager winces and then offers an *I'm about to disappoint you* smile. "The thing is..."

"You don't have our reservation," I blurt out.

"We do," Harry reassures me. "But it seems whoever took your change last night was mistaken. We can't make any changes to a non-refundable booking."

He flashes a smile that both says *sorry* and *you're shit out of luck.*

"But the person I spoke to last night said it was no problem. That you upgrade all the time," I say, panic rising in me right along with my pitch. *Harry, help a girl out!* How am I supposed to share a room with these two men and all my desire? It's like an elephant tromping around. I'll call her Ellie the Elephant. She's a very dirty girl.

Another grin from the man behind the counter. This one says he's a brick wall. A nice brick wall but an unscalable one, nonetheless. "Yes, and I do regret the misunderstanding. I'll have to see who was staffing the phones last night and educate them on the policy. But our non-refundable suites are also *not changeable.*" He swivels his tablet screen around to show me the policy, like that'll soothe the wild thrashing of lust and worry in my chest.

"Harry," Dev says with his customary warmth, "I hear ya. And that makes perfect sense. But you probably have other rooms. I'd be happy to handle it," he says, and I can't let him pay for another room. He already booked a private freaking jet.

I set a hand on Dev's arm. His very big, very strong, very touchable arm. "You don't have to," I say, taking my hand off right away. I don't need more temptation.

Dev's green eyes meet mine, flickering with tenderness and concern. "I know. I want to. For you," he says, holding my gaze.

My heart pounds.

I feel foolish for *not* wanting to share with them. It'll be fine. Of course it'll be fine. I handled getting dumped at the altar yesterday. I've handled my mother's emotions for the last few years. I've weathered the grief of my father's death. There is no need for my little internal freak-out. Ellie the Elephant will be fine, and so will I. "It'll be fine," I say, meaning it. "I swear."

"We want you to have a good trip," Ledger puts in.

Dev turns back to the man with the magic tablet, trying again. "Can you get us some more rooms?"

One more *sorry* smile comes our way. "We don't have any other suites available. There's a wine festival in town and every room is booked." Harry pauses, peering at the screen again. He holds up a finger. "This is interesting."

He found a room! For Ellie the Elephant and me. "You found something?"

His brow knits, then he lifts his face. "It seems whoever made the change last night put you in our Ultra-Deluxe Honeymoon Suite instead of the Deluxe Honeymoon Suite."

I perk up. "Does it have three beds?"

Harry shakes his head. "No, but the tub is bigger."

Oh, great. Thanks, Harry. I'll just put my lust in the tub for the next few days. No problem.

"Thanks," I say.

"And the beds are bigger too. So, there you go."

Wait! There's hope on the horizon from Harry Titterington. "*Bedssssss?*"

I mean, surely there are honeymoon suites somewhere, someplace, with beds plural? Like, for sets of twins honeymooning together. That has to be a thing.

"This suite has one very big bed."

One big bed for my brother's two best friends and me.

16

THE BED PROCLAMATION

Aubrey

Act normal, act normal, act totally fucking normal.

After we grab the bags from the car, Dev thanks the valet and tips him well. With suitcases in tow, the three of us head to the elevator. No one has said a real word since we left the front desk with key cards in hand. Just the basics. *Here's your bag, I'll carry it, what floor are we on.*

The tension is thick as we step into the small elevator. If this isn't a metaphor for the next week, being trapped in this small space with two hockey studs, I don't know what is.

But this kind of uncomfortable silence is familiar to me. And since I got us into this situation, I'll have to see us through. "There's probably a couch," I say, looking on the bright side as the doors to the elevator shut.

"Maybe even two," Dev offers, equally hopeful.

"Guys, I'll take the couch," Ledger says, laying down the law like that.

And what? Give the bed to Dev and me? That's even weirder, sharing a bed with just *one* of the guys. "I'll take the couch," I say, eagerly volunteering. Then I jut out a hip and gesture to myself. "I'm not a big hockey player."

"No way," they say in unison.

"I'll take it," Dev says.

"I'm sure we can get a rollaway bed," Ledger counters.

"When was the last time you saw one of those in a hotel?" Dev asks his friend, clearly skeptical.

"When was the last time *you* saw one?" Ledger fires back.

"On TV," Dev says. "Some Christmas movie where there was, gee, only one room at the inn."

"You and your Christmas movies," Ledger says as the elevator chugs slowly. "I'm pretty sure in real life hotels offer rollaway beds and stuff."

"They do," Dev says, acknowledging Ledger's point. "But when was the last time you slept on one?"

Ledger seems like he's about to answer but his brow knits, as if maybe he's trying to remember if he has conked out on one lately.

"Exactly," Dev adds quickly. "It's been a while. They're hell on backs. Like in the movie when the rollaway bed was fuck-all uncomfortable. You want to wake up with your back trying to murder you?"

Ledger huffs but finally concedes, grumbling out a "no."

Which means we're back to square one. My heart speeds up uncomfortably. I've got to find a solution. But I don't know how to fix this conundrum.

Maybe Ledger has an ace up his sleeve, though, because he waggles his phone. "But here's another idea. I'll just find the nearest Walmart and get an air mattress." He barks into the device. "Google, where is the nearest Walmart?"

Spoiler alert: it's not going to be close. But I'll let him find that out on his own.

Ledger's phone is cheery with its reply: "The nearest Walmart is thirty miles away. Two hours by car and ferry."

Undeterred, Ledger asks again, "Google, where is the nearest camping supply store?"

This is going so badly. No matter how uncomfortable this whole situation is, I can't let them go buy an air mattress to solve this problem.

Another upbeat response comes as the elevator slows: "The nearest camping supply store is four miles away."

"Guys," I say as we reach the fourth floor. "There's no need for an air mattress. I'll just get a tent at the camping store."

Dev's brow crinkles, and the furrow is adorable. Ledger's lips part, but he's speechless. Their double confusion over who's getting what at the camping store is too cute—and precisely what I'd hoped for. This isn't my first defuse-the-tension rodeo. "I'll set it up outside. I've always wanted to sleep under the stars. It was actually on my adventure list for the honeymoon," I say as I wheel my suitcase off the elevator, pretending like I really will pitch a tent to fix the situation.

Ledger growls. "You're not sleeping in a tent, Aubrey."

Dev nods fiercely. "You're going to sleep in a big, comfy bed. We're not letting you have anything but the honeymoon you deserve."

But they deserve a good trip too. When we reach the room, I stop outside the door, turn to them, and lay down the rules. "Harry said it was a big bed. We're friends. We'll just share it as friends. It'll be great."

There. Sometimes a girl has to take charge and issue a bed proclamation.

Ledger swallows roughly, his Adam's apple bobbing up and down. Gruffly, he says, "It'll be fine."

True to his fun-loving nature, Dev gives an easy shrug. "I don't move when I sleep, so I'm basically the best bed companion in the history of the world."

A laugh bursts from Ledger. "There's nothing you can't turn into a pat on the back, is there?"

Dev's smile is pure devil as he says, "Nope."

He unlocks the door, opens it, and without giving a girl a warning, he scoops me up in his arms for the second time in as many days. His eyes meet mine, glimmering playfully as he says, "Let's carry the bride over the threshold."

My stomach flips.

Ledger RSVPs to Dev's invitation without a second thought. "Yeah, let's do it," he says as he moves next to him and slides his strong arms under my calves.

I don't need them both to carry me together. Hell, I don't need a man to carry me, period.

But they seem to want to.

Together, they carry me into the room, and I try not to think about how good it feels to be in their arms.

17

THE CURSE OF AN ASS MAN

Ledger

There are fucking rose petals on the bed. To make matters worse, they're strewn into the shape of a giant heart. The second Aubrey steps into the bedroom of the suite, she lays eyes on them, then groans out a long and plaintive, "Seriously? *Seriously?*"

We're right behind her in the doorway. I turn to Dev, feeling a little helpless. Is it the roses, the bed, or the whole damn suite? Or the reminder of what could have been?

She drops her head into her hand.

Ah, hell. Maybe she's sad again. Or, more likely, maybe she's going to beat herself up once more for *almost* marrying that turd bucket.

What do we do, I mouth to Dev. He's way better with this emotional stuff than I am.

But Dev is at her service in no time, striding past

her toward the bed. "I'll just get rid of those bad boys right now," he says.

Aubrey lifts her face, shakes her head. "No, that's not it."

He stops as she spins around and flaps a hand to the living room. We passed through it to reach the bedroom, but now she's turned back and is pointing to the coffee table across from a couch. A bucket of ice sits on the table, a bottle of champagne peeking out. Two flutes are next to it on the table. "It's just..."

Maybe that champagne is getting to her? Hell if I know.

She cuts a path to the bottle and picks up a white envelope leaning against the bucket. Sliding a pink manicured fingernail under the flap, she opens it, reads, then bursts into big, rich peals of laughter, like she did on the grassy hill outside 7-Eleven yesterday.

I don't get it.

Dev shrugs, seeming equally perplexed. When Aubrey looks up from the card, a smile has tipped her glossy lips. She must have reapplied her lip gloss in the car. Her mouth is shiny and entirely too kissable, especially when she laughs like that, all carefree.

Before she lets us in on the joke, though, she heads to the hotel phone next to the couch and stabs a button. In a few seconds, she says, "Yes, I'm curious if this champagne is complimentary."

She's quiet, but her grin grows wider. Wilder too. "Thank you."

After she hangs up, she clears her throat and reads the card. "Surprise! Just a little something extra from your groom. Because you deserve it, my beautiful bride," she says, then meets our eyes with glee in hers. Like it's a graduation cap, she tosses the card high in the air. Her brown eyes twinkle with wicked delight as she grabs the neck of the bottle, tugs it out of the bucket, and waggles it in a way that's far too sexy. But she *is* holding a phallic object, so it's not unreasonable for me to think dirty thoughts. "Champagne's on Aiden tonight, boys!"

"I'll drink to that," Dev says.

"Such a shame he remembered to book his super-saver fare but forgot to cancel the Cristal he paid for." I shake my head in mock sympathy.

"Karma's a bitch." She sings out the last word like it has ten syllables and heads toward the en-suite bathroom. She freezes in the doorway, though, turning into a statue of a woman, all long, lush red hair curling down her back, leading to a fantastic ass.

Wow. Just look at that backside.

That black skirt is doing illegal things to her body, hugging her nice and tight. But I really shouldn't think about her curves, especially after last night, especially after Dev and I made a gentleman's pact to give her the honeymoon she deserves.

Yet I can't look away. Call it the curse of an ass man. I want to bend her over the bed and spank that fine flesh, to hear her yelp, then moan in pleasure, then beg for more.

After a few seconds in the bathroom entrance, Aubrey unfreezes, glancing over her shoulder, and... fuck my dirty fantasies. She's even prettier like that, lips parted, something sly and clever flickering in those irises. "The tub *is* big. Hope you brought your bathing suits like I told you to."

She heads into the bathroom, and I've got no choice but to follow her.

"Holy shit," I say once I turn into the spacious room.

It's not a bath.

It's a hot tub set into the corner of a giant bathroom, with a big marble step heading up to it. From the tub, you can enjoy a view of the water and the emerald trees below.

But I'm not thinking about that view.

I'm thinking about the future view of her in the tub. And whether I'll be stupid enough to get in it with her.

Chances are, I probably will.

When I catch Dev's gaze, he's staring at her like he's picturing the same damn scene.

This is going to be the hardest honeymoon in history.

18

THE DAILY DOSE OF GOOD

Dev

I'm not disciplined for nothing.

The way I see it, all my training in the weight room, on the ice, and at the dinner table when I resist carbs will come in handy tonight.

I can resist the woman I want just like I can resist bread.

I'll have to be my own goalie, saving me from me.

The key will be routine. First, we'll grab some food, and as we eat, I'll make sure we chitchat about anything else in the world besides sex, beds, and romance.

Starting now.

On the walk to the restaurant, Ledger waggles his phone and tells us he needs to return a call to his dad, so he ambles ahead, and we give him some space. I reach into my grab bag of fun facts and turn to the woman by my side. "Did you know there's a prehistoric bird once thought to be extinct that's now roaming through the wilds of New Zealand again?"

Aubrey tilts her head. "What kind of bird?"

"Takahē. An iridescent flightless bird and now a conservation success story. My parents sent me an article on it. That's their shtick. Happiness," I say.

"Do you mean that's their schtick as therapists?"

As we turn the corner, we pass a sundry shop with a rack of postcards out front. I'm tempted to thumb through them, but I resist the pull. "A lot of their clients are dealing with anxiety and depression due to, well, the state of the world. Climate change and all. So they're both big on trying to teach them about finding happiness in the moment. Compassion. Kindness. But those two often stem from finding personal happiness. So, they look for the good news in the world," I explain. "And they send it to me each morning."

Aubrey's smile is soft, almost enchanted. "They send you stories every day?"

"*The Daily Dose of Good*, they call it." Maybe it's cheesy to share this. But I'm proud of them. "Their theory is that focusing on some of the good things happening can help you experience more happiness, and that can offset, I suppose, the shitty things."

"I love that. I think I believe it. I want to believe it," she says, clearly giving it some thought. "What about you?"

"Hard to do, but I try," I say.

Except a dark cloud floats over me. Do I try hard enough? Sometimes I get too caught up in the intensity of my job, the drive needed to play at the top of my game. Happiness sometimes takes a back seat to ambition, that powerful motherfucker.

"What else do they send you in the daily dose? Like, what was in it today?" Aubrey asks, her ankle boots click-clacking on the sidewalk as we pass a vintage shop peddling antique road signs right beside blouses and teacups.

"Honestly, their stuff is the antidote to the regular news. For instance, I read a story about a landfill in Latin America that became a mangrove forest. Or, there was one about a dude who used discarded vape batteries to build an electric scooter."

"Oh! I keep meaning to try out a scooter. I'd love to get around on something upcycled."

I picture Aubrey on a scooter, her flaming hair fanning out from under a helmet, her legs lean as she cruises from her place in the Mission to her hair salon in Hayes Valley.

Would she wear those little black ankle boots she has on now? Or maybe those tall pink ones from the plane? Or a pair of dark red thigh-high socks that peek out over the tops of her black boots like the ones she wore to that Christmas party a few years ago?

That party before Eva. For a sliver of a second, I wonder—was that my chance?

Did I miss it?

The cloud darkens more.

So much for the daily dose of good.

* * *

I'm back on track a little later as we finish dinner at The Green Pantry, a farm-to-table restaurant that she had on her restaurant research list.

All the tension from the room mishap vanished long ago thanks to the lube of good food and friendly conversation.

We've shot the breeze about the upcoming hockey season, though Ledger kept his mouth shut, for the most part, about the sport we both love. I can guess why, but I sense I shouldn't poke around there.

Aubrey told us about a photography class she's been taking online, since she wants to improve her photography of clients and their styles. "I've found that a good picture makes people happy, like a good hair day or a good chat," she says, then sets down her fork with a clink next to the remains of her mushroom and snap pea polenta. "And a free meal. So maybe Aiden will surprise us and have paid the bill."

Yup. We're back on track, keeping things in the friend zone. "Maybe he even surprised you every day of the honeymoon. Tomorrow could be a...surprise spa day," I offer building on this tale of Aiden's clearly unintended generosity. Aiden is a cockblocker. This will for sure do the trick.

"Don't get me excited," Aubrey says.

"I bet he has chocolate-covered strawberries waiting for us when we return to the room," Ledger says.

"Now you're really teasing." The spark in her brown eyes tells me she loves that idea.

Immediately, I want to find berries for her. I grab

my phone. "Siri, does the Blackberry Inn have chocolate-covered strawberries?"

Siri responds quickly with, "The number of calories in chocolate and berries is—"

With a groan, I punch the volume on the phone. "Shut it, Siri. No one needs your calorie buzzkill."

Another time, I'll check on the option. Maybe back at the hotel. With a contented sigh, Aubrey tilts her head. A soft smile tips her pretty pink lips. "Guys, seriously. Thank you. I know the whole 'sharing a suite' thing is awkward, but I appreciate you just rolling with everything on this trip," she says.

My heart warms. It's worth it, tabling all these feelings. Worth it to make her see there are good guys in the world. "You say it like it's a hardship to handle a change in the schedule." I lean back in the chair, my empty plate in front of me since I polished off every last bit of my seared salmon and summer green beans.

"I don't know. Change is hard for a lot of people." She sounds a little resigned, maybe disappointed too. "Aiden didn't like it one bit when things didn't go according to plan. He'd get very antsy and agitated."

I want to roll my eyes and tell her how damn glad I am that he's the ex, but then I realize she doesn't need to hear that. *She's* glad he's the ex. She's telling me this because she's worried we'd be the same. "That must have sucked. When he acted that way," I say, gently.

She brightens. "It definitely made me tense at times. Wondering how he'd handle it if I had a last-minute client or a schedule change," she says, then she dips her face, lifting it a second later and saying to us in a shy whisper, "Is it weird that I feel seen right now from what you just said? Because I do. I just do."

Too many people are used to being treated like shit. They assume it's the norm. I hate that she's felt that way. "You should. What you said makes all the sense in the world," I say, emphatic.

After Ledger takes a final drink of his wine, he adds, "Doesn't sound like fun to go through the day always looking behind you."

"It wasn't. Though, the weird part is my dad was so sure Aiden was a good guy," she says. "He was so happy when I dated Aiden briefly after college, and so convinced he was my *one who got away*."

And the picture of Aubrey colors in some more. She must have felt the pressure of expectations. "Was that one of the reasons you said yes to his proposal? Because you thought your dad wanted it for you?"

Like it costs her something, she nods. "I think so."

"That's gotta be hard. Wanting to live up to someone who's not here anymore."

Ledger shifts closer to her, tapping the table, perhaps to make his point. "That's normal though. Most of us are wired that way. Hell, I want to make my dad happy and he's around. That's why I called him back earlier. He wanted to talk all things broadcast booth," Ledger says. "It's hard to want to make someone else happy. But to have to think about it when someone you love is gone? Hell, Aubrey. That's a lot."

Aubrey sighs, sounding a little relieved. "Thanks for understanding. I guess Aiden tricked a lot of people. I just wish I'd figured it out sooner."

"Hey," I say, sitting up straighter, leveling her with my gaze. "That's just what some people do. That's what some people are good at. Don't beat yourself up."

"It can take you a while to figure it out," Ledger adds. "Took me a while with my ex."

I give a nod of solidarity. "Same here. With mine."

Aubrey leans closer, her gaze focused on Ledger, then me, like she wants to know both of us better. "What happened?"

She's so curious, so earnest as she asks that I know I'll tell her. I'm sure I'll start to open up.

Guess I'm not such a good goalie when it comes to keeping her out.

19

IT'S A WHOLE THING

Aubrey

I latch onto Ledger's last comment. *It can take you a while to figure it out.*

Like I did last night at the diner with Dev, I wonder again if Ledger's speaking from experience. I don't know much about Ledger's marriage, only that it was short-lived and ended about a year ago. I'm gentle when I press, asking, "You feel like your ex-wife tricked you?"

I wouldn't be shocked if Ledger shuts me down. He's scrubbing a hand across his stubbled jaw, clearly working through something, then he says, "I don't want to make this about me. I was just saying I get it."

This poor man. He's clearly got walls up. "I asked you. And guess what? Not everything has to be about me. Plus, you know all my stuff now."

That's not entirely true. But they know enough.

With a heavy exhale, Ledger gives in. "She cheated on me with her personal trainer. This guy Ben, who she begged me to hire for her. The best personal trainer in the city," he bites out, sarcastic, but masking real hurt.

The sound I make, low in my throat, surprises me. It's protective. Animalistic. Angry. "That's awful," I hiss.

"Especially since she was always saying I wasn't available for her. I was hardly around. I was either at the arena, or on the road, or seeing the team trainer, or doing yoga. Or something. And she wanted to stay busy, she claimed. She stayed busy all right, screwing her trainer."

The edge in his voice makes me want to march over to Marla's place and give her a piece of my mind. "What really hurts is that you wanted to believe in her," I say.

When Ledger looks up, there's vulnerability in his blue eyes. "I did," he says, then he's quiet for several seconds. "But I'm fine," Ledger says, resigned perhaps to his romance fate. "I haven't had the best of luck with relationships. But that's the past. I'm over it. The point is..."

He runs out of steam, then laughs, dragging a hand over the back of his neck. "I don't fucking know what the point is."

That must be Dev's cue to jump back in. "The point is—relationships are hard, people get hurt, and thank fuck for hockey."

In one sentence, that tells me multitudes about Dev. Despite his sunny attitude, he's got his own baggage, too, and hockey is his salve. I don't know much about Eva, his last girlfriend, except that he was involved with her at the start of the last season, maybe even the one before. Part of me wants to give him the space to offer up that story on his own, but I've learned in the last few years of running my booth at the salon that people often want to talk but few want to go first. Few want to "inconvenience" others with their emotions. Most of us want to be asked so we can either decline or open up.

"Did hockey get you through your breakup?" I ask him.

Dev seems to give it some thought, but the answer must come easily since he's nodding sagely. "Yeah, it did. Especially since I thought everything was going well. But then, bam. It wasn't and I just mainlined hockey after that."

"She ambushed you, man," Ledger says, his jaw ticking.

"And can you believe it, she did it right before Christmas too. Which is my second-favorite holiday."

"What's your first favorite holiday?" I hope he doesn't say April Fool's Day.

"National Grilled Cheese Day," Dev says, eyes glinting like a cartoon character lusting after a leg of turkey. Yup, he's back to light-hearted. "Whoever invented that deserves a prize."

"You're not wrong," I say as I stay in this light zone with him, since that's clearly where he wants to be. "But do you even eat cheese? Maybe, since it's not a carb. But I'm doubtful."

Dev scoffs. "I like cheese."

"But do you eat it?" Ledger presses.

"Sometimes," Dev mumbles. "Like on National

Grilled Cheese Day, and when the team captain takes us out for pizza. So there."

I give an obvious glance to Ledger, pointing my thumb at Dev. "We should take him out for National Grilled Cheese Day. Let's pretend it's sometime this week."

Ledger's grin is devilish. "I'm in. You in, Ryland?"

Dev stretches his neck back and forth, like he's hemming and hawing and mulling it over. "Fine, we'll have grilled cheese as part of our Ambushed by Exes club."

"It's a plan," I say, and I leave the relationship talk at that, not pushing into how he's doing now. But the door's been opened at least.

We settle into a comfortable silence, and I glance around the small restaurant. There are only a dozen or so tables at The Green Pantry, and we're pretty much closing the place down. A couple at a table in the corner is paying their bill. He touches her arm as he signs the check, and she angles closer to him, a soft smile on her lips. There's a sensual energy between them, so I look away quickly.

Soon, we'll have to deal with the honeymoon bed. "This place was good," I say, delaying the inevitable. "Did you guys like it?"

Ledger eyes his empty plate. Then Dev's. "Was it not clear that we liked it?"

"Finishing isn't the same as liking something," I say.

Ledger's blue eyes sparkle. His lips curve into a slow grin. "Might have to disagree with you there, honey," he says, his voice shifting to a bedroom husk.

Dev picks up the baton of the conversation, his raspy tone hitting the same sexy, innuendo-laden notes. "I definitely like finishing."

I shake my head as heat tinges my cheeks. But I glance at my plate, where several forkfuls of my dish remain. "I didn't finish, but I liked it. *A lot.*"

Dev keeps his gaze locked on me, his green eyes bright with dirty delight. "Things you wouldn't say with us," he says.

Us.

That word clangs, rekindling my desires. Would they share me? Are they trying not to think of me as much as I'm trying not to think of them?

I shouldn't, but I search their eyes for answers—first Dev's, whose gaze glimmers my way, then Ledger's. His blue eyes don't stray from me, either, and neither man seems bothered that the other is checking me out.

My mind floods with a fresh wave of images. Hungry kisses, curious hands, questing mouths determined to make me finish, maybe many, many times.

That'd be an adventure, for sure.

But what would happen in the morning? We're three lost souls, wandering around this desolate, post-relationship landscape, trying to figure out what's next.

Thirty-six hours after a failed *I do* is not the time for me to say *make it a double.*

I swallow, trying desperately to reroute to Platonicville. I fiddle with my napkin and fold the linen neatly on the table. "I'd heard great things about The Green Pantry when I was planning. It's a woman-owned business, and I try to support ladies when I can..."

I'm not rambling at all.

"Like Beverly's diner," Ledger points out.

I smile. "Yes."

"That's why you should root for the Golden State Foxes over the Sea Dogs. We're a woman-owned team," Dev says, and I picture Jessie Rose, the badass billionaire boss lady behind his team. Ivy's not only the mascot for the team, but she also does some work for Jessie as a personal stylist and has said how much she looks up to the tough and brilliant team owner.

Ledger stretches his arms across the back of the chair. "But when you're thinking about who to root for, don't forget I've won two cups."

The smug smile says *try to best me.*

Dev glowers a moment, then he straightens his shoulders, game face on. "And I'll fucking play till I claim one too."

More solemnly than I expect, Ledger offers a fist for knocking. "You will, bro. You will."

"I will," Dev seconds, and his faith in himself is admirable too. I imagine you need that steely faith to strap on skates for eighty-two games a year, to train every day, to keep your body in tip-top shape.

The moment remains solemn until Ledger yawns. An unstoppable yawn that has me laughing, and Dev rolling his eyes. "C'mon, old man. Let's get you to bed."

"Fuck you. Not old," Ledger grumbles.

"But it is late," I add gently. "So let's go."

Ledger doesn't protest as we leave. We walk back along Main Street. I take a certain amount of personal pleasure in the fact that neither man glances twice at one of the pie shops Aiden wanted to check out for *competitive intel*.

At the corner, Dev's attention snaps to the local convenience store we passed on the way here, the one with a wooden sign on its door advertising *McDoodle Goods and Stuff*. He stops right in front of a postcard rack by the door, like he's helpless to the lure of the brightly colored pieces of cardboard. "Guys, go ahead. I'll catch up," he says, then heads inside the shop. As we keep walking, I reach into my pocket for my lip gloss, my room key slipping out too, then falling to the ground. "Shoot."

I bend to grab it from the sidewalk, but Ledger's faster, kneeling to grab it and handing it to me in no time.

"Thanks," I say.

"Welcome," he says, but he winces as he rises.

After I slick on some gloss, I swear I see him favoring one leg over the other for a few steps. I furrow my brow. "Is your knee injury acting up?"

"It's nothing," he says, shutting that down.

But is it? I rack my brain, trying to replay his recent career history. He didn't have an injury that I'm aware of. I'm pretty sure he played regularly on the Sea Dogs last season, but a couple years ago he had a slight tear that took him out for a few weeks. Garrett mentioned it when he took me to a game that Ledger didn't play in.

Maybe the knee still barks now and then? I'm about to suggest he use the hot tub when he snaps his gaze to me, saying quickly, in a surprisingly cheery tone, "You said on the way to the ferry that you want to hike, visit a ghost town, go grape stomping. You up for hiking tomorrow? That'd be a fun start."

"Sure," I say, going with his one-eighty.

"Let's do it," he says, upbeat once more.

"Okay. Sounds fun." It also sounds decidedly friendly, and I suppose that's for the best. What's sexy about a hike, after all? It'll be the perfect platonic honeymoon activity.

He spends the rest of the walk to the hotel chatting about hiking trails.

One thing is clear—this is the end of the knee conversation.

20

THE BANG PREDICTION

Aubrey

We're back in the suite a little after eleven. The stars wink in the night sky, the quiet of the Pacific Northwest surrounding us. One by one, we take turns getting ready for bed.

The men insist on ladies first, so once I brush my teeth and slip into my sleep shirt and shorts, I return to the room while Ledger roots around in his suitcase and Dev heads to the bathroom.

I slide into bed. Adjust myself under the crisp covers. Paddle my feet to loosen the tight sheets some more. Arrange the pillows. Tug up the duvet.

What now? Do I read like I do at home? I don't need the light on since I brought my Kindle, but will it bug them if I'm lying in the middle of the big bed reading the latest book club pick? I do want to know what happens next in *The UnGentleman.*

Dev emerges from the bathroom, but he hasn't changed into sleep clothes yet. Maybe he just brushed his teeth. He trades with Ledger, then grabs some clothes and toiletries from his suitcase, along with a Kindle.

He sets it on the nightstand on top of the postcards he picked up at the store. "Gotta read before bed. Hope you don't mind."

I don't even try to hide my smile. "I insist on it," I say, then I hop out of bed and grab my Kindle from my purse.

I'm back under the covers as Ledger returns from the bathroom, wearing basketball shorts and a gray T-shirt. With a nod, Dev heads back into the bathroom, and the sound of the shower turning on reaches me.

As Ledger comes over to the big bed, there's a mischievous look in his eyes. Before he can say something, a lightbulb goes off in my head. "You want *that* side?" I ask, pointing to Dev's nightstand.

Ledger's eyes sparkle. "Yeah, and since Dev's in the shower, I don't even have to call shotgun."

"Go for it," I say, his partner in crime.

Ledger goes to the other side and gets into bed *before* he moves Dev's things. Then, he grabs the Kindle and stretches all the way across me to set it on the other nightstand. His chest is inches from my face. His body is over mine, and I'm staring at the breadth of his muscles, the size of his biceps, the cords in his neck, all while water patters rhythmically from the room nearby.

This is such an unusual bird's eye view of the man.

I don't mind it one bit. I hold my breath so I don't... gasp.

When Ledger moves back, I watch him again, retreating over me. And for a second, he stops, pressing a hand into the mattress on one side of me.

"You have..." His eyes travel over my face, then he tips his chin at me. "An eyelash."

"I have many," I say, but I know what he means. I lift my hand, gently brushing at my cheek.

He gives me a faint smile before he pushes up on an elbow and ever so tenderly brushes it off my cheek, then blows on it.

My heart squeezes. "Did you make a wish?"

"I did," he says, then gives me another soft smile that turns into another yawn.

I wonder what he wished for, but suspect he's reached the end of sharing tonight, so I don't push. Instead, I try to give him what he needs—*not pushing, not asking.*

"Good night, Ledger," I say, tugging up the covers and playfully tucking him in as the shower forms our soundtrack.

He grumbles. "I'll just kick them off."

"I have no doubt," I say.

He sighs, a contented, sleepy sound as he settles into the pillow, then looks back at me once more. "Good night, Aubrey."

It's a soft wish against the quiet night.

But it's his gaze, even in the dim light of the room, that tugs on something inside me. That same impulsive part of me that was compelled to kiss him on the cheek last night in the parking lot.

Maybe it'll ease the tension of sharing a bed.

Or maybe I'm just an impulsive girl. I lean over and give in to the urge. But he must have shifted as I moved, because my lips don't touch his scratchy cheek. They dust against his lips instead.

His lush, hungry, masculine lips.

"Oh!"

The surprised sound comes from me. He doesn't move. I don't either. Instead, I linger for one, two, three delicious seconds on his mouth. In that shadow of a kiss, I feel a pull toward him. The sense that he needs something. That I could be the one to give it. It's there, unspoken between us.

Finally I break the silence. "I didn't mean to." It comes out staccato, and it's probably a lie.

His expression is stony till his lips quirk up. "I wouldn't stop you," he says, and on that tempting note, he turns around, shuts off his light, and, like it's his superpower, he's asleep in ten seconds.

I'm not tired at all. Replaying what just happened, I open a book and try to read the next chapter of *The UnGentleman*. The hero is either a bodyguard or a billionaire or a billionaire bodyguard, and the heroine could be his childhood sweetheart or his red-hot enemy.

I can't focus on the words. I'm too busy running my finger along my bottom lip, reliving that teasing touch.

An accidental one but sexy nonetheless. Only...Was it accidental?

I close my eyes, but I don't stop the trail of my fingertips until I hear a door swing open. My eyes fly open, too, and I drop my hand. My Kindle tumbles from my other hand and smacks the covers.

Dev arches a brow. I gulp, and I mean to look away, except...I can't. The man is shirtless again, his hair wet, a lone droplet of water traveling down his massive chest, roaming along his abs.

I take a longer look than I did in the diner parking lot. He doesn't have any ink. That's a surprise. He seems like the kind of guy who'd ink dogs, or cats, or a line from his favorite book on that muscular canvas. Instead, his chest sports a fine covering of light brown hair, the kind I could run my nails through. The kind I *want* to run them through—there's just something about polished pink nails trailing through golden brown, wiry chest hair that gets me going. Like Dev gets me going. He's wearing only a loose pair of gym shorts, and it would be a gold medal feat if I could take my eyes off the freshly showered athlete as he walks to the bed.

He gives the sleeping arrangements on his side of the bed a final once-over, then glances at Ledger's side. "Bet he thinks he stole my spot."

"Well, he did," I point out.

"Can I tell you a secret?"

Does it involve you wanting to pound me into the mattress after your friend and I just kissed?

I swipe that thought away, smiling innocently as I say, "Sure. I love secrets."

Dev leans closer, and I catch a whiff of his scent. It

goes to my head, with his cedar and suede notes. "I had a hunch he'd do that. But this is the side I really wanted."

"Strategic."

"Every good athlete is," he says, then lifts up the duvet and slides under.

Right next to me.

I hold my breath for a few seconds. Here I am. On my double honeymoon with my brother's two best friends. It's just the goalie, the forward, and me in this big bed. This isn't awkward at all.

Dev dims the light, then cracks open his Kindle too.

I try not to glance at him as I flip through pages about the billionaire who *operates* a security firm and *hires out* bodyguards, which makes so much more sense now. But as I read about his new leggy client, who just showed up in his sleek corner office, I'm hyperaware of the inches between Dev and me. Of his finger sliding across the screen every fifteen seconds or so. Of his strong legs under the covers, shifting a little restlessly. Of the rise and fall of his naked chest.

Am I too close to him? Does he need more space?

"Do you need more room?" I whisper.

He looks my way. "Nope. I'm all good." He tips his chin toward my e-reader. "Whatcha reading?"

The dreaded question. I'm not ashamed of my tastes, but I also don't want to explain myself to someone who doesn't get it. "It's a book about a billion-aire," I say tactfully.

He arches a playful brow. "Same!"

I jerk my gaze to him, doubtful. "What?"

"Well, it's not a book. It's a long piece from a tech site about how a bunch of billionaires hired an economist to help them prep for a future with scarce resources. He had to train them to realize they can't just buy everyone off. He taught them that money doesn't solve everything, and they might need to trade resources and skills and, you know, treat people with kindness and stuff."

That's not exactly what I'm reading. "Sounds interesting," I say, evasively.

"Is yours good too?"

"Yes." I hope he doesn't ask more questions. Before I reconnected with Aiden, I was on the dating apps, where I encountered more than a few judgy men who felt entitled to comment on my choice of books. *Why would you read that stuff?* Fuck them, but I don't want to burst the bubble of good feelings I share with these two guys. If Dev's book judgy, I'd rather not know.

"Read some to me," he suggests.

I freeze.

"C'mon, Aubs."

"It's a romance novel. For book club," I say.

That would deter most men, but not Dev. "Cool. Read me a bedtime story," he demands, setting down his own Kindle and parking his hands behind his head. The move sends the covers snaking farther down his body, revealing more of the toned, trim abs that make my fingertips tingle to explore every dip and groove.

"I don't want to wake up Ledger," I say, even though I'm feeling a little fizzy at Dev's request.

He throws back the covers and swings his legs out

of bed, nodding to the adjacent living room. "Let's read out there."

Is he for real? "You really want me to read to you?"

"News flash: I like books."

"And you heard me that it's romantic and stuff?" Also, it's kinda naughty, but I don't add that little nugget.

"Did you hear the part earlier where I watch Christmas movies? I like this stuff...well, in entertainment form. Important distinction."

Yes, it is. Especially after what he shared about Eva at dinner.

I'm not tired in the least, so I follow him out to the living room. He parks himself on the couch.

"Ready?" I ask, arching a skeptical brow as I sit next to him.

"Yes. Or I can read to you," he offers, gesturing for me to give him the device.

A hot hockey player reading a romance book to me? I didn't turn down the private plane. I'm sure as hell not turning down this adventure. I hand him the Kindle and catch him up to speed on the story. "So, Mariana just came into Hayden's office, and she's driving a hard bargain on hiring his firm."

With a *got it* nod, Dev clears his throat, then begins. "And there's one more thing I want, she tells me, those sharp eyes lasered in on me. *Too bad it won't be for me to bend her over the desk*," Dev says, and to his credit, there's not one snarky remark the rest of the scene. Not as he reads about them arguing, not as the hero and heroine trade dirty glances, and not as the hero talks about all the filthy things he wants to do to her.

When the chapter ends, Dev waggles the e-reader. "How long will it take for them to bang?"

A grin takes over my face. "We place bets in book club on that."

"Yeah? How do you usually do?"

I blow on my nails. "I'm a pretty good bang predictor."

He lifts a brow in admiration, then holds my gaze for a long moment—a moment that sends a rush of warmth down my chest, straight to my core. "And what's your prediction for this one, Aubrey?"

Those tingles spread across my skin. Heat flares brightly inside me. Even though I'm sitting on the couch, my knees feel weak. I try to catch my breath, but it's hard to breathe with his gaze pinned on me.

"Hard to say," I finally manage.

He's quiet, but his green eyes speak volumes. They flash with dirty thoughts till he drags a hand down his face like he needs to recalibrate all his systems.

He mumbles something that sounds like *sorry*. "We should..."

"Yeah. Go to bed," I say, feeling both heady and hollow at the same time.

He gestures to the bedroom, making it clear I should go first. I get up, and I'm tempted to look back. But I don't. I'm pretty sure what I'd see, though—the evidence of his desire tenting his shorts.

It takes him a minute before he makes it into the

bedroom again. Once he's under the covers, he says hoarsely, "Night, Aubrey."

"Good night, Dev."

I don't fall asleep for a long time. But when I wake in the middle of the night, I feel him against me. His big body is pressed against my back, his hard length prodding my ass. His steady breathing coasts over my ear.

He's asleep.

So is his friend, who's flat on his stomach, with one hand resting gently on my shoulder.

Sparks shimmy over my chest. Arousal pulses in my core. Wild thoughts flood my brain.

I don't know how I'm going to survive in this bed with Ellie the Elephant since she takes up so much space.

21

THE BIRDS AND THE BEES

Aubrey

Twigs crunch under my feet as the summer sun sneaks its rays through branches canopying the trail. Wildflowers bloom along the path while birds chirp from nearby branches.

Bees buzz too.

But nope. I refuse to think about the birds and the bees. I've got a better plan for Ellie the Elephant today.

Keep the guys talking about hockey, like I've done all afternoon on our hike. "So that game last year when you went into overtime when you were playing the Sabers," I say, cueing Dev on my next round of hockey chatter.

Another hockey tale will keep my mind where it belongs. *Off my lust.* "They were working you hard in that game. Taking shot after shot on goal. Were you exhausted at the end of it?"

Dev's ahead of me, hiking in trim khaki shorts and a T-shirt, and fine, the clothes look good. But I'm not checking out his ass. Nope. I'm not at all admiring the gloriously firm shape of it whatsoever.

I so am.

With a quick glance back at me, he gives an easy shrug and winds past a small boulder. "Yes, but no. I've got pretty good stamina," he says, a twinkle in his green eyes.

Great. Just great.

I try to laser in on a question that can't become wordplay. "What about you, Ledger? What's the wildest game you've ever played in?"

From behind me, the Sea Dog forward hums, clearly giving it some thought. I steal a glance at him as he says, "That'd have to be—"

"Fuck. Shit. Hell."

I startle, whipping my gaze back to the man in the lead who's backing the fuck up, right into me.

"What's going on?" I ask Dev, setting my palms on his back.

Dev flails a hand at the dirt path in front of him. "I thought I saw a—"

"My sweet summer child." I laugh softly then sidle past him to handle the scary creature. I bend and pick up...a long brown twig. I waggle it, not meanly, just playfully. "This thing?"

Dev shudders, then breathes out hard, a dragon disturbed. "It looked like it."

"Dude. *Dude*," Ledger says, unable to stop chuckling.

"I saved you from the twig," I say to Dev, then I wing the stick into the woods, away from the path. I turn around and squeeze his shoulder, reassuringly. "There, you're all safe now."

Dev closes his eyes, his expression pained, like he's embarrassed. When he opens them, he mumbles, "Fucking hate snakes."

We're jumbled together on the narrow path. A thicket-covered hill stretches up on the left, and the other side of the trail slopes to a gently flowing river below. This proximity, this intensity—it's like it was when we were in bed.

Which means we should keep going, maybe all afternoon and all night. Anything so that I don't have to face the temptation of sleeping next to these two men again.

"Want Aubrey to walk in front of you?" Ledger goads Dev. "Protect you from any more woodland threats? There might be a chipmunk ambush ahead."

Dev flips him the bird.

Ledger smiles, then says genuinely, "No worries, man. If a Ferris wheel jumped at me, I'd freak the fuck out too."

"What is it about Ferris wheels?" I ask Ledger while Dev resumes his pace. "Is it heights you don't like?"

"Nope. I hate the thought of getting stuck," Ledger says, owning his fear. "Do not want to get stuck in something that I can't escape from."

"What about you, Dev?" I ask as he hikes past a willow tree, its branches sweeping the top of his head.

"I don't entirely know. I looked it up—the fear of

snakes. Did some research. I can't figure it out. I just fucking hate them," he says darkly.

"I shouldn't have suggested we go hiking," I say, guilt clawing at me. Why didn't I realize this would trigger him? I was so focused on finding an activity that felt fun and adventurous for three people on a makeshift honeymoon.

But Dev stops again, tilts his head my way. Glares. "It's not stopping me. I like hiking. I like moving. I like exercise. Don't you even for a second think about *not* doing something because of me."

His eyes are blazing. And they heat me up. Or maybe it's the way he's facing the fear anyway. *For me.* "Thank you," I say.

"You're welcome. Now let's go. Dammit. Everyone knows honeymoons are for hiking," he says dryly.

A laugh bursts from me. "Yes, they are."

We soldier on, wandering past the water many feet below. Supposedly, there's a bench around a loop in this trail with a view of the clear, bright blue waters, then the mountains all around us. I want to take a picture there, a memento of the trip.

We stop talking for a minute or so as the path narrows. We meander along, farther away from the water, till Ledger breaks the silence by clearing his throat. "What about you, Aubrey? You're not afraid of S-N-A-K-E-S," he says, and Dev turns back, rolling his eyes. "What's your irrational fear?"

As we trek away from the water, deeper into the cool of the evergreens, I give it some thought, then avoid the truth. "I'm not actually sure."

"You have to be afraid of something," Ledger says.

He's right. No one is fearless. But I don't love saying mine. I try to turn his question around. "It's funny that you ask. I hear so much of my clients' fears. We tend to talk about everything. Their worries, their days. Fear of getting old, fear of dying, fear of spiders. Fear of intimacy. I try to listen to all of them. I try to help them if I can."

Dev peers around me again. "Are you afraid of that?"

"Of what?"

"Feeling helpless," he says easily.

Oh. Was I that obvious? Maybe I was.

Up ahead, I hear a rustling of leaves, then a gurgling sound. "Yes," I admit.

"When do you feel helpless?" Dev asks as we reach the stream. There's a huge log across it, a makeshift bridge.

My throat tightens. We shouldn't be talking about things like fears on a platonic honeymoon. It makes you closer. It makes you like someone. It makes you care.

"When do I not?" I ask as I step onto the huge, felled tree. When we reach the other side, we're deeper into the woods. It's both quieter and noisier. The sounds are birds chirping, branches crunching, water bubbling. But the place becomes more serene, and quieter in that way.

"Do you mean because of your dad?" Dev asks gently after another minute of silent walking.

"Yes, but sometimes I feel like I can't help my mom

either. I think I can, but I don't have what she needs," I say.

"What's that?" Ledger asks.

I turn to him, feeling helpless all over again. "She misses my dad."

Sadness crosses his eyes but understanding too. "I'm sorry."

"I shouldn't be such a downer. It's a trip. An adventure. It's not time for being sad," I say, and as I walk, I hunt for happier topics. Games. Events. Food. Something. Anything. "What's your favorite—"

My foot stumbles on the edge of the path.

Dev grabs my hand, jerking me close to him. My heart skitters. "You were about to step off the trail," Dev says calmly, right as Ledger's hand comes down on my hip, holding me firmly

Dev's eyes swing to the side of the path. Slowly, fearfully, I follow his gaze. Then gasp. There's a sharp drop-off. A steep hillside. Maybe ten feet or so into the stream.

Right now, I'm up against Dev, my heart beating in my throat. I'm in front of Ledger, his hand curled on my hip. Neither man lets go.

I'm not afraid of a thing now. Although the fear of never kissing your brother's best friends is a new one to add to the list.

I lift my chin, meet Dev's eyes, and whisper, "Kiss me."

22

THE PATH TO PROPER KISSING

Aubrey

Before I can even take back my words, and before Dev can even answer, Ledger's hand curls tighter around my hip, holding me in place.

For his friend.

We're standing on the narrow path, tall emerald trees protecting us on one side, the water bubbling several feet below us, the quiet of the afternoon cocooning us.

Dev's eyes darken as he searches my face, like he's making sure I mean it. Like he wants to be certain.

Ledger breaks the silence though. "You want this, honey?"

I shiver then nod several times. "I do."

"You heard her then. Kiss the girl," he says to Dev in a clear command, then ropes his other hand around my left hip.

He's keeping me safe on the path so his friend can kiss me.

My head swims with desire.

Dev's hand is still wrapped around mine. But as a sly smile tilts his lips, he lets go, lifting his big hand and touching my face instead. He slides his thumb along my jaw, and I shiver. His smile grows deeper. Hungrier.

Slowly, he traces my jawline under the afternoon sky, coasting from my cheek to my chin then back up, like he's memorizing me with his hand. Time slows deliciously, melts into this gorgeous moment where he's lingering on my face.

Anticipation thrills me. It races through me in a hot rush. I feel wobbly everywhere. Maybe it's dangerous to kiss where I nearly stumbled.

But they've got me. I'm literally trapped between them. Ledger is pressed up against my back, his hard-on nudging my ass. Dev is crowding me, his strong frame molded to my body.

Ever so gently, Dev slides that thumb down, stopping at my chin and holding me as he dusts his lips against mine.

I gasp at the first touch.

I don't know who murmurs—if it's Dev or Ledger. But then I realize it's both of them. There's a soft groan behind me. A louder one in front. And lips tracing mine.

It's the softest tease of a kiss. It's temptation. It's flirtation. It's a promise of pleasure. A slow, unhurried kiss that pours through me. It's a kiss that reaches the ends of me as Dev takes his time tasting, nibbling, ghosting his lips across my mouth.

It's an ache of a kiss that makes me want so much more.

And it ends too soon when Dev breaks it, but he doesn't look at me. He looks at Ledger with wicked intent. "You need to kiss her too. Really fucking soon."

My knees wobble.

"It's all I've thought about all day," Ledger says, flooring me with his admission, turning me on too.

He tips his chin and nods ahead. "But not here."

They march me along the path, and five minutes later, we've reached the bench set just beyond some trees, overlooking the water.

I'm heady with a new kind of anticipation. No one has talked; no one has said a word. I can't wait a second longer. "Are you two going to kiss me again?"

Dev sounds unrepentant as he says, "We promised we wouldn't."

I'm double floored. "Wait. You talked about...this? About me?"

"Yes, before the trip," Ledger says, and there's no guilt in his tone either.

"So, before the trip you said you wouldn't touch me?" I'm a little electrified from this news.

"On Saturday night," Ledger says. "We set the rules. Made a deal. To resist you."

One question zips through my mind—*would you share me?* Only, I don't have to ask. It's clear they would. "But now...are you going to break that promise?"

Ledger yanks me against his chest, threads a hand in my hair possessively. "Want us to?"

I pant out obscenely hard. "I do."

"Then rules are meant to be...broken." Ledger's lips crash down on mine as Dev cages me in from behind, hands on my back, lips on my neck.

It's a whole new kissing adventure on my double honeymoon.

23

THE VIEW, PEOPLE

Ledger

Walking behind her that whole time was not a good idea if I wanted to keep those platonic honeymoon rules.

The view, people. The motherfucking view of her ass in those shorts fried my brain, then scrambled it good.

Pretty sure an hour's worth of visual torture, watching the way her copper waves cascaded down her back, how her ass curved so deliciously like a peach, then how her strong legs moved with every step, is the new definition of erosion. That hike wore down all my resistance.

Although maybe walking behind her was the best idea after all.

Since...*this.*

Her.

In front of me. Sandwiched between *us*.

Holding her face, I consume her lips. I swallow her sighs. My whole body whirs to life like a machine turned on, lights flickering in a darkened room. I'm lit up everywhere. My bones vibrate as Aubrey melts into me.

And into Dev.

It's like she can't decide if she'd rather press against me or back against him. She chooses both, her lithe body subtly rocking between us. Back and forth, back and fucking forth.

She's as hungry for us as I am for her. As she wiggles against my friend, she parts her lips for me, asking me to kiss her deeper, maybe sensing I fiercely need to have her. It's been a long while since I enjoyed the feel of a woman.

Hope I'm not rusty. What a way to re-enter the kissing atmosphere though.

Aubrey's lips are soft but curious. She's pliant but eager, letting me taste her thoroughly, then tugging on my lower lip in return. Kissing me back confidently. Giving as good as she gets.

As she nips on the corner of my lips, my dick jumps, pressing almost painfully against the zipper of my shorts. I push against her, and she trembles all over.

I can't get enough of her lush mouth.

I deepen the kiss, clasping her face tighter while Dev's hands thread into her hair from behind. He lavishes kisses along the back of her neck.

I don't even need to see him kissing her to know that's the way he's touching her. Her long, needy gasps tell me she's getting a very sensual treatment from my buddy.

Good. She fucking deserves the twin attention. I hope she knows it. Hope she feels it in our hands, our mouths, our bodies.

Her hands stay busy, roping around my shoulders, jerking me close. "Mmm," she whimpers, and yes, fucking yes.

She knows it, and she likes it.

Desire winds tighter in me, climbs higher. She gives me the controls, parting her lips in a *take me now* move. And I take. I devour. I consume as she tilts her chin, her way of asking me to kiss her ravenously.

"Ohhh," she murmurs. It's barely a word—an encouraging sound as we get closer, and like that, my dick isn't just hard. It's granite.

My muscles are so tight. My control is breaking. One kiss and I'm already vibrating with the need to fuck her.

Images snap ruthlessly before my eyes. Her naked flesh. Her raised ass. Her breathless demands for *more, harder, again.*

Tension ratchets up in me, and I'm walking a tightrope of desire—do I wait till we get back to the room, spread her out on the bed, and shower her with endless foreplay?

Take our time. Kiss, lick, suck, then fuck.

I want it all then. I want it all now.

Screw granite. I'm *granite-er.*

I break the kiss for a second to get a grip. Need to calm the fuck down. No way will she want sex in the woods. She came here for grape stomping and hiking, not banging under the afternoon sun.

Hell, I've never fucked alfresco.

I try to catch my breath and maybe locate an ounce of, I don't know, logic or restraint.

But a few seconds after I've stopped, she moans out a plaintive "*more.*"

And, Dev, the enabler, doesn't relent. He heeds her prayers, cupping her jaw, turning her face to his. She leans back, lips parted, offering her mouth for a possessive kiss. She moans and whimpers against him, soft, little needy sounds that turn me on.

I'm imagining the sounds she'd make in bed as I moved down her body, kissed between her thighs. Edged her.

I grip her hips, holding her against me, picturing all the ways I want to please her as she gives herself to him.

He finally breaks the filthy promise of a kiss, rasping, "You can have anything you want."

Aubrey's eyes float open. Her gaze is dreamy and trained on him, then slowly, she turns her face to me. Her lips tilt, curving into an intoxicated grin. She looks like she has a secret. It's the sexiest thing I've ever seen.

"What do I want?" Aubrey repeats, but the question isn't for us. It's for her. A woman navigating her own pleasure.

The answer? She crooks a finger my way.

Hell yes.

I'm there in no time with my answer.

I kiss her harder, rougher. I feel wild in my own skin. She's moaning into my mouth, and I don't know if it's from my kisses, or his, or all of us together. The circuits in my brain overload as I explore her sweetness while she rocks her hips, back and forth, him and her, her and me.

My cock thumps, ready to charge full speed ahead in the woods. I've got to get a handle on myself though. She said she wanted *more*, but we can give her *more* in the suite. She'd like that better, I bet.

I jerk away. "Should we leave?"

I make no move to go though. I can't stop staring at the disheveled sight of her.

Hair a wild mess.

Lips bee-stung.

Eyes sparkling.

Skin glowing.

Bold, adventuresome, wants-to-make-everyone-happy Aubrey. My agent's little sister. My platonic honeymoon companion.

She shakes her head. "I want to stay. And I know what I want."

I'm nothing but nerves crackling as I grit out two words. A rough, hard demand. "Tell us."

That smile of hers is going to be my undoing, especially when she says, "Don't stop."

The last shred of my restraint snaps. I grab her hips and yank her against the outline of my stiff cock.

"Oh god," she gasps, then grabs my T-shirt. She doesn't let go of me as I grind against her.

"You like that, baby?" Dev whispers to her.

"I do."

"You want to feel more of him?"

With a hot shudder, she nods. Desperately, savagely, she whispers to him, "I do."

Dev slides his hands up and down her arms, coasting his lips along the side of her face. "Tell us what you want, sweet thing." Dev drags a finger along the hollow of her throat, over her chest, toward those beautiful tits. "And be very specific."

Aubrey breathes out hard. Heady too. Her lips part. I wait, a man on edge, and hold my breath.

She lifts her gaze, pins me with big brown eyes, then leans back into Dev's touch, trusting him completely, taking all that he'll give her while she never looks away from me.

"Fuck me here and now," she says, and then the last word is even better. It's my name, breathed out: "Ledger."

24

THE LUCKY ONE

Aubrey

Someone might hike past us. Someone might hear us. But I just can't find it in me to care.

Not as Ledger catches his breath. Not as Dev tucks a finger under my chin and says confidently, "I'll get her ready."

But I'm pretty sure the water park in my panties means I'm ready. "Oh, trust me. I'm more than ready," I say to the bearded man. Except. Wait a hot minute. They don't think they're double teaming me right here? I hold up a hand. "I mean, give a girl some time. I don't have any lube. I've never done *that*."

Dev dips his face, laughing. But quickly, he stops chuckling, swipes a thumb over my lower lip. "We're not fucking you together for the first time."

First time. Does that mean I'll get a honeymoon's worth of dicks?

Better stop that train of thought. This might be a one-time-only thing.

Dev guides me to the front of the bench and slides his hands around me, smoothing them up under my shirt, then over my stomach. I shiver.

"I meant...I'll get you ready as in...the right position," he says in my ear, his voice like butter.

Oh. That makes more sense. Glad he has a sex plan. Didn't want to have to rely on all the threesome diagrams branded in my brain. What if I remembered wrong from all that Internet research of pics of Barbies and Kens, and extra Kens? "Okay."

"Grip the back of the bench," Dev instructs, and I reach forward and grab the high back. He slides a hand down my shoulder blades approvingly. "He can fuck you while I play with those perfect tits that have been taunting me for the last two days."

I gulp. Swallow. Tremble. I'm dying to ask how they know the best positions, but I want sex more than I want to talk about it.

As Ledger reaches into his pocket, he tips his chin at his friend. "Take her shorts off. Leave the panties on."

"Marching orders. Got 'em." From behind me, Dev unzips my shorts, slides them down my legs, then taps my ankles so I can lift my feet.

I comply. While Ledger fishes the condom from his wallet, Dev folds my shorts and neatly sets them on the wood of the bench seat.

I'm half-naked in a tiny clearing in the woods, a big boulder forming the only shield between us and anyone who might hike by and look at the lake beyond me.

A sharp panic rises in me, but arousal beats louder. I'm not an exhibitionist. At least, I don't think I am. I've never been turned on by the possibility of getting caught. I've never even craved it. Right now though? Outdoor sex is all I want. And I want both men urgently.

I gasp, shivering as lips sweep up my legs. Dev must have kneeled behind me. He's kissing my thighs, then he angles up my ass and presses a kiss to the wet panel of my panties, inhaling me deeply.

"You lucky fucking bastard," Dev says to his friend as Ledger sets the condom on the bench. "You get to fuck this sweetness."

Ledger watches with hooded eyes as Dev pulls the panel to the side of my pussy lips, exposing me. I quiver in anticipation.

"Looks like you're the lucky one," Ledger says to Dev, a cocky smirk on his face.

I groan when Dev flicks his tongue up my seam, licking me. "Pretty sure I'm the lucky one," I murmur.

Dev's kissing my pussy, and the man isn't teasing me sensually anymore. He's hungry, eating me like I'm his one meal at the end of a long day, and he can't even wait long enough to remove my panties. He just keeps them tugged to the side, giving him all the room he needs. Sparks race up my thighs, straight to my core. I grow wetter. He groans again.

I grip the bench tighter while Ledger strokes my hair. "That's right, honey. He's gonna make sure you're good and ready for me. I like to fuck hard. Think that'll work for you?"

"Yeah," I pant, nodding, unable to say more. Dev is devouring me with the loudest, greediest groans. I'm helpless to the onslaught of his attention, to the ferocious licks and relentless kisses, to the press of his hands, the scratchy feel of his beard, the wildness of his desire.

In front of me, Ledger unzips his shorts, pushes down his boxer briefs, and frees his cock.

Hello, hard-on. Nice to meet you.

Ledger's dick is pointing at me, and my shoulders heave in excitement. He grips the base, then slides his fist down his shaft to the head, squeezing out a drop of liquid arousal.

The sound I make is downright feral. My mouth waters for him. For *them*. I stick out my tongue. Ledger swipes off the drop, presses his thumb to my top lip. Wantonly, I lick it off, my eyes on him the whole time.

"Fucking beautiful," he praises as he strokes himself again. All at once, reality hits me. All my jokes, all my wisecracks, all my comments about a double dicking are no longer sketch comedy.

I'm both turned on and nervous. But the nerves are the kind that pop and fizz under my skin. The kind that make the hair on my arms stand on end.

Dev stops, stands, then removes my panties at last. He sets the useless scrap of lace on top of my shorts, then smacks my ass with an approving groan. "She's yours now, man. And she's fucking soaked," he says to Ledger, then Dev bends, drags his beard against my cheek. "I'm gonna need more of that sweet pussy later. When I can spread you out on the bed and feast on you. I'm gonna spend a good long time eating you out till you can barely handle the number of times *we* make you come."

I sway. From the words and the *we* in them. I'm so outrageously excited that they like to share.

Dev circles the bench till he's facing me from the other side while Ledger moves behind me, grabs the condom, and covers himself. "Your ass is just..."

That's it.

That's all Ledger says.

He slides his big palms over my cheeks, squeezing them, kneading them and coasting down, down, down to where my ass meets my thighs. He presses his thumbs there, angles me up, spreads me open.

"What a perfect fucking pussy," he praises. "So fucking wet."

"Tastes so good too," Dev says from in front of me.

I raise my face, trying to play sex choreographer, but I don't know how this position will work for Dev. He's taller than me by many inches. Plus, I'm sloped down, so I don't know how he'll play with me while Ledger fucks me.

Ledger pushes in, slow, but powerful. I shudder from the delicious intrusion.

"Oh god," I moan as he fills me.

"That's my girl," Ledger praises. "Look at you. Taking me all the way."

Ledger stretches me open till I'm full, and then I'm

moaning as Dev's hands cover my tits. I roam my eyes over Dev.

I get it now. This position makes sense. He's a goalie after all. They're always the most flexible. The man's got his feet planted wide, almost in a V. He's lowered himself to me so he can play with my tits as his friend fucks me alfresco.

Dev pushes up my T-shirt, tugs down the cups of my bra, then squeezes my breasts.

A sharp inhale. A burst of pleasure. A loud moan. *From me.*

Ledger eases out then grunts as he slams back in, burying his cock inside me. "Yes, so fucking hot," he murmurs, then does it again. I grip the bench harder, rising on my toes.

I angle up my hips too, asking for a deeper fucking, and Ledger delivers. He's not sweet or kind. He's rough and relentless, pounding into me.

My body jolts from each thrust. He grunts. I groan. Dev plays, green eyes dark with lust. A rumble seems to escape his lips as he pinches my nipples. "These tits," he says.

"This fucking ass," Ledger says from behind me in a chorus of praise. Ledger rubs his palm against one cheek. I tense in excitement. I've never done this either. Impulsively, I blurt out, "Spank me."

Dev grins like they've hit the jackpot. "You heard her," he says.

A thrill rushes through my veins in those seconds as I wait for the slap. It comes sharp and bright. My skin stings, but then my core pulses. A sweet, hot ache builds as the pain turns to pleasure.

"Again," I demand.

Ledger smooths a hand over my other cheek, lifts it, and waits. I hold my breath, but not for long since Dev wets his thumb, then glides it over my nipple. The cool sensation makes me bow my back more, lift my ass higher.

As Ledger's hand comes down, I yelp. It hurts, but it hurts so good.

"Look at you," Ledger rasps out.

It's rhetorical. Of course I can't look at him fucking me. But I crane my neck regardless, watching Ledger. His hands curl tight around my ass as he pistons his hips, easing out, sinking in. His gaze is locked on where we meet, his dick sliding into my wet heat. "Look at you taking my dick so fucking well. That's so hot, honey. So fucking hot."

He's lost in the moment. Caught in the way we're coming together. With his filthy praise, his relentless strokes, and his friend's strong hands entertaining my tits the whole time.

It's like a full-body fucking.

The temperature in me shoots higher. My fingers curl tightly around the wood. I brace myself, holding on for dear life as Ledger owns my body with a fearless pounding. I'm getting closer, pleasure flooding my cells as Dev somehow manages to grab my chin and bring my mouth to his.

He bestows a hot, messy, passionate kiss on me right as a hand comes down on my ass again.

Spanking and kissing.

Kissing and spanking. It's sweet bliss and sharp pain mingled together under the evergreens, not far from the bright blue sea.

One man is mercilessly pounding me. The other is ruthlessly kissing me. I'm being fucked. I'm being kissed. Fucked. Kissed. Smacked. Squeezed.

I'm a toy. I'm their plaything. I'm the girl in between.

Pleasure marches through me, invading my body. It coils low in my belly. A pulse, insistent, undeniable.

Then, oh my god.

Dev has slid a hand between my thighs, and he's stroking my hungry clit. That's it. That's all.

I'm flying.

I break apart, coming without warning as Ledger fucks me, and Dev strokes, and I have the time of my life with two men in the woods.

Seconds later as my brain flatlines, my vision blurring, Ledger shoves deep into me, and stills, then jerks. He grunts out a carnal *yes*, spilling into the condom inside me with a final brutal thrust.

Groans soften. Movements slow. Pleasure ebbs.

Still, I'm tingling everywhere.

When I look up, Dev's standing in front of me. He looks happy, and very, very horny. I glance down at the bulge in his shorts. Following my gaze, he rubs his palm over it.

"Want me to...?" I ask.

He shakes his head. "Later, baby. I like delayed gratification."

Later.

This is not a one-time thing.

Not at all.

Ledger slumps over me then kisses the back of my neck, whispering, "I think you broke my dick, honey," he says, and he sounds like that's all he wanted.

It's the best compliment I never expected to get.

* * *

Soon, we clean up as best we can, and we leave. When we reach the car, I remember I never took the picture of the little bench at the loop in the trail. Or the view of the water.

But I'm pretty sure I won't forget this double honeymoon hike.

25

THE OTHER KIND OF HANGING OUT

Aubrey

Spank me.

Did I really say that?

Fuck me?

Who am I? I stare at my reflection in the bathroom mirror, alone in the suite that evening as the guys work out. I finished a yoga video, doing my friend Briar's twenty minutes of downward dog with her dog Donut, but now I'm unsure what to do next.

It's six. We didn't even make dinner plans.

When they return, do I say, "That was fun. Fancy a burger and another fuck? I picked a spot for food. Do you want to pick the position?"

I have no idea how this works. I did a great job fantasizing about the sex but not the in-between sex.

I flop down on the couch in the living room. Of

course we'll have dinner. We have to eat, but is this a dinner date?

Oh, shut up. You just had sex and broke rules. It's like National Grilled Cheese Day—that's all.

But what do I even wear to dinner? Do I put on a cute sundress? Jeans? Boots or heels?

I groan, sinking deeper into the cushion, then do the only thing I can. I commiserate with my phone, searching for an outfit of the day for a platonic honeymoon. Surely, I can't be the only person who's ever faced this fashion dilemma. But Google refuses to even acknowledge the adjective *platonic*, serving me up a barrage of pretty honeymoon outfits.

Because no one goes on platonic honeymoons.

Wait. Ivy would know! She's a fashionista. I hop over to my text app, spotting one from my sister and my brother, and some new ones in my group text with my friends. I go there first, clicking open that thread.

> Ivy: Ahem. Details.

> Trina: Also, I'd like a medal for having waited twenty-four hours to check in.

> Aubrey: Yes, you get a prize for amazing self-restraint.

> Trina: That was not an answer.

My fingers hover over the keys. I'm not sure if I want to confess. I mean, what happens in the woods stays in the woods, right? I'm also in a different situation than they are. They're both ensconced happily in their committed throuples.

> Aubrey: I'm sorry, but was there a question?

> Ivy: Yes, how is everything going? We wanted to know how you're doing.

> Trina: Are you having fun? Are you getting to do all the things you really want to do? The things Aiden wouldn't do?

Oh. They weren't even asking about sex. I just went there in my head. They're asking about me, my heart, my soul. Of course they are, because they're my girls, and two days ago I was left at the altar.

> Aubrey: I feel…okay. And I mean the good kind of okay not the meh kind.

> Ivy: The kind of okay that's said upbeat :)

> Trina: Okay, like it's a nice surprise to be okay!

.   .   .

They get me. They always have.

> Aubrey: Yes, exactly. Though, it's more than that. I feel good. We went for a hike today, and tomorrow we're going to a ghost town, and it feels like...

I stop, pause, look at the words I'm typing. Then, screw it. I add exactly what I'm feeling.

> Aubrey: It feels like the wedding that didn't happen was a lifetime ago.

> Ivy: That's great!!

> Trina: Good. You deserve good things, my friend.

I don't know if anyone deserves anything. Life has a way of delivering what it wants when it wants. But so far, this honeymoon has been a very good thing.

Aubrey: And I suppose I should get ready for dinner. Which brings me to my question. What do I wear, my scrappy little fashionista friend?

Ivy: Something that makes you feel sexy. Like, say, that cute, pleated skirt we found for you at Champagne Taste. The one that's purple and black plaid. Black lace stockings if it's not too hot. You have the best legs. So show them off.

A skirt does make me feel good, especially that one with its schoolgirl vibes—innocent but also...not.

I say goodbye to my girls, then shower, and get ready for dinner.

As I'm getting dressed, I keep myself busy with a playlist. I scroll through some of my options, finding one from Briar, since she's the queen of playlists. She has one for when she needs to kick ass, one for when she wants to unwind, and one for when she has to deal with a cantankerous person. I find one she shared called It's Not A Season—It's A Lifestyle. That feels apropos, so I text her that I'm listening to it now.

She replies instantly.

> Briar: Because you're the best year-round! Also, you and your birthday wishes are so cute. I love them. I have so much to tell you when I see you in two weeks for a blowout. Well, a blowout and therapy.

> Aubrey: I'm all about the double-duty hairstyle.

> Briar: And I seriously appreciate it.

As I put on some of my silver eyeshadow, I turn to the texts from my family. First, my sister.

> Claire: I got the veil from Mom. I will take good care of it. Do you need anything else? Let's talk when you get back! I want to make sure you're okay. Also, can you give me Aiden's address so I can send a couple metric tons of dog shit to him?

> Aubrey: What a thoughtful gift.

Then, I turn to my brother's note.

> Garrett: Are my guys taking care of you?

. . .

In the best of ways, big brother.

My cheeks flame. I glance behind me even though no one is watching. Even though no one knows. But I reply with the truth.

> Aubrey: Yes, they're great to hang out with.

When my honeymoon companions return a little later in their workout clothes, sweaty and muscly and all kinds of manly, I'm thinking about the other kind of hanging out.

Which means we need to set some rules, not just break them.

26

THERE WILL BE FOREPLAY

Dev

Why food?

Seriously, like why is food even necessary?

We're heading to the upscale Italian restaurant by the sea, my stomach growling, but all I want is to make a meal of Aubrey.

It's not the way she looks in that little skirt as she walks down the street that's making me ravenous. Or those sheer black thigh-highs that make me just want to peek under that fucking skirt. Does she have on garters too? My dick is offering up hopes and prayers that she does.

But more than that, it's how she *is* that's been winding me up all afternoon. The way she lifted her chin in the woods and demanded *kiss me* lives rent-free in my head and will for days. Hell, for weeks. Maybe even years. Nothing twists me up faster than a woman who knows her mind.

Last night, I forced myself to stay in the fun zone so we wouldn't push her. But now that she's made the first move, hell if I can hold back.

Instead, I'm holding the door open for Aubrey, letting her lead the way into the restaurant. As much as I want to bring her to bed and spread her out on the covers, I fucking love the seduction. I love taking a woman out, seeing her enjoy a meal, flirting with her at the table.

Making her feel good in every way.

It's like foreplay was made for me. Just like I'm certain I was meant to be a goalie, I'm certain, too, I was meant to work up a woman all night long. I'm not even sad there's no hockey on this honeymoon since there will be this—the celebration of this woman.

Together, Ledger and I hold out the chair for her at the table. The twin gesture isn't lost on her. She's grinning but seems to be trying to rein it in at the same time. She sits. "Thank you. You two make quite a... team."

There's a wink and a nod in her tone that tells me she's enjoying this shift too.

"Just glad you like the partnership," Ledger says, but then the server appears and does a quick double take before he rearranges his features and asks for drinks.

We order wine and he leaves us with menus. I file away that the server *maybe* recognized us but also said nothing about it. Once we get through the business of ordering and trying the pinot noir he brings, Aubrey looks to Ledger, then me, then back. That's a little new. This shy side of her. She dips her face, and ah hell.

I only want her to feel good. I slide a hand under the tablecloth, touching her knee. The server can't see that. But Aubrey sure must feel it since her breath catches. I roam my fingers along the silky, sheer fabric. "I like these," I say.

"Yeah?" She sounds breathy.

I nod toward my friend across the table. Ledger's dark gaze is fixed on her as well.

"He does too," I say.

"Do you speak for him?" Aubrey counters.

"No. I just know they drive him wild," I say with a knowing shrug.

She's quiet for a beat, strands of auburn hair framing her face. "I noticed he did. In the parking lot the other day. Outside the convenience store."

"When I was cutting your skirt," Ledger confirms, not even bothering to hide it.

"You seemed a little distracted," she says to him.

"I was way more than distracted," he admits, rolling up the cuffs of his black button-down. She watches him reveal a little forearm. "Just like Dev at the high striker game."

"I was very, *very* distracted," I say, and I'm not telling her anything she doesn't already know. But it's a relief to finally give voice to these desires.

My longing for her, but the thrill, too, in sharing her. Not gonna lie—that fling with Zahra four years ago was the hottest, sexiest month of my life.

Before today with Aubrey.

I didn't even get off, and it was hotter with her. I'm not sure why. Maybe her excitement. Her eagerness. Her wide eyes and bold mind.

I don't want to take a chance with Aubrey's heart, but I'd fucking love to show her how good we can make her feel together.

If she's willing.

If she knows the score.

If she wants the same things we do—orgasms and an end.

She shifts her focus back to me. "You also know what Ledger likes in a woman. And Ledger knows what you're into, Dev," she says, clearly adding up the evidence from this afternoon, and perhaps from this whole trip.

No point keeping this a secret. Not after the hike. "We've shared before," I say.

Her breath comes out in an excited rush. "I was hoping you had."

Well, that's a horse of a different color.

"That so?" Ledger jumps eagerly on that comment.

Aubrey nibbles on the corner of her lips. "I've been thinking about it for...the last few days."

My neck burns. "You wanted us to share you?" My voice is rough with lust. It's hot to hear her voice her desires. Even hotter to explore them with her.

Her smile is sensual, confessional. "Yes. I couldn't stop thinking about the possibility," she admits, then waves a hand in front of her face like she needs to cool off.

I don't know that I'll survive the heat either.

"Me neither," I admit.

"Same fucking here," Ledger says, then takes another drink of his red wine. Bet he needs to cool off too.

There's another smile again from Aubrey—sexy, but wholly innocent at the same damn time. That's her specialty, it seems. "I sensed it. But today confirmed it. The way you knew what to do in the woods. The position. The bench. Even just how you held me." She shivers.

I strip away any flirting, any humor as I tell her about our experience. "One summer a few years back, we were both in Los Angeles. We met a woman at the gym. We were both into her. She was into both of us."

Aubrey's eyes widen with each sentence. "Did she tea—?"

Holy shit. She's so fucking into this she can't even finish.

"She taught us everything we know about sharing a woman," Ledger supplies, answering the almost asked question.

Her cheeks flush. "I nominate her for teacher of the year." Then her brow knits, and she gestures from Ledger to me and back. "Were you two ever together? With each other?"

There's no concern. Only curiosity.

I shake my head. "We were only with Zahra. We both like women. It was a summer fling. We all knew the score. And when she returned to Beirut before the hockey season, she gave us each a Leatherman and a note—*now you've got all the tools.*"

Aubrey sighs happily. "I love Zahra."

And I fucking love that there's zero jealousy on Aubrey's part. Not that there should be. But her girl support is yet another thing I like about her.

Too bad I don't need more things to like about this beautiful woman.

Best to focus on sex. Only sex. "Good. We want to make it good for you. Great for you. You like what we did today on the hike?"

She's a little breathless as she answers with, "I did. It was better than I imagined." She turns her gaze to Ledger. "But did you?"

She sounds nervous, like she's worried he didn't have a good time.

"Honey, I fucking loved every single second of kissing you, touching you, and fucking you," he says, meeting her gaze straight on. "Don't doubt that one bit."

Her shoulders relax. "I won't."

But her brow knits, her eyes going serious. "Does it bother you that this is all new to me?"

Smiling and shaking my head, I slide my hand up her thigh. I can feel Ledger doing the same to her other leg, roaming his palm along her skin. Heat races down my chest, heading straight to my balls. "Sweet thing, it fucking excites me," I say.

"The things we can introduce you to," Ledger says in a rasp, his eyes hooked on her.

Her skin flushes as she murmurs something like *yes.*

"The ways we can touch you," I add. Her chest rises and falls, her breasts heaving beautifully as we seduce her together.

"The places we can take you in bed," Ledger rumbles.

I tease my fingers along the silky fabric of her stocking. She lets her legs fall open, looking the slightest bit intoxicated. She feels warm. Her eyes are glossy.

This is my favorite thing. To make a woman feel like she's the center of the world.

"I hope dinner goes by really fast," she says.

I couldn't agree more. "Me fucking too."

27

THINGS ARE BETTER

Ledger

Dinner goes by so quickly that less than two hours later, I'm in my board shorts in the hot tub. Bubbles froth around the three of us. Aubrey's between us, her skin dewy in that skimpy pink bikini that makes me want to tear it off so I can play with her fantastic tits.

But first things first.

We've already broken our pre-trip rules. Time to lay down some new ones for the rest of the vacation.

Currently, Aubrey's focused on enjoying the hell out of this bottle of Cristal, courtesy of Aiden, so I don't press the topic yet. I'll search for the perfect moment like I hunt for opportunities on the ice every game. She lifts her glass high. "To free champagne."

"It just tastes better when someone else accidentally buys it for you," I say after I take a sip of the

Cristal, savoring the taste. Dinner, jacuzzi, champagne. The hallmarks for a good night.

With a satisfied post-sip sigh Aubrey declares, "I'm going to start a line of champagne and call the first one...*I Never Liked You That Much Anyway*."

What a treat to see her laugh about the situation. I smile, getting in on the fun. "Let's make it a whole collection."

"The three of us will launch it," Dev adds, then tips his glass my way. "It'll also include the *Thank Fuck I'm Single Again* for you."

I snort-laugh at his champagne name for me, then he points at himself and adds, "And we'll add the *So Glad I Didn't Marry Her*."

"Ooh!" Aubrey sits up straighter, eyes bright. "Can we call it the *Better Off Without Them* collection?"

"Honestly, if this wine line doesn't already exist, I'm going to be disappointed in all the entrepreneurs in the world," I say.

"Me too," she says. "There's a whole cottage industry out there celebrating breakups. A friend of mine in the city is actually a breakup party planner. Juliet throws these fantastic parties to celebrate moving on."

Briefly, I consider that kind of fete. The meaning behind it. Then decide I fucking like it. "You know, I think she's onto something."

"Hell yeah," Dev says, then sets his glass down. The look in his eyes says he's trying to make sense of something. He's always trying to find connections and twists on the conventional. "Think about it," he says, getting excited. "When you hear someone is getting divorced, what's your first reaction? *I'm sorry to hear that, bro.* But...what if we turned it around and said, 'Congratulations! May things get better.'"

Aubrey rolls her eyes, but with obvious affection for him. "You're so cute."

Dev growls. "I'm not cute."

"You are. That's such a cute thing to say."

"I'm a goalie. I'm programmed to be unhinged. I am not cute," he insists with a grumble. She slides up against him, then threads her hand through his hair, and...*hello.*

That's nice to see too. Her taking the lead with touch after the hike. Feeling free to do it. To give it. "I love that you see the positive in everything," she says warmly. "It's your gift."

"Yeah, maybe time to rethink that whole *I'm unhinged* thing," I say dryly, and that earns me a scowl from Dev. But I'm right and he's wrong. "Look, if you threw tires in the parking lot before a game maybe you'd be unhinged."

"Or ate a dozen raw eggs," Aubrey puts in, getting in on the teasing.

"Then barfed them up before you went on the ice," I add.

"But only after you had all your teammates punch you to prove how tough you are," Aubrey adds.

Dev looks horrified. "Who does that?"

"Unhinged goalies," I say with a grin.

He shudders. "Fuck that. Fine, fine. You've made your point. I'll be hinged. Happily hinged."

Aubrey laughs. "Like I said, you're a positive guy."

"Also, that whole 'congratulations on your divorce' is *such* a shrink's kid thing to say, Dev."

"News flash: I *am* a shrink's kid," he says, full of pride and self-awareness. "You can't escape how you were raised."

That's too accurate. "Truer words," I say flatly.

I am my parents' son. My mom and dad wanted the best from themselves and from me. Mom's an architect, designing beautiful buildings around the world. McBride Design is her firm name. Dad's a hall-of-fame hockey player who believed in always climbing higher. *Don't stop. Don't relax. Do, do, do.*

That's what Dad did. He retired at the top of his game, but that wasn't enough for Ansel McBride. He went on to coach juniors for a year, then became a legendary broadcaster, and he's won awards for that too. He thinks I should go into the booth with him when I retire. Like father, like son. *We can be great together*, he's said.

I shudder at the thought. All I want is to play a game. And to play it for a little longer.

Or a lot.

I think.

But I don't want to get lost in my cloudy future tonight. I want to live in the present, here with Aubrey. When I catch her gaze, she looks like she's elsewhere too, sadness flickering in those brown eyes.

"We are who we are," she says, perhaps resigned to the weight of how she was raised as well.

This is getting far too serious for the hot tub. "All

right. Let's drink to hikes in the woods," I say, taking back the moment for all of us, then my gaze roams to the water and to her body below it. "And to that sexy bird tattoo on your ankle."

Aubrey's smile spreads again, flirty and fun. "Glad you noticed," she says, then pokes her foot high in the air.

She's right next to me, so I take that offering, sliding my hand down her calf, then tracing the tiny stencil of a bird on her ankle. She lets out a soft gasp. I meet her gaze and run my finger along the outline once more. "So pretty," I say to her.

"Thanks." She sounds delighted, like she's not used to compliments, even simple ones. Bet Aiden the Selfish Fuckcake didn't dole them out. I dip my face, brush a kiss to her ankle, giving her a compliment in another form—the physical.

She shudders, then I gently let go of her foot.

"What's it for? Your ink."

"My dad."

"Oh shit," I say, coughing immediately over my faux pas. "I'm sorry I called it sexy then."

"It's okay," she reassures me. "It was for him. But for me too. If that makes sense."

Not entirely, but I go with it. "Sure."

"And yours?" she asks, moving on as she nods to my wrist and the arrow wrapping around it, then the vines and leaves snaking over my shoulder. "I can figure out the vines and leaves, Plant Daddy."

I hide my smile over how much I like her nicknames, from Stern Brunch Daddy to Plant Daddy.

"But the arrow?" she continues.

"Got that when I signed with my first team. Just to remind myself that even if I didn't know where I was going, I wanted to *keep* going."

"It's a good reminder."

Yeah, it is. And tonight I want to *stay* in the here and now and keep going with *this*. Drinking to hikes and to women who know what they want.

I lift my glass in that toast at last. She clinks her glass to mine and then Dev's. Her gloss leaves a faint trace on the rim of the delicate glass as she sips.

I'd like to do other things with those lips than talk. I finish the wine in my own glass and then set it down on the edge of the tub. "We should set some rules," I say finally.

I brace myself for her reaction. A lot of people don't like to set rules.

"Rules?" she asks, like she's confused or maybe surprised. Shit. I don't want to ruin this night or this trip.

"I just think they're a good idea," I say diplomatically.

Aubrey gives me a skeptical look, her red hair curling in little damp tendrils by her face. "First you wanted to break the rules. Now you want to set them?"

This is why I've avoided relationships post-Marla. They're fuck-all confusing. But I try to stay cool as I answer. "I think it's a good idea."

"You mean rules for the hot tub. Like we should be really careful when I get out of it?"

I release a huge breath. "I thought you were pissed."

She tilts her head, smiling. "I get it, Ledger. But this is fun. I know it isn't the start of a relationship."

Even though it seems she's on the same page we are, it's better to lay out the expectations clearly. Learned that with Zahra. Everything was clear from the start. No one got hurt. Everyone had fun. "Maybe we can just do this for the honeymoon," I add.

"I was going to say the same thing...but also, guys?"

Dev sits up straighter. "Yes?"

"This is between us," she adds, firm. "We don't need to tell Garrett. Yes, he's your friend and your agent. But this isn't a situation where my brother is overprotective of me. Or where he thinks you're jerks and not good enough for me. He trusts both of you completely. I trust both of you too."

"That's what's really important," I add.

"It sure is," Dev says, meeting her gaze. "We want you to trust us."

Trust is vital in bed. It's even more vital the more people that share the bed.

"This is a situation..." She pauses, perhaps to collect her thoughts, "Where there's a start and an end date. That's why my brother doesn't need to know." Her voice pitches up at the end, like she wants to make sure we're on board.

I can only speak for myself, but I get Aubrey's point completely given everything going on in her life. "That all sounds smart. You just got out of a terrible situation and deserve a good trip."

"We can definitely give you a good trip," Dev adds.

Besides, we've all got too much going on when the trip ends to continue anything. That's no secret.

Dev's focused on having the best season of his life starting next week. When we return, Aubrey will need to deal with the fallout of her failed wedding. And I've got all sorts of what-ifs weighing me down.

This can only be a fling.

"It's a honeymoon deal," she says, then smacks a quick kiss on my cheek, then his, before her gaze turns contemplative. "You know...I was just thinking about the waiter. How he kind of did a double take when he saw you two."

I flash back to dinner, remembering that. "Right."

She shrugs but not in resignation—more acceptance. "I suppose no PDA would be a wise rule too. You guys are kind of famous."

Dev scoffs, then pokes his chest. "Kind of, woman? I was the star of the *Hockey Hotties* calendar."

I laugh so hard. "So that's like...D-level celeb?"

"Fuck you. I have a sponsorship with Ding and Dine, and my videos on healthy eats for them fucking rock. Another with Peak Fitness. And—"

I hold up a hand. "—Let me just stop you right there before you turn off Aubrey."

Dev swivels his gaze to the woman between us. "Did that turn you off?"

"No, I kind of tuned it out, to be honest," she says dryly, and fuck, I think I might fall in love with her for that.

I mean, not real love. Just momentary affection. Amusement. Yeah, that's what this is.

I don't mention my sponsorship with a watchmaker or a cologne company. Instead, I turn to Aubrey again. "Got any other rules?"

Her eyes twinkle. She stretches her neck from side to side, exposing soft skin I want to kiss and lick, then says in a seductive whisper: "Yes. I want you to take turns with me."

I'm not about to correct her since that's not technically a rule. It's just a very good idea. So good that I'm out of this hot tub in seconds.

* * *

The best part of sharing a woman is watching her get turned on. If you do it right, she melts into your touch, into your mouth, into the two of you, falling apart in a new kind of exquisite bliss.

But every woman is different. Every woman has her own likes and dislikes.

Learning *her* is the fun of it.

I am here for all the exploration. I stand at the side of the bed with Aubrey then gently take off the towel that's wrapped around her breasts, letting it fall to the floor.

I've still got a towel hooked around my waist. Well, undressing *is* part of the fun in bed. Dev is at the foot of the mattress, waiting for her.

"Lie back," I say, and she complies, then I move her up to the pillows at the top of the bed. "Want to take our time with you. You want that, honey?"

"I think so," she says, but she sounds uncertain.

I'm pretty sure we can help her along. I join her, lying next to her, stroking her hair as Dev climbs onto the foot of the bed, pressing light kisses to her calves.

"You're not sure though?" I ask, kissing her shoulder.

She trembles. *Yes, let the melting begin.* "I just don't know."

"That's fair," I say, roaming my fingers down the soft skin of her arm, layering more kisses along her collarbone.

"You want us to take the lead, sweet thing?" Dev asks in between kisses along her shin.

"Yes. I think so," she says, breathy, but there are those nerves again in her voice.

One way to quiet them. By soothing that busy head of hers. I stop, then lean over her, capturing her mouth in a hot, hard kiss that has her writhing, reaching for my face, tugging me close. She's grabbing at my hair and revving my engine all at once.

But, I hope, relaxing too. As she cranks up my desire, I break the kiss to say, "You can tell us anything you like or don't like. Anything you want more of or less of. Anything at all."

She nods, faster this time, and I glance down. Fuck yes. She's tilting up her hips, offering herself to us. Our girl is already turned on from his mouth on her legs and mine on her lips.

I spread a hand across the soft flesh of her stomach, then bury my face in the crook of her neck, kissing hard, then nipping on her earlobe.

As Aubrey stares down at Dev with amazed eyes, I

whisper hotly in her ear. "How badly do you think we want you?"

She shudders, then gasps an "oh god."

I grin wickedly. Good. So fucking good. She can barely even answer my question, she's so aroused.

With noisy groans, Dev doesn't relent his path up her calves, kissing her behind the knee now.

My hand travels up to her tits, squeezing one roughly. "Tell me," I command as I pinch the nipple. She gasps. "Tell me. Scale of one to ten," I urge. I want her to know, to really know, how much we want her. The more she feels worshiped, the more she'll surrender to the pleasure.

"Um," she says, but her eyes go glassy again.

"Aubrey," I chide. "How badly?"

With a shudder she looks at me, then him, then she reaches for his towel.

"Ohhh," she groans.

She feels wanted, and that's the sexiest thing ever. Then, she's even sexier when she falls back on the pillow, her back arching as she meets my gaze and lets out a feathery "one hundred."

I groan approvingly, then slam my mouth to hers, taking her lips in a possessive kiss. "Good girl," I tell her when I break it. "Now take mine off too."

She shifts to her side, tugs at my towel, and her eyes widen. "Guys...things are definitely, *definitely* better."

28

DELAYED GRATIFICATION

Aubrey

Look, I'll admit I've watched some porn. I'm even a devoted monthly subscriber to a particularly delicious site that's run by women, made by women. Spanking, hair grabbing, pushing her down to her knees, coming on her tits—those are all my faves.

While I've read some spicy threesome stories in romance novels, I've never watched a threesome before. Probably because I didn't want to seem like I was perving on my friends and their lifestyles.

All the times I fantasized about two guys, I didn't know entirely *what* to picture. Here I am now, surrounded by men devoted to...me. Ledger's behind me, his big, strong legs hooked around my body. I'm leaning back against his thick cock, his abs, his chest.

Dev is between my legs, sliding those calloused hands from my ankles, over my bird tattoo, then all the way up my thighs. He stops at the apex, letting out a heady groan. I'm so vulnerable like this, spread out before him, wide open and...outrageously wet.

As he stares at me, his green eyes flash with unchecked lust. His big chest heaves. His mouth parts, and he unleashes a carnal rumble.

"Worth waiting for," he murmurs.

Then he dips his face to my center right as Ledger cups my tits.

And...I gasp.

Dev's mouth. Oh my god, his fantastic mouth. His lips are soft and hungry, and he kisses my pussy in the most intoxicating touch I've ever felt. It's desperate and greedy.

I arch up into him. Ledger squeezes my tits more, and I wriggle against him.

While Ledger runs his thumbs across my nipples, Dev flicks his tongue along my wetness then swirls it around my clit.

I suck in a long, needy breath, my hands reaching for Dev's thick hair. I need to grab on to something, on to him. Finding him, I thread my fingers in his strands.

He slides his hands under my ass like he's scooping me up, bringing me closer. But before he devastates me again, he whispers against me, "You're fucking delicious, sweet thing." Then he drags his beard along the inside of my thigh.

I moan. "Yes, I love that."

"Mmm. You taste so fucking good," he says, then obliterates my senses by doing the same thing to my other thigh.

Meanwhile, Ledger's kissing my neck and fondling my tits.

I feel like a power grid, lighting up block by block. The more they kiss me, the more they touch me, the more I feel like I could light up the whole city.

"You feel sooo good," I say, unsure who I mean. Except I am sure. I mean both of them, together. "Both of you. You both feel good."

My words are so basic. Am I even saying the right thing? I've never dirty-talked before. I've never been dirty-talked to like this either.

"Give her more, man," Ledger commands Dev. "She's fucking trembling in my arms."

I'm shaking as sparks rocket through my thighs.

Dev shoots a look at Ledger. "Spread her wider for me, then."

What? How the hell?

But they know how to play me, evidently, since Ledger stretches his arms down, reaching for my ass with one hand.

Oh. My. God. He tugs the back of my upper thigh on one side, yanking up my leg.

Holy fuck.

He's opening me up to his friend. I lift my other leg higher, finishing the *V.* "That's it. Nice and wide. He's gonna want a lot of room to feast on your pussy," Ledger rasps out.

"I fucking am," Dev says, then buries his face between my thighs again.

I fly into sensory overload. Dev devours my wetness, licking, flicking, sucking. Ledger plays with my tits, squeezing my nipples while coasting his talented mouth along my neck.

I hold my legs nice and wide. Dev kisses relentlessly in between, praising me with words like "so fucking good," "so hot," and "so sexy."

Pleasure bears down on me, smothering me in its hot, merciless grip. I'm buzzing everywhere, vibrating from the inside out with this quivering, intense need.

Then, all at once as Dev sucks on my clit, I detonate, breaking apart and shouting. Incoherent, wild, fevered noises come from deep inside me.

My vision goes black, and I'm lost—just lost to the pleasure.

I've never felt anything like this before. Bliss pulls me under to a new land. I float on a brand-new high that doesn't end.

After I come down, I can barely register what's happening, but when a mouth crashes against mine, the man tastes like me.

The other man is tasting my pussy. I reach my hands into short hair between my thighs as Ledger eats me out while Dev kisses my mouth like he can't get enough.

They don't stop trading off.

Not for a good long time. Not until I'm drunk and limp from orgasms.

But I'm not so blissed out that I've forgotten about the two fantastic cocks waiting for my attention. Besides, Ledger orders me, saying, "Now take care of my friend."

I return the favor, all right, crawling between Dev's

legs, taking his thick cock in my hand, and savoring—absolutely savoring—the grunts he makes the first time I touch him. Like he wants this so badly. Wants me so badly. I grip the base, then twist my fist up and over the head, squeezing out a drop of liquid arousal.

"Suck him off, Aubrey," Ledger commands from his post on the bed, lounging on the pillows.

I comply, dropping my mouth on Dev's delicious cock, taking him deep, letting him fill my throat.

"Mmm. Yes. Worth waiting for too," he mutters. His words drive me on until I swallow his release, warm and salty on my tongue.

When I let him fall from my mouth, Dev looks drunk on me. He swipes my hair from my face, as he tips his chin toward Ledger, who's working his cock in his fist while staring wantonly at me.

"Looks like he wants you badly too," Dev says.

"Don't worry. I'm a helpful girl," I say, and this people pleaser gets to pleasing, taking care of Ledger as well.

When he finishes, I collapse with a stupid, woozy smile on my face, glad their gratification is no longer delayed.

* * *

But when I wake at dawn, Ledger's not in bed. He's sweating, staring out the window and looking utterly lost.

MORNING DREAMS

Ledger

I can't get the images out of my head. The dream—
nightmare, really—keeps replaying.

I'm trying to blink off the awful reel flashing over
and over. I'm really trying, but it won't leave my head.
With one hand pressed to the cool glass, I stare out the
living room window, trying to make out the edge of the
water, the height of the trees, but dawn hasn't chased
away the darkness yet. Only a hint of soft blue light
tugs at the horizon. But the images feel like flies
chasing me.

Until the soft pad of feet lands on my ears, then a
gentle voice, full of concern, floats across the room.
"Hey. Are you okay?"

Ah fuck.

With a heavy sigh, I barely turn to Aubrey. I don't

want her to see me like this, yet she's seeing me like this.

I scrub a hand across the back of my neck. "I'm fine," I mutter.

She comes up behind me but doesn't touch. She's careful as she asks, "Are you sure?"

"Yeah," I say, lying. "Just couldn't sleep."

"Do you want to come back to bed?"

More than you could ever know.

But I don't want to wake up sweaty, startled, and fucking haunted again. Prior to last night, I hadn't had a nightmare in ages. Not since I was injured two years ago. Not since it took me longer than I'd have liked to get back on the ice.

"I'm good," I say.

After an exhale, she says, "I get bad dreams too."

I snap my gaze to her. "What do you mean?"

"I do. I have dreams about tsunamis. Earthquakes. Waves that pull me out to sea."

"That sounds unpleasant," I say, and that's putting it mildly.

"Yeah. It was. I still get them, but not as often as I once did," she says quietly, and then moves to the nearby couch and sits down. Can't let her sit alone, so I join her. She came out here to check on me after all.

"Was there a reason you were getting them?" Maybe if I focus on her my stupid brain will let go of the remnants of my nightmares.

"Happened a lot after my father died," she admits, then her eyes shine, but she fights off the threat of tears. "Maybe I was processing my feelings. I'm not sure I entirely understand dreams. Or that anyone does. But I think I felt a lot of anxiety about wanting—" She stops, and this is clearly tough for her but she pushes on. "To be a good daughter for him even when he wasn't around."

Ah, hell. My heart thumps harder for her, my throat tightening too. "I'm sure you are. He'd be proud of you."

"I don't know about that."

"Hey," I say, then tuck a finger under her chin, making her meet my gaze. "You're kind and funny, and you care about people. And you look out for your mom, and you're a good friend, and your clients love you."

"How do you know?" she counters with a sassy little smile.

That's a very good question. But I man up and tell the damn truth. "I looked you up online," I say. "When I saw you at Sticks and Stones late last year. I was curious about you. I'd just gotten divorced, and I'd known you so long but didn't really *know* you. So, yeah, I looked you up. Your salon. You have great reviews. Everyone says you're great at hair and a good listener."

Maybe I had ulterior motives. Hell, of course I did. She was pretty and witty and warm. But she was seeing that other guy. And she's my agent's little sister, so I shut the search down pretty fast after that.

"That's nice to hear. I try," she says, then tilts her head and runs her hand across my knee in a tender touch. "When I had these dreams, I would try to do breathing exercises after. Or visualize something pleasant. Sometimes I would listen to music to ground myself in reality rather than the unpleasant dystopian world I felt stuck in."

She's hitting close to home, and it's stupid to keep playing the tough guy. Not after she's opened up. I slump against the couch, drag my hands through my hair, then meet her gaze. "I sometimes dream I can't run. I'll be outside jogging, but my legs won't move. They're stuck on the sidewalk. And I can't really control my body anymore. Can't lift my legs or move my arms. And then I feel stuck, and I yell, and nothing happens. I can't even make a sound," I say, embarrassed that I'm a grown man with recurring nightmares. "That sounds fucking stupid as I say it."

She rubs my knee some more. "It's not stupid, Ledger. We're just processing things all the time. I'm no expert, but I'm pretty sure that's what dreams are. We're working through the day." There's a pause, then she adds, "Is your injury acting up?"

Was I that obvious? "Yeah," I admit. I guess I don't want to keep it to myself anymore. Or I don't want to keep it from her. "But it's just a twinge. No big deal."

"Was it the hike?"

I shake my head adamantly. "No. Hell no. I can walk, run, skate. Work out." I sigh. "It just hurts sometimes. That's all. I can handle the pain."

"Of course you can," she says sympathetically. Then she runs her hand through my hair, her touch soothing. My heart rate calms some more. "It's probably just because the season is starting soon."

That has to be it. "Yeah, probably."

"And if you ever want to get that free haircut and talk about it, you know where to find me," she says.

After.

After this honeymoon is over.

It's a nice offer.

But right now, I *do* want to return to bed with her. I stand and hold out my hand for her. "Let's go back to bed."

She takes it, and we return to the bedroom. She gets in, sliding to the middle, next to Dev. He stirs, blinks his eyes open, then flashes her a dopey grin. "Hey," he mumbles, then closes his eyes, slinging an arm around her when she settles back in.

She's facing me and when he falls back into slumber a few seconds later, she glances down at his arm wrapped around her, then whispers to me, "He's cuddly."

Yeah, I know my buddy. And he really, *really* likes her.

I don't say that. I just smile, feeling a little better than I did ten minutes ago.

30

WHY CAN'T I PUNCH GRAPES?

Aubrey

Things no one tells you—grapes are icy.

Also, there's no real stomping involved. I'm in a short barrel on the wraparound porch of a picturesque white bungalow-style home that's part of Valenti Winery, massaging the grapes with my toes, trying not to freeze my feet off.

It's warmish outside. But inside this barrel? It's chill-ay.

"I think my feet are going numb," I whisper to the guys. Dev's in a barrel next to me, treading on some grapes too. It's a funny sight. This big, burly man in khaki shorts, squishing grapes with his bare feet.

"Woman, this is nothing," he says.

From my other side, Ledger scoffs. "Yeah, have you felt ice?"

I huff as I tread some more. Nearby there are a few

other visitors engaged in similar squishing activities and also a winemaker walking by, checking on our stomping.

"But you don't go on the rink in your bare feet," I hiss as I flinch, then wince. Damn. "I think I got a stem between my toes."

"Will you survive?" Dev deadpans.

"Want me to call an ambulance?" Ledger counters.

I deserved that. "I'll live," I say, chin up.

But seriously. What is the proper etiquette at an early morning grape stomping? Do I pull the stem from my foot like it's dental floss?

I don't even know, so I try to ignore the interloper between my toes as the winemaker strides past the group, a calm, instructive tone to her voice. Her name is Isabella, and her jet-black hair is wildly curly. Her Mediterranean complexion and last name suggest she's from Italy.

"We harvest our grapes in the early morning hours for a couple reasons," she explains, her peach linen pants and blouse as flowy as the breeze. She stops a few barrels away from us to give a tip to a man with a mesh cap touting "Everything's better in Texas" across it. Then, she continues her lesson for the group. "We can better control the sugar levels and avoid oxidation when the grapes are a little colder. And it's easier for our staff to harvest them before the temperature rises." She sweeps a tattooed arm, bangles jingling on her wrist, toward the trees and peaks hugging this vineyard. "Yes, we have some warm days in Washington." Her tone turns conspiratorial. "But please don't tell anyone.

We want Washington to remain the best-kept secret of all the states."

"But doesn't it rain here all the time?" the Texas cap man drawls.

The winemaker smiles approvingly. "Exactly. All the time. Every day," she says with a serene smile, clearly doing her best to prevent an influx of people moving to her state. I rein in a grin as she plays him.

She continues on, explaining more about the process as I steal glances at my travel companions. Dev's like a large cat, shifting his legs in a languid rhythm, his attention lasered in on his movements, his body able to handle anything he throws its way.

Ledger's confident, too, in his repetitive steps, but his gaze is fixed on Isabella as he tosses out curious questions about the vines, the amount of sun they need, then rain, then drainage.

I furrow my brow as he goes, trying to assess his interest. Is he a wine connoisseur? But he barely asks about the grapes. Then I remember when he spouted off facts about oleander a few days ago.

His plant daddy-ness runs deep and wide. I smile privately at this little detail about him.

When Isabella spins around the other way, I wince since I just stepped on another stem. "I swear they're trying to get me," I whisper to the guys.

"Pain, honey, pain," Ledger says, like he loves getting hurt. Well, he *is* a hockey player.

Dev shoots me a devilish grin. "You get used to it."

I roll my eyes. "Great. Just great. I'm grape stomping with two hockey players who love pain."

"It's all part of the game," Ledger quips, but there's no joking in his tone. He sounds legit.

Dev seconds him with, "It's proof you're alive." But then, he tilts his head my way in concern. "You want to stop?"

His tone is so sweet, full of genuine concern. "I'm no quitter," I say before I realize that's not entirely a compliment. I should have quit my relationship with Aiden well before my wedding day. But I try to shove that bad decision away and focus on *this* choice—grape stomping was *mostly* a good decision. "And this *was* on my adventure list."

This honeymoon is definitely an adventure, too, and I'd better savor every second of it since it'll be over before I know it. It'll end, taking its place in the memory banks, and I'll return to cutting hair and reading books and dealing with the pity looks from everyone in Duck Falls when I return to town to see my mom.

On those sobering thoughts, I glance down at the squishy substance oozing through my toes. "Too bad you can't punch grapes. That'd be fun," I say.

"Maybe add that to your entrepreneurial list, along with the breakup champagne," Dev says, then mimes punching.

But Isabella Valenti is unamused. With a stern glare, she stops in front of him. "Please be careful. If you fall and crack your head, I'll be liable. I don't like being liable," she says, then looks to me. "Make sure your partners behave."

Whoa.

Partners.

That's a first. Not the word *partner*, because everyone uses that term now. But the plural, the assumption she made is all new, and I don't want to look like I'm overstepping my role with them. "Oh they're not—" I begin.

She's already walking away though. As she goes, I have to wonder—do we come across as partners? All three of us?

As we finish and hop out from our barrels, I'm stuck on that word.

And the way it felt sort of nice to hear.

* * *

After we hose off our feet by the side of the bungalow, Ledger asks, "Was it what you wanted?"

Not entirely. I thought it'd be more of a wild time. Silly, outrageous, a little goofy. In reality, it was harder and less pleasant. But they're such good sports that I don't want to sound like I'm complaining, especially since it was my idea.

"Sure," I say brightly as I dry off my feet, then hand the towel to Dev. We're sitting on the wooden steps, and everyone else has straightened up already, so it's just us and the morning sun rising over the mountains. "It was a blast."

As he rubs the towel down his calf, Dev arches a dubious brow my way. "A blast?"

"Yeah. It was great," I say, even peppier as I pull on

my sandals. Then, I adjust the buckle, making sure it sits just so. "Look. No stains."

But then a gentle hand on my chin draws my attention. Dev turns me to face him then drops his hand to my thigh. "It's okay if you don't like something," he says, reading my mind.

Is it okay though?

I didn't like it when my parents were icy to each other years ago. I didn't like it when they fought like cats either. I'm not sure it's okay to dislike something. It's better if everyone gets along.

"I liked it," I say again right as Ledger finishes putting on his sneakers, then parks himself next to me, setting a hand on my other thigh.

Does this violate our PDA rule? Probably not. We're all alone back here. And these are friendly touches. "Aubrey," he says, stern.

I sit up straighter, feeling trapped. I can't just say I didn't love it. I'd sound ungrateful.

Nerves prickle inside me. I'm about to tell them once more that I'm fine, but the words stop before they make landfall. I should have said something sooner about Aiden. To someone. My friends, my brother, my mom.

I take a deep breath. "I didn't love it," I admit.

Dev smiles affectionately. "Good."

"Why is that good?" I ask, still feeling out of sorts.

"Because it's good that you're honest with us. We want to know. We don't want you doing things you don't like."

"You mean in bed?" I ask.

"Well, yes. Of course. But I meant in general," Dev adds.

I pause, take my time, then speak from the heart again. "I'm glad I did it. I like to try new things. But it wasn't what I thought it'd be."

"That happens," Dev says casually.

"Good thing you tried it," Ledger adds.

There. I said it and the sky didn't fall. They're not walking away. They're not annoyed with me. They're all good. I take another breath, letting it fill me with confidence. With courage too. "And I'm glad you insisted I tell you."

"Me too," Dev says, with a genuine smile. Like he really wants to know my true heart.

These guys are doing so much for me. They're going where I want to go. They're doing what I want to do.

I desperately want to do something for them.

On the way out, we walk through the winery's gift shop, where I spot a postcard on the counter. I tell the guys I'll meet them at the car. We're heading to a ghost town next.

But even as I buy the postcard, it hardly feels like enough. I tuck it away in my canvas bag unsure if I'll give it to Dev or not.

31

THE NICE MAN

Aubrey

I'm chased by those thoughts as we explore a nearby mining town. Is this what they want—to be traipsing around a small town on a replacement honeymoon? Just because I had a room reserved?

Is this even fun for them?

Maybe Ledger's having a good time. He can't seem to get enough of the history of this ghost town. He's reading all the plaques in the museum as we check it out, then chatting with the tour guide who takes us through the tiny town, showing us creaky old cabins where miners once lived, then the local watering hole.

"This was once a saloon," the grizzled guide says before he swings open the twin doors of the erstwhile bar, taking us into the abandoned establishment. "A lot of folks think California was the only gold rush territory, but we had plenty of mining here too."

But do my guys even *want* to be here? Would they rather be someplace else? What's on *their* dream list? Well, besides National Grilled Cheese Day for Dev. Maybe I'll ask them later, because right now Ledger seems happy enough.

As Ledger launches into his reporter's list of questions about the town, Dev and I take that as a cue to wander a bit, checking out the old wooden bar, a piano that doesn't work in the corner, and a sign for the outhouse out back.

Is he happy enough?

I'm about to ask, but he's faster to the question draw. "So, this is another Aubrey thing?" Dev asks as we survey some old mining equipment outside the bar.

"I'm a little obsessed with ghost towns," I admit. "I loved visiting them in California on family trips when I was a kid. Garrett hated them. Maybe that's another reason I liked them. Vexing my brother."

"A damn good reason," Dev says, then stares off in the distance at the train tracks several hundred yards away. "See, I think you've got a traveler's heart."

I feel a little giddy from the comment, from the way he seems to see me. "You do?"

"You like adventure. You like trying different things. You're not afraid. I think it's just who you are."

I seize the chance to understand him better too. "And who are you?"

With a playful grin, he says, "You tell me."

It's said like he wants me to know him. He folds his arms, waiting, with a tease of a grin. I study him, thinking about his Daily Dose of Good. His genuine affection for people. But his superstitions too. "You like learning things and seeking the positive. You like understanding the world. You want everything to go well though," I say, and...wow. I might as well be looking into the mirror.

"Yeah, I do," he says. "I really want this trip to go well for you." Then he leans closer, his voice husky. "In and out of bed."

"Spoiler alert: it *is* going well," I say, feeling a little tingly from the compliment, but also how he's managed to weave one in so seamlessly.

Still, that nagging voice doesn't let up. But with Ledger enrapt in the tour, now's not the time to ask them about their adventure lists. Instead, I grab the winery postcard from my bag and thrust it at Dev. "It's not the same as offering to be my honeymoon tribute, but I wanted to get you a little something," I say.

He takes it, his smile spreading slow and pleased as he regards the image on the front—a grape harvest. "This is an awesome gift."

I roll my eyes. "It's just—"

"Nope. I love it."

My heart beats a little faster. Maybe this is his daily dose of good. "Why do you collect them?"

"I started when I was, I dunno, thirteen or fourteen. We'd just moved back to California from Minnesota," he says, jogging my memory. He was born in San Diego, moved to Minnesota, then returned to Northern California. "And I'd had a run of bad games. I was trying to get my footing in a new place, and then I grabbed a postcard from a road trip to Monterey and my game-play started to turn around. It felt like a good sign."

"And it has been?"

"I haven't looked back since. So yeah, maybe it has. Maybe if I collect enough, I'll get a cup."

There's that ambitious side of him rearing up. It's so strong in him, maybe just as strong as the side that's upbeat and kind.

I wonder how hard they war with each other.

* * *

When the tour ends and we head to the town gift shop, I find him another postcard, then I grab a book—a brief history of ghost towns for Ledger. After I pay surreptitiously, I sneak both into my bag. As we head out the door, we weave to the side, ducking out of the way of family photo hour. A girl with long black braids strikes a playful pose near the porch railing as someone down the stairs takes her pic. A young blond boy stands on the porch of the museum gift shop, likely flashing a grin at his mom who's down the six or seven wooden steps, snapping a shot of him in front of the old town sign.

"I want to grow up to be a ghost in a ghost town," the kid declares.

"Or maybe a person who visits ghost towns, Travis," the mom offers as she lowers the phone.

"Nope. I'm going to be a ghost. I'll be one for

Halloween," he says, then heads for the steps. But he smacks his forehead. "I forgot my candy."

A whirling dervish of energy, Travis spins back around, races into the store to grab his nearly forgotten sugary goods, then with half a Nerds Rope in his hand, he barrels out of the shop seconds later right as we reach the steps.

The tornado of a child scurries past us, flying toward the stairs.

But he trips on his laces. He tumbles face-first toward the step when a big hand reaches out to grab his arm, the other grabbing the railing hard so they don't topple down together.

I gasp.

A second later, Dev lets go of the railing, sets that hand on the kid's shoulder, then yanks him upright.

I breathe again as the goalie places the kid safely on his feet.

"Did he just...?" I can't even finish the sentence my heart's beating so fast.

"He sure did," Ledger says, awed, too, as the mom rushes to her son.

As she flings her arms around Travis, she thanks Dev profusely. "I'm so grateful. I can't tell you how grateful I am," she says, words coming in a rush.

The kid turns around, squeezing the Nerds Rope. "And my candy's safe as well."

"Travis, thank the nice man," the mom says.

"Thank you, nice man," Travis says, and after a few more thank-yous, she turns around to go, her arm draped around her kid.

The hair on my arms is still standing on end when Dev turns and meets my gaze at last.

I'd expected a *no big deal* smile, or a *right place, right time* quip. Instead, he's shaking out his left hand and grimacing.

32

I SEE PLAYS

Dev

I'd like to find the person who invented splinters and give them a piece of my mind.

"What the—" I bite off the rest of my words as I jerk my gaze away from Aubrey's careful, methodical work on my hand.

I can't even look. That makes it hurt even worse.

We're at the car in the mining town parking lot, the driver's side door open. I'm side-saddling the seat, and she's bent over my hand like a good nurse, working out all the evil pieces of wood from my palm. Before she began, she swiped my palm with an antibacterial wipe from her bag, then cleaned the tweezers too. Even though it's afternoon, Ledger's holding his phone, the flashlight on, to help Aubrey see every single awful piece of it.

"You're doing great," Aubrey coaches me as she plucks the tweezer at a two-by-four in my palm.

I clench my jaw as she fishes it out, then unleash a long, "Fuuuuck. Did it go all the way through?"

Ledger tries but fails to stifle a laugh. "Let me get this straight. You can handle a puck to, I dunno, pretty much any portion of your body, but not a couple splinters?"

Looking up, I hiss at him. "Dude, there are not a couple splinters in my hand. There are ten thousand."

Ledger arches a dubious brow my way as Aubrey soldiers on. "Math is still hard for you."

"I hope you get a splinter in your—ah fuck," I howl as Aubrey hunts for a jagged plank. "Ahhh! I think that one's lodged in my love line. I'll never be able to have kids now."

Aubrey laughs. "That's not how love lines work."

"Feels that way," I grumble.

"I need a little more light," Aubrey says.

Ledger lowers his phone, the flashlight shining brighter on my wounded hand. "Who knows? You might never be able to jack off again," Ledger muses.

"I'm right-handed," I spit out. "Also, a puck to the collarbone hurts less. A puck to the stomach. A puck to the ass."

"Maybe you should wear pads when you're doing hero duty."

"These are nasty little splinters," Aubrey says sympathetically as she hunts another bastard down. "I have to pull them out slowly so they don't break off in your hand."

"That can happen?" I sure hope my voice isn't as high-pitched as it feels.

Ledger doesn't chuckle this time. He actually frowns. "That one is jagged and shit," he says when Aubrey expertly tugs one out.

I stare up at him. "I told you so."

"They're so painful and so big," she says, stopping to squeeze my shoulder.

And that's nice. All her touches are so nice. She inches closer, straddling my thigh, her hair brushing against my chest as she bends over my hand, searching and plucking.

And that's not too bad. Her hair tickling my face. The scent of her shampoo is kind of tropical. Not coconut, not pineapple—more like the tropical rainforest.

Tonight, I'm going to dream of tropical rainforests populated by one very hot nurse. "You just have tweezers in your bag?" I ask, circling back to how fast she whipped the tool out a few minutes ago when she'd assessed the damage to my palm.

I can feel her smile as she says, "Yes, I do. Tissues too. Also Tylenol and Advil."

I look up at Ledger, smiling dopily as I say, "I love women."

"I do too."

Then I look to Aubrey again. "You're a perfect nurse."

With a teasing grin, she asks, "Are you going to get Florence Nightingale effect because I'm taking out your splinters?"

No. Only because I'm pretty sure I fell for you a while ago.

I don't answer. I grit my teeth, taking the pain as I let her finish.

"Last one," she says victoriously as she holds up the final sliver of wood in the sunlight.

I let out the biggest breath. "Thank you."

Ledger claps my shoulder. "Thanks go to you for saving that kid. That was badass."

"It really was, Dev," Aubrey says.

My chest warms from the praise. I do love compliments. But the truth is, I did what anyone would have done. "I was just in the right place at the right time. That's all."

Aubrey scoffs. "No. You don't get to downplay it."

I roll my eyes. "I swear it was no big deal. Anyone would have done the same."

"But not anyone did. *You* did," she points out.

"That was baller," Ledger says, then he shoots me a cocky grin. "But if you need me to take care of Aubrey tonight so you can rest..."

I growl. "Nothing can stop me from fucking. Even a broken dick."

Aubrey's laughing. "The two of you and your broken dick jokes." But then she stops laughing, her lips curving into a seductive smile. "And speaking of non-broken dicks..."

Ledger gets behind the wheel faster than he flies down the ice.

* * *

The elevator up to our room is just too tempting. We're all alone in it, the three of us, so I slide a hand down Aubrey's arm, slow and tantalizing, savoring the way her breath catches.

She's so responsive, it's addictive. She seems to crave touch, and Ledger must sense it, too, since he brushes strands of that copper hair away from her face, eliciting gasps.

Yeah, that's our girl. She loves being touched, being played with, being the center of attention. "She loves it when we play with her hair," I observe.

"I've noticed. Bet she'd love it if we tugged on it," he adds.

Aubrey's big brown eyes widen. "I might..."

"...And pulled hard," I say, dragging a finger down the side of her neck as I test out ideas. She likes it, too, when we tell her what we want to do to her. "What do you think, sweet thing? Think you'd like a little spanking again? Some hair pulling?"

"I think so," she says, and Ledger gathers some strands, gives her a tug toward him. She gasps.

What else does she like though? How much does she want?

The questions make the adrenaline in me spin higher, and I'm grateful when the elevator slows to a stop on our floor. We reach the suite quickly.

The second the door to the room opens, I've forgotten those evil splinters. I've got only one thing on my mind.

Taking care of her. Introducing her to new vistas of pleasure. Ones that, ideally, involve her riding my cock.

I grab the waistband of her shorts and tug her against me, letting her feel how much she's turned me on. "This is what you do to me," I say, pressing my hard-on against her lithe frame.

Ledger crowds her too, lining up behind her, sweeping her hair to the side and exposing her neck.

She bites the corner of her lips, then whispers excitedly, "This is all from...the elevator?"

I scoff. "No. The car, the lobby, the elevator. Last night, this morning, the last several days."

I cut myself off before I say too much. Before I tell her I've wanted her for a while now. I just had to come to terms with my feelings. Had to accept them. Face them head-on.

Not just...hard-on.

But I'd really like to deal with the latter right fucking now. "You want to know something about goalies?" I ask her as my hands roam up and down her waist while Ledger keeps busy kneading her covered ass.

Aubrey's trembling in our arms. Looking dizzy in the best of ways.

"What is it?" she asks in a breathy voice that gives away how very, very turned on she is.

"Goalies watch the whole game. We see pretty much every play. We see them *before* they happen," I tell her.

She puts two and two together. "You're making a hockey analogy for sex?"

"You bet I am. I can see the action before it unfolds and picture where they're skating to. I can see it like a movie, how they're chasing the puck." I brush my lips along her jawline, inhaling that tropical scent that's frying my brain. "And right now, I've got this play unfolding before my eyes."

As I pull back, her eyes spark, radiating with desire. "Tell me."

"I'd like to strip you naked, put you on your—"

But I don't get to finish because my phone brays.

With Garrett's ringtone.

33

THE GODDESS

Dev

Does he have a camera in the room? My pulse spikes faster than before a fight on the ice.

Then my brain takes over. Of course there aren't any fucking cameras in the room. That'd be illegal. Maybe the elevator though? That's possible, and if so, damn, Garrett moves fast.

But I'm a sloth as I grab the phone from my pocket in slow motion then angle the screen away from my face, like it's an X-ray and Garrett can see inside my soul and read my filthy mind as he rings and rings.

Aubrey eyes the screen.

"What do I do?" I ask, flabbergasted. I mean, I've answered calls before. I should know how to do this.

"Um, answer it?" Aubrey suggests, but the look in her eyes says she's freaking out too.

I swing my gaze to Ledger. He's not the wise old

veteran now. He's got his hands up in the air, as flummoxed as I am. But then he snaps his fingers. "Maybe we need to...talk about this first. What to say to him. Hit ignore."

"Yes! That's brilliant. Talking. That's what we'll do. Communication. Right, right." I send my agent to voicemail then rub my palms together. "What do we tell him?" I shift my focus to Aubrey. "Last night you said he's not the kind of guy who would say *don't touch my sister*, but—"

My phone cuts me off when it buzzes with a text. I scan it so fast. ***Hey, remember that time you saved a kid?***

I blink. "What the...?"

Then the rest—*give me a call.*

I'm too intrigued not to call back, but I also don't have to since he's ringing again. I answer it with a casual, "Hey, G-man."

At least I hope I sound casual—not like I was just caught stealing. I head to the couch, Ledger and Aubrey right behind me.

"The Dev Save is going viral, and I think we need to get in front of this right now," Garrett says, businesslike.

"The Dev Save?" I ask as I sink down onto the cushions, but I've got a hunch I know what that must be.

"Or was that some other goalie on McDoodle Island who looks like you and is on a vacation with my client and my sister?" His tone is playful, and that's such a relief.

I breathe easily, my pulse steadying. I stab the speaker button right as Aubrey whips out her phone. Ledger's fast at the draw too, grabbing his mobile like he's a gunslinger in the old west. They're likely searching *The Dev Save.*

"The mom called me a *nice man.* She didn't ask for my autograph or anything," I point out. "How does she know it was me?"

Garrett chuckles. "It's seriously hilarious that you think hockey players aren't recognizable. They're not recognizable to non-hockey fans. But, guess what? Travis's other mom *is* a hockey fan. She was in the store when it all went down, and when she came out and saw the video *another* family had taken, evidently, she lost her mind over the goalie saving her kid. Life imitating art. The art of hockey. Damn, I love it."

Aubrey's shoulders relax. "She posted the video then? One of Travis's moms?"

"And it went viral in no time. Everyone's calling it The Dev Save. You're a fucking hero meme," Garrett says, and I can picture him with his feet up on his desk. "Also, I need to apologize."

We all look at each other like *what's Garrett talking about now?*

"Why?" Ledger asks carefully.

"I should have had you three do this sooner, what I'm about to ask you," Garrett says apologetically. "But now's as good a time as any. Remember when I said if any fans spotted you on this trip it'd be a good thing that the three of you are friends?"

I wince a little from the reminder. He said that during golf. We were friends with Aubrey then. Now we're a little more.

"Right," I say tentatively, letting Garrett steer this convo.

"So, what do you want us to do?" Ledger asks, and I can hear the hesitation in his voice too.

"I'm calling it The Garrett Save," our agent says. Then he gives us an assignment.

* * *

An hour later, we're standing in front of the Deception Pass Bridge in the ultimate tourist photo, the three of us smiling for the camera in a selfie ordered up by our agent.

On the surface, we look happy. But everything feels off. When I'm done playing shutterbug, I show Aubrey the pic, trying to shove aside the weird feelings.

"We look...friendly," she says, her tone a little worried. But I'm not able to deal with it since I've got to get this shot to G-man so he can get in front of any potential double-honeymoon stories.

"Should I send it?" she asks.

"Yes," I grit out.

After she hits send, we trudge to the car.

As I reach the rental, Garrett pings me with a text, showing that he's already posted it on his social feed, along with the caption—*One guy broke my sister's heart, so I sent my two buffest players to make sure no one gets that close to her again.*

It feels like a lie.

Because we did lie to Garrett. I can't shake the gloom descending on me.

I get back into the car, shutting the door a little harder than I should. We're all a little quiet on the drive. I feel like I just sobered up. Too bad I was really enjoying being tipsy in the room.

After a few minutes, Aubrey points out the window at a mountain peak we're passing. "That's pretty."

"Yeah," I mutter.

She's quiet again, and I have nothing to say. What would I say anyway? *I'm a big, stinking liar?*

"Hey! Do you guys like kayaking?"

That's random. "I don't know if it's forbidden in our contracts," I answer. *Like you're technically forbidden.*

The gloom grows thicker, tries to dig roots in my chest.

"If you can, that might be fun," she says, cheery and bright, like she is, and I wish I knew what to do with her. "Ledger, have you ever gone?" she asks.

He doesn't answer. When I peer in the rearview, he's staring out the window. A moody motherfucker too.

But why should I have to be the only one to try to keep up the uncomfortable convo? I don't want to say *that felt too close for comfort.* "Ledger?" I prompt.

A few seconds pass before he says, "What?"

"She asked you a question. Have you kayaked?" I ask, annoyed with him too.

"Oh. Yeah. I have," he says, flatly, letting the topic die.

Aubrey sighs, then fidgets with her cuticles. "I just wonder if..."

But she doesn't finish the thought either.

When we reach the main traffic light on McDoodle Island, the red light feels like a metaphor.

The sun is setting. Maybe we should just get some chow. "Want to get food? Something from your restaurant list."

Aubrey lifts her face, then like a goddess calling upon her powers, she turns to me. "Earlier today, you made me admit I didn't like grape stomping. I need something from you two now. Is *this* over? Was it a one-night thing? If it was, that's fine. But I want to know. And I *deserve* to know."

Holy shit. That's hot, the way she's just laying down the law.

But that's the problem. Am I allowed to keep acting on all these wild wishes? Plus, this isn't my decision alone to make. I peer again in the rearview.

Ledger drags a hand down his face. "I'm just thinking about Garrett," he says heavily.

"I gathered that." Aubrey stands her ground. "But if we're done with...*this thing*, don't I deserve to know? If that's the choice you're making just tell me. I can go back to being friends. What I don't want to do is drive around in silence that I try to fill when you won't tell me why you're moody." She looks at the time on the dash. "In fact, you can take me back to the hotel. I'm going to do some yoga with my friend Briar and give you some time and space to sort out whatever is going on with you two."

The light changes and I head to the hotel on her orders. Once there, she marches into the suite, leaving us behind.

34

SHOW ME

Dev

As twilight spreads across the sky, we wander around the hotel grounds. "I feel bad not telling him the truth," I say.

"Yeah. Me too. But..."

"But what?" I ask, jumping on the way he trailed off just there, eager to know if he found a loophole while he was a quiet, broody bastard in the back seat.

Ledger stops, scratches his jaw, a sign he's still thinking. "Do we tell him about other women we sleep with? Separately or together?" It's a rhetorical question, but I get where he's going.

"No. We don't," I answer so fast, then I jump on the bandwagon. "We aren't lying to him. It's just not his business, right?"

Ledger holds up a hand. "Not so fast though."

I groan. Of course he's going to look at the other

side of the story. I'm full speed ahead, but Ledger's measured and steady. "We don't *have* to tell him," he says. "But does keeping it from him mean we're the assholes? My ex lied to me. She cheated on me. I don't want to be the asshole here, man."

"This is not the same," I point out. It's like I'm on the ice again, and I'm seeing a whole new play. "And here's the thing. Aubrey made it damn clear she doesn't want a relationship. This is a rebound hookup and only that. We're not going to tattle on her to her big brother. That'd be shitty."

"I wasn't saying that," Ledger says evenly.

"I know, but my point is...women have agency. Women get to make choices. We get to make choices. We don't need permission, and withholding something doesn't make us liars," I say, and I wish I'd seen this an hour ago, but I'm damn glad it's crystalline now. "This is her choice and our choice and no one else's."

Ledger shakes his head in amusement. "Once a shrink's son, always a shrink's son."

"And you fucking love my progressive opinions," I say.

"I do, man. I really do."

Time to bring it home. "This is about us and Aubrey. And when it's over in a few more days, we're all going to be fine. We're all adults," I say, making the closing argument to him. I'm going to sell this to the judge and the jury.

He's silent for several seconds, perhaps weighing my arguments, then he nods and says, "Let's go tell her we fucked up in the car."

But we don't just march back to the room. We make a pit stop in the restaurant kitchen and ask for a special dessert order, stat. Fifteen minutes later, Ledger's knocking on the door to the suite. I'm holding a silver tray.

When Aubrey swings open the door, her gaze is wary as she assesses us. She's not welcoming us with open arms. But one look at her wearing pink yoga pants and a sports bra, and I know we made not only the right choice, but the only choice. It's not because of how good she looks in those clothes I want to peel off. It's because of who she is and how she stood up for herself.

I hand her chocolate-covered strawberries. "A peace offering?"

She opens the door wider. "Come in."

Grateful she's not still pissed, I head to the couch, Ledger by my side. I set down the strawberries on the table, then I meet her gaze and give her the truth. "Listen. Your brother's been my friend for a long time. Since I moved to Northern California when I was thirteen. He's been my agent for years too. He's always done right by me, and I don't want to be a jerk. I've worked really hard to be a good guy."

"I get that," she says.

"And I need him now, maybe more than ever," Ledger says, letting some rare vulnerability show in his tone.

Aubrey pauses to process what we're saying. "So this means...?"

"It means I just needed to make sure I wasn't being a jackass," I admit.

"And I didn't want to lie to him," Ledger says heavily.

Aubrey nods, her lips a ruler, like she's bracing herself for bad news. "Okay."

"But the thing is, like we've said—this is private," I say.

"And even if he knew, he'd want to make sure we were treating you right," Ledger adds.

Aubrey tries to fight off a smile. "Well, you definitely are."

"But you deserve better than us giving you the silent, broody treatment," I say.

She lifts her chin. "You're right. I do."

Ah, shit. I hope she's not done with us. "We were jerks in the car," I add.

"Kind of," she says.

"You've had enough of that," Ledger says. "You don't need that from us. We want to be so fucking good to you."

Her smile grows wider. "You do?"

"Yes," I say, emphatic. "Because you deserve chocolate-covered strawberries, and champagne, and king-size beds, and three-Michelin-star restaurants, and all the orgasms you could possibly want."

"That is, if you still want them. And us," Ledger says, with openness and hope—the same damn hope I feel.

Aubrey's gaze softens. Her eyes go warm. Then, in a strong, certain voice she says, "What we do behind closed doors is our business. No one else's. We're friends in public. But in private we're..."

With wide eyes, she waits for us to fill in the dots.

Ledger gives a nod that makes it clear he's taking this one. "We're your men," Ledger says, answering her with certainty too.

"We fucking are," I say.

Her eyes roam over us like she's a woman who knows exactly what she wants. "Then act like it," she says.

I grab my phone and make a show of turning it off. Ledger does the same. Once Aubrey's phone is off too, she says, "That play you mentioned earlier? Show it to me."

35

JUST THE TIP

Aubrey

Look, I don't mean to brag, but I've always been good at multitasking. I rock at walking and talking, exercising and listening to a book, eating and hanging out with friends. *Fun things*.

So yeah, bring on the two dicks any second. At the moment, though, these two men are stripping me. Ledger pulls off my sports bra while Dev tugs down my leggings. I'm left standing in the middle of the room in my undies.

But they're fully clothed, and sometimes a girl just wants to enjoy the view of two hard dicks. "No fair. I want you guys naked. Cocks out," I say.

I feel more free in bed now than I did last night. Today at the winery, then moments ago, unlocked me. I *can* speak my mind in bed. I *can* voice my wishes.

Dev comes at me, and without warning, tosses me over his shoulder.

"Dev!" I shout, but maybe it's a squeal. I pound his back. Damn, that's a strong back.

"You'll get our dicks when you're good and ready to take them," he says as he carries me to the bed, then tosses me down on it.

I like that he doesn't treat me as if I'm delicate. I push up on my elbows, and gaze at the two of them with wide, eager eyes. What will they do to me next? But neither lets on. Dev's green eyes, flecked with hazel, linger on me. Ledger's blues travel along my body. They're appraising me.

Are they going to give me instructions? My skin prickles with dirty hope. I'm about to ask what they want me to do when Dev turns to Ledger. "Let's get her ridiculously wet," he says.

News flash: I already am. But I'll let them find out for themselves.

Only they don't go for my panties. Dev covers me with his big body, kissing me hard, a little ruthless.

I melt into the bed, reveling in the weight of him on me. But the moment barely lasts. Seconds later, he's shifting off me, and Ledger's taking over, devouring my mouth.

They don't kiss the same, even when they're rough like this. Dev's more passionate with deeper, hungrier kisses. Ledger's merciless, kissing like a hunter.

But both kinds of kisses melt my brain. My thoughts float away, and I can't even try to catch them.

Soon, Dev's moving down my body, kissing my

breasts then pinching my nipples, all while Ledger continues to own my mouth. It's so much stimulation. So much foreplay. I feel like a liquid woman. Every touch makes me wetter, then Dev barks out a command: "Push her hands over her head."

Ledger breaks the kiss to maneuver my wrists toward the top of the bed.

I'm pliant under them. "Do what you want to me," I say to them as warmth flows through me.

I feel powerful as I give my power to them. They take it, and they devastate me with attention. Ledger grabs my face, holding me roughly as he kisses me, his other hand stretched above us, pinning my wrists tightly to the mattress. Dev travels down my body, flicking his tongue against my nipples, then tugging down my panties.

He slides them off, then groans out a long and carnal, "So fucking pretty."

The compliment spreads confidence through me, and I part my legs for him. Dev rubs his beard against my thigh. Then he presses a hot kiss to my core right as Ledger crushes my mouth in another bruising kiss.

I burst with pleasure. It's radiating throughout my entire being as Dev sucks on my clit. It's so much, all at once, then it's even more when Dev stops and rises to his knees. "Hands and knees," he says.

Ledger wrenches apart, giving me the filthiest smile. "Good. Because I'd really like to feel those pretty lips wrapped around my dick."

Dev grabs my hips, then flips me over so I'm facing

Ledger. I meet his hungry eyes, then tell him, "Yes. I
want to taste your cock."

Dev slides a palm down my back. "Be a good girl
and give his dick some attention while I eat this pretty
pussy. I can't seem to stop going down on you."

My insides clench. "Yeah. That's not a problem for
me either."

A few seconds later, we're all rearranged. Ledger's
shorts are undone, and he's lying down on the big bed.
I'm between his legs, playing with his dick. Dev's at the
foot of the bed, behind me.

His hands curl over my ass, and he angles me up,
exposing my pussy farther. Pleasure snaps and crackles
through my body. It's hard to focus on giving and
receiving, but I'm up to the multitask. As Dev goes
down on me, I swirl my tongue around the head of
Ledger's dick.

"That's so good. Gimme more," Ledger says,
sounding like he's begging.

I like the sound of his pleas so much, I deny him.
"But maybe I want to do *this*." I lick off a drop of
arousal. "And play...just with the tip."

"Aubrey." My name is a warning. Ledger's growl
turns me on.

I tease him some more, flicking and kissing till
Ledger's arching his hips. I'm about to take him deeper
when Dev moves like lightning. He buries his face in
my pussy. He eats me ferociously, with a greedy mouth
and a filthy moan that sends electricity sparking
through my whole body.

My thoughts unwind into only sensations as I try, I

swear I try, to focus on sucking Ledger's fantastic dick. But I can barely focus on Ledger. Hot sparks spread through my belly as Dev devours me.

"More, honey. Take more," Ledger urges desperately, fisting the base of his cock, encouraging me to go deeper.

He needs me to suck him off. Just like he needed me this morning when he woke up.

I want to give him everything he needs, but before I can Dev breaks the contact and smacks my ass. The sharp sting radiates through me, forking into pleasure. Until I was with them, I never knew I was into spanking, but holy hell, am I ever. I'm learning I'm into asking for it too. "Smack me harder," I whisper.

Dev lets out a low rumble. "You like that, sweet thing?"

Another smack of my ass. Then a squeeze of my flesh as I manage a breathy, "I do."

"And I like your mouth," Ledger says, all hungry too.

Yes. That's right. Can't lose sight of my multitasking mission.

"Just the tip," Ledger adds and he's playing by my impromptu rules now, asking for anything I'll give him.

I'm not sure I can suck him properly, though, since Dev's returned to my wetness, and he's going down on me like it's *his* mission. With his thumbs pressed hard at the crease of my ass, he holds my pussy open, sinking his face against me, rubbing his beard right where I want him. I rock back against him, seeking out more, more, more, while I try to tease, tease, tease.

Then, Dev slides a finger inside me, then another,

and I'm moaning around Ledger's dick, whimpering as I try to suck him off.

Dev crooks his fingers inside me, and it's like a pinball machine in my body. Buzzers whir, sounds clang, music blasts.

I can't suck and be eaten.

Not like this. Not when I feel everything in every corner of my body. Pleasure, pressure, bliss. Dev's playing me perfectly with his fingers, his tongue, and his hands. I'm moaning and groaning, then crying out as Dev curls his fingers as he sucks on my clit just right.

My world bursts into bright, bold fireworks, the finale at the end of the night.

I drop Ledger from my mouth, shouting *yes, yes, yes* as I come harder than I ever have in my life. White spots dance before my eyes. Warmth floods me. Hands tangle in my hair. I don't know how long I come, but soon, I hear a zipper, shorts coming off, and a shirt too, then the crinkle of foil. A rip.

Ledger's moving as well. He's no longer lying on his back, stretched out. He's off the bed, clothes vanishing in record time. In a second, he's back on the bed, up on his knees in front of me while Dev nudges the head of his covered cock against my soaked pussy.

"So wet. So fucking pretty," Dev says, and I can tell he's staring down at me.

"Please," I say. It's the only word I can get out as Ledger strokes his dick at me. Like it's a weapon of pleasure. His eyes are savage. My mouth waters, and I just *want*.

All of this. All of them. The way they treat me in

bed is everything I never knew I wanted. I feel worshiped and owned at the same time as they manhandle me and praise me.

As Ledger squeezes a drop of pre-come out of the head, he arches a brow. "No more teasing, Aubrey. You gonna let me fuck that pretty mouth now?"

His tone is stern, just the way I like it from him. But I don't know that I *can* let him fuck my mouth. I don't know that I can handle deep-throating. It's a little terrifying but thrilling too. So I meet his gaze with brutal honesty. "I don't know. But I want to try."

Ledger runs a hand over my hair gently, his gaze softening. "Pinch my arm if it gets too rough."

"I will," I say, comforted and excited by the fact that he's thinking about my safety. I've never had the kind of sex where I'd need a safe word or gesture. I want to though.

I show him as much as I lick the offered drop, but then I gasp because Dev's rubbing the head of his dick against my clit. I want to bask in the feelings, but I want to please Ledger too.

I can do this. I can totally fucking do this. I open my mouth for Ledger as Dev glides his cock against my clit. I ache for him to fill me.

But Ledger needs me too. His cock is throbbing, and I brace myself on my palms as Ledger wraps a hand around my head, gathering my hair. Ledger slides into my mouth an inch or so while Dev taunts my clit with his cock.

I feel so empty, and I want so much. I moan as I suck Ledger.

"She's getting so worked up," Ledger says to Dev, and that turns me on more, the way they narrate my arousal.

"Yeah, our greedy girl wants my dick deep inside her," Dev says, all casual, like he's just talking about coffee. Does he want it with cream or sugar? "But I'm gonna tease her even more."

Dev rubs the crown against my clit again, then barely slides inside, giving me just the tip.

I shake with need, but I don't let go of Ledger's cock this time. I've teased him long enough. "Yes, you look so fucking good like this," Ledger praises as I draw him deeper past my lips.

Relaxing my throat, I focus solely on pleasing Ledger. I lick and suck, swirling my tongue up and down his length, savoring the salty taste of him, the feel of his rough hands in my hair, the hard grip.

He pushes into my mouth, fucking me deeper. I nearly choke. He pulls out. "You need me to stop, honey?"

I shake my head, grab the base, and bring him back to me.

Then I show them what a good multitasking girl I am. I suck Ledger with everything I have while Dev relentlessly teases me with his cock. Dev gives one thrust of the tip, two, three. A few more. Pretty sure he gets to ten. He stops, then shoves inside me without mercy.

Yes. I don't want mercy. I want to be fucked.

"Fuck me," I groan against Ledger's cock as I revel in

the feel of Dev inside me at last, like he's reaching every part of me.

"Yeah, you like that don't you, sweet thing? When I give you all of my cock," Dev says.

I nod with my mouth full of Ledger's dick.

"Then you better finish him off so I can fuck you hard," Dev says, punctuating his demand with a smack to my ass. The smack stings deliciously.

I like being smacked.

I like being roughed up.

Being filled at...both ends.

As Dev feeds his dick in that one, two, three move, he's swatting my ass. As Ledger fucks my throat, he curls his hand tightly around my hair, staring at my lips stretched wide. "Look at you. So full of my dick."

I maneuver his dick against my cheek so he can see the outline.

"Yes, fucking yes," Ledger rasps, his breath turning ragged, the tell-tale sign he's close.

Just. Like. Me.

I'm aching for Dev to slam into me, to pound me ruthlessly. But Dev is a man of restraint.

And I am a woman on a mission. I focus on giving Ledger the blow job of his lifetime. Showing off how much I want him till he bites out a strangled, "Take it all."

I swallow every last drop right as Dev slams into me.

"You were so fucking good, baby. So fucking hot. You want me to pound you into the mattress now?" Dev asks.

It's hardly a question. Still, I answer with a *god yes*, right as Ledger's dick falls from my lips.

In no time, Dev's fucking me so hard I can feel his balls slapping against my clit. His hips smack my ass. His hands grab my ass hard. He made the fucking part of the foreplay, and now he's bringing it home. Nailing me into the bed. One hand coasts up my spine to my shoulder blades as he shoves me down on the mattress.

I'm ass up, face down, and on the edge. Don't even know where Ledger is, and I can't care.

"Yes, please, more," I gasp as I grab at the sheets, struggling to hold on. Seconds later, I succumb to the biggest, hardest orgasm of my life, shattering underneath Dev who doesn't stop, who fucks me through the aftershocks to his own release, grunting out a strangled *yes* as he shudders inside me.

I'm spent.

Utterly spent.

Well, multitasking takes a lot out of you.

SEX MATH

Aubrey

Later, as the stars wink in the night sky and an upbeat tune floats from my playlist, I grab a chocolate-covered strawberry and take a bite. We're stretched out on the couch. I'm curled up against Dev, my legs resting on Ledger's thighs. We're all in our jammies. We ordered dinner in and now we're finishing dessert.

"Did Fitzgibbons assist you with locating the strawberries?" I ask.

"He was most decidedly helpful," Dev says, adopting the British tone again.

I raise my chin haughtily. "Do thank Fitzgibbons for me."

"Are you playing *Bridgerton*, Aubrey?" Dev asks, back to his voice now, his bedroom tone.

"Well, it's a sexy show," I say. "And I do kind of want to go to London."

"To pretend you're in *Bridgerton*?" Dev asks.

"Sure," I say, picturing drawing room trysts and library canoodling. "There really should be a season where one of the heroines has two suitors shagging her at once."

Dev seems to give that some thought. "There should be."

"Seriously, I'd watch the hell out of that. Wait, wait." I sit up straighter, ideas pinging through me. "What if, and hear me out, there was a whole spin-off devoted to unconventional pairings? I can see it now. Lord Whackoff and Lady Aycock bring Henry Cummings into the bedroom," I say, then finish my strawberry, savoring the sweetness of the fruit and the decadence of the chocolate.

"And what would be the bang prediction on that?" Dev asks.

Ledger arches a brow in question. "What's that?"

Dev quickly explains about the book club and the bets we make, then Ledger flashes a cocky grin. "Well, we hit at the forty-two percent mark."

I furrow my brow. "How do you figure?"

"Third night. Of seven on the trip," Ledger explains.

I give him a look like *where are you getting those numbers from*? "We've only been on the trip two nights. We had sex *yesterday*."

With a dry laugh, Dev says, "Dude, your sex memory needs a tune-up."

Ledger rolls his eyes. "I remember yesterday. But I'm counting Saturday night. We hung out then, so..."

Dev shakes his head. "No. That's not how this works."

"Oh, you're an expert now on bang predictions?" Ledger fires off.

I cut in since, well, this is my area of expertise. "I'm pretty sure in our case it's two out of six. Since we return on Saturday. So, that's thirty-three percent."

"Which means we have sixty-seven percent more opportunities," Ledger adds, looking delightfully smug.

"I'm not entirely sure sex math works that way," I say.

"It does," the guys say in unison, and I suppose it's not surprising they agree on that.

I grab another berry. "Fine, I like your sex math, and I like these so much better than the champagne." When I finish, I offer one to Dev.

With an affectionate grin, Dev takes it. "Good," he says, and judging from the flicker in his eyes, the meaning isn't lost on him—I like their gift more than Aiden's bubbly freebie.

I take another strawberry from the silver tray and give it to Ledger.

Dev breaks off the chocolate covering, setting that down on the tray, then eats his berry. Ledger doesn't give him a hard time about his regimented eating. I don't either. It's the choice that works for him.

I draw a deep, contented sigh. I feel so damn good with them, and yet there's still that nagging issue unsolved.

What do they want?

But I've been good at using my mouth today and

not just for sucking cock. I set down the stem of the berry on the silver tray, then wipe my fingers on a linen napkin. "Guys, this trip has been amazing. You've been such great sports," I begin.

Dev sits up a little straighter.

"But what?" Ledger asks, his guard up.

"There's no *but*," I reassure him, and this is going out on a limb, but I do it anyway.

"You've given me a dream trip, and I've done the things I wanted to do. But I want to know where you'd like to go," I say, opening the conversation that way.

Dev squeezes my shoulder. "I'm having a great time."

I believe him. I can see it in his enthusiasm.

"No place I'd rather be," Ledger seconds.

"Thank you, but what I'm trying to say is...what if we went somewhere else? What if we did the things you wanted for the rest of the trip?"

"Like fucking you every second of the day?" Dev asks.

Ledger shoots a hand in the air. "Sold."

"Seriously. Do you want to pick the agenda? This was the trip I was supposed to take with someone else, and I'd really like to make new memories. Where do you like to go?" I ask, determined to get an answer.

With a twinkle in his eyes, Dev says, "I love Vancouver. The food is amazing."

"Supposedly the nightlife is too," Ledger says. "Last time we were there we were pretty beat from this youth hockey camp we did with Sanchez on the Vancouver team."

Before I can even ask, Dev grabs his phone, opening Google. "Let's take you there and take you out."

With a glow inside and out, I sink back into him as Ledger massages my calves. "Yes," I say.

It's a new honeymoon, and it's a good thing we packed our passports.

In the morning, we pack up and leave.

37

NEW HONEYMOON

Aubrey

"We got you a surprise."

We've just pulled up in our rental car. They insisted on handling the hotel reservation, which didn't surprise me, given Dev's earlier insistence on the jet. They even handled any potential awkward hotel staff observations by booking two rooms this time, even though we only plan to use one. The hotel is renowned for its opulent rooms—but also the discretion of its staff. Better safe than sorry though.

Still, they're doing so much, and I feel the imbalance, even as I feel the glee of their generosity. I'm standing in front of this bustling luxury, high-rise hotel, with its sleek, mirrored facade, next to these men who look so satisfied with whatever this surprise is for me. But I can't burst their bubble by asking *why are you doing this for me?*

Instead, I go with the moment. "Well, what did you guys do?"

The corner of Dev's lips quirk in a grin. "Let's just say...we got a nice room."

* * *

Nice is the understatement of my entire life. This room is a palace. "It's bigger than my apartment," I say, before I backtrack. "Well, actually everything is bigger than my apartment. It's pretty much just a studio. So of course it's bigger than my tiny place," I say, and then I'm a little embarrassed. Why did I just bring up my apartment and how small it is? Oh, maybe because I feel like Cinderella with them. Well, Cinderella and her two princes. "What I'm trying to say is that this is incredible, and I seriously appreciate it."

"It suits you," Dev says, and I'm not sure I'm a penthouse gal, but I'll take the compliment.

The place is sun-drenched in the late afternoon. There's a gorgeous sunken living room and a huge bedroom suite off to the side.

Dev walks to the floor-to-ceiling windows overlooking the city, and he looks so outrageously pleased. So does Ledger when I find him a minute later, checking out the bedroom.

The bed is bigger than any I've ever seen. "This is so much more amazing than the honeymoon suite at the Blackberry Inn," I say in an awed sort of whisper as I stare at the bed.

It's covered in a thick white duvet with mountains

of pillows in sapphire and dove gray, and a quilted headboard that begs to be banged against. Everything smells fresh, like clean linen and springtime.

"Check out the bathroom," Ledger says, and I follow him in there, drinking in the marble vanity, the plush towels, the sunken tub.

"It's big enough for a party," I quip, because I don't know what else to do but joke. This is overwhelmingly incredible. There's a huge rainfall shower with five showerheads.

Dev comes up behind me, moves me in front of the mirror, presses a kiss to my neck. "What do you think?"

He sounds hopeful. I'm confused but thrilled.

"Is that even a real question?" I ask, incredulous as Ledger joins him, sliding a hand down my back, curling it over my ass.

But when I look at Dev, then at Ledger, I see nerves flickering in their eyes. What is going on? They're normally so steady, so strong, so confident. But I can tell it's truly important to them that I like this. As if I could do anything but love it madly.

I exhale, breathing out the surrealism of this moment in my life. I'm just a hairstylist, living in a tiny studio in the Mission District, sending birthday greetings to clients, going to book club, grabbing mango smoothies and lattes with my girls, and seeing concerts with them, too, way up in the nosebleed seats.

But somehow, incomprehensibly, I'm in a beautiful city with two strong, funny, caring, deliciously filthy men. I don't want to come back to earth.

"Yeah, I like it, I like all of this," I say, but other

words bubble up on my tongue unexpectedly. Words I'm dying to say like *I like you guys. I like you two so much*.

"It's amazing. You're amazing. Thank you," I say.

Whatever worries flickered in their eyes have vanished now.

"Come see the city," Ledger says and takes my hand. He guides me back out to the living room, and we head to the floor-to-ceiling windows.

Together, the three of us gaze at the Vancouver skyline, the sun-kissed waterfront below, the blue sky stretching for days.

We're on top of the world with the city at our feet.

But my gut still twists.

I don't feel bought. I just feel unequal. They're doing something so tremendous to make up for my bad luck as the girl who was jilted.

I step away from them and hold up my hands in surrender. "You're doing so much for me. I can't return the favor. This is so huge. You're too kind, and I don't even know what to say."

Dev looks at me like I've lost my mind. "Who said anything about returning it?"

"But I can't do anything like this," I say, a little desperately as I flap my hand toward the vista. "I can barely afford taking you out to the nicest taco shop in town."

"Hey, we like doing this," Ledger says.

"You do?"

With a sigh he turns to Dev, shaking his head. "Just tell her the plan."

"The plan?" I ask.

"When you were in the shower this morning. Back at the Blackberry Inn. We came up with a new plan for you," Dev says as he closes the distance and turns me around so I'm facing the window again. "Over there. That's the concert venue where Amelia Stone is playing tomorrow night."

I only mentioned to them once that my friends were going to that concert. There's no way. There's no way at all...

"We got front-row tickets," Ledger says. "We're going to meet up with your friends and their guys tomorrow night. That work for you?"

It's like bubbles are flowing through me, bright and frothy. "Y-yes," I say, stumbling on the word.

Ledger adds, "And on Friday we made a reservation at a three-star restaurant. Do you like shopping?"

My mind is popping. I can barely speak. I can barely think. "Yeah, sure. I love it. I mean, yes, of course."

"Good. We'll take you shopping for a dress beforehand—"

"But you hate shopping," I point out to Dev. "You died a little inside when you thought we were going to shop for clothes on my wedding day."

Dev smiles then brings me to the couch, sets me on his lap, and runs his hands through the back of my hair, kissing my neck. Ledger watches us from his post by the window, a satisfied smile on his handsome face.

"I do hate shopping," Dev says. "But I really like

making you feel good. And I bet you'd like to get some sexy pink dress, and some of those stockings you like."

"Some trendy...um...boots," Ledger adds, and my god, they're trying so hard, rattling off the things they've seen me wear—colors and styles, and it's so endearing my heart is thumping fast.

Ledger strides across the carpet, looking powerful in those jeans and his black Henley. He bends, cups my cheek, and gives a firm, quick kiss to my lips.

When he pulls back, he says, "Let us spoil you."

I've hit the honeymoon jackpot.

"If you insist. But I *might* have planned something for the rest of the day."

I can spoil them too. In my own way. And it'll start like this.

38

AN ERECTION SELECTION

Aubrey

I stand, backing away from the couch and fiddling with the buttons on my cami. That gets their attention. I push Ledger's shoulder so he knows to sit on the sofa. "I don't want you to think I'm getting on my knees to thank you for the room, the tickets, the dinner."

Two pairs of eyes pop as I sink to the plush carpet. I'm wearing a short jean skirt, and I seriously appreciate this hotel's commitment to luxury floor coverings.

"I'm getting on my knees to say thank you for your... sex math," I say.

Their smiles are full of filthy anticipation, but they say nothing.

This is my moment to be in control. "Now, this time, boys, I'm going to expect you to listen to me when I say take out your cocks."

This time, they do.

Faster than they fly down the ice, both my guys unzip and show me their shafts. The best part? They're already hard. From zero to aroused in seconds.

I tap my chin and my gaze shifts back and forth, back and forth as I appraise my choices.

It's an erection selection.

"Gee. I just don't know which one to suck first. Want to flip a coin?" But before they can say a word, I answer with, "Wait. Silly me. I've got hands and a mouth. Why don't you guys just enjoy the view?"

I wrap a hand around Ledger's cock, and I swirl my tongue over Dev's. He tosses his head back, grunting out, "Your mouth."

I preen from the compliment.

"Your hand," Ledger rasps. "So fucking good, honey."

The thing is, I've never been that great at math, but I've always been very, *very* good with my hands. *Both hands.* I stroke Ledger's length with my left hand, sliding from base to tip then back again, all while I wrap my right hand around the base of Dev's and draw his dick deeper into my mouth.

As I wrap my lips nice and tight around him, he ropes his fingers through my hair, watching me suck him off.

But I can't let him get too comfy. Right when Dev lets out a bitten off grunt, I pop off. Then smile. "Musical dicks," I say with a bob of my shoulder, then turn my face to Ledger's cock. "Your turn, handsome."

Before I take Ledger deep, I spit in my palm, and wrap that hand around Dev, jerking him.

"Yes, fucking yes," he groans, sounding like it won't take him long at all.

He punches up his hips into my hand while Ledger grips my hair.

But even as he's fucking my fist and losing his mind, bossy Dev can't seem to resist giving orders, since he says, "Tug her hair harder. That makes her lose her mind."

Ledger threads his hands tighter, then fucks my mouth faster.

Bossy Dev is right. I'm so turned on, I'm moaning against Ledger's dick and rocking my hips. Sparks race across my skin, and I'm so aroused. I can't keep it to myself though. It'll go a long way to get Dev over the finish line. I let go of his dick to shove my hand up my skirt. After I coat my fingers, I return them to Dev's cock once more, tunneling my fist along his shaft.

"Fuck, baby. That's so fucking hot," Dev says on a strangled groan.

"She gets so wet, doesn't she?" Ledger says while I swallow more of his cock. "She looks so fucking good on her knees. Can't wait to tie her up later. See how pretty her pussy looks when she's bound on the bed."

And I gush.

"Yeah, she wants that," Dev says, but he can barely finish the sentence since he's grunting and groaning.

Excitement rushes through me, knowing he's this close to coming in my hand. But before he can climax, Ledger eases out. "Honey, open wide for my friend. So he can come in that pretty mouth of yours."

Oh. My. Fucking. God.

"Yes, take it," Dev growls.

I obey, taking Dev's dick in my mouth right as a warm splash of come hits my tongue, sending electricity cracking across my whole body. I drink down his release, swallowing it all as he curses in pleasure while Ledger works his dick in his fist.

God, it's so hot when the men you want jerk off to you. In front of you. *On you.*

But I know he'll want to finish in me.

I shift back to Ledger, opening wide. Ledger jams his hand into my hair, practically pushing my head back before he groans, shudders, then comes down my throat.

I'm sweating, shaking, trembling all over as I swallow.

I can barely take how aroused I am. As Ledger eases out, I thrust my hand between my legs, crying out in relief as I stroke my eager clit when Dev cuts me off.

"Get on the couch and fuck his face. You want to come like that?"

Oh, god. I do. It turns me on even more that he asks *and* demands at the same time.

"Yes," I say, barely getting out the word.

I'm so excited I could cry. But like, good tears. Sexy tears. Is that a thing? It feels like a thing.

Dev jumps off the couch immediately and peels off my panties as Ledger lies flat, patting his shoulders. "Sit on me and ride me hard," he says, then grabs me, pulling me on top of him, hiking up my skirt to my waist. This won't take long.

I straddle his face, rock against his mouth, and I

ride his wild need for me till I'm shouting, screaming, then flying into bliss in this palace of a room.

When I come down, Ledger wraps his hands around my hips and lifts me off him, setting me onto the couch.

He wipes his face, then says, "Now, I really need you to come again. All over his beard."

And Dev's on his knees on the floor, spreading me open and eating me till I fall apart once more.

Yes, I am Cinderella with two very filthy princes.

39

NATURAL PAINKILLERS

Dev

This is seriously not fair.

When Aubrey stops in front of Plant Parenthood in the early evening, my dumb heart thunders.

I'm not even a plant guy. But she found this little shop to show Ledger.

My buddy's grin is nothing short of electric when he stares at the window bursting with green. Plants hang. Vines dangle. Leaves take over all the real estate.

Aubrey looks so proud, it's sexy.

"I can do trip research too, Plant Daddy," she says to Ledger with a lift of her chin, all her attention on him.

Pride suffuses me too. She pulled this off, and it's damn fun to watch her shine.

He turns his gaze away from the buds and blooms, focusing only on her. "I'm never leaving." It comes out serious.

She jerks back, maybe surprised by the intensity of his remark. Me too. It's said in a soul-deep way.

It's clear that he's touched. Like an eager explorer, he strides into the plant shop.

We follow, and I draw a deep inhale once inside. The air is cool and sort of refreshing. "Why does the air seem different?"

Ledger tosses a glance my way as he stops at a potted plant with tall stems and oval-shaped leaves. The name next to it reads Chinese money plant. "Photosynthesis, dude," Ledger says, like it's magic.

I roll my eyes, but the truth is I'm intrigued. "I mean, yeah. But really?"

There's no joking or ribbing in his tone when he says, "They purify the air. Plants remove pollutants from it."

When he says that, of course it makes perfect sense now. I snap my fingers. "Right, that was like biology class and shit? Did we learn that in school?" I ask, making light of my studies even though I was an A student. I like to be good at things. But I haven't given plants much thought.

As Ledger peruses the snake plants like he's an archaeology professor let loose in an ancient museum, he adds, "I bet your parents recommend plants to their clients. There are studies showing that they reduce anxiety. They also make you happier."

I'm about to ask what's his excuse for the sullen moods he gets now and then, but I'd be a dick if I said that. Besides, maybe he'd be grumpier if he wasn't a plant daddy. Yeah. That makes sense. Plants are his natural painkillers.

He wouldn't want me to make a joke about that, so I say, "Cool info. I think you just gave a Daily Dose of Good."

He growls, narrowing his eyes. "I did not."

"You did too," Aubrey says, like she's caught him in the act. "Plants are your Daily Dose of Good. Admit it."

Ledger narrows his eyes, wags a finger at both of us. "I don't believe in that."

"Right. Sure," I say as we walk past a cactus. "Here. It's you in plant form."

Ledger rolls his eyes.

Aubrey smiles. "You're a little prickly, Ledger."

"Am not," he counters.

"You are," she says, and he harrumphs as a lanky man sporting messy black hair and trendy plaid pants emerges from a back room. A Japanese flag hangs behind the counter next to a Canadian flag. The man spots us and says, "Welcome to Plant Parenthood. Let me know if I can help you with anything."

"I'd love some help," Ledger says, then heads off, leaving me alone with Aubrey, who's studying a shelf of small house plants.

"Maybe when I return to San Francisco I'll buy some plants for my booth," she says as she checks out a Boston fern.

"That one is boring. Get a money tree instead."

"I'll put it on my to-do list after..." She stops, blinks, then says, her tone a little heavier, "...this trip."

I don't want to think about the end either. "Good plan."

"What about you? Will you get one?"

Me? Nah. I'm not a plant guy. But is that the real issue? "I don't know if I could take care of one when I'm on the road. Hockey is pretty demanding."

That demand is going to start next week at training camp. My fingers tingle at the thought of getting back on the ice.

"You could just get a plant sitter," she offers.

That's a valid idea, but here's another one. A dangerous one. One where I almost say something like "Or maybe you could take care of them when I go out of town and then we will see you when we return?"

But that is not, *not* going to happen.

This ends when the trip ends.

I dodge the topic, turning it back around. "Do these plants make you happy?"

She considers the money tree some more, running her polished nails along its leaves. "I think they could. They're like a mango smoothie. The contented sigh of a dog. A good haircut. Getting your nails done. Going shopping with friends and finding a great discount. Listening to a song that just feels like it moves your soul. I think all of those things do it." She drops her hand from the plant with a happy sigh and turns to me. "What about you? What makes you happy?"

Improving my stats as a goalie like—shots against and save percentage. Not to mention winning it all.

But also, *this second.*

The problem is I keep thinking about next week,

too, and the antsy feeling that kicks in when the season nears. The urge to skate. To spend my time on the ice, to work out harder, faster, better. The tingle in my fingers. The buzzing in my bones.

A few seconds later, Aubrey tilts her head. "What are you thinking, Dev?"

Oh. I drifted off. "Hockey," I admit.

"You miss it."

It's a relief to just tell the truth. "I can't wait for it to start. I just want to play."

I want to dominate. I want to crush the competition. I don't say those things because I'll sound like an athlete with a one-track mind.

She smiles, understanding. "See? You do need plants. You need them to unwind at the end of an intense day."

Is that what I need to balance all this drive? I'm not sure anything could be a strong enough counterweight.

Aubrey nods toward Ledger. "I'm going to join him."

I let her go, staying back, checking out plants I know I'll never get.

As she joins him, I watch from a distance. They look good together. I pick up bits and pieces of their convo. He mentions a plant shop he goes to in the city —Late Bloomer. She says she'll check it out someday. Then, I tune them out, letting them have their moment. Seeing them enjoying each other's company like this makes me happy enough right here, right now. But I also feel like I don't quite fit. Like they're both at a certain place, and I'm not sure I'm there.

Or that I want to be.

No matter how much bigger these feelings for Aubrey grow by the day. No, by the hour.

And really, no matter how big they get, they still aren't going anywhere after.

40

MELT YOUR HEART

Ledger

"Time to confess. Where did your plant daddy side come from?" Aubrey asks as we walk along Robson Street, passing eclectic local shops peddling candles and stationery alongside flashy designer brand-name stores hawking handbags and sunglasses. We're en route to a dinner place she's picked out.

She won't tell us what it is. It's part of her *spoil us* plan.

I do want to answer her question, but the more I let down my guard with her, the more I want to let it down. I've still got the wounds from my marriage ending. On the other hand, can Aubrey really hurt me? Come Saturday, we say goodbye. I'll be back with my monkey plants, my mean cat, and the ticking clock of the big decision looming over me.

"Can't a guy just like plants?" I say, avoiding the topic a little longer.

"Sure, but cigars aren't always cigars. Why plants?" she presses.

Because my dad wasn't into them. Because they weren't sports. Because it was no one else's thing in my family.

Ah, fuck it. She deserves to know. As we stop at the corner of a bustling street, traffic whisking by on a Wednesday night, I turn to the redhead with the beguiling brown eyes. They're big and deep, and they make me open up to her. "Because they were all mine," I say with a shrug. The shrug is for me—resignation to the effect she has on my closed, cold heart.

"When I was a teenager, I needed something that had nothing at all to do with hockey," I add. There, I said it. "An interest that was entirely separate from the ice."

"You needed an escape," she says thoughtfully.

"Yeah, I did." I scratch my jaw, weighing how far I want to go. This is getting heavy. This is getting close to the stuff I keep locked up tight. The nightmares, the twinge in my knee, the sense of dread as the season marches unstoppably closer. I want to play hockey. Truly, I do. But I want it to be fun. I just don't know if it is anymore. I meet her gaze again. "Sometimes I still do."

"We all do, bro," Dev says with genuine understanding.

I'm not sure he ever needs an escape from hockey. He's lived it and breathed it since my dad coached him in juniors, when we were younger, and I helped my dad. Dev was eager, relentless, always ready. There was never ever a day in his life when Dev wasn't the *put me in, coach* guy.

I was that guy for a long time.

But I'm different now. Eventually, Father Time catches up to all of us. It's happened to the greats in football, basketball, and hockey. It's the one phenomenon no man is immune from.

"We all do, don't we," I echo, since it's easier than pointing out the differences between us. As we cross the street—and maybe it's psychosomatic—my knee barks, then I look at Dev, spry, five years younger.

Maybe he is right about dog years.

"I think I was expecting you to say your grandma liked plants or you had an aunt who was a botanist," Aubrey says, picking up the plant thread. "But it's very you that you found this interest on your own."

I fight off a smile. She observes me too closely, sees me too well. That awareness makes my pulse race a little faster. I do still want to jump over the boards and slam my stick against the puck, but that desire is mixed with others now. With unexpected new ones. Like this —I want to see her at a game, skate over to her, and press a sweaty, exhausted kiss to her pretty face at the end of a hard-won victory.

Things that'll never happen.

I shove those thoughts aside when my phone pings with a text. I swipe it quickly, nerves prickling. Maybe it's Garrett again.

But it's a text from Hollis, and there's a video

attached. "Hollis sent me something," I say, intrigued since the thumbnail is him and Jack.

I waggle the screen at Aubrey and Dev, and we stop in front of an awning in front of a bar. I hit play. "Thought you might want to know your cat and I are besties. Check him out," Hollis says, then strides across my home with my cat riding his shoulders.

"You have a parrot cat," Aubrey says, awed.

"Evidently."

"Does he do other tricks?"

"He's never done a single trick for me," I grumble, but with begrudging admiration for Hollis's determination to teach a cat.

A second video lands.

I shake my head, but I'm laughing. I can only imagine what he's sending now. I hit play once more.

"High five," Hollis says to the cat, who's sitting across from him at the kitchen table. The cat lifts his paw and high fives my cousin.

"Ohhh! He is the cat charmer," Dev declares.

"Dude, you're killing me," I say to the video.

Hollis turns to the camera almost like he's heard me. "Sorry," he says with zero contrition. "Should have called it the high paw."

He smiles and the video ends.

"Your teammate is too charming," Aubrey says to Dev, then to me, she asks, "And the cat? Is he named Jack because he has only one eye? Like Calico Jack the pirate?"

"No. It's short for Jackass because ever since I adopted him from Little Friends Animal Rescue, he's been a jerk," I say, feeling terrible now I named him that.

Aubrey pats my back. "Maybe you should have named him Calico Jack. Maybe he'd have liked it more to have a badass pirate name."

I heave a sigh. "You might be right."

With her other hand, she taps her chin for a few seconds. "When did you get him from Little Friends?"

"Couple years ago. At the *Hockey Hotties* calendar fundraiser in the park."

"I remember that! That's when Trina and the guys announced their relationship," she recounts.

"And distracted the media with their romance," Dev adds.

"Now everyone's used to hockey throuples," Aubrey says with amusement, then she meets my gaze again. "So you got a cat that day? Was it...sublimation?"

I scrunch my brow. "For...what?"

"Trina said she thought you were checking me out then," she teases, giving my back a bit of a squeeze now.

I flash back to that day. To noticing Garrett's little sister in the park. To thinking she was off-limits, but so damn pretty too. "Trina's right," I admit. "But then I met Marla shortly after, married her quickly, then lost her just as quickly."

Timing. It's really everything, isn't it? Maybe if I hadn't been so worried about her being Garrett's sister, I'd have said something that day. But maybe not. "Guess I should have swooped in before Aiden did."

There's regret in my tone.

In Dev's sigh, too, when he adds, "And I was with Eva."

Aubrey goes quiet for a few seconds, maybe contemplating her own what-ifs as well. Wondering what it'd have been like if we'd all connected when we were truly free.

"Well, one good thing came out of it. Or two, really. I started volunteering with Little Friends, and you got a cat. Who's probably getting a new name very soon." That's Aubrey. Looking on the bright side.

"Calico Jack," I say, trying that on for size.

She doesn't let go of my back for the rest of the block. I want to walk all night. But when we reach the corner, we're clearly at the place Aubrey picked out. I crack up at the orange name written across the window in a vintage font. *Melt Your Heart.* "You did it," I say to her, impressed.

She smiles proudly. We're standing in front of a grilled cheese restaurant that *she* found for my friend. "Let's make it National Grilled Cheese Day. It's your cheat day, Dev," Aubrey says.

Dev drops his head, shaking it in delight, perhaps trying to hide his smile but utterly failing. "I'm all in," he says.

I bet there's a double meaning there.

We go inside, and my pulse kicks up again. I want to kiss her. I want *him* to kiss her. I want to tell her that taking me to that plant shop and taking him to this grilled cheese joint is just doing it for me. Making me feel like I could escape into her. Because of what she does for me, for him, and for us.

Feelings are such dangerous fools though. Best to focus on food instead.

Ignoring the mushy thoughts and the squishy things she's doing to my heart, I order a gouda on sourdough while Aubrey picks a cheddar and apple, then nudges Dev, who's perusing the chalkboard menu. "Get the Ultimate. You can do it," she goads.

He draws a deep, fortifying breath, then nods a few times. "All right. I'm going in."

After we order, we grab a table in the corner. The place is pretty empty. Aubrey glances around, then something flashes in her eyes. A decision, maybe? Like something's been on her mind, but she wants it off her heart too?

"The bird on my ankle?"

"Yes?" I ask.

"I said I got it for my dad. And that's true. I did. Just to remember him by. But also to remember things he said. His words about being happy and doing things you love. So it was for him, but it was also for me to remember those words. To do those things. Except, I think I messed it all up," she says, her tone stretched thin.

"What do you mean?" I ask, concerned.

"I told you I only wanted to marry Aiden because my dad thought he was the right guy for me," she blurts out and she said that at dinner the other night, but the emotions in her eyes tells me there's more to the story. "My mom was so sure of it too. I thought I was making them happy. I always wanted them to be happy when I was younger," she says, barreling on. I was not expecting this new confessional, but judging from the speed and her vulnerability she needs to share this.

"But when I was in junior high," she continues, "they went through a rough patch, and I was pretty much the only kid at home. I tried really hard to make them happy. To entertain them. To tell them stories. To cover up the silence. The tension. The way everything felt so strained. Later, after they stayed together, working through whatever it was, I just became that person. Always wanting everyone to have a good time. Making sure everyone has everything they need."

I get why she's telling us this. "Are you saying that's why you took us around today?" I ask, but I'm not mad if that's the reason. I am, however, intensely curious.

"Because you don't have to make us happy. I can only speak for me, but I already am," Dev says.

Her smile is soft, relaxed as she shakes her head. "I *don't* feel that way with you guys at all. That's what I like about...*this thing*. I *did* feel that way about my family. I just wanted you to know the deeper reason for why I almost got married. I wanted to share it since you've been so good to me. I'm glad Aiden showed his true colors, I'm glad you guys were there for me at the church, and I'm glad I'm here now with both of you," she says, then breathes a sigh of...not exactly pure relief. More like delighted relief.

"Me too," Dev says, meeting her gaze with utter sincerity and something else—a look in his eyes I haven't seen before. One that's not hard to read at all. A look that says he's falling for her. "Really glad."

It feels too easy to say the same thing. Instead, I say,

"Then you're going to sit back and enjoy the hell out of it as we make you happy the next few days."

"Fine. If you insist, then I'm all in." Her smile turns a little naughty. "And there are some things I want to try…"

She shares a few of those *things,* and it's not my heart that melts this time. It's my brain.

"Yes. We're up for that," I say immediately, certain I can speak for Dev in this regard.

And I need to since he's speechless.

The naughty conversation ends when a server brings our food. After we thank him and he leaves, I blurt out impulsively, "This will be my last season."

I didn't plan on saying that. Hell, I wasn't even sure this was going to be my last season. Until now. But now feels like the right moment to declare myself, alongside all these other confessions. Just voicing what's been swirling inside me lessens some of the tension, some of the uncertainty.

I feel lighter. More free.

Aubrey's eyes are warm as she reaches for my hand across the table and squeezes it. "Good for you."

"Why is it good?"

"Because you sound ready. Ready is good."

"Should I have a breakup party?"

She smiles, answering sincerely as she says, "Maybe you should."

Dev offers me a fist for knocking. "Man, you've had a great career."

I don't knock back. Instead I push my hands against the table, downplaying it. "Yeah, yeah."

I feel better, but not completely. Something is still nagging at me. The inevitable *what happens next*. There are too many choices for life after hockey and that pressure to work hard and be the best—to be chasing the next big thing—has been drilled into me since I was a kid.

But now is not the time to deal with what's next. There will be plenty of time for that when this trip ends.

We tuck into our grilled cheeses. Mine's absolutely delicious. Dev looks like he's in heaven as he moans around his sandwich, permitting himself this one transgression on his diet, enjoying this moment for all it is. It's not what we planned a few nights ago—grilled cheese as part of our Ambushed by Exes club.

It's grilled cheese for us.

The moments are all you get. They end before you know it, so you have to make the most of them while you're in them. If that's the case, and I'm pretty sure it is, I pull Dev aside after the meal. "About those things she wants to try..."

"I'm all ears," he says.

I tell him my plan.

Later, I'll pull her aside since there's something I think she and I can do for him.

41

_____

TASTE TEST

Ledger

I'm relaxing on the couch, holding a glass of scotch, debating the merits of various whiskeys with Dev.

"Scotch is smoother," I say, just stating the facts of my drink of choice as the faint sound of the blow-dryer whooshes in the background. Aubrey just got out of the shower. "It goes down better."

Dev knocks back some of his bourbon, then paces some more. "And bourbon is sweet, like vanilla or caramel."

"Smoky is better," I say as the hair dryer turns off. "Just like the Sea Dogs are better than the Foxes."

Yeah, that'll wind him up even more.

He growls, then paces as he bites out, "We are stacked up and down the line. Including yours fucking truly in the crease."

I smirk. It's hilarious to see him like this. "Be careful

or the vein in your neck might burst," I tease, but then I shut the fuck up when Aubrey emerges from the bathroom, slides a hand up along the doorframe, and juts out a sexy hip.

She's a vision in black lace, creamy skin, and lush red locks.

"You wanted to spoil me in this?" she asks, coasting her hand down the black corset to the matching lace panties before she teases the top of her thigh-high stockings.

And my dick's about to burst now.

"Yes," I grunt, my voice like gravel.

"You." It's all Dev can seemingly manage to say.

"You look stunning," I rasp out, then set down the glass on the coffee table and lift a finger, beckoning her to me.

In black high heels, she crosses the living room, passing Dev, whose eyes widen by the second. He doesn't look away. He follows her every step till she reaches me.

I run one hand down her right thigh, taking my sweet time appraising her in the lingerie we bought for her this evening before we returned. We stopped at a sex toy store and bought lots of things.

I pat my thigh. "Sit on me, honey," I tell her.

Like a good angel, she parks that sweet ass on my thighs, then crosses her strong, sexy legs. Dev doesn't do a thing but gawk from across the room, too mesmerized by Aubrey's sexiness and obedience to speak.

"You like scotch?" I ask her.

"I don't know. Never tried it."

I reach for my drink, making sure she watches me the whole time as I lift the glass to her lips, then say, "Just sniff it."

She draws a quick inhale.

I raise the tumbler, take a small drink, and hold it in my mouth. I set the glass down on the table, then press my lips to hers, giving her the liquor, letting her taste it from me while I run my hand down her throat as she swallows.

When she finishes, she trembles.

"You like?" I ask.

"I do," she says, her breath feathery. "It's a little smoky."

"Smoky's good." I slide my tongue between her lips, licking off the taste.

"So good," she says when I break the kiss.

"Good. Now let Dev try some. I need to prove I'm right."

Aubrey straightens, then lifts her finger and beckons Dev.

He's across the living room in no time, setting down his bourbon as she drinks a swig of the scotch, then lifts her chin toward him—an offering from a goddess.

She stays on my lap, looking like sin and salvation in all that black and lace as she gives him the gift of her lips. He bends and covers her mouth, then swallows the liquor with a satisfied sigh.

"Better, isn't it?" I ask.

He doesn't answer. Instead, he takes his tumbler, then roams his gaze up and down the beauty on my lap.

"Lean back, sweet thing. Against the couch," he instructs.

Aubrey complies, stretching next to me, her back arching, her tits rising up.

Slowly, purposefully, he pours a small splash of bourbon between the valley of her tits. "Try the bourbon sampler, Ledger," he instructs.

The sneaky fucker.

He knew I couldn't resist. I dip my face to her sweet skin and flatten my tongue, licking off the bourbon drop by drop as Aubrey trembles, murmuring an *ohhhh*.

I lap up the liquor that I can catch, along with the taste of her. Her scent—something tropical and lush—fries my brain. Makes my blood burn hot and fast. Makes me want to peel away the satin of her corset and expose the flesh of those tits.

Before I know it, I'm doing exactly that, devouring her lush tits while Dev chuckles.

"Guess you do like bourbon better," he says.

I don't answer him. I'm a prisoner to this lust. I need to get a grip. Take my time. Slow the hell down.

We have a scene mapped out.

Somehow, I tear my face away from her breasts.

Her shoulders shudder as she raises her face to gaze up at Dev with mischief in her brown eyes.

"Maybe Ledger needs another taste, though," Aubrey says in a playful purr, rubbing her lush ass against the denim of my thighs.

Dev's playing with her hair, tucking it behind her ears as he says, "Bet he does too."

I'm strung tight with anticipation. What the hell is up his sleeve?

"Aubrey, baby," Dev says.

Like a good angel, she lifts her chin, bats her lashes. "Yes, sir?"

He cups her ear and whispers something I can't hear.

When he steps back, she wriggles off me. Standing and striding to the bed with the confidence of a club dancer, she sinks down on the mattress on her side, like a supermodel posing, before she shifts to lie flat on her stomach.

She's giving me a perfect view of the back of all that lingerie that we bought her.

"Now, tug those panties down just a tidge," Dev says, his dirty smile indicating that he's having a blast with his instructions.

I swallow roughly, my throat dry as a desert, my dick hard as a statue.

Aubrey pushes her panties lower, exposing the crack of her ass before she stops. "This good?"

I hiss in a breath.

"A little lower," Dev urges.

Like a helpful good girl, she pushes them down more till they hit the bottom of her cheeks. She smiles up at him, eager to please. "Like this?"

He leans in and presses a kiss to her face. "So good." With the scene set, he turns and meets my gaze. "Want a taste?"

I stare at the scene unfolding on the big bed. Dev

standing with his tumbler of bourbon, holding it a few feet above Aubrey. Then trickling it onto her ass.

"Oh!" She wiggles as the amber liquid hits her skin. In seconds, I'm there, pulling down the panties way past her ass cheeks and lapping up every last drop.

I keep going. I pull the lace down her thighs, bringing it to the tops of her stockings. With her gorgeous ass exposed, I wrap my hands around her front and jerk her up. "A little higher," I mumble against her soft flesh.

She moves under me, raising her ass, and yes, fucking yes. I can't resist. I lick a long, hungry line down. She told us in the restaurant that she wanted ass play tonight. We bought her toys and lingerie, and we're ready to introduce her to some starter fun.

But first, I need *this* unplanned moment.

I press a kiss to her ass, and I go up in fucking flames. A wildfire ignites in my body, blazing out of control. As I splay my hands across her belly, she angles her ass up in the air, her body telling me how much she likes it.

Her noises, too, as she moans, "Oh my god, so good, so good."

Yeah, it's so fucking good that I might spend the whole night here. But there's so much more of her to explore so I find the willpower to tear myself away from the goodness.

I lift my hand and bring my palm down hard on all that sweet flesh. She yelps. I slide a hand between her thighs, where she's slick and wonderful to touch.

On a groan, I bring my fingers to my mouth and lick

off her taste as I stand. Get my bearings. Try to blink off the fog of lust.

I spot Dev already turning on a toy, grabbing the lube.

Good. I need a moment to recover. "Get her ready, but leave the shoes on," I instruct, then I head to the bathroom, but not before I toss one more glance behind me at the scene.

Aubrey looks sex drunk, spread out on the bed, hair fanned out, cheeks flushed, panties twisted by her knees.

She's about to get introduced to the first step in the double fucking she wants really, *really* soon.

42

TAKING TURNS

Aubrey

My arms are spread wide above my head, tied to the headboard with silk restraints from the toy shop. I'm wearing only my corset and the stockings and the shoes.

Because...*orders.*

Dev is shirtless, jeans on, kneeling between my legs, lazily stroking my wet pussy with one hand while pressing a lubed toy against my ass with his other.

I'm a hot, wild, wet mess already. Well, I do *enjoy* booty action. Discovered that on my own, thank you very much. I've got a collection of toys at home. Being a curious cat, I picked up some plugs online from Just For Her several months ago and experimented with them. *Frequently.* I've never used them with a partner though. Aiden was pretty vanilla, and since my fantasies strayed to the more adventurous shores, self-care became a regular item on my nightly to-do list. Maybe that's another reason I never pushed Aiden to move in with me. I suppose in hindsight I enjoyed my solo time more, exploring my own pleasure.

Now, Dev's in charge of my pleasure.

Ledger's back from the bathroom, kneeling next to me on the bed, lazily stroking the outline of his erection through his jeans too.

It's an erotic overload. I want this so badly. Want to watch them jerk off to me. Play with me. Explore me.

I want it all, everywhere, all at once.

I'm vibrating everywhere too, then I'm moaning as Dev presses the lubed toy against my ass. But before he pushes it in, he dips his face to my center and sucks on my clit. Hard, eager, a little ruthlessly. But full of passion.

"God!" I shout.

A few mind-bending seconds later, he lets go, rises again, and slides the toy into my ass. An inch, maybe less. I tense.

"Breathe, baby," he urges.

Ledger strokes my hair. "You've got this."

Deep breath, then I let air spread through my body as I take more. Another inch. But this time, I welcome it, even as it's stretching me.

"Good?" Dev asks with genuine concern but obvious excitement too. His green eyes flicker with desire and restraint. That's my Dev.

"So good," I say as he eases out the toy, then glides it back in while fingering my clit.

I moan, throw my head back. I don't even know

what to feel. I feel so much. All this pressure and plea-sure and a fevered ache between my thighs.

"I want your cock," I murmur, begging.

"Take his for now," Dev says carelessly. I turn my face to Ledger on the bed next to me.

I'm greedy, so damn greedy as I demand, "Gimme."

Ledger unzips his jeans, frees his dick, and offers it to me, squeezing out a drop of arousal.

My mouth waters. I stick out my tongue. Ledger rewards me, giving me the head of his dick while Dev plays with my pussy and my ass. It's so much, all these sensations. And I still want more.

I swirl my tongue around the salty drop right as Dev slides the toy deeper, then strokes me faster.

My belly tightens and I can barely hold on. I don't want to hold on. I let go of Ledger's dick, begging Ledger, begging Dev. "Fuck me. Please just fuck me."

"Give our good girl a break," Ledger says, going to bat for my sex drive. "I'll fuck her if you won't."

Images flash before my eyes. Dev fucking me. Ledger fucking me. Dev, Ledger. One, the other. Why choose, really?

"Take turns with me. Please take turns fucking me," I beg, and I'm not afraid to ask for anything in bed with them anymore.

I want it all.

Dev eases out the toy, sets it on a hand towel on the bed. Seconds later, he's naked, covering his cock as Ledger sheds his jeans too.

Two gorgeous naked men, ready to give me anything I ask for in bed. Is this my honeymoon?

Yes, yes, it is.

Dev grabs my hips, hauls me close to his cock. Then, with my hands bound, Dev slides into me, filling me beautifully as Ledger grabs the lube and pours some on his dick.

Ledger kneels near me but not too close. He gives me room to watch Dev or to watch him.

But I can't choose where to look—at the man pounding into me or the one getting off to the sight of it.

I'm snapping my gaze back and forth, back and forth, helpless to the fucking, surrendering to their control. Dev's braced above me on one hand, hooking my leg over his shoulder with the other, then taking me mercilessly. Ledger's watching me, jerking his cock with hard, determined strokes.

"You want him to fuck you too, don't you, sweet thing?" Dev grunts out as he drives into me.

"Yesss," I moan as warmth floods my body.

He eases out almost all the way, leaving me empty, leaving me wanting. "Say it. Say how much you want us fucking you," he demands, leaving me dick-free for the moment.

"So badly," I cry out.

He slams his cock into me, and I scream in pleasure.

But he eases out again, giving me just the tip. "Then you need to do one thing," Dev demands.

"What? I'll do anything," I babble.

Dev bends over me, brings his face to my lips, and bestows a hot, passionate kiss, answering at last with, "Come really fucking soon."

He pulls up to his knees, grabbing my hips tight

once more, yanking me down on his cock. Dev drops one hand between my thighs, and he strokes my aching, eager clit.

Pleasure spins in me, higher and higher, faster and faster. I'm panting, moaning, then begging to come.

Shouting, babbling, *please, please, please.*

I'm not begging them.

I'm begging my body because I'm so damn close. I take one look at Ledger, and he's working his fist mercilessly on his cock, grunting and groaning.

I detonate without warning.

An orgasm bursts inside me like stars lighting up in the sky. One after another after another.

It feels endless.

My vision is blurry; my world is silver and neon. I'm screaming in bliss, then for a flash of a second, I'm empty. And *boom.*

I'm full.

I blink, look into Ledger's eyes. He's above me now, rocking into me, swiveling his hips just so. "You did such a good job, honey. You fucking deserve all the orgasms. Untie her now," he instructs Dev.

I'd have thought Ledger would rail me too.

Instead, he's taking his time with long, tantalizing strokes, letting me come down from the prior climax while Dev works on untying me.

First, the right wrist.

Dev kisses it, soothing away the sting. I reach for Ledger's face, cupping his cheek as Dev moves around the bed, coming to the other side as Ledger delivers a long, dizzying stroke.

"Oh god," I pant.

"So fucking pretty," Ledger praises.

Dev unties my left wrist, then kisses that.

When he's freed me, I throw my arms around Ledger, who fucks me slow and deep till I'm boneless, till I've melted into the bed, till I don't know whose name I call out as pleasure crests in me once more then breaks in a long, lingering orgasm that I feel in my soul.

Seconds later, he's coming too, grunting, groaning, burying his face in my neck.

All while Dev watches us from a chair I didn't even know was in the corner of the room, stroking his cock, looking in my eyes like I'm the sexiest thing he's ever seen.

As I come down from my release, he spills in his hand, shuddering.

It's the most surreal sexual experience of my life—the things that get them off, the ways they get me off, and how the three of us come together.

After we're all cleaned up and showered, Dev's the first to conk out.

Well, sex twice in a day, plus travel, will do that to you. I can barely even crack open my Kindle. But before my eyes flutter closed, Ledger whispers, "Need to talk to you."

With nerves prickling me, I get out of bed, wearing only my T-shirt, and follow him to the living room. He's in boxer briefs. He shuts the door to the suite behind him.

"Been wanting to grab a minute with you ever since the restaurant," he says when we reach the couch.

"What is it?"

"Oh, shit. Didn't mean to worry you," he says, then reaches for my hand.

I sit next to him, somewhat mollified but still curious.

"There's something I want to do for Dev tomorrow. But it's going to take a lot of planning, so I want to see if you're interested."

He's speaking my language now. "Tell me."

He shares his idea and I nearly bounce. But then I say, "But I can't afford that."

Ledger sighs, then tucks his finger under my chin. "Aubrey, you need to stop worrying about money. I don't expect you to pay for this. I don't want you to pay for it. I just want to do it with you. Do you get that?"

Finally, I think I do.

The imbalance has been all in my head. It comes from my worries about being good enough.

Being happy enough.

Being entertaining enough.

The fear stems from the same place—am I interesting enough to keep a family together?

Only, I don't have to do that with these guys.

I flash back over the last five days, picturing the grape stomping, the ghost town, the plant shop, the grilled cheese, the dinners, the hot tub, the hikes, even the amusement park, and all the conversations.

All the moments that we've spent together.

I *am* giving so much to them. I'm giving time. I'm giving myself. I'm giving enough.

I can see it in their eyes. I can hear it in their voices. I can feel it in my own heart.

"I understand." Then, with new confidence, I say, "Let's do it."

43

NOSE BREAKERS

Dev

"Almost there," Aubrey says as Ledger maneuvers the car onto the next street, heading toward the outskirts of the city.

I can't wait. "I love surprises," I say, rubbing my palms together. That's all they told me this morning— that they had a surprise for me.

That was all I needed to know. I was sold. Now it's early afternoon, and I'm buzzing with anticipation as Ledger drives us farther away from downtown.

"Of course you love surprises," Ledger says dryly as I glance out the window at the Vancouver neighborhood. Something about the curve in the road feels familiar. It tickles my brain. Wait. I *might* know where we're going. Pretty sure I've been here.

But I don't know why we're going now. I keep it to myself though.

In the passenger seat, Aubrey nods at Ledger in agreement. "Surprises suit Dev."

But what about her? I lean forward, curling a hand around the back of her seat. "You like surprises, Aubs?"

"Good surprises," she says, hedging her bets.

"Everyone likes good surprises," Ledger says with a harrumph.

"I bet Aubrey could get you a brand-new money tree plant and you'd be like 'I hate surprises.'"

With a cocky glint in his eyes, he glances in the rearview mirror. "I liked the surprise of bourbon last night."

Excellent point. I turn my focus back to the woman who's captivated me. "Me too. Now, Aubs, what's a good surprise to you?"

She taps her chin, meeting my gaze with her eyes sparkling. "This," she declares as she gestures to the windshield.

I follow where she's pointing to the end of the street.

Yes!

That's what I was hoping for. The road felt familiar because I was here last summer. The big sign on top of the structure reads *The Sharon Abreau Ice Rink*. This is where the Vancouver goalie holds his off-season camp. Ledger and I went to the camp last summer as guest coaches, playing with some of the junior high school kids. "We're going to play...hockey?" My voice pitches up, and I'm not even embarrassed.

"It was Ledger's idea," Aubrey says, and her smile is as wide as the city.

"We both put it together," Ledger says, giving credit where credit's due.

My heart warms a little more, knowing both of them planned this. I squeeze his shoulder then I lean forward and give Aubrey a kiss on her cheek.

"You seemed like you were missing it," she says.

"I sure was," I say, in the understatement of the century.

I don't even try to smother the joy that's rocketing through my cells. We park, and I try not to run to the entrance of the rink. A sandwich board outside the doors says Austin Sanchez Skills Camp for Local Youth, then the hours for today and the rest of the week. The man behind the camp waits next to the sign. The sturdy goalie from the Vancouver team has his big arms folded across his chest, tattoos of vines snaking along his light brown skin. There's a twinkle in his eyes.

When I reach him, he offers a fist for knocking. I knock back. "Sanchez, I have to crash your camp to see you? What's up with that?"

"Maybe play a little better and you'll get an invite to guest coach again," he says.

I clutch my chest like I'm wounded. "See if you can drive the knife in a little more."

"Sure. I can. Try to have a season as good as mine," he ribs, since he's no stranger to trash talk.

I hold up my forefinger. "You saved *one* more goal than I did."

"Yes. Yes, I did." Then he smiles brightly and claps me on the back before he turns to Ledger, giving him a quick greeting. "Good to see you, McBride."

"Thanks for doing this," Ledger says.

Aubrey's next, and for a few seconds, I just hesitate. Do I introduce her? Does Ledger? Obviously it's no secret we're here with her since Garrett posted that pic, but I don't expect Sanchez to be stalking Garrett's social. But when his eyes swing to Aubrey expectantly, I don't hesitate.

"This is Aubrey Emerson," I say, and I'm dying to add, *"She's this woman we're seeing."*

But nope. I shut down that desire, stat. Swallowing those words, I add, "She's a good friend."

"Nice to meet you, Ledger and Dev's friend," Sanchez says smoothly.

The word *friend* lodges like a stone in my heart. It's all wrong. She's so much more than a friend.

She takes his hand. "And nice to meet you, Ledger and Dev's...*co-worker.*"

Sanchez chuckles, then he lets go of her hand.

I steal a glance at Aubrey. There's no weirdness in her expression. No awkwardness that says that moment was as wrong for her as it was for me.

Because...when this ends in two days, we'll be just that. Friends.

That word twists in my gut, souring.

Sure, friendship ought to be enough for me. I shouldn't linger on what the future definitely doesn't hold.

This is the good stuff, the here and now, when your *friends*—and that's what Ledger and Aubrey both are— know you so well, they surprise you with an impromptu chance to play the game you love.

"I'm ready. Let's do this," I say, full of the bravado I bring to the ice.

There's one little problem. No gear. But Sanchez *is* running a camp. "You got pads and shit for me?" I ask him.

Sanchez scoffs. "What do you take me for? A newbie?"

"Cool. I can borrow your stuff."

Another scoff. "We've got yours."

Wait. What? "H-how?"

A wicked grin comes from the man running the camp. "Your teammates are here too."

Not that I keep tabs on everyone, but I don't remember any of the Golden State Foxes mentioning they'd be in Vancouver when I saw them a week ago at the gym. "Yeah? Which ones? Did you know about this?" I ask Ledger.

He shrugs, but he's trying to fight off a smile. Aubrey has the straightest of straight faces as well.

"Some of his too," Sanchez adds, pointing to Ledger.

"Sea Dogs?" I feel like I'm missing the punchline.

Ledger sheds his stoicism. "Stefan, Hayes, Chase, and Ryker flew up this morning for the concert. We called them last night and asked them to bring our gear. We'll play with the kids. But first, get ready. We're going to practice shooting. *On you.* You better hope your summer ass is in shape."

"It. Is. On."

I step inside the arena right foot first. Like I've always done.

* * *

The ice is smooth as glass, and the sound of blades cutting through the rink is my favorite song on the best playlist ever.

My pads are tight, and my helmet is snug. Gloves on, skates laced, stick in hand. Everything fits perfectly. Just the way I like it. I'm standing between the pipes, ready to face the barrage of shots from my friends, some of the best players in the league.

Now they're my enemies, trying to score on me.

They're circling the ice, weaving around each other, laughing, casually passing the puck before we start.

The crowd is loud. As in Aubrey, Trina, and Ivy. They're standing by the boards, shouting, hooting, hollering.

And singing too? Is that "Livin' on a Prayer?"

Yes, the ladies are belting out Bon Jovi. It's adorable but I'd better tune it out.

Doesn't matter that this pre-game warm-up is for kicks. I'm here to play hard. Sanchez watches from the stands as Ledger flies down the ice, passing deftly to Chase. They're aiming for me, but that's not gonna happen today.

Nope. Aubrey is here, and I want to show her what I can do.

Chase takes aim, lifting the stick high and sending it flying. But there's nothing quite as satisfying as stopping shot after shot, including this one that's hurtling toward me at Mach speed. I stretch out my glove, slapping that rocketing disc down.

Take that, puck.

Stefan comes at me next, racing with Hayes, passing that bad boy back and forth. I'm at the ready, crouching in the crease as Hayes tries to fool me with a backhand shot.

I catch it with my blocker.

From the side of the rink, Aubrey catcalls, "Ha! You can't score on him. Go back to LA."

Damn, she is a heckler, and hell, if that doesn't fire me up some more.

Player after player come at me. It's just like shooting practice at morning skate when the guys fire off shots from all directions, trying to score on me. Ryker slams a wrist shot that I knock down with my glove. Chase flies around the perimeter of the rink, trying to sneak up on me as he comes in fast and hot, but I kick out my leg and say *see you later* to that one.

Jaw tight, eyes lasered in on the action, I watch as Ledger flies down the ice. I can't believe this season is going to be his last. He's still as fearless and as terrifying as ever. When he smacks a slapshot at me, I stretch as far as I've ever stretched. I've got this, I swear I've got this, but it whizzes past, and lands right in the twine with a loud thwap.

"Ledger! You show him how to get in the hole!" Aubrey's voice is loud and exuberant and downright filthy.

I fucking love that she cheers for both of us. No issues, no jealousy—she just switches back and forth.

As Ledger turns and skates the other way, there's a

pang in my chest. An ache. I wish it weren't his last season. I wish he could play forever.

But a man's got to do what a man's got to do. What will he do, though, when he retires? Will he spend more time with Aubrey? Without me?

What the fuck? Where did that thought come from?

I don't even know. This fling has an end date—two days from now. Not a year from now. Not at the end of the season. It ends in less than forty-eight hours when the plane lands back in San Francisco.

I blink away the sobering thoughts.

Here on the ice, there's no room to get lost in my head. Scrimmage or not, there are always stakes—playing my best.

For the next forty-five minutes, I soak up every second, reveling in each save as if it were happening during game seven in the playoffs.

That is where I want to be at the end of the season.

* * *

When our session ends, Stefan rips off his helmet and skates over to me, tapping his stick to mine. "You could do better," he deadpans.

Asshole. He knows I only let in three.

"And you're slow as shit," I reply.

Stefan adopts a serious expression. "It's all the sex I've been having."

I roll my eyes. "Then stop having so much."

He scoffs. "Please. I'll just work out more to balance

it. Yeah, that's it. This Sunday. The gym at my place. It's on," he says, pointing my way as Hayes glides over, joining us.

"I'll be there." I have to—training camp starts the next day.

"Me too," Hayes puts in when he stops at the net, jerking up his helmet as well.

"No shit. You live there," I say to Hayes, and damn, this feels good too, ribbing these guys, seeing my teammates.

"You can work out by your lonesome then," Hayes says to me.

"Nah, I like the kale smoothies the Viking brings me," I say, tipping my forehead toward the team captain.

Stefan shrugs with the confidence of a king. "I do make excellent smoothies."

"Why don't you just open a kale smoothie truck?" Hayes suggests to his friend and his partner since they're both married to Ivy.

Stefan's blue eyes twinkle. "I already own a restaurant. Why not add a smoothie truck? Thanks, New Guy."

Hayes growls. "Nope. You're not calling me that anymore."

We haven't called Hayes that in ages. He joined the team a year ago and outgrew that moniker quickly. "Yeah, Hollis has that name now," I add.

"Actually, Hollis needs to be Surfer Boy, I decided," Stefan says, then gestures to Hayes. "We picked it."

I furrow my brow like *what gives?* "You picked a

nickname without me? You know I love doling out nicknames. Also, I have a much better one for Hollis."

This intrigues Stefan, judging from the quirk in his brow. "What have you got?"

"Hollis is...wait for it...the fucking Magician. He trained a cat to high five," I say.

Stefan blinks, seeming impressed. "I might just call him that next week."

Seconds later, Chase and Ryker skate over to us, tugging up helmets too.

The Golden Guy on the Sea Dogs offers me a fist for knocking. "Not too shabby. But I did go easy on you," Chase says.

I stare him down menacingly. "Don't make me challenge you to get back out there, Weston."

"Don't make me go easy on you again," he taunts, then glides over to the boards, heading Trina's way. Probably to meet her at the tunnel for a kiss.

Ryker nods at me. He's always been the more serious of the two. "Good to see you. Still can't believe you went to the enemy."

I roll my eyes. "Dude, I didn't leave. You did. You left us," I point out since he was traded to the Sea Dogs a season ago.

"Details," he says, waving a hand.

Ledger joins us, and he's smiling as well, looking loose and easy. It's a good look, and I hope he's enjoying himself. "Did you have fun?"

Like he's giving it some serious thought, he nods, then says, "Yeah. I did."

"Good. I think you needed this too."

He's quiet, then he says, "I probably did."

Then, my gaze strays to the boards. It's only us here, and Chase and Ryker are surrounding their wife, Trina, chatting her up while Stefan and Hayes take selfies with Ivy.

Watching them warms my heart and makes it hurt a little too. I wish that we could have that with Aubrey, that kind of free and easy life. Maybe in some other world, we could. She'd lean over, offer one kiss to me, one to Ledger. We'd snap pics. We'd walk down the street together, unafraid.

But the woman I'm falling for isn't ready for even a date. I'd thought I wasn't either. Only the more time I spend with her, the more I want another day, another week, another month.

That can't happen though.

Five days ago, she was ready to get married. I don't want to be her rebound. I'm just going to enjoy what I have for a few more days since it's going to end very, very soon.

Right now, the kids from the camp are heading down the tunnel, ready to join us on the ice.

It's game time.

* * *

The Freezer Burners are tied with the Nose Breakers, and that is not okay. I'm a Nose Breaker after all, tending to the net for a motley crew mix of hockey kids and my teammates.

I'm guarding it like a hawk. Nothing will get past me. Not even the determined spark plug of a kid racing down the ice from Lord knows where, hell-bent on scoring. He takes a killer shot. I lunge for it. I've saved these goals before. I can save this one. I'm diving to the side, since it's caroming toward the pipes, but it sneaks between my legs.

The kid shouts in victory. "I got one on the Brick!"

I try not to smile. I swear I don't. But the kid knows my nickname.

We go on to lose.

When the game ends, young players mob us and thank us.

"You played great," I tell the kid who scored the winning goal. "What's your name?"

"Kaio," he says.

"Keep having fun, Kaio, okay? That's the most important thing. Got it?"

"Got it, Brick," he says, nodding dutifully.

Later, after I've shed my gear and packed it up, Sanchez pulls me aside in the hallway. "I took some pics today. Would love to post them on social. You cool with that?"

"Of course."

"Thanks, man. And you should do this again next year. You're good with them."

"I thought you didn't want me."

"You're always welcome here. The kids like you."

"I'll do it," I say, and really, this feels like where I belong.

Especially since it's not ending. At least, it'd better not.

I'll need hockey even more come Saturday.

44

TOLD YOU SO

Aubrey

My friends don't ask. They don't have to. The second Dev and Ledger head off the ice to go and get changed, Trina grabs one arm. Ivy grabs the other.

"I have one question. Was I right?" Trina wiggles a naughty brow.

There's no point denying it. "Yes." I don't grumble the admission. I lift my chin and own my choice, right there in the ice rink. "And you were right not only about that but also..." I fan my face. "Holy shit, so fucking good." I smack her arm playfully. "Like, why did you keep it a secret from me for so long?" I ask, mock annoyed.

Ivy tosses her head back and laughs. "Right. We kept it sooo secret."

Trina gives me the biggest *told you so* look. "You were banging them when we texted on Monday."

I hold up my hands in surrender, picturing that moment when Ledger bent me over the bench in the woods.

Trina points. "Look at you. You're blushing."

"Well they fucked me alfresco."

"Are you a pasta dish?" Ivy inquires.

"I felt pretty—what is the opposite of al dente?"

"*Scotta*. Overcooked," Ivy says.

"Yes. That. I felt like a noodle. A spaghetti noodle. Is that normal?" I whisper. I mean, I don't want the kids skating around the ice to hear us comparing notes on the effects of double dicking.

Trina bobs a shoulder. "Yes, but normal good. And then your new normal. And then you're like...*mama, my new normal rocks*."

"This week has been one huge new normal, then," I say, already wistful for the new normal even before it ends.

"Or two huge new normals," Trina whispers.

I smile and Ivy rolls her eyes, then quickly shifts, asking, "But what does this mean?"

I can't stand thinking about Saturday. I know that's what she's asking, so I dodge the question. "It means I need to stretch tomorrow night. If you know what I mean."

She doesn't take the bait. "No. What does it mean for after?"

I sigh, feeling a little lonely as I think about *after*. "It means I wish this weren't the honeymoon I was supposed to take with another guy."

* * *

"What do I even say to her?" I ask Dev as we enter the venue before the Amelia Stone concert, making our way to the VIP door. Because the tickets are freaking VIP tickets.

Nerves jump around inside me. "What do people say to you after a game?" I hang back with Dev as our friends walk ahead, following a tour assistant. "What if I sound stupid? How many times a day does she hear people gush, *I love your music*?"

"Babe," he says, gently. "Just tell her you like her music."

"Is that what people say to you?"

"Yes, I make sweet music in the net," he says, straight-faced.

"Seriously. What do you say when fans are all *I love you*," I ask, feeling a little desperate. "Isn't it boring?"

He stops, tugs me around a corner, gives me a serious look, full of understanding and vulnerability. "It's not boring when someone tells you they love you."

My heart sweeps up like an amusement park ride. I know he's not saying those words to me, but still, I feel a little floaty. "It's not?"

"I like meeting fans. It doesn't get old," he assures me.

"You're sure?"

"Of course. And if she's a dick, fuck her. Tell her you like her music because it's what *you* want to say." He taps my sternum as if transferring some of his courage to me. "Want to practice with me?"

I take a deep breath. "I love your music."

His eyes sparkle with pride and maybe something else.

Something that scares me and thrills me.

Something that feels all right and all wrong at the same time. *Possibility.*

"Good." He runs his hand down my cheek and adds, "Have fun, babe."

"Am I babe now?" I ask.

"It felt right," he says, like he doesn't need any further justification for the nickname.

And really, he doesn't.

I grab his hand, holding it tight for a second. "Thank you."

We catch up to our friends, and I feel a little less jittery. Ledger shoots Dev an inquisitive look, but Dev just gives him a reassuring smile. Ledger nods in return. A wordless exchange, and yet they have their own language about me.

I've grown to understand them in just a few days too.

So much of this week has been out of sync with my regular life in San Francisco, which involves waking up for blowouts and balayage, for yoga and smoothie dates, for book club and volunteering at Little Friends.

For lazy Saturdays when I don't get out of my sweats or my hoodies, when I binge books and TV shows. When I see my mom, or my brother or sister. When I fritter away the day.

That's my regular life.

This is my temporary, supercharged, high-voltage

one. But I'm going to enjoy it because I fucking deserve it.

* * *

The VIP experience doesn't stop with the tickets and special seating. Amelia Stone's stage manager shows us around backstage, including where the pop star does one of her whizz-bang costume changes. "That's where she goes from the red sparkles to the jean shorts and cowboy boots, right?" I ask excitedly when the woman gestures to an area just offstage. I've watched countless videos from her tour this summer.

"Someone knows her Amelia Stone." The stage manager sounds impressed. I think I'm glowing.

Dev and Ledger weren't kidding when they said they like to spoil a woman. From the penthouse suite to the concert tickets to the private jet, these guys are serious about their indulgence.

It's almost too much. I've felt a little guilty from the beginning, letting them lavish me with experiences and luxuries and knowing I couldn't return it in kind. Then I understood—*really* understood—that repayment is not what they want from me. Now my guilt has a different flavor. Are they imagining what it'd be like to do things like this in San Francisco?

The look in Dev's eyes when we arrived at the rink earlier today was magic. I wish I could be the one to put that look in his eyes again and again, to plot little surprises for him with Ledger and vice versa. I want to make them happy.

But I can't bear the thought of failing at that. I can't stand the idea that I might hurt them.

My heart is full and heavy at the same time.

As we tour backstage, I remind myself to savor every second of the peek behind the scenes, the pre-show sound check, and most of all, the photo op with the pop star.

When Amelia strides into the wings after the sound check, bubbles flow through my veins. She smiles as she heads our way, but one of the wind machines comes on unexpectedly, blasting her bright red hair in all directions.

The stagehand rushes to turn it off, apologizing, "My bad, my bad." But the damage is done. The hair has blown loose from the vintage silver barrette holding the pop star's hair to one side. With a laugh, she tries to brush the hair from her face and say hello at the same time. "Hi. I'm Amelia Stone and I'm having a bad hair moment." She seems to have no problem poking fun at herself.

"Oh, you can just do this," I say, demonstrating how to tuck the strands back in a quick fix.

The star grimaces, trying to untangle the clip, then says to me, "Can you do it?"

I'm sure she has a hair person. In fact, I see a man with a makeup bag scurrying across the stage. But when your favorite rock star asks you to fix her hair, you snap up the chance.

Quickly, I tuck the loose strands back into place. "There you go. I'm a hairstylist, actually," I say.

She smiles warmly. "Then maybe it's kismet you were here today."

Perhaps it was. But not because of the hair. Because I know what to say to her after all. "What if you fail?" I blurt out.

She furrows her brow, processing the question. "Like when I get onstage?"

"Yes. Exactly. What if you get it all wrong?"

She's quiet for a spell. "Then, you pick yourself up and you try again the next time."

During the concert, my girls and I dance and shout and cheer in the front row, singing as loud as we can to songs we know by heart.

Here like this, with the music flowing through me, I do feel like I am picking myself up.

But the next part? Trying again? I'm not so sure.

Especially when the music slows, cross-fades to something deep and soulful. It's a number that makes me want to grind against one guy, then another. That has me picturing nights at music clubs in San Francisco, dancing with my men, one behind me, one in front, arms all over me, and around me.

I want it so badly my chest aches.

But that's not part of *this* deal. I know, too, that photos could be easily posted. By anyone.

As my friends dance with their partners, I dance alone. I steal a glance at Dev on one side of me. Arms are crossed, he looks at the stage, but every few seconds, his gaze cheats to me.

Ledger is on my other side. His hands are in his jeans pockets. His expression is stoic, but every now and then he checks me out.

Like he did at the calendar event in the park?

Maybe.

What if we'd all been available that day—not just single, but truly free?

What if we hadn't been hurt? Hadn't made bad choices in the past? Hadn't hemmed ourselves in to others' expectations?

What if we'd gone to a concert that night and I'd danced for them *like this*?

Arms in the air. Hair trailing down my back. Hips swaying.

Dev and Ledger have eyes only for me, like it's impossible for them to look anywhere else.

Like they have to fight off the devil himself not to touch me.

Dev looks like he wants to pounce on me, Ledger like he wants to throw me over his shoulder and haul me away.

In the middle of thousands upon thousands of people, I dance, letting the music turn the three of us on. It's some of the best foreplay I've ever had, and we're not even touching.

But I also can't wait to leave.

45

DID THE BUTT PLUG LIE?

Aubrey

The second we reach the hotel suite, the two men break

If I'd thought it was hot when one man pushed a woman up against a door, that was nothing compared to Dev and Ledger claiming me.

Ledger slams my left hand to the wall above my head, calling dibs on my mouth with fresh, new ferocity. Dev pins my right wrist to the doorframe and blazes a hot, needy trail along my shoulder, up my neck to my ear.

These men and their obsession with my neck—they've unlocked a new kink in me. The more they kiss my neck, the more I'm convinced *neck-gasm* is a thing.

I'm flush with desire from Dev's fierce devotion with his lips, from Ledger's bruising possession with his mouth, and from their questing hands.

Four.

I get four hands all over me.

Hands in hair, hands on tits, then hands down my belly, coasting across my ass. They're touching me everywhere, and I know, with terrifying certainty, that nothing will ever compare to them.

But I'm determined to suck every last ounce of pleasure and passion and joy from my last thirty-six hours with them.

There is no time for sadness when Dev cups my jaw and jerks me away from Ledger. "Need this mouth. Need you."

I ache at his words. My panties grow wetter. I grab Dev's shirt and moan into his mouth, not sure if I'm moaning from his kiss or Ledger's hand snaking under my skirt and inside the lace of my undies.

Finding my wetness.

Hissing against my neck.

Biting down as Dev kisses me.

"Fuck, honey. You're so fucking wet for us," Ledger praises me.

"I am," I gasp in between kisses, grasping at his shirt too, holding onto him at the same time.

Ledger strokes my clit then runs his fingers through my slick heat like he's mesmerized by my arousal.

"Fucking beautiful." My desire has put him in a trance. "Look at how turned on you get," he says against my shoulder before he nips my flesh.

I gasp, letting go of Dev's lips just to catch my breath. "Need you both," I whisper.

Dev gazes at me. "Where do you need us?" He

sounds like he's holding onto the edge of the world, waiting for me to answer.

I tremble as Ledger strokes me sensually, his fingers coasting reverently across my pussy, stopping at my clit where he draws maddening circles and repeats the same question. "Where do you need us?"

My answer won't be a surprise. Since the first night, we've been talking about what we all want in bed. We've been direct and open. But they want to hear me say it as much as I want to admit it.

I slide one hand over the steely ridge of Dev's erection, the other over the hard outline of Ledger's.

"I want you both inside me." Tingles race down my spine at my own words.

I want my two men to fuck me tonight.

* * *

I'm new to threesomes, but I know this basic rule—lube is like books, batteries, and sunshine. You can't have enough of it.

My guys know this too.

Ten minutes after I make my request, I'm perched on the edge of the couch in just my lingerie. It's one of my favorite positions with them —Dev standing behind me, playing with my tits as Ledger kneels on the floor. I'm angled for all access, and I love it. His mouth worships my pussy while he teases my ass open with a well-lubed plug.

Pretty sure they bought the whole toy store, and pretty sure I want to use every toy with them.

I'm sweating from desire. I'm hot everywhere from Ledger's mouth, Dev's hand, the toy, the sensations. The *unholy* sensations as Ledger preps and pleases me.

He flicks his tongue against my clit while he taps on the plug with his finger, sending a wild zing through me. A zing that I give back to Dev as I hunt for his mouth, lifting my face to his. "Kiss me, please," I pant.

His mouth comes crashing down as his hands squeeze my tits. Ledger sucks harder, wiggles the plug just a little deeper.

Everything in me ignites. I'm a flare on the side of the road at night, bright and beckoning, and I'm coming on Ledger's tongue, gasping into Dev's mouth.

I'm shaking and crying out, and the hair on my arms stands on end. Before I know it, Dev's carrying me to the bed, then easing out the plug as Ledger grabs a towel. Dev sets the toy on the towel, next to the lube, and immediately I want to be filled again. I'm getting so addicted.

Dev tells me to strip him.

Once I get my bearings, I tug at the bottom of his tight, trim polo, yanking it off, revealing his strong, firm chest covered in golden brown hair that I love roaming my fingers through. He shudders as I touch him. I travel down to his jeans and unbutton them.

Dev steps back and sheds the denim, then he tips his forehead to his friend. "Get your man undressed too," he says.

A smile lights up my dirty soul. Everything they say includes all of us. Everything's an acknowledgment of the way the three of us work together.

I peel off Ledger's black shirt then yank down his jeans and boxer briefs.

Then I sit back and inhale a very satisfied breath at the sight at the foot of the bed—two hot hockey studs standing there with hard, bobbing cocks pointing at me.

I'm the one they desire. I'm the one they want.

They've seen me at my worst, when I was dumped on my wedding day by a man who never deserved me. And they rose to the occasion. Judging from their eager dicks, they've just kept rising.

I take a moment to relish in my power, my femininity. I slide a hand down my black cami and over my stomach, stopping at the thatch of hair between my thighs. Then I lean my head back and let out a long, sensual *ohhh*.

Their cocks jump.

I smile.

I run my hand back up my body, grabbing the bottom of the cami and tugging it off. Then I let them stare at my naked form, gobbling me up with their dirty gazes. I send them another smile. Another bite of the corner of my lips.

Then, I whisper, "Well, boys. Why don't you spoil me with your dicks?"

"We fucking will," Dev says as I get on my hands and knees.

Ledger's behind me in no time, kissing a path down my spine to the top of my ass, grabbing the lube, drizzling some on his fingers, then teasing my ass open.

Dev strokes his hungry cock. Watching us.

We discussed this. Mapped it out. The kind of

choreography you need to pull off a double boning doesn't happen magically. It requires a little bit of planning. Some pre-game stretching.

Ledger gives that to me as he slides his fingers into my welcoming ass and then scissors them. My breath comes hot and fast as I grind down on his hand. He plays with me for a minute or two, praising me as he goes. "Nice and open, honey. Almost there."

I rock back against him while my patient Dev strokes his cock, then stops suddenly to grab a condom, tossing it next to Ledger.

The man behind me smacks my ass.

I tense, then sigh into the pain. The joy of the sting. The way it radiates through my belly to my toes then ebbs.

He eases out his fingers.

I glance back. Ledger opens the foil, then rolls on the condom. My pulse spikes and then soars as he pours more lube on his shaft.

He nods at Dev, who steps closer, gathering my hair to the side as Ledger kneels behind me, then smacks my ass with his dick.

"You like that?" Dev asks, stroking my hair.

"I do," I tell him, then draw a sharp breath as Ledger pushes against me. The blunt head of his cock stretches me, and I try to relax.

There are butt plugs. There are dildos. And then there are big dicks.

I swallow roughly, nervously as he pushes into my ass another inch.

I grit my teeth. Dev bends, cups my face. "You okay, baby?"

I nod into his hand, but I'm still bracing myself against these new feelings. What if the butt plug lied? What if the vibrator is all I like in my backside?

My worry fades when Dev pets my hair. "You're so fucking pretty all the time."

The compliment is a rush of warmth and a shot of relaxation.

My muscles loosen.

Ledger sets a hand on my lower back. Pressing down. Angling me and holding me in place. It's possessive and purposeful.

"Breathe, baby," Dev says like a coach.

I do as I'm asked.

Ledger groans, pushes his hand down more firmly, sinks deeper into my body.

I'm stretched as far as I can go, I think. It's so different and I'm so full, and I don't know if I love it. But as I wiggle my butt the slightest bit onto his cock, I gasp.

Oh.

Yes.

That feels...good.

Oh god.

The butt plug didn't lie.

I'm pretty sure I like this.

When Ledger sinks in the rest of the way, the sound he makes is feral. "Oh fuck, honey. You look so fucking hot taking my dick. Look at you."

A squeeze of my cheek, a smack of my flesh, then he slides out. Back in. Out. In.

Then he eases out all the way.

Trembling with pleasure, I turn around, so I can sink back onto him with my ass, but in a new position. "Now lie down so I can ride your dick like this," I say with a wild smile I don't dare hide.

"Like a good fucking cowgirl," Ledger says, his voice rough with excitement.

He shifts, lying flat on his back on the bed. With him supine, I kneel and hover over his dick.

"Yes, get that sweet ass back on my cock," he bites out, holding his dick for me.

I'm facing Dev, who doesn't stop stroking his cock as he watches me sink back onto Ledger's dick.

The pressure is intense, like I'm riding the razor's edge of pleasure the whole time, balancing with this tight stretch that's just shy of mind-blowing, but not quite.

The way they treat me though? How they touch me? That's so arousing.

And so is this position. I can play with myself easily, and I slide my hand between my thighs, stroking my clit as Dev unleashes a growl. "Yeah, play with that perfect pussy."

"You're doing such a good job riding my cock," Ledger grits out, and I rise up on him, then down, playing with myself.

I'm the center of attention, the apex of their world.

Then, I shift my legs from under me, so I can lean down against Ledger, my back to his chest. Like that, me lying on him, he reaches for the back of my thighs so he can hold them open while Dev kneels between my spread legs.

I've never felt more vulnerable or more wanted.

Quickly, Dev covers his cock and then nudges the head against my slick entrance.

I shudder, over and over, wave after wave. This is it. The moment I've imagined. The moment I've been so curious about. This moment is mine, and if life is all about moments, if it's about squeezing joy out of the seconds that fall too quickly from our fingers, then I want all the filthy joy I can get from life right now.

"Fuck me, Dev. Fuck me, please," I whisper, greedy and desperate.

The green-eyed man gazes down at me with lust and something I've never seen before. Worship, perhaps? Dirty adoration? Maybe both.

As he sinks into me, it's like he's luxuriating in the feel of my pussy welcoming him home. Once he's all the way in, his eyes flicker darkly. His breath comes in a sultry, guttural groan, and he murmurs, "Yes, baby."

I am just...stuffed.

I am full. Stretched in ways I barely knew were possible. Thank god yoga keeps me limber. Nothing, though, could have prepared me for this deep and wickedly forbidden fullness or for the intimacy, and vulnerability, of the position. Ledger's hands on my outer thighs, opening me for Dev. Dev kneeling before me while rocking into me, his hands on my knees. Me, under him, on top of the other, being fucked both ways by both men.

Wanting both of them.

Wanting this wild, new, erotic adventure.

Pleasure races through my body as they fuck me. I fuck myself, too, my fingers flying against my clit. Heat spreads from my core to my belly, down to my fingers. Sparks rocket in my chest, and everywhere, noises fill the suite.

Grunts, groans, slaps, growls.

Words like *yes*, and *this*, and *fuck*, become *yeah, so close, so pretty.*

I rub faster, moan louder as Dev powerfully fucks down into me, as Ledger thrusts up into me, and I take everything they have to give.

Sharp, hot spikes of pleasure spread deep in my body till I'm shouting, "Make me come."

Giving them a command.

But really, it's *us* I'm asking.

The three of us are triple-teaming me. Cocks and fingers and passion and trust all at once—they coil, then burst. I shatter, the world blurring as I fly into a new one. I'm hostage to the orgasm, breaking apart, shaking everywhere as it pulses to the ends of me.

I'm still moaning as Ledger thrusts and then growls out a carnal *yes* in my ear. Dev sinks deep, jerks, then shudders out a *goddammit, Aubrey.*

He doesn't stop groaning for a long, long time.

* * *

Later, after they clean me up in the shower, taking their time washing me, we lie in bed, and I feel tingly, loose, and a little sore. But also, renewed.

"That was a Daily Dose of Good," I say with a satisfied sigh.

Ledger chuckles softly. Dev smiles. And I feel joy too.

But moments can contain more than one feeling, and this one is chased by wistfulness.

We have one more full day, and then this will end. We'll go shopping and I'll get a dress, then we'll go to dinner, then we'll leave. I'll just have to embrace the last day and live it as fully as I lived tonight.

That's my plan as I drift to sleep. But I wake to Dev pacing around the bed with his phone to his ear, asking the person on the other end of the call, "This morning?"

46

FAIL AGAIN

Aubrey

I push up in bed, tugging the covers tighter around my chest.

Dev prowls in silence, listening, then finally stops in the doorway, his back to me as he says to the caller, "Don't apologize. I get it."

Another pause.

Who's apologizing? For what?

"That soon?" He drags his free hand through his messy morning hair.

Leaving the bedroom, he pads into the living room. Maybe I should wait here. Maybe I should be patient. But my pulse surges painfully at the prospect.

Screw that. I need to know what's going on.

I toss the covers aside and swing my legs out of bed. I'm naked and I feel exceedingly vulnerable, so I take a quick detour to the palatial bathroom, grab a robe, and tie it as I head to the living room.

Dev stands by the window, his palm pressed against the glass, and stares at the sparkling Canadian city as the sun rises.

He's so serious as he listens to the call. Is someone hurt? His parents? My worries spiral into full-blown fears.

"Yeah, just send me the info," he says, his voice even but resigned. "Of course I'll go."

Okay. No one's hurt. That's a huge relief.

"No problem. And hey, it's all good." His tone brightens like he's trying to convince the person on the other end of the line that he's truly cool with this change.

He ends the call, then lets out a long sigh, kind of mournful and kind of frustrated. He scrubs a hand across the back of his neck, shaking his head before he chucks the phone at the nearby couch like he's annoyed with the device for bringing bad news.

Dev startles when he turns and sees me, then, seeming chagrined, says, "Didn't mean to wake you up."

"What's going on?" I tug the belt tighter as I join him in the living room, swallowing down my worries.

He comes around to the couch, pats the cushion. I join him, my stomach churning.

"That was Garrett," he says.

My heart twists and then jackhammers. I'm not worried my brother's figured us out. That's easy enough to handle. But if my brother's calling Dev, and Dev has to handle something right away, and it's nearly training camp...

"Were you traded?" I ask, my heart pounding with fear. "Is that why you have to go back early? Are they trading you before the season? *Where* are they trading you?"

I picture Dev leaving town. Playing somewhere else. I cycle through teams that might need a world-class goalie. "New York? Miami? St. Louis?"

My voice hits the sky. I'm freezing, horror-struck, and he knows it.

I don't want him to go. I need him to stay.

He chuckles softly, then drags his thumb down my jawline. "No, baby. I'm not being traded. But it didn't go unnoticed how you sounded just now." Like he's just discovered a wooden chest with hidden treasure, he tilts his head my way. "You don't want me to go."

Said with wonder. Said with total delight too.

The way he looks at me is disarming. It warms my heart. Fills it up. Completely terrifies me. "Of course I don't want you to go," I say, like it's no big deal.

When it *is* a big deal.

And he knows it.

He lifts a brow, then taps his temple. "I'm filing that away in the good things drawer."

I grab his arm, frustrated. "Dev! Just tell me what's going on? I'm dying to know."

"Sanchez posted some pics of the game yesterday. Which is fine. We knew he was doing that. Apparently, with the 'Dev Save' thing going viral..." He shrugs, looking embarrassed to be at the center of a trend. "The pics took off, too, and became the next thing in the whole 'Dev Save' saga. And this local camp in San Francisco that Jessie's husband runs wants me to stop by."

"Oh," I say, processing this news. "The Sea Dog's owner's husband."

"Cade's a sports agent too. A buddy of Garrett's. He gave him a call. And..."

I fill in the dots. "The owner and the owner's husband asked your agent. Of course you need to do it," I say before reality hits me. My shoulders sag. "It's today, right?"

He winces, then nods. "This afternoon." He sighs heavily. "I can say no though. I can say I can't cut the trip short." But then he hesitates. "It's just I feel like it'd be really shitty to G-man then, you know?"

I get it. "I understand completely. It's important that you do this stuff for you."

"It is," Dev says. That's the bigger issue. Not so much that my brother asked for his help, but that Dev wants to do it. That's who he is—a man who shows up. "But I told him I'd check with you."

I love that Dev's asking. He's including me. "You should go," I say, meaning it, so he feels free to get on that plane.

Dev looks unconvinced. "But it's our last day."

"Go," I add, more brightly. "And have fun."

The longer I hold onto these guys, the harder it'll be to say goodbye tomorrow. There's just one little problem. Ledger and me—do we stay behind?

I hadn't thought about that till just now.

Footsteps pad across the carpet, then Ledger's standing in the doorway, dressed in black boxer briefs and a scowl. "What kind of animals are you? Up at this hour?"

"I need to take off," Dev says, explaining the details quickly.

Ledger's sleepy morning grimace vanishes, replaced by a more thoughtful expression. "That sounds cool, man," he says as he sits next to me on the couch.

"It really does," I say since I want Ledger to know that I support this choice.

I want both guys to know I'd stand behind their careers rather than in front of them. But why am I trying to impress this upon them? I'm not their girlfriend. I am their friend, though, and I know what it's like when someone doesn't support you. I know the anxiety that produces.

Everyone goes quiet. This is where things get awkward. Do we part ways now, with Ledger and me staying behind to traipse around the city, shopping and eating fancy food? That feels all wrong.

But the guys won't ask me to leave early. They'll want to spoil me, even with one here and the other remote. Here is where my make-everything-better skills come in handy.

"I think we should leave, too," I say before they can try to convince me to stay.

"What?" Dev asks, his brow pinching. "You guys don't have to."

But honestly, we do.

The more I stay with one of them, or both of them,

the harder I'll fall for these men. I set one hand on Ledger's strong chest and the other on Dev's.

"I came here with both of you. This isn't how it should end, with one person leaving."

Ledger's expression is stoic, but his eyes flicker with sadness. There's resignation and understanding too. "I agree," he says, tone heavy.

Dev scoffs, tossing up his hands. "That's ridiculous. Stay and have a good time."

"It wouldn't be the same."

He rolls his eyes and then breathes out hard, like a horse at the track, insistent and ready to race. "There's no reason you two shouldn't have fun."

"Dev," I say, gentle but firm. "We did this trip together. The three of us work well together."

Before he can protest again, his phone beeps for his attention. "My flight details," he says after a glance.

Yes. Planes. Agendas. Like on the day we arrived, I need to focus on practicalities and book our flights back home instead.

* * *

A half hour later, we're packed and getting ready to leave, the three of us now booked on the same flight back.

We won't shop for a dress today.

We won't go to a three-star restaurant tonight.

We won't sleep together one more time.

We'll leave and go our separate ways. I'll return to my simple life of blowouts and balayage, and they'll return to their star-studded lives filled with team jets, long workouts, tense games, and all the hardships and joys of professional sports.

As I head to the door, I replay the last six days on a loop. It's not only about the sex we had. I learned a lot of things unintentionally: Saying what's on my mind. Speaking up even if it means rocking the boat.

No time like the present to put that into action.

At the door, I stop, hand on the knob, then I turn to my travel companions. "I want to tell you something," I say, my pulse racing.

Dev's eyes flicker with excitement and maybe some hope. "Yeah?"

"What is it?" Ledger's tone is more measured, but there's a touch of excitement there too.

My throat tightens with rising emotions. I look into Ledger's soulful blue eyes, which have seen years of change, then into Dev's eager, bright green gaze. "This was a fun trip, but I learned a lot too. More than I expected. I learned to say what I'm feeling. Not to hide it," I say, and it's hard to speak the truth, but I have to do this.

"What is it?" Dev asks, as if he's hanging onto my words.

Go for it, I pep-talk myself. "I'm tempted to ask you to meet up after training camp," I begin, speaking from the heart.

Dev's eyes spark with hope. "Yeah?"

Ledger's flicker with possibility. "Yeah?"

I soldier on. "I want to keep doing this more than anything," I say, and holy shit, I'm breaking all the rules of our tryst, the ones we set in the hot tub. "I know we said we had a start and end date. But part of me wants to say *screw that.*"

Dev lets out a big breath, then smiles. "Screw it."

"Really fucking screw it," Ledger echoes.

My heart rockets, wanting to fly into their hands. I want to dance with them, laugh with them, have fun with them. "I don't want to hurt you," I say.

Dev scoffs. "I get hurt every day."

Ledger glances down at his knee like, *C'mon*.

"But I can't risk that," I say. "I have a lot to figure out, and I care about you guys too much to keep going while knowing I'm not ready. I won't ask you to wait for me. I just want you to know." I dig down deep and I do what I should have last week. I speak up. "This week has been..."

I take a second to gather my thoughts, but Dev's faster. "It's been everything," he says.

Ledger's quiet at first, but then he nods. "*You're* everything."

My heart thumps harder and heavier. "I wish this had happened at another time," I say, resigned to our fate—right guys, wrong time.

At the door, Dev leans in to press a poignant kiss to my lips. It tastes like salt and goodbye.

He lets go, and Ledger brushes his mouth against mine. I taste all the what-ifs, chased with regret.

Then, we go, ending the trip far too soon.

Maybe that's better—one less day to fall harder.

Because I'm just not ready to fail again at love.

47

MISTER CUDDLES

Dev

I take off across the ice, catching up with my team as they start drills at one end of the rink. My feet feel like lead as we skate in a speed drill. My mind keeps drifting back to a few days ago, when we left Vancouver, when Aubrey opened her heart but closed the door.

I get it. I fucking get it. I understand why she said what she said. But goddammit, my hopes soared and crashed in the same damn second.

I've got to shove it out of my mind.

It's time to take my place in the net, so I set up camp where I belong. This is my home. Me, and the goal, my stick and my pads. But mostly, my body blocking the other team from doing their job.

There's something very lone wolf about being a goalie. Your job is the opposite to most of the other guys. They move around the ice. I move around the net as they attack during practice.

Like right now. Half the shooters are lined up in one corner. The rest at the other end. After each shot, the shooter camps out on the other side to be a rebounder for the next guys. Keeps me from being lazy.

Like that'd happen.

Stefan comes at me first, taking a shot on goal.

Then he rebounds to Hayes, who makes his move.

Next Hollis.

Then Fisher's coming at me.

I make save after save against some of the best shooters on the team. A cold thrill rushes through my veins when no puck gets past me. I need to just keep up this focus for the rest of training camp, the pre-season, the long season, and into the next year.

Without Aubrey.

I blink away that thought as the drill ends, and Coach moves into the next one, mixing it up so my teammates are coming out of the corner, from behind the net, or across the zone.

Coach barks out commands, but my concentration is shot this time. It's back in the hotel suite with Aubrey. It's on the streets of Vancouver with her. It's in the woods with her. It's in the ghost town saloon when she asked *who are you*, then proceeded to show how well she knew me.

I really wanted her to know me.

She saw me for who I am just like I saw her.

And I fucking miss her. Hell, I practically miss the splinters she removed from my hand. My palm tingles with the memory of shards of wood as a puck whips past and lodges cleanly in the net behind me.

"Fuck me," I mutter, then slam my stick into the ice.

Rookie move.

"Ryland, take five," Coach Riley shouts.

I rip off my helmet and skate away, jaw clenched, irritation coursing through me as our backup goalie comes in.

I'm on the bench knocking back some water when Coach comes over. "What's going on out there?"

"Nothing," I grumble.

"I'm not sure about that," he says.

"It's nothing."

"Then get back out there and let's get these plays down."

Yup. That's the key.

That's all that matters.

This is my year, my chance, my time. Garrett and I have plans. Lock up a long-term contract and play my ass off till we win the big one.

With that in mind, I hit the ice again. Nothing will get past me.

Except everything does, and I'm so fucking pissed as I stomp to the locker room at the end of practice, tossing my helmet in my stall, ripping off my jersey, and yanking off my skates.

"Brick."

The nickname comes from Stefan, the first one in the locker room.

I don't even look his way. Don't want him to see me so angry. "What?"

"It's just practice. It's just training camp."

I shake my head. "It's not."

"It is," he says.

"I don't want to play like that," I mutter.

"Everyone has bad practices. Everyone has bad games."

"No."

He laughs. "What? Just no? You can't say no."

Finally, I turn to him, feeling vulnerable and hating it as I drag a hand through my hair. "I can't have a bad practice. Don't you get it?"

Hockey doesn't disappoint me. Hockey doesn't break my heart. Hockey is always here. Hockey is dependable when nothing else is.

"Dude. This is not like you," he says.

"I need to play well. All the time," I bite out, building up a new head of steam.

Stefan comes closer like I'm a rabid dog, then sets a hand on my shoulder. "Let's get a beer after practice."

I stare at him like he's nuts.

"Fine, fine. A water with no carbs and a salad or what-the-fuck-ever," he says.

At least he understands me.

* * *

Later, we're at The Great Dane. That's the restaurant/bar Stefan owns. Hayes is there, too, along with Fisher, who joined the team recently. Hollis is here too and he's telling us a story of a guy he knew in college who was tired during a game from an all-nighter. "So then Brody says to the captain, 'Well, it'd be helpful if I could get an espresso during inter-mission.'"

Wait. That perks me up. "Did he get one? Did he actually order an espresso during a game?"

"Said he was feeling a little sluggish," Hollis recounts, "and that an espresso would do the trick."

This I have to know. "And did it?"

Hollis's eyes widen as he nods. "He fucking attacked the puck after that. Went on a tear."

Hayes tilts his head, seeming to consider this. "Are you saying we should get an espresso cart rink-side?"

"I was promised espresso when I was traded so I say yes," Fisher puts in dryly.

I say nothing, knocking back some seltzer as Stefan looks my way. "What do you think, Brick? Next time you're sluggish during a game, want a cup?"

I roll my eyes, then grab onto the trash talk. "I'd think a whole jug for you."

Hollis smiles as if he likes the idea. "Nothing wrong with a little caffeine."

"When are you ever tired?" Stefan counters to the laidback new guy who's magic with cats.

Hollis draws a deep breath, seems to give it some thought. "Fair point. It's rare. But that's because I'm married to sleep."

"What hockey player isn't married to sleep?" Hayes asks.

"This is like a serious devotion to it. I've got a sleep mask and a special pillow," Hollis says, as if he's proud of his bedtime accouterments.

Stefan sits up straighter, blue eyes twinkling. "Wait. You bring a special pillow on the road, Hollis? That's fucking gold. Your new name is Mister Cuddles."

Hollis groans, leans back in his chair. "I don't bring it on the road, and I'm not Mister Cuddles."

"Mister Cuddles," Stefan says, having a grand old time, pointing to Fisher next. "Because Fisher's *other new guy*."

There's too many new guys to keep track of.

Fisher grins with relief. "Glad I got that one."

The nickname wars perk me up. I meet Stefan's gaze, a little accusatory. "We agreed Hollis's nickname was Magician. Fight me on this."

We spend the next hour arguing over the nicknames for Hollis and for Fisher, and in the end I win.

* * *

When we leave, Hayes, Fisher and Hollis walk ahead and Stefan hangs back with me, a paper bag of leftovers from the restaurant in his hand. We're shooting the breeze about the season and the city, then Stefan tells me he wants to take a detour. We say goodbye to the other guys and swing by the park. It's dark and late, and I'm not sure what's up but he finds an old guy on a bench doing a crossword puzzle by the duck pond.

"How's the puzzling going, Henry?" Stefan asks the guy.

"This one's easy. A five-letter word for penance. Atone," Henry says, answering it before we have the chance.

Stefan gives him the bag. "Chicken risotto special tonight. Not too shabby."

The grizzled man smiles. "Thanks, kid."

"Henry, this is my buddy, Dev."

Henry turns to me, arches a brow. "You like ducks?"

"Sure."

"Don't feed them then."

"I won't," I say, grateful for the unsolicited advice.

Henry returns to his crossword puzzle book.

We leave, and I understand completely what Stefan did for me tonight. "Appreciate this, man," I say to the captain as we stand at an intersection, the evening traffic passing us by.

"Anytime," he says.

But when I'm home alone, wandering through my wide-open living room, the spacious kitchen, and the balcony with a view of all of Pacific Heights, I'm just that.

Alone.

48

CALICO JACK

Ledger

There's a clean shot to the net. I take aim, slam the puck, and send it flying past the goalie.

Sweet!

It still feels good to score, even in practice. Nothing's hurt much for the first few days of training camp. Empirically, that's good, even if something's been nagging at me all week.

Namely, this empty feeling in my chest.

"Looking sharp," Chase says once we're off the ice and in the tunnel. "You looked like you could play forever."

I wince. But it's not from the knee. "You never know," I say evasively as we head to the locker room.

"I bet you are. Nothing can keep you down," he says, and that's Chase for you. Optimistic. Full of sunshine. No wonder he's the team captain. He's like Dev, always seeing the positive.

"Let's hope so," I say, and eventually I'll tell the team that I won't play forever. I just need to tell Garrett first.

I hate letting him down.

But I'm not sure that's what's dogging me either.

After we shed our gear, we hit the weight room in the arena. It's so familiar, all of this. The routine, the weights, the machines, and the random conversations about who's looking good in football this season, or what new video game the guys are playing, or some rando debate about big questions in the universe—like Marvel versus DC. The weight room is like a dog park for men.

It's fun enough.

I really should try to enjoy it since I'm sure I'll miss it when I'm no longer here. At least I think I will.

But I'm missing something else more. Someone else.

* * *

After practice the next day, I spot my father waiting in the tunnel.

Shit.

He's not entirely unexpected. As a national broadcaster, he's got all access. But I don't think he's here to do a game play-by-play. Since, well, there's no game.

He flashes me his big, TV smile. The friendly one that wins over the whole world. He's wearing a suit, no tie. He looks like me, except older and happier. He's the social one. The outgoing one. "How's it going? Can you believe they let me in here?"

The senior McBride can get in anywhere. "I can," I say, wishing I knew why I felt so apprehensive about seeing him.

"Practice looked good. You're playing strong," he says.

"Thanks," I say, hoping the conversation ends there.

He claps me on the shoulder. "Listen, have you thought any more about going into the booth with me?"

And it doesn't end. I haven't even told him I'm going to retire and he's planning my next career, wanting what's best for me.

"When it's right," he adds. "I'm sure you won't hang up your skates for a while. But when you do, we'd be a great team."

I wish I could say I was surprised by the suggestion, but he's been dropping anvil-sized hints for some time.

"I haven't really thought about n—" I stop myself from saying *next year*. "About then."

As if my retirement is some nebulous time in the distant future.

He seems to take this fable for truth. "You should. It's good to prepare." He sweeps out an arm, indicating way down the road. If he only knew. "We never got to play together, but if we could call games together...can you imagine?"

I'm not sure I can. But he takes me out to dinner and chats about it all through the meal. When I go home, all I want is to tell Aubrey how weird this makes me feel even though I don't know why. She'd know what to do. She'd know what to say.

The next morning, I wake up sweating, heart pounding. I try to blink off the remains of the dream. If you can call it that.

This time I couldn't make a sound. I was stuck in some too-silent land, unable to make a noise.

Back on McDoodle Island Aubrey said when it happened to her she'd try to *visualize something pleasant.*

I think of her. And I hope those thoughts will keep the nightmares at bay.

The next night after a day doing drills on the ice and lifting weights in the gym, I head over to Sticks and Stones, where Garrett's waiting for me at the bar. He's got a beer in front of him and is chatting with Gage as I join them—dad stuff, from the sound of it. Gage is telling my agent that his daughter is playing softball and he's trying his best not to be *one of those coaches.*

"The kind who intervenes and stresses them out?" Garrett asks the man behind the bar.

I sit on a stool and nod a hello.

"Exactly. I'm the cool dad," Gage says to Garrett, and I scoff.

Gage arches a brow my way. "You doubt me?"

"No. I just think every dad thinks he's the cool dad, but really, aren't dad and cool antithetical?"

Gage pokes his sternum. "No. I'm the cool dad. I'm the hot dad. I'm the best dad."

I turn to Garrett, laughing. "We really need to work on his confidence." Then back to Gage, I say, "All right, where's bartender dad? Can you find him and tell him to get me a pale ale?"

"Maybe if you're nice to me," Gage says, then parks his elbows defiantly on the counter.

I roll my eyes. "Fine, fine. You're a cool dad."

"I know," he says, then pours me a beer and heads to tend to some customers down at the other end of the bar.

Garrett meets my gaze, his agent face on. "Tell me stuff. How's the knee doing?"

"It's fine," I say, but is it? Sure, technically the knee feels good. *This week.* But will it feel good in a year? That's the big what-if. Ah, fuck it. Telling Aubrey and Dev was such a relief. Keeping it from my dad the other night was stressful. "I'm going to retire after this year."

Blinking, he sits up straighter. "Oh. Yeah?"

"Yeah. Sorry, man," I say, feeling like shit. I hate disappointing him.

Garrett leans closer, concern in his eyes. "Why are you sorry?"

"Because I won't earn money for you."

Garrett shakes his head. "This is about your career. I've only ever wanted to guide you through it."

"I appreciate that," I say, then sigh heavily. I wish I were in a better mood. I wish I wanted to tell my father. I wish I were a better client. I wish telling Garrett eased the ache inside me.

I wish for...a lot of things.

But I've been in a bad mood since I left Vancouver. Imagine that.

"You're in a funk," Garrett says, reading me perfectly. My poker face sucks today.

Maybe I should say something about...*anything.* "Just a lot on my mind," I begin, trying that on for size.

"Anything I can help with?"

My life doesn't spark without your sister. But can I say that? Well, considering I just told him I'm going to retire...Considering I feel like a schmuck for keeping shit from him...Considering there's a way to say it without violating Aubrey's confidence...yes, I can.

I straighten my shoulders, meet his eyes. "I...care a lot about your sister," I say honestly.

Garrett's still for a second. Brow scrunching. Eyes intense. "Yeah?"

"Yeah," I say. It's not just a relief. It's a necessity to have spoken the truth.

Garrett nods a few times, as if he's taking in this new data point. "Are you going to do anything about it?"

I wish I could do everything. "Not right now," I admit, and you couldn't miss the moroseness in my tone.

Garrett turns his beer glass in small circles. "Makes sense," he says, understanding the situation completely.

The timing is awful.

"It does," I say, and there's not much more to say than that. But at least I'm not sitting with a lie of omission between us. That has to count for something.

But I don't know what.

* * *

When I get home that night, I check the moisture levels of the plants, watering some, chatting with others, then I grab a feather toy I picked up at a pet store and wander through the living room, dangling it in front of the cat. "Hey there, Calico Jack," I say, calling him by his new name.

The black one-eyed critter bats the feather, and all I want is to tell Aubrey she was right.

But I don't.

I do sleep better that night. No nightmares. I'm not saying one night has cured me. But maybe voicing my desire to retire to Garrett has lessened some of the anxiety. Maybe Aubrey's right about that too. I was working through my decision to retire. Some of working through it is telling people.

I still wish I could wake up next to Aubrey though. Wish I could tell her I'm making progress.

* * *

The next day is light. Just a morning skate then the team has the rest of the day off.

When we're done with the skate, I head down the hallway toward the players' exit, along with Chase and Ryker.

"Free afternoon. We can take Trina to that bookstore she wants to go to in Sausalito," Ryker says to Chase as we near the door to the parking lot.

Damn, that sounds nice.

"Pretty sure you want to go to it too," Chase says to his friend.

"Yes, but so does she. So let's do it."

"If we can bring Nacho," Chase says, and now I'm picturing taking Aubrey and a dog we don't even have out shopping. Great. Just great. I'm imagining future dogs with her now.

Ryker rolls his eyes at Chase. "Obviously. Dude loves bookstores."

Chase turns to me, and for a second, I think he's going to invite me along. I fucking hope he doesn't. Not that I hate bookstores—I do not—but the last thing I want is to be a third wheel for their trio. Fourth wheel actually.

I make a preemptive move with, "I've got to...get some plant food."

Chase shoots me a look like I've said the equivalent of *I need to rearrange my sock drawer*. Which I suppose I have.

His brow knits. "Have fun...shopping for plant food?"

It comes out as a question because who the fuck says that? But as we reach the lot and Ryker breaks for his car, Chase motions that he'll catch up with him, then pulls me aside.

"Hey," he begins in the universal tone of *I'm about to give you some unsolicited advice.*

I brace myself for what's coming. Not sure I want advice. I probably can't follow it.

"You seemed happier in Vancouver," he continues, slinging my words back at me. A couple years ago, when he went through a rough patch with Trina, I said as much to him.

This situation with Aubrey isn't the same. Back then, I told Chase to get Trina back no matter what.

That's not a thing I can do with Aubrey. She set a boundary. I respect it. Still, I appreciate Chase's gesture, so I give him a nod and say, "I was."

"Maybe do something about that," he adds.

I sigh heavily. "Not sure I can."

He lifts a brow. "You sure about that?"

On that mic drop, he walks to his car. As I head to mine, I replay those words. Turn them over. Then inside out. Am I sure?

Come to think of it...I'm not.

Not at all.

I hop in my car and call Dev. "What are you doing?"

"Working out," he says in between heavy breaths. Sounds like he's on the elliptical at his gym.

"I'm coming by," I say.

"Okay."

Fifteen minutes later, I'm walking into the gym with a renewed sense of purpose. I march over to the cardio machine that he's attacking with the ferocity of a man who's as lonely as I am. I stop at it as he rips out his earbuds but keeps on running. "What's up?"

"I can't stop thinking we messed up."

His eyes spark. "How? Tell me how? Because then we can fix it. I've been dying to fix it, but I have no idea how."

"I think I do," I say, and for the first time in a week, I feel a spark.

49

HAT DAY

Aubrey

It's been over a week since I saw the guys but I'm doing my damnedest to live in the moment.

This second, I'm doing something I've loved since I was a kid. Playing with hair.

My friend Briar's at my salon this Saturday since she has a photo shoot this afternoon for some promos for her new series of yoga videos. "Don't ever leave me. Or it'll be hat day every day for the rest of my life," she says into the mirror.

"Aww, I love hat days. But I'm happy that you need me," I say above the hum of the dryer.

"Need you. Refuse to leave you," she says, meeting my gaze in the mirror. "Especially since the struggle to master the art of the blowout is real."

I smile back slyly. "I know." Then I stage whisper,

"And I love it. Now tell me more about the videos," I say as I move to another chunk of her hair.

"They've been taking off. Ever since I started working with the Golden State Foxes," she says, since she teaches yoga classes for the team.

Stay in the moment. Don't start thinking about the hockey guy you're pining for on that team.

That's what the therapist I saw a few days ago said. A woman named Elena Alvarez that my chocolate-loving friend Elodie recommended.

She talked about focusing on the present. Not the future. Not the past. But each moment. I told her about the wedding that didn't happen and the honeymoon that did. I'll see her again next week too. It was cathartic to talk to someone. There's a lot I've been holding in. A lot I'm no longer holding in too.

I finish Briar's hair and turn off the dryer, then do a final perusal of my friend, her blonde hair blown into voluminous curls and glowing against her fair skin. "You look gorgeous."

"So do you." She arches a brow in question. "Does that mean it was a good trip?"

It's an interesting question from someone who doesn't know every detail of my unusual double honey-moon—just that I went on one. "You know, it really was," I say. "I learned a lot about myself. What I want. What I don't want."

Her smile brightens as the salon owner scurries by, waving at us as he goes, adding a "Hi, gorgeous."

Bronze is a friendly guy.

"Hi, boss," I answer.

He rolls his eyes like he still hasn't accepted he's the man in charge.

Once he's past, Briar returns to our convo. "Good. You deserve everything you want."

"So do you," I say as I snap off her smock. "How was your birthday?"

"It was good. I've been making some plans about expanding my business. I might take on a business partner," she says.

"Ooh, that sounds exciting."

With the smock off, she stands and gives me a thoughtful look. "You seem good for someone who didn't get married. I'm glad. Sometimes the things that don't happen are the best things."

I let those words of wisdom sink in. Yeah, I think she's right. "Words to live by, bestie," I say, and we hug, then she leaves.

I clean up my booth for my next client and try not to think about the guys.

Truly I do.

I try to follow Elena's advice.

But it's not easy. I miss them so much. I do my best to put them out of my mind the rest of the day, and it's a battle.

By the time work is over I'm worn out fighting it. I just want to go home and linger in memories as I take a shower and listen to music and binge a new show on my couch.

But I'd like my badge for resisting calling, texting, seeing, or asking them to see me.

When I get home, though, they're waiting at the foot of the stoop of my building in the Mission.

50

IS THIS A KIDNAPPING?

Aubrey

I take slow steps out of my car, like I'm seeing things. This feels like a mirage. Or a very good dream. Dev with his light brown hair and winning smile. His beard is thicker, and that makes me happy and sad. Happy because I like it. Sad because the fact that I can see the change reminds me I haven't seen him in eight days.

Ledger's all Ledger-y, in a black polo that hugs his muscles and shows off his ink. His expression is intense, borderline glower-y. He's the storm to Dev's sunshine.

But my heart flutters wildly since I want the storm and the sunshine.

Dev's holding a postcard, Ledger a plant.

"Hi," I say tentatively as I reach them. It comes out breathy, full of hope. I shouldn't want to see them so badly and yet I do.

Ledger closes the distance between us, his stern expression locking with mine. "No."

What? That's what he's saying to me? That's his first word? I jerk my gaze back. "No what?"

Dev straightens his shoulders and steps closer too. "No. This isn't ending now."

A laugh bursts from me. I'm shocked. Speechless. Still, I manage to say, "Um, it's not?"

Ledger's eyes turn more serious. "We respect the hell out of what you said eight days, nine hours, and thirty-five minutes ago. But we're also not letting you go."

Way to tell time.

But still, since these guys aren't mafia bosses, I'm a little lost as to this *we're not letting you go* declaration. I am damn curious. "Are you kidnapping me?"

Dev smiles, his eyes glinting with mischief but also with hope. "No. Because here's the thing, Aubrey." His smile burns off. "I get where you're coming from. We both do," he says, gesturing from Ledger to himself and back. "I get that you're hurt. I get that you're questioning everything. I get that there's all sorts of stuff we need to sort out and put on the table. But you're..." He draws a big breath, his eyes all swoony. "...fucking amazing."

Oh. Wow. Is this how two men tag team telling you they're into you? My heart thunders, but my head is warning me to be careful. I don't want to tell them I need time a second time. That feels mean.

Ledger jumps in. "Exactly. So we want you to take your time. To do what you need to do. But I'm just saying this." He pins me with a smoldering, important stare. "We'll wait for you."

Oh.

Oh, my.

They're giving me time. They're giving me all the time. Is this happening?

"You're saying...?" It's almost too much to breathe aloud.

"We'll wait for you," Ledger repeats. "We're not going anywhere. You said you'd want to go out, but you need time. So how's this?" Ledger says, then a small smile shifts his lips as he hands off to Dev.

"We came over here to ask you on a date," Dev says.

"For a year from now," Ledger adds.

My eyes pop. I swallow in pure surprise.

"You are?" I can barely speak I'm so amazed.

"Same time. Next year," Ledger says, strong and certain. "Will that work for you, honey?"

My hand flies to my chest. "You'll really...wait for me?"

"Yes," Dev answers with a smile that's like the sun in the morning. You see a hint of it at first, then it rises, all at once. "We will."

I'm overwhelmed. Overjoyed. And flabbergasted. They must know that sometimes you just have to leave on a high note, since they start backing down the steps.

"Same time," Ledger says, then hands me the prickly cactus in a small terracotta pot. "Until then."

"Next year," Dev adds, then gives me the postcard. From Vancouver.

It's my turn. The invitation is in my court. The offer

is big and beautiful and simple. A postcard, a plant, and a promise.

Something from each of my guys. Like I could forget them in a year. "It's on my calendar," I say, then tap my temple.

They start to leave, to head down the street, but I set the postcard and the plant on the stoop and catch up with them.

I grab Ledger's face and plant a quick, firm kiss on his lips.

Then Dev's, doing the same.

I turn around and go inside on a promise, with a postcard and a plant.

I'm still alone, but I don't quite feel so lonely anymore.

51

MAN-BATICAL

Aubrey

One month later...

"It's been thirty days," I say to Elena, who's sitting serenely in a purple chair, a painting of a snow-covered cabin behind her.

"Not that you're counting," she says playfully, and I like that she's not all serious all the time. She knows when to poke fun.

"Just a little bit," I say, but old habits die hard. I'm not entirely being clear, and I know I need to be.

She turns more serious. "But are you?"

"I'm not counting what you think I'm counting," I admit.

She knits her brow. "Oh. I thought you were saying that's how long it's been since you saw the guys."

"It has been," I say, but we've kept in touch. I've texted, sending them ideas for our champagne line, like We All Hated Him Anyway, and suggestions on new holidays for Dev, like National Arugula Day, and videos for Ledger like "How to charm your cat and other impossible tasks."

But I'm *not* counting down to our date next year.

Really, what Elena and I have worked on is *why* I felt compelled to marry someone I didn't really love because I thought it would make someone else happy.

That someone else isn't here anymore.

And it's been thirty days since I started to let go of the idea that I should keep trying to make him happy—especially when it's not what I want.

I swallow past the guilt and the shame. "I think I should say something to my mom."

Elena's smile is pleased, proud even. "That's your countdown?"

I let out a big breath. "Yes. I think that's what I've been working through with you. And I needed to really understand what to say to her, and what *not* to say. I don't think she needs to know all the burdens she and my dad placed on me, whether inadvertently or not."

Elena shakes her head. "Probably not. That's lovely of you to think of her emotional health."

"She misses her husband still. I don't want to say *this fucked me up when I was younger.*"

Elena nods, tucking a strand of silvery hair behind her ear. "That's a gift, in a way—to know what needs to be said and what needs to be left unsaid."

I let those words sink in. "I wish I'd figured it out

sooner. I feel like I've spent way too long trying to figure it out."

Her smile is sympathetic. "Generally, it takes a life-time," she says.

When I leave, I head to my mom's salon in Petaluma.

* * *

Before she gives me a trim, we head to the break room in the back of the salon and pore over some new looks and styles in her look books, debating our favorites. But a few minutes of discussing beach waves and layered cuts, and I know it's time to cut to the chase.

"You'd look pretty like that. Or that. Or that," she says, flipping from page to page.

My stomach's flipping with nerves. I shut the book. "Mom," I say with some gravitas.

"Yes?" She sounds nervous.

"I need to talk to you."

Her eyes flash with worry. "Are you okay? Are you sick? What's going on?"

I squeeze her arm. "I'm fine," I say.

"Are you sure? Is it about the gifts? I returned them all," she says.

The wedding seems like a lifetime ago. I've learned so much in the last six weeks.

"I know, and I'm grateful for that. But this is about why I thought I should marry Aiden in the first place," I say.

"Oh." She fiddles with her wedding band. She hasn't taken it off.

A stone lodges in my heart. This will be harder to say than I'd thought. "I wanted to make Dad happy. I wanted to make *you* happy," I add, but I fear I said that badly. I don't want to blame her.

"What do you mean?"

"It's my fault," I say, trying to correct. "I made the choice. I thought it was the right one. I thought I was doing the right thing since Dad was friends with Aiden's dad, and he had this idea that Aiden was perfect for me, and you did as well."

"I did," she says, sounding horror-struck. "I'm sorry."

"Don't apologize. I did it. I should have said something sooner. I should have said he wasn't for me. I didn't, and that's mine to own. But I want you to know that I'm not going to try to live my life for someone else anymore. I'm going to live it for me," I say, my throat tightening.

"Oh, sweetheart. That's all I've wanted. I'm so sorry you felt otherwise. I only ever wanted you to be happy. I didn't realize I was pressuring you."

A lump pushes past all that tightness, and everything hurts, but it's a good hurt, the kind that needs to come out. "It's okay. I wanted you two to be happy," I say.

She sighs but offers a resigned smile. "I'm learning how to be happy again. Just promise me you won't walk down the aisle unless you're in wild, mad, incredible love. I was with your dad, and even when it was hard, even when we fought to stay together, even when I was afraid we wouldn't make it, it was worth it. Every single day."

A tear slips down one cheek, then another. "I think I needed to hear that," I say. Then I rip off the Band-Aid a little more. What the hell, right? "What would you think if I cared about two men at once?"

She blinks, takes a moment, then lets it register. "Well, isn't that just totally in right now, what with your friends and all?"

"Maybe it is," I say, and I feel unburdened from the past. I feel free of all the fears I put in front of me so long ago.

"If it makes you happy," she says.

I hug her and I feel...happy enough.

* * *

A few days later I'm at Little Friends, snapping pics of pups for their adoption photos.

I'm in the tiny yard at the back of the rescue in the city, working with a little Jack Russell mix in a blue bow tie with rubber duck illustrations on it. "Say cheese," I say to the guy.

The direction doesn't do the trick, but the biscuit I'm dangling in the air above my phone camera sure does. The handsome boy tilts his head just so, and I snap a few shots.

When I'm done, I turn to Trina. She's been volunteering at Little Friends, and she enlisted me to take dog beauty pics. I'm now a stylist for people and pets. I help bathe them, then make them look fabulous for their "dog glamor shots."

"The dude is all set," I say of the energetic guy.

"Perfect. I love the pic," Trina says, then walks me to the sidewalk after I've packed up my things. It's Monday, my day off, and when I reach the car, she gives me a curious look.

"How's the man-batical going?"

That's the million-dollar question. "It's...not my favorite diet," I joke. "But I guess I need it."

She nods sagely, seeming to understand. "I hear you, but don't be so hard on yourself either. Sometimes things happen at what we think is the wrong time, but it turns out time is just...time. And if you don't grab it, it'll pass you by."

She should know. She met her husbands only two weeks after she discovered her ex had cheated on her. But she'd only been living with her ex. She hadn't been poised to walk down the aisle to him.

Still, her words linger with me the rest of the day as I go home alone, then as I hop onto my laptop and search for photos of Dev from the start of the past few seasons, confirming visually what he told me on the plane.

I send him a text.

Aubrey: I know you always get your haircut before the first game. If you think I'm letting anyone else touch those locks, you're sorely mistaken. My chair. Tomorrow. Five p.m. Be there.

Dev: Someone's possessive.

Aubrey: Yes.

Next, I send a note to Ledger.

Aubrey: I have something for you. For good luck for the new season. Meet me at my salon on Wednesday at five p.m. so I can give it to you.

Ledger: That message seems clandestine.

Aubrey: But that won't stop you.

Ledger: With you, nothing will.

52

JERSEY GIRL

Aubrey

I pace the salon after my last client has left. Dev is due any second. I'm all jittery, touching my recently polished nails with their bling sparkles then checking my reflection.

Bronze must notice my overactive attention since he stops on his way to the back of the shop and whispers, "You look gorgeous, hun."

"Thanks, Bronze," I say. He winks then mouths *anytime*. I smooth a hand down my sweater.

Dev isn't late. He's not due for three more minutes, but I've already swept my booth, wiped down the chair, and straightened up the station. I've got scissors and clippers out. I have hair products. I have nothing else to do but wait.

Do I look okay?

I steal a glance in the mirror again. My little skirt

lands mid-thigh and I'm wearing thigh-high socks and lace-up boots. A cute argyle sweater hits at my waist. My hair is long and wavy.

And my heart is all fluttery. Too fluttery.

I close my eyes. Breathe in, out. Imagine I'm relaxing in one of Briar's yoga classes. I focus on this moment. Not the next one, or the next, or the one after that.

When I open my eyes, I startle. Dev is striding across the shop and I watch him in the mirror as he gets closer, my pulse thundering. When I turn around, my skin is tingling too, and I want to throw myself at him.

"Hi," I say, hoping that one syllable contains everything I'm feeling. Hoping he can hear it.

"Hey," he says, flirty and full of emotion. It feels like we have a private language. His gaze travels up and down my body. "You look...incredible."

I finger the hem of my skirt. "Thanks. I..." I pause, weighing which words to choose.

They told you they're waiting for you.

With that in mind, it's not hard to say the next thing. "I want to...look good for you."

His smile is dazzling. "Mission accomplished."

But I replay what I just said. *Look good for you.* It feels so weak. Like it's not enough. "I want to look special."

He steps closer, shaking his head in amusement. "You could be wearing a stained sweatshirt and ripped pants. You could have on clothes that are ten sizes too big. You could be wearing no makeup—you could not even have brushed your hair. You could have a cold. Or the flu. I'd still think you're the most beautiful woman I've ever seen."

And I fall a little harder. No, *a lot* harder.

"Sit," I say, and I can't wipe the smile off my face.

"So bossy."

"If you keep showering me with compliments, I'm not going to be able to focus on your hair. And I know you have a superstition about getting a haircut before the first game."

"I do," he says, acquiescing to my argument as he sits.

We talk about the style he wants, how much to trim, and what he likes. Then I take him to the sink where I wrap the smock around his neck and tell him to lean his head back.

He leans against the dip in the black sink bowl, looking relaxed as he lets me do my thing. It's such a privilege to give him a shampoo. Such a treat to do this thing for this man who's done so much for me. To shampoo his hair, run my fingers through it, massage his scalp.

It's a joy to experience the sighs and little moans he makes as he lets himself savor this indulgence. I feel like I'm the only one he'd let touch his hair, and I cherish that feeling.

When I'm done, I run a towel over his wet locks and bring him back to the chair at my booth. I take my time cutting and snipping, buzzing and clipping, asking him how he's feeling about the season.

"Better," he says, meeting my gaze and holding it.

"Yeah?"

"Yeah." He sounds steady, calm, certain.

"Maybe I should come to a game," I say impulsively. I'm not sure why I hadn't thought of that yet.

"You absolutely should. Maybe the first one?" he says, and I nod. "You should go to a Sea Dogs game too."

"Maybe I will."

We both know I'm going to both.

The next day, Ledger strides into the salon at the end of the day. Tall, broody, handsome, and here for me, he takes my breath away. He's inscrutable on the surface, but I know deep down he's soulful, gentle, thoughtful. He scans the place as he walks over. "So this is where the magic happens." He pats the back of the chair, looking around, really surveying the salon with its crisp white walls and sleek steel booths.

"It is."

There's a modern but welcoming feel to my home away from home, and he seems to see that. "This place is nice."

"You knew that. You looked it up," I point out.

"I did. But it's nicer with you in it," he says.

My stomach flips. It's going to be an occupational hazard if I keep inviting them to my work.

But just now, I'm a woman on a mission—to let them know I'm worth waiting for. "I have this for you." I reach into my purse and take out a little box. I hand it to him.

The corner of his lips twitches. I bet he's not used to getting presents. Well, he'll have to get used to them with me. He opens the box and fights off a smile. It's a key chain with a small cactus charm on it.

"Prickly. Like me," he says, repeating what Dev told him in Plant Parenthood.

"Like you," I echo.

He leans in, and whispers deliciously against my cheek. "And you like prickly."

I shiver. "Seems I do," I say, then I take my turn whispering. "It's a good luck charm. For your final year."

He pulls back, then tosses the chain in the air and catches it before he holds my gaze again. "It's going to be a very hard year."

He's not talking about hockey.

"I know," I say, and I'm not either.

* * *

A few days later, I head into the Golden State Foxes arena with Trina, excitement bouncing in my cells. It's the first home game of the season and the place is jumping. The new logo—a badass fox—is all over the walls.

I've got a jacket over my shirt since it's fuck-all cold. Well, ice is like that. We gab about customers—the good ones and the bad ones at my salon and her bookstore—as we head to our seats.

When the mascot hits the rink a few minutes before the puck drops, Trina and I shout the loudest.

"Go Foxy!" we cheer like madwomen.

That's our girl after all. Ivy's the mascot and she's racing around the ice in her tawny fox costume as the announcer tells a story about the Golden State Foxes. She whips up the crowd, and we're shouting till our throats go numb as the guys emerge from the tunnel.

They hit the ice skating fast and furiously.

"Yay Seventeen," I shout when I see the goalie, my heart tripping over itself. He's covered in pads and a helmet, and I doubt he can see me. But I cheer for him again and again as he saves goal after goal, some with his legs, some with the stick, and some with his whole body. He's the brick wall they want him to be, and damn, it's hot that he doesn't let a thing get past him.

When the first period ends, he yanks up his helmet, turns to the stands, and flashes a smile my way. I tug on my shirt so he can see it.

Well, he sent it to me today. I'm wearing his Number Seventeen jersey.

* * *

Two days later, Ivy and I join Trina for the first game of the Sea Dogs across town. We don't go to the former wives and girlfriends' section, now called The Partners' Suite.

For this game, we have seats rink-side.

"My, how times have changed," I tease Trina. "You were slumming it in the VIP suite with me, holding up revenge signs to get even with your ex. Now look at you. You're Mrs. Hockey," I say to the double wife.

She rolls her eyes, then nods to Ivy too. "Pretty sure we all are."

I raise a *who me* brow. "Not me."

But even to me it feels like the lady doth protest too much.

"Not you *yet*," Ivy corrects, as the team hits the ice, and all my attention turns to the veteran forward.

Ledger flies across the ice, tough and stoic and focused.

Does his knee hurt? Is he masking any pain? Or is he hanging in there and enjoying his swan song? I hope it's the latter.

Before he heads to the bench, his eyes find mine and his smile feels private, just for me, when he sees me wearing his jersey—the one he sent me today.

These guys and their need to claim me.

When the game ends, I text my brother and ask if he can have dinner with me on Friday night after book club. He says yes.

I breathe deeply and try to just keep in this moment right now.

* * *

That Friday night, Briar and I head into An Open Book for Trina's Page Turners club. "Finally," I chide playfully as I push open the door. "Took you long enough to come with me."

She shoots me a look with those crystal blue eyes. "You act like I've been avoiding book club."

"You have," I tease.

"You only invited me a month ago," she points out.

"Details," I say airily. Then I narrow my eyes at her as we wander past the new release shelves. "And it turns out you were secretly reading romance without telling me."

"Well, I needed some...tips," she says, lowering her voice.

"Tips? Like on how to date?"

She leans in and whispers even more quietly, "Toy tips."

Ah, I've got this one. "I love books with toys. I'll rec some." We head to the back, where Trina's setting up with Ivy. The regulars are here, like Prana and Kimora, who's petting the paperback in her hand.

The book has a red cover with a brown cartoon couple kissing swoonily under the title *Overnight Shag*. In the story, the heroine meets a hot Brit named Naveen who stays at her B and B in a small town. Prana suggested it because the heroine is Desi, like her.

Kimora's loving on the paperback so hard. "This book. This freaking book. Yes. Finally. When I said I'm over bad communication, I am over it. Like forever. And I am so glad it's not in this story."

Prana taps her chin, ever the diplomat. "Me too. I'm not into it when something can be worked out with a simple convo. But miscommunication is a thing. It happens in real life."

"It does, but so do periods and UTIs. I don't need

any of that stuff in a book," Kimora says, no ifs, ands, or buts.

"In real life I don't really *O*," Briar blurts out.

Whoa.

We all whip our gazes to the blonde by my side. "You don't?" I ask.

"By myself I do. Not really with...a partner." Briar winces like it pains her. Well, it pains me on her behalf.

Kimora's voice softens as she turns to Trina. "Give her the mug. I don't care who got the bang prediction right. This girl needs the mug."

"You really do," Trina says with sympathy, reaching for the gift for the bang prediction winner. It's a "We Are Well and Truly Fucked" mug.

Briar clutches it like it's a precious gift. "It's the *I have no O*s mug."

I consider the slogan, then turn it around in my head. "Or maybe it's a promise for the future. Like, you're going to be well and truly fucked."

She rolls her eyes. "I'll just start with the *O*."

"I'm rooting for you to be well and truly fucked, B," Kimora says, then flicks her black braids off her shoulders.

"I'll bring the pom-poms," Prana seconds.

As we sit and debate the banter and the tension in the story, my mind drifts to my own bang prediction.

To Dev reading me a scene from *The UnGentleman*.

To Ledger's sex math.

To the guys coming over and declaring they'll wait for me.

Then, Kimora's saying to Briar, "Just ask for help with the O. Life is too short."

And you know what? It really is.

On that life lesson, I head out to meet my brother for dinner.

53

FAIRY GODBROTHER

Aubrey

The second Garrett arrives at the table, he sweeps his shrewd gaze to the left, then to the right, then to his watch. "Is there a warp in the time-space continuum?"

"Oh, shut up. I'm not normally late," I say, patting the chair so he can sit down.

"But I'm always early," he says. "Never have I ever arrived after you."

This won't be the only surprise he gets from me tonight. "Well, I plan to keep you on your toes," I say.

He motions for me to stand, then wraps his arms around me. It's nice, his brotherly hug. I've come to rely on it my whole entire life.

Garrett's dependable, trustworthy, and good.

And as he hugs me, I *know*—I just know—that he won't be the wrench in my love story.

But I still need to give him the news.

When he sits, he's first to speak, older brother style and all. "Listen, I've got to head to New York tomorrow to work on some sponsorship deals. And I've got some VIP tickets to the Renegades game this weekend that I can't use."

"Say less," I say, since I love football.

He's laughing already. "I didn't even offer them to you yet."

I rub my fingers together. "But you were going to."

Grinning, he drags a hand through his hair. "Fine, fine. Maybe I was."

"You love me best," I say with a sweet little sister smile.

He gives me a stern glare. "Don't tell Claire."

"I don't have to. It's obvious," I say, but what's obvious, too, is that if life is all about moments, I need to take this one, and I need to do it now before we become too comfortable with the teasing and the talking.

I asked my brother to dinner for a reason. Yes, I made a pact with the guys on our honeymoon. That pact was to keep our honeymoon times private, and I plan to stick to that.

Still, here goes. "I want to date your friends," I say.

There. It's that simple.

Garrett blinks. Several times. A line digs into his brow. He tilts his head. "I'm sorry. What?"

"Ledger and Dev," I add, keeping my shoulders straight, my gaze locked on his.

He's quiet, his lips parting like he's trying to speak, but he's a fish and no words come.

Which means it's still my turn. Briefly, I flash back

to some of the novels we've read in book club—romances where the heroines have to say the hard thing. That's my life lesson I have to keep learning.

"I kind of fell for both of them," I continue, and it's not truly hard to say this. It *is* necessary. "And I want to see what's there."

"With both?" he repeats.

This isn't a new concept to him. He lives in a city that's home to a hell of a lot of sports throuples. But sometimes people need to adjust in their own time.

"Both of them? Together?" Garrett doesn't sound shocked though. He sounds like his lawyerly self, clarifying the points.

"Yes." That's all I say.

He leans back, scratches his jaw, then shrugs. "Well, since you aren't even asking my permission, I guess all I can say is...*enjoy the suite Sunday night.*"

I crack up. "Wait. For real?"

He rolls his eyes. "Dude. I pretty much walked right into that one."

I laugh. "So you're a matchmaker now? A wing brother? A dating coach? A set-up man? A fairy godbrother?"

He holds up a hand, as if he's fighting off the laughter. "Stop. Just stop."

But really, I can't.

54

FAST FORWARD

Dev

I'm almost home from the rink after a shutout, thank you very much to me. I bound up the steps to my home in Pacific Heights, still high on the game, when my phone pings with a group text.

I stop in my tracks.

Hell, my heart stops beating.

It's her. Yes, we've been talking. Yes, we've been texting. But the preview pane has me all kinds of hopeful. I click it open faster than I stopped that shot flying toward my face tonight.

> Aubrey: You know those scenes in the movies when there's a montage to show the passage of time?

· · ·

Yes. Fucking yes.

I reply, though, in the way she'd want me to.

> **Dev:** Yes, like in a Christmas movie when they show a Christmas party, a tree farm visit, and a stop at the Christmas fair. Go on.

>> **Ledger:** Are you saying it's Christmas, Aubrey?

>> **Aubrey:** It seems my calendar just went into fast-forward mode.

Best. Gift. Ever. But just to be sure, I write back.

> **Dev:** So it's ten months from now… now?

>> **Aubrey:** If you guys want to see a football game with me Sunday night it is.

Our answers land simultaneously. *Yes.*

I punch the sky, then once I'm inside, I call Garrett and I waste zero time. "I'm wild about your sister."

He sighs heavily, but it's not an annoyed sigh. It's more like a *tell me something I don't know* sigh. "I figured as much."

Some things in life are just simple.

* * *

But I do give him a hard time that weekend as I'm getting ready to meet Aubrey. "It's your fault," I say on the phone as I trim my beard in the mirror.

"I did not intend to set you and Ledger up with her," Garrett grumbles.

"And yet you did. Admit it. This was your grand plan."

"Yes, Dev. You figured me out. On my sister's wedding day, I was really hoping to hook her up with you two clowns," he says.

"The evidence says so," I say as I set down the trimmer, then run a hand over my stubble.

"I never planned to be a matchmaker."

"It could be a new calling," I say, since this is too fun. Hell, everything is too fun. Life is fucking good. I have a date with Aubrey tonight.

TEN MONTHS EARLY.

And there's no way I'm going to let her slip through my fingers. I'm keeping her, dammit.

"Why do I put up with you?" Garrett groans.

I could keep hassling him, but that time has passed. I turn serious, like I was when I called him last night. "Seriously, I appreciate you being cool about this."

"Was I supposed to be an asshole?"

"No. But you weren't, and I'm grateful," I say, meaning it from the bottom of my heart.

He's quiet for a few seconds. "I'm grateful she's dating...a good guy. A couple good guys," he says, like those words don't quite fit.

But they don't *not fit* either.

"I'll treat her right."

"I know," he says.

"We both will."

"I know that too."

I say goodbye, then head to the garage and hop into my car. I head to Ledger's place to pick him up because we have business to take care of.

Once he gets in the car, I turn to him. "You know what this is?"

He's as stoic as he's ever been as he says dryly, "A date?"

"Yes. But it's *also* the start of a future with her. We're not going to lose her. We're going to do everything we can to keep her."

He rolls his eyes. "Obviously."

55

YES, BABY

Dev

But I'm a little concerned after what I just learned about Aubrey during the first half of the game.

Maybe this drive will clear things up though. The quarterback drops back into the pocket, scans downfield, finds no one open. He scrambles for two, three, four tense seconds until he launches a missile that sails fast and beautifully into the arms of the open receiver, who hauls it in and escorts that baby into the end zone.

Aubrey bursts my eardrums with her cheers of "yes, baby" and "that's how we do it."

Yup. It's clear. She's a feral football fan. I root for the Renegades too. But still, I need her to say *yes, baby* for me. For us.

When the cheers in the suite settle down, I nudge Aubrey. "Do we need to talk?"

She's still exuberant from the touchdown. Her cheeks are pink, her eyes bright. "About what?"

Even though I'm in a suite full of other VIP fans of the city's most decorated football team, I narrow my brow and ask pointedly, "About that *yes, baby*. Are you a bigger football fan than hockey fan?"

Aubrey rolls her eyes. "Seriously?"

Quickly, Ledger gets on board. "It's a legit question, come to think of it."

"I didn't see you cheering this hard at the hockey game you came to," I say.

She parks her hands on her hips, looking too sassy, too sexy, too just fucking perfect for me as she says, "I didn't realize you were the jealous types."

"I didn't realize you were loyal to the gridiron," I counter.

"Just seems you'd have *double* the reasons to like hockey," Ledger deadpans.

"But football is sooo fun," she says.

I cough to cover up my shocked laugh. "But it's not hockey."

"I thought you had good taste, honey," Ledger says, waggling his eyebrows so his double meaning is clear.

"Aww, is it hard for you, handsome?" she asks him before setting a hand on my chest. "Does it bother you too, babe?"

Ah, hell.

We're *handsome* and *babe*. I'm so far gone for her. But I try valiantly to give her hell about this. "No, I'm just thinking we need to get you season tickets to the better sport," I say. "Right, Ledger?"

His nod is decisive. "We sure do."

"But what if you're both playing the same night?" Aubrey asks, all flirty and playful.

I lean in close, sweep some of those auburn locks off her ear. "We can share you."

She shudders under my touch, then nibbles on the corner of her lips, turning her gaze to him. "That work for you?"

"Yes, yes it does," he says.

She sits down in the tall, leather chair, then lets out a shaky breath. Looking at him, then looking at me. Just as it should be. I sit, too, put a hand on her thigh. Ledger drops down, wraps an arm around her shoulder. Yes, this is us, dating our girl.

* * *

But dating her also means surprising her. She does like to be thrown for a loop.

Once the game ends, and the suite clears, the three of us hang back, Ledger and I making small talk about the game before he holds up a finger and says he needs to chat with the suite attendant.

He bounds up the steps, tugs the guy aside. The man smiles and nods, then disappears into the hall.

The door clinks shut right as Aubrey reaches for the knob.

I cover her hand with mine. "Not so fast. You need to understand there are consequences for your actions."

Her eyes flicker as she lets go. "There are?" Her voice sounds breathy. Just shy of excited.

"We can't let you get away with that kind of defiance," Ledger says, then locks the door.

"You can't?" Her voice pitches higher.

"Nope," he says, then tosses her over his shoulder and stalks down the steps to the glass of the suite, overlooking the field.

The Renegades have won, and the field is clear, but fans are still trickling out of the stadium. He takes her to the second row of seats, obscured behind the tall backs of the seats in front.

He sits then sets her down across his lap, ass up, hair spilling beautifully. Ledger tosses me a careless look. "Raise her skirt for me, will you?"

"Gladly," I say, joining them in the second row to give a helping hand.

Aubrey gasps, then looks my way as I tug up her skirt, exposing...holy fuck. She's wearing pink low-rise bikinis, showing off some of her fantastic butt. I yank the fabric higher up the crack of her ass.

With her skirt bunched at her waist and her panties a string, Ledger raises a hand, then lowers it with a quick thwack.

"Oh god," Aubrey gasps, then wiggles on him, like she's rubbing her pussy against his thigh.

"This will remind you that you're not a football girlfriend," he reprimands.

"I'm not?" she asks, clearly playing along.

He smacks the other cheek. She writhes again as he soothes away the sting. "You're a hockey girl. Got that?"

She nods a yes, breathing heavily.

"You sure about that?" I ask.

"I don't know. Am I?" she asks, taunting me, fucking taunting me.

Ledger shakes his head, like *can you believe this defiance.* "Show her, man," he says, then lifts her up, setting her on her booted feet. "If memory serves, she likes taking turns."

She faces me, her brown eyes wide and brimming with arousal, her expression saying *please take your turn.*

"Go to the window." I point.

The stadium isn't quite empty yet, but close enough. She starts to tug down her skirt.

I shake my head. "No. Leave it up. I want to look at that perfect ass as you go."

"Okay," she says, her voice feathery. She walks down the steps, reaches the window, and looks back at us.

"Hands up."

She slides her palms up the glass. Then waits. I don't go to her yet. I cross my arms and enjoy the view. Aubrey Emerson, copper hair falling down her back, jean skirt rucked up, ass exposed, creamy pale flesh on display for her men.

"Yes, this is a motherfucking date," I say, then stalk down to her, cup her face, and claim her mouth right as I smack her ass.

She yelps into my kiss. It's such a rush, her reaction to kissing and spanking. I swat her other ass cheek, and she kisses me even more greedily. I crush my lips to hers, grab her by the flesh, and haul her close. I need her taste, her sounds, her sweet, soft body melting into mine. And I want her to know, too, that we can take care of all her needs.

I break the kiss. "Now go give him a kiss. But kiss him like you love hockey best."

When she turns around, Ledger's right there, dragging her into his arms. I let them have their kiss since she's sinking into it, whimpering against him.

A few seconds later, I bark out, "That's enough."

They break apart. We move to the corner of the suite. "Now, listen, sweet thing," I say, tugging her against me while he stands behind her, playing with her hair.

I spread my hand over her mound, then inch it lower. She quivers under my touch. "I fucking missed you. I need to show you how much," I say "Ledger, you want to help me out? Get these off her, maybe?" I pluck at her panties.

"Yeah, I want to see her beautiful ass. All of it. That sweet pussy too," he says as he slides the undies down her legs, then helps her step out of them.

Aubrey's breath comes in soft little puffs of desire. Of anticipation. When her undies are off, Ledger brings them to his nose.

Her eyes pop as she watches him inhale her. I slide a hand between her soft thighs and indulge in my favorite thing—my sweet, slick girl.

"She's already so fucking wet for us," I say to Ledger, who seems to be getting high on her scent.

Then he stuffs the panties in his pocket, moves

behind Aubrey, and palms her ass. "Because she loves it when we play with her."

"I do," she says breathily as I stroke her slick heat.

"I missed this mouth," I say, then kiss those lush lips. Her taste goes to my head. Lip gloss and mint. Her desire goes to my dick as I coast my fingers through her wetness.

It's too much and never enough. I'm so high on her in seconds. I break the kiss, drinking in her lust-struck expression. "I missed the way you look when you get so worked up for us," I say.

"Missed you two touching me, looking at me, toying with me," she rasps out, rocking her pussy into my fingers then arching her ass against his hands.

Back and forth, him and me.

"That's our girl. Needing her men to get her off," I say.

Ledger dips his face to her neck, murmuring, "You deserve double the pleasure, honey. You give so much of yourself to us."

"I want you both to have me," she murmurs as she seeks her pleasure, rocking faster against my fingers, her mouth parting, her head falling back. "I need you both."

"I fucking know you do," Ledger says, coaxing her along.

"And we need you, sweet thing." I brush my lips over hers, hungry for her. "Need you so much."

She moves, fearlessly, freely between the two of us. Making it crystal clear she missed *this*, missed us— what we give her together.

"Let's remind our girl how good we can be to her," I say to Ledger, but the message is for Aubrey.

Everything's for Aubrey as I slide my fingers across her clit until she breaks apart in my arms. Then, as she's gasping, Ledger moves around her, gets down on his knees, and pushes her against the wall. She's grabbing his face, dragging him against her pussy as she tips her chin toward me, begging for a kiss.

I move in next to her, kiss her face, her jaw, her hair while he wrings another orgasm from her in mere minutes. When she comes down, she's gasping and moaning, then smiling as she whispers, "I've missed you so much."

I look her in the eyes. "Good." Then I cup her jaw, tug her to me. "Now say it."

Her brow knits. "Say what?"

"What you said when they scored a touchdown. Say it for us."

With a loopy smile, she murmurs, "Yes, baby."

"That'll do," Ledger says, and we leave.

We make our way to my car in the nearby parking lot, when a whimpering in the alley catches my attention. Then a scrabbling of paws.

A second later, we reach the source of the noise. A little black-and-white pup is pawing at an empty carton of takeout food. He's not wearing a collar, and he's skinny and dirty.

When he turns to us, he looks hungry and hopeful.

56

THE THIRD MAN

Aubrey

"I'm soaking wet!" Ledger shouts, but there's laughter in his voice, booming through my little apartment.

"Well, yeah. Dogs shake," I say.

"That's clear," he says, then peels off his shirt.

Mmm. Nice. I shamelessly stare at his sturdy chest while keeping my hands on the wiggly, wet body in the tub. "And I don't mind that dogs shake," I say.

"I'd strip, too, if I wasn't busy helping this little dude be presentable," Dev says. He's kneeling on the floor of my tiny bathroom, scrunched in front of the world's smallest tub, giving this puppy a bath.

I snap my focus back to the critter.

As I spray the nozzle over the wily guy, who's maybe fifteen pounds, Dev scrubs some more of my cruelty-free tropical paradise shampoo into the pup's short-haired coat. The dog was more black and gray when we found him. Now he's gleaming.

But he's no fan of getting clean. The little guy whines, then rears up on his back paws, hell-bent on scrambling out of the tub. His black-and-white legs reach the edge, then he hoists himself up and onto Dev's chest.

The goalie wraps his arms around the sopping wet, soaped-up mutt of all mutts, and hugs the busy boy. "It's all right. I've got you."

Deep, but soft. Commanding, but caring.

There goes my heart. It thunders as the burly, bearded man embraces the homeless dog and then gently sets him back in the tub. "Let's just get you rinsed off," he says to the new guy, and I'm almost too fluttery to focus on the task.

But I manage, spraying the dog till he's spick and span and both Dev and I are as waterlogged as Ledger. My sweater is dripping. Dev's burgundy Henley is sticking to his pecs and abs.

When I turn off the water, Ledger snort-laughs at the two of us. "Join the club," he says, then holds out his arms with a towel draped across them. Dev hands him the dog and Ledger wraps the dry, fluffy towel around the canine. "There you go, buddy," Ledger coos.

My heart flip-flops again.

Ledger stands and carries the pup out of the cramped bathroom, drying his head, then his belly, then carefully blotting each paw.

I follow him, plucking at my wet sweater.

There's not much room in my home, and every square inch is filled with wet dog, big men, and me.

After rubbing the towel down the dog's bony spine one last time, Ledger puts our new companion on the floor. The pup shakes again, leaving a huge circle of water droplets on the tiles.

"How does he have any more water on him?" Ledger sounds amused and a little bit in love.

I get it.

"He was a dirty boy," Dev says, crouching down and offering the dog a palm for sniffing.

Nervously at first, then boldly, the boy scampers over to Dev, then downward dogs him, shaking his butt, gone from scared to friendly in a few hours.

On the way home with the dog, we'd stopped at a grocery store and grabbed some kibble, a collar, and some dog toys. It's one a.m., too late to call Little Friends, but I'll do that in the morning, see if he's someone's dog who got out. For now, the pup runs around my kitchen, then barks at the bowl where we fed him earlier.

It's empty now. "Maybe he's hoping he can conjure more food into it," Ledger says.

"He needs a dog butler," Dev jokes, then looks my way. "He needs a—"

"Fitzgibbons," we say in unison.

Dev scratches him under the furry chin and nods to Ledger. "Give this boy some more kibble, will ya?"

Ledger grabs the bag, shakes some nuggets into the ceramic dish with the paw-prints pattern, and then returns the bag to the counter while our sleepover guest chows down.

I head to my bedroom to strip off my soaked clothes and tug on some sleep shorts and a cami.

I haven't technically invited the guys over, and though it seems a fait accompli, I've been learning that words are actions. They matter. When I return to the living room, my guys are yawning, so I hook my thumb in the direction of my bedroom. "There's only one bed here, but I think it can fit all of us."

Ledger grins. "I bet it can."

A few minutes later, I'm under the covers with Ledger. Dev's in the bathroom, brushing his teeth. "Well, looks like you two finagled a sleepover pretty quickly," I say.

Ledger scoffs. "Don't put it past us to pull out all the stops to get one. But no, we didn't plan a dog rescue to get into your bed," he says, then slides closer to me.

But a dog rescue is doing things to my heart. "How's your knee? I've been wondering. Been thinking about you."

A smile tilts his lips briefly, then he inhales deeply to answer, "It's okay."

"Does it hurt when you skate?"

"Sometimes. Sometimes it hurts when I don't skate. Mostly it doesn't."

"Is that good?" I ask, trying to read between the lines and determine if he's really okay.

"I'm good. Don't worry about me."

But I do worry. I stare at him with the same intensity he gives to me. "Are you being Stern Brunch Daddy?"

"Maybe. But you love that." He swipes a finger down my cheek.

"Ledger," I implore.

"Trust me. I feel good, especially right now."

My heart cartwheels. "I don't want you to get hurt though."

He pushes up onto an elbow. "I know you don't." He comes in for a brief, hot kiss. "And I can't tell you how much that means to me." He pulls back and meets my gaze with vulnerable blue eyes. "My dad wants me to go into the broadcast booth with him when I retire."

Oh. I hadn't even realized that was an option. "Do you want to?"

"I haven't told him I'm retiring." He drags a hand across his hair. This is hard for him. I set a palm on his chest so he can feel my support.

"Maybe you're not ready to tell him yet."

His soft laugh stirs the air. "Yeah, I'm definitely not. I'll need to soon though. I saw him before the season started, and he mentioned working with him. It's my last year on the ice, and I couldn't tell my dad." Another pause, the kind where it's clear he's deep in thought. "Aubrey?"

"Yes?"

"I don't know what I want to do when I retire." It must be a hard thing to say, but he sounds utterly relieved to have said it.

I meet his gaze again. "That's okay."

"Yeah?"

I nod. "Yeah. Maybe you'll just...take time off."

A smile shifts his lips. "Maybe I will."

It sounds like he's giving himself permission at last to think differently. He drops another kiss to my forehead. "I wanted to tell you all that for a while."

"I'm glad you did," I say, then pause. "Are you still having nightmares?"

"Not as often. Actually, a whole lot less. I think you were right. I was just working through stuff."

"You sound like you're coming out on the other side."

"I think I am." He slides his hand down my arm, clasps his fingers around my wrist. "I didn't realize how much I wanted to see you at my games till you started showing up. Seeing you in the stands..."

My heart stutters as he trails off, the words clearly hard for him to say. I get that. He's a man who's been burned before. He's a man who's closed himself off. But he's also a man who's demanded the best from himself his whole life. Whose family expected the best from him too.

And he's a man who possibly no longer wants the life that's been ordained for him. "I'll be there," I say.

"Yeah?" His voice sounds like it contains all the hope in his heart.

"Yes."

He squeezes my wrist, his fingers encircling it.

Before my heart performs an entire uneven bars routine, I hear Dev's footsteps, and he pointedly clears his throat. "Hello? Did you forget about Puck Fitzgibbons?"

The other shirtless man in my home bends and scoops up the dog from the floor beside the bed. I laugh and Ledger snorts, letting go of my wrist.

"You already named him?" Ledger asks Dev.

"Dude. He needs a name," Dev says defensively, then sets the precious cargo down on the mattress, not even asking me if he's welcome in the bed.

Because Dev knows me. *Of course* the dog is welcome.

The mutt seems to know it, too, bounding up the bed then whining tentatively for my attention. I stroke his soft snout till he sighs and then curls into a dog ball by my side. "He might be someone's dog," I point out.

"We do need to see if someone is looking for him," Ledger adds.

Dev rolls his eyes. "Dude is skinny, hungry, and collarless."

"But he might have gotten out a few days ago," I say.

Dev turns on his side and pets the dog. "Puck, did you get out, or were you looking for Aubrey?"

Ledger drops his face into the crook of my neck, chuckling. "There's no way you're not keeping this dog."

I sort of knew that the second we found him, but I take issue with one word. "You mean *we*."

When Ledger lifts his face, he smiles softly. "Yes. *We*."

I let that sink in for a little bit—the ease of the *we*. The comfort of it. The way we all seem to know that a year became two months. That a first date is only the beginning. That this is us. "You know, the place where I used to live didn't allow dogs," I say, musing on the seemingly random as I pet the new bedmate.

"But this place does?" Dev asks with some concern.

"Yes. Definitely. One of the reasons I moved here. But then Aiden was allergic..."

Another pause. Another contented sigh from Ledger. Another pet of the pooch from Dev.

"Looks like it all worked out," Ledger says.

Maybe it did. Like Trina said, sometimes time is just time. It doesn't have to flow perfectly. It doesn't have to line up according to rules. Life is short and real love doesn't come around often. If you don't grab it, it might pass you by.

Ledger falls asleep first, like he always does. I turn to Dev, who's petting the dog. "Damn, you fall fast." I've never seen someone bond so quickly with an animal. "Even faster than me."

He meets my gaze, his green eyes flickering with heat and vulnerability. "Yes. I fell a long time ago."

My breath catches. My skin tingles. "You did?"

He nods solemnly. "I did."

My neck is warm. My insides are melting. "Really?"

He slides a thumb along my jaw. "Yes, really."

"That's why you said you'd wait for me?"

He shakes his head. "No. I fell for you before that week. During that week, I knew you were worth waiting for."

So much for going slow. I'm not sure I can now either. I lean in to give him a quick, firm kiss. When I break it, I say, "How are you feeling about the season? I know you want it to be the best."

"I do. But that's not the only thing I want now," he says.

The dog breathes evenly against my neck as I drift off after my first date with my two men. I'm pretty sure I fell in love with them while we were together on the honeymoon.

And then I fell a little more while we were apart.

57

THE HOT VET

Aubrey

"Let's see if this guy has a home," the calm vet says.

I bring my clenched fist to my mouth, offering a prayer to the universe as Doctor Lennox runs the scanner along the dog's scruff, hunting for signs he has a home.

It's only been a few seconds, but I can barely take it. "Does he have an owner?" I blurt.

"Yeah, what's the word, Doc?" Dev stares at the microchip scanner so intently he could burn a hole in it.

Ledger reaches for my hand and squeezes it. His steadiness settles my nerves. I need his steadiness just like I need Dev's exuberance.

Doctor Lennox pets Puck Fitzgibbons' head. I mean, the dog's head. The potentially-owned dog's head who I shouldn't keep calling by the name I might not be entitled to give him.

"I'm checking. Sometimes these microchips roll around," Doctor Lennox says, cool and confident, and friendly as he talks to the dog. "What's your story, little buddy? You gonna tell me?"

I have no chill. "Tell us." I can hear the desperation in my tone.

"They're a little eager, Doc," Ledger adds while rubbing my arm.

"I can tell." Doctor Lennox turns off the scanner and looks up from the table. The vet has golden brown hair, fair skin, a trim beard, and kind eyes. He's empirically good-looking, the hot vet and all, but all I can think is *I need dog details now. Right now.*

"He's not microchipped," he announces, and it's like he's telling new parents, *Your baby is healthy.*

I beam, I soar, I fly. "That's great," I say. Or maybe I shout it.

Dev spins to face me. "Can you keep him?" Then, before I answer, he turns back to the vet. "Can she keep him? Can we keep him?"

He's plowing through the pronouns, but the change to *we* isn't lost on me.

"You might want to check with Little Friends next door and make sure no one has listed him as missing," Doctor Lennox says.

Dev nods, turning serious. "Right, right. That's our plan. We're already going over there next."

"Good, because if he were my dog, I'd be looking for him," the vet adds.

"Do you have a dog?" I can't resist asking about people's pets.

"I have two."

"Are they microchipped?" I ask, when I really want to shake him and say, "Tell me my dog would be microchipped if he belonged to someone."

"Yes, neutered and spayed, microchipped, and they have GPS trackers. I kind of like them," he confesses in a whisper. "The dogs."

"You picked a good profession," I say. "We'll stop in at Little Friends. But otherwise, how is he? Is he healthy? What is he? How old is he? How big will he get?"

I have a million more questions, but I hold them back as the doctor studies Puck Fitzgibbons, who's sitting on his little butt on the table now, behaving like a good boy. He's black and white—with black socks and white gloves, a harlequin face, and a standard-size snout. He's strong for a little critter. The vet runs a palm down the pup's haunches. "I'd say he's a cocktail. Some Border Collie. Some Chihuahua. Some hound."

Ledger pats the dog's head. "I'm not a vet, but it sounds like you're just covering your bases there."

The vet's eyes twinkle. "I am." He scratches the dog's chin. "You're a good boy."

"And you're a good vet." I catch the doctor's eyes and say sincerely, "You saved my friend Trina's dog a couple years ago."

"Nacho, right?"

"Yes, that's him."

"The goodest three-legged dog around. That was quite a story when he ate those panties," he says.

"It sure was," I say.

* * *

Five days that feel like five years later, Little Friends has good news. Puck Fitzgibbons is mine. Or ours, really. Both guys are out of town at games, but I text them right away.

> Aubrey: Puck has a new home.

> Dev: Yes, he does.

> Ledger: And you will soon too.

I think I know what he means. But I don't even feel rushed from the veiled suggestion.

Over the next few weeks, we see each other as often as we can, given our schedules. We're dating, and somehow, it's all working out. In fact, it's going so well that a few weeks later, when they're at practice and I'm walking my cocktail dog, I text Trina and Ivy and ask them to join me on a special errand this weekend.

58

GAME TIME

Ledger

December...

I'm not a superstitious guy. But lately, since Aubrey's been coming to the games, I've become a man of habit. When I hit the ice, I look to the stands, find her in her usual seat, then wrap my gloved hand around my other wrist ever so briefly.

A sign. Just for her.

She wraps her right hand around her left wrist, making the gesture back.

Then I play my heart out. Not for a place in the hall of fame, or for the next phase of my career, or for a top rank in the sport.

Just because...I love the game.

Tonight, when the puck drops, that's how I play. The crowd roars as we win the face-off, then as I move fast and aggressively down the ice, weaving in and out of the Phoenix defense, angling for the puck.

I miss the first shot.

But so does Chase when it's his turn.

I grit my teeth, narrowing in on the opportunities with every line change, dodging the bloodthirsty D-men on the other team. Then, near the end of the first period, Chase spots an opening and passes to me, and just like that, I'm flying on a breakaway. My heart rate speeds up as I get closer to the net.

The bite of blades cutting through ice echoes off the walls of the rink as I race toward the goal with the black disc. As soon as the puck leaves my stick, thunderous applause erupts.

And I choose to enjoy every moment of the goal.

* * *

Later, after the game ends with our victory, I leave the locker room hoping to meet my girl in the hallway, but someone cuts me off.

My father.

My shoulders tighten.

Of course he's here. He broadcast the game tonight for the national network. He's in his tailored navy-blue suit, no tie, his affable smile pasted on.

Tension slams into me, hard and brutal.

"Great game tonight," he says, then claps me on the back.

Why the fuck am I so tense? He's only ever wanted the best for me.

But maybe that's the issue. After years of wanting the best, I'm just not that interested in it anymore.

"Hey, Dad," I answer, glancing down the hall to the redhead in the white knit cap who has my heart in her fucking hands.

"Have you given any more thought to my suggestion? We can do a trial run at the house in my media room. Call some past games from YouTube for practice. Really make a go of it, so whenever you're ready, we'll get you a plum assignment in the booth."

Damn, he has my future all mapped out.

I look to Aubrey, ten feet away, wearing my jersey. I don't answer his question. Instead, I raise a *hold that thought* finger, "Be right back."

I close the distance to her, my tension melting. "Come meet my dad. Well, come meet him again. Okay?"

"Sure," she says with a smile.

That's how things are with her. Easy. I've never felt so understood. So accepted.

I take her hand and bring her over to the man whose career has defined mine. "Dad, this is Aubrey. You probably remember her. Garrett's little sister," I say, threading our fingers together more tightly.

"Good to see you again, Mr. McBride," she says, as friendly as ever.

Dad doesn't miss a beat. "And you too. Garrett's doing great. Making deals. He's a terrific agent. Bet his little girls grow up to be hockey players too." He's always focused on business, the next thing, the big opportunities for everyone.

Aubrey's smile is guileless. "Or maybe they'll be farmers. Or pilots. Or museum security guards. You never know."

He blinks. He's not used to being told he might not know everything. But that's my girl. She knows there's more to someone than an expectation. She knows there's always a choice.

"Maybe," he says as if he's not sure what to make of her. He looks to me, decisive again. "We can talk more about the offer another time."

Actually, we can't.

"No thanks," I say, surprising myself by the strength of my conviction.

His brow knits. "No thanks?"

"I don't want to be a broadcaster." The statement feels like freedom.

"You don't?"

Aubrey squeezes my hand, saying, *Way to go,* without words.

"Nah," I say. "I don't want to work in hockey when I'm done." That feels wholly true too.

Another blink. Another awkward silence, then Dad tilts his head. It's like life without hockey is completely alien to him. "What *do* you want to do?"

"No idea. We can talk about it more later." I give him a quick hug. "Good to see you, Dad. But, if you'll excuse me, I'm heading out with my girlfriend."

Then I leave with the woman I adore.

The woman who makes me better. Stronger. Calmer.

I steal glances at her the whole of the drive to her home. Dev's out of town, so it's just us this evening. I love our time together as a trio, but I love time alone with her too.

Though, we're not truly alone. Puck Fitzgibbons is bouncing against the walls when we get home. He whines happily when Aubrey opens the door then whimpers as he jumps to greet her, then me, with kisses all around.

"You are such a lover," Aubrey says, and I fall even more at the way she talks to our dog.

After we walk Puck Fitzgibbons, I show her how much I love my solo time with her, spending a good long time stripping off her clothes, laying her on the bed, and kissing my way down her body, starting with her earlobe. Then, I move to her chin. The hollow of her throat comes next.

The valley of her breasts.

Her soft belly.

One hip, then the other.

She's writhing, arching, panting, and I haven't even settled between her thighs yet. But I can't deny her. I bury my face in her pussy and devour her sweetness till she's coming hard and fearlessly.

Then I put her on her hands and knees and fuck her and spank her, giving her the good hard fucking she deserves.

I want to tell her soon she's the love of my life. I hope she's ready to hear that.

But while I like to do some things alone with her, there are others that involve all of us. Which means I need Dev's road trip to end really fucking soon.

* * *

Two nights later, we gather at Dev's place. He's just returned to town and he's *seriously hungry and can't wait to eat.*

His words.

I'm drinking a scotch as Aubrey plates the dish Dev's been cooking. It's some new chickpea, kale, and tofu number that's making my mouth water thanks to the rosemary in it.

"I'm still amazed you can cook," Aubrey says, clearly impressed with his kitchen prowess.

He turns off the stove, then he wraps an arm around her waist. "Woman, I've got lots of skills. Haven't I told you?"

I scoff. "Only five hundred times."

"Can't wait to try *your* dinner," he retorts, knowing full well I can't cook for shit.

"Fair enough," I concede.

We sit at the counter and tuck in. The food makes my taste buds sing, and I moan in culinary delight. "Turns out I don't mind having a chef," I say.

He lifts his fork. "I wouldn't mind having someone to take out the trash. You game?"

"Boys, boys," Aubrey says as if breaking up a fight. "There are enough chores to go around. Just like there's enough of me. You simply have to take turns."

"Your favorite thing to do," I say, leaning in to kiss her cheek.

"It sure is," Dev says, kissing her other cheek.

As we eat, I'm still thinking about the conversation with my dad at the stadium the other night. I'm glad I told Aubrey my decision about post-hockey life, but if we're doing this thing—this throuple thing—I can't leave out one third of us. I need to tell my friend.

I set down my fork and look my buddy in the eyes. "I told my dad I didn't want to go into the booth with him."

"Damn!" Dev seems briefly surprised before he offers a fist for knocking. "Excellent."

There. It's that simple with Dev. Some things are, and for that I am grateful.

Aubrey lifts her glass of wine. "While we're at it, I told my mom I never wanted to marry Aiden in the first place."

Dev whistles, looking from her to me. "Look at you two being all emotionally adjusted and shit. I almost feel left out." He strokes his chin like he's deep in thought. "Do I have something *I* need to tell my parents?"

I laugh. "No, dude. You'd worked through all your emotional baggage by the time you were ten."

But he stays strangely quiet, unusually serious.

Later that evening, while Aubrey's sending birthday emails to clients, I leash up the dog and then motion for Dev to join me for a quick walk.

"There's something I did talk to my mom about last week," he begins. "Something I want to do for Aubrey."

He tells me his idea, and the nice thing about falling in love with the same woman is that you can make plans for her together.

59

DATE MATH

Aubrey

This is the way to wake up.

To scruff against my neck. To a hungry groan. To a request. Well, a demand, really.

"Sit on my face, baby," Dev says.

I stretch and then rise up. "Since it's an order."

Dev growls, pats his bare shoulders. "It is. Fuck my face. Do it now."

Ledger's not in bed, but I wouldn't ask his permission anyway. The three of us made a deal long ago so that there's no jealousy. Some nights, Ledger fucks me. Some mornings, Dev does. Most of the time they both do.

I slide off my panties but leave on my plain white cami as I straddle him. Dev grabs my hips and tugs me down. I ride him like a cowgirl till I'm falling apart on his mouth, his beard, his desire for me.

A desire that feels a lot like love.

So much so that when I disappear that morning to meet my girls and finish the errand I started a few weeks ago, I know I'm not making a mistake.

*　*　*

That afternoon as I leave No Regrets, the tattoo shop, my arm's a little sore, but not much. Trina and Ivy sat with me the whole time, like good friends do. When we arrive at my apartment, I fetch the dog, take him around the block, then hand him off to them, giving Puck Fitzgibbons a scratch on his chin before I toss on a dove-gray hoodie over my tank and meet the guys at Dev's place.

We hop into Dev's electric car, and the three of us cruise over the Golden Gate Bridge, heading north past Marin County, winding our way into Wine Country like we did that September day when my life was upended.

The best thing that ever happened to me was Aiden walking away. Now, I'm walking into something better with two men.

But first, I'm walking into Beverly's diner. The guys picked this spot and said they wanted to take me here. Once inside, the woman who runs it flashes me a grin like she knows me. "Hey, you! You're not in your wedding dress today?"

"Good memory. But nope. Just my regular clothes," I say with a smile I feel all the way to my soul.

"Well, you look pretty in jeans and a hoodie. Let me

get you your table," she says, then guides us to the very same spot we once sat.

After we open our menus, I say to the guys, "Is this your date math at play?"

Ledger nods. "Yup. Since this was definitely our first date."

No one argues with him on his two plus twos this time.

After we order and Beverly retreats to the kitchen, Dev clears his throat. "And speaking of date math, we don't want it to be our last one."

I lift a curious brow. "Last one? Why would it be?"

His expression is serious. No joking.

I turn deadly serious, too. "Okay."

I don't know where we're going but my heart is already racing. My pulse surges again when Ledger chucks off his jacket, reaching into the inside pocket as he does. He takes out a box from Elodie's Chocolates.

Ah. I get it now. They do love to spoil me with chocolate. "My favorite," I say, feeling all fizzy for them. The last time they gave me chocolate was the start of our honeymoon.

"Open it," Ledger says, a bit stiffly, as if this is uncomfortable for him.

Curious, I undo the bow with excited fingers. But when I open the box, I don't know what to make of the treats.

There are five pieces, each in the shape of a number.

I do the math. It's the date of the football game last

month. "It's when we got back together," I say, pleased I figured it out.

Dev shakes his head. "Yes, it's the date of the football game, but it's also the code to my home."

Ledger leans closer to me, holding my gaze. "*Your* code."

My heart flutters. "I love it."

Dev shakes his head again. "Aubrey. It's a permanent code. We want you to live with us. I want us all to live together. Move in with me," he says, eyes locked with mine, full of vulnerability and hope. "Ledger will move in too. We can all be together with you. And Puck Fitzgibbons, as well."

My heart stops. The hair on my arms stands on end.

I knew this was coming. I knew it was coming a month ago, yet it's still more thrilling than I'd expected. Maybe I didn't entirely believe it would happen. After last summer and all the expectations I placed on myself, all the expectations I took on, right or wrong, I've been reluctant to put more on us.

But Dev and Ledger exceeded all my dreams with their offer. "You do?" I want to be sure I'm not imagining this.

"Yes. I want us to be together. I want to cook for you. And walk the dog with you in the morning. And see you after games, and when you come home from work. I want to hear about your clients, and your boss, and your book club."

Ledger reaches for my hand with a smile that says he has something to add. "I want the same. Because I love you, honey."

My throat catches.

Dev reaches for my other hand. "I love you so damn much."

Here, where we began, I'm between my two men, starting a whole new chapter before I expected to. But I have zero doubts. I'm ready. There is no second guessing. No voices in my head telling me to run away. All I want is to stay.

"I love you," I say to Dev, then to Ledger, "and I love you."

I take off my hoodie. I'm wearing a tank top. My right arm is bare.

Dev's eyes widen. "That's gorgeous."

"I got a new tattoo," I whisper, and I'm a little giddy for them to check out the dainty, delicate script on my shoulder.

Dev traces the air near my ink with his finger, as if he's outlining each of the five letters. "Baby," he says to me reverently, his tone telling me how he feels.

I shift to Ledger, showing it off to my other man. He drops an air kiss to each word.

A commitment to them.

All in.

EPILOGUE
TAKING TURNS

Aubrey

A week later, I move in. I sublease my little apartment to another stylist who wants to stay close to the salon.

It's like it was meant to be. I move my books and candles and lotions and potions and more hair products than anyone else in the city owns—count 'em—and a few pieces of furniture and all my clothes.

Doesn't take me long to settle in. I hang up my clothes by color, and I organize Puck Fitzgibbons' jackets in the mudroom the same way.

That night, after the pup settles into a dog bed and Calico Jack climbs to the top of his cat tower to enjoy his one-eyed view of the city at night, Dev, Ledger, and I head to the kitchen to break open a bottle of champagne.

This one isn't on Aiden. It's on Chase and Ryker and

Stefan and Hayes. "*Welcome to the double-team team,*" their note says.

After we toast, Ledger roams his eyes up and down my body. "I'm wondering how this really tastes..."

A few minutes later, I'm on a big towel on the couch in the living room, and he's licking champagne off my back, then the top of my ass.

When he flips me over, Dev gets in on the action, pouring some on my tits, then licking it off each one.

Soon, I'm squirming and wildly aroused, but they keep pouring more on me. Ledger leaves drops on my nipples for Dev to suck off. Dev pours some on my belly for Ledger to lick.

A drop slides down between my thighs.

They fight for it. But I hold up a hand. "Take turns, boys."

They both growl. But then they take turns with me.

Ledger manhandles the fuck out of me, yanking me off the couch and bending me over the edge of it. He presses a firm, strong hand to my back. "Just like this," he says coarsely, then takes out his cock and fills me to the hilt.

No protection this time. We've had the talk, and we've all been tested, and I'm on birth control.

With me bent over, he grabs my hair in his fist, my ass cheek in the other hand. Then he fucks me to a screaming orgasm while Dev leaves the room for a few minutes, then returns to down a glass of champagne as I finish.

I'm panting and moaning when Dev hauls me onto the couch, puts me on my hands and knees, and gets behind me. He fucks me like a wild man, just the way I like it.

Yeah, I think I like living with my guys as much as I like when they take turns.

* * *

One evening after work in January, I find Trina waiting for me outside the salon, a scarf wrapped around her neck, a cute red hat on her head. She doesn't have an appointment, but I'm always happy to see her.

"Want to grab a drink? I have a proposition for you," she says.

"Ooh, baby. I love it when you talk dirty to me."

She leans in and whispers, "It's definitely a little dirty."

Color me intrigued.

We head to Sticks and Stones, and over a glass of wine, she draws a deep breath and says, "I want to open a romance-only bookstore. I'd like to call it Once Upon A Good Time. There's a block on Fillmore Street that has some spaces. And," she says, and her words are shaky with excitement, "one of them is perfect for a little hair salon. Right next door. We'd be neighbors and it could be a combo bookstore/hair salon. We could call our pair of stores Books and Beauty, and market them together. What do you think?"

My jaw falls open. I'm not even sure what to think, except running a business with my bestie sounds like another dream I didn't know I had. But now it's one I desperately want to come true. Bronze has always been supportive. He's said he thinks I could run my own place someday. Maybe that someday is now.

"And I think I know how I can pay for it," I say.

* * *

That weekend, I'm in a jewelry shop. A silver-haired man with crinkled eyes peers through a loupe at my engagement ring. "Big spender." He whistles.

I furrow my brow. No way was Aiden generous in the ring department. "He said it was maybe worth a few thousand. But he was just guessing," I say. "He picked it up at an estate sale and didn't see the point in checking the value since he said it was such a good deal."

I'm hoping the value of this ring and some of my savings on apartment rent might be enough for me to pay for the first few months of a salon lease.

The man looks my way with the loupe still in his eye. A sly smile curves his lips. "Your ex-fiancé is a dingleberry. He should have had it appraised. But his loss."

I might love this man. "Why?" I ask, holding onto the display case, eager to hear the real value.

He lowers his voice even though it's only us in the shop. "The cut and clarity are excellent." Then he tells me the value. I nearly stumble. It's several times what Aiden *guessed*. "He didn't know what this was worth."

Story of Aiden's life.

My grin turns electric. "And it's all mine."

* * *

That night, neither of my guys has a hockey game, so the three of us take Puck Fitzgibbons, who's a whopping twenty-seven pounds of energizer dog now, to the park. As I toss him a frisbee, I tell the guys about the place I want to turn into a salon. "It has brick walls, which I love. But I'd install black sinks and silver mirrors to mix a homey and a modern feel."

"It sounds perfect," Ledger says.

"It is." Then, I hesitate. "The only issue is it's a small space. I always imagined a slightly bigger salon. But it'll be fine for my first salon. I think if it's just me and one other booth, I can make the rent for the place. *I think.*"

At least that's what I tell myself.

"And this is what you want?" Dev asks as if he wants to be absolutely certain.

I weigh his question, but the reality is it just feels right—in my gut. And I've been learning to trust my gut. "I do want it."

"You should go for it," Ledger says.

"You absolutely should," Dev echoes.

I cherish their support.

* * *

A few weeks later, Trina and I are working to finalize the deal. I'm crunching numbers over Saturday morning coffee at the kitchen counter when an email lands on my phone.

My heart drops like an anchor as I read the disappointing email from the landlord. Last night, he writes, he got a better offer on the lease for the little space. But there's real estate on the other side of the bookstore which is a lot bigger and could be retrofitted. I could rent that one, he suggests. But it's much more expensive.

That sounds too daunting, and I definitely don't have the money for a bigger space.

"Maybe it wasn't meant to be," I tell the guys as they grab their water bottles before heading to the gym for a morning workout.

"But you liked the space," Dev says, annoyed on my behalf.

"It was perfect for you," Ledger adds, equally irritated.

"I did and that's true." I shrug sadly. "But what can you do?"

Two hours later, they come home, but they're not sweaty. "Did you not work out?" I ask, eyeing them up and down.

Ledger smiles like a cat and shakes his head. "Nope."

"We made a deal instead," Dev adds, his eyes twinkling.

"What did you do?" I ask, a little giddy, a little nervous.

Ledger reaches for my hand. "We'll show you."

I leash up my pup and the four of us head down Jackson Street to Fillmore. We turn onto the busy shopping street and weave through Saturday crowds until we reach the empty block.

There are three spaces here. The little potential salon, the bookstore space, and the bigger potential salon.

They stop in front of the planned bookstore. The small place that would have been my own salon mocks me. But the bigger spot on the other side? It is huge, and also too big for my little wallet.

Ledger takes a deep breath. "We bought them both," he says. "Both spaces next to the bookstore."

My head spins, and I stutter, "You did?" They can't be serious.

Ledger's smile is sweet, a little unsure. "When you mentioned the bigger space this morning, everything clicked. I had a wild idea, and you can say no. I swear you can say no, honey," he assures me. He sounds so vulnerable but so excited too. "We saw the landlord an hour ago and made an offer he couldn't refuse for both places. The little space and the bigger one. I thought this one"—he gestures to the big place—"would be a perfect hair salon for you. And the little one? That seems perfect for an ex-hockey player who wants to try his hand at running a plant shop."

My hand flies to my mouth, then I let go and jump into his arms. "That's so perfect for you. I love it. And I love you. You have to do it. I insist. I insist so hard."

"But if you want more space and don't want to work next to me, I'll find another place in the city," he says, clearly wanting to make sure this works for me.

But it does. Oh yes, it does.

"We want you to have the space next to your friend, though," Dev puts in. "So we bought them both."

I hug Ledger tighter then let go and throw my arms around Dev. "I love you guys so much."

When I break the embrace, Ledger still looks unsure, his smile tentative. "If you don't want to work close to me, it's fine, Aubrey. I get it."

I swat his arm. "I do. I really, really do."

I can picture it now. My salon next to my best friend's bookstore next to my guy's brand-new plant shop.

* * *

A few months later, a neon sign in bright, bold pink lights up the front of my salon, reading *Hello, Gorgeous*. It's right next to the fabulous bookstore Once Upon A Good Time. On the other side is the cutest plant shop in the city—Welcome to the Jungle.

It's my favorite block in San Francisco.

Especially when the first day is bustling, and Ledger sells more succulents, prayer plants, and ferns than he'd ever expected.

When the clock hits closing time, we lock up and head together to the arena. His team is out of playoff contention, but the Golden State Foxes aren't. Ledger and I have on our matching jerseys, and we're going to cheer on our favorite goalie.

When Dev wins that night, advancing to the next round, the whole crew celebrates at Sticks and Stones. As our friends head off to play a round of pool, Dev wraps an arm around me. "We have another gift for you."

"You really do spoil me," I say, chiding him, but not really.

"We do," Ledger says, then hands me a card.

I open it. There's a gift certificate they made, and it says, "For a lifetime of adventures."

The start is in June, when we return to Vancouver to finish the trip we started last year.

Then go on to have many, many more.

And I say yes with no reservations.

THE END

Can't get enough of Aubrey, Dev and Ledger? Scroll below for access to an exclusive bonus scene of their life together, then binge the rest of the series FREE in KU!
Double Pucked: (Trina + Chase and Ryker)
Puck Yes: (Ivy + Stefan and Hayes)

Also, I have a surprise! Everyone's favorite bartender is getting a romance! Gage's story is coming in The Almost Romantic, a spicy standalone single dad marriage of convenience romance coming to KU in March! And stay tuned for Briar's romance with a couple of hot hockey hunks in Well And Truly Pucked!

Click here for the Thoroughly Pucked Bonus Epilogue! Or scan this QR code!

EXCERPT - PLAYS WELL WITH OTHERS

Rachel

Where are my lucky spatulas? I swear they were in *this* box in the corner of the kitchen. The one marked *Very Important Things*.

Because my baking supplies are vital. They're therapy, dammit.

Wait.

There's a box next to the stove labeled *VIP Things 1* and a box on the counter designated *VIP Things 2*.

Which one has my spatula in it? And why didn't I label any of these things specifically?

Oh, right. Because I fled Los Angeles faster than a twelve-year-old could stack plastic cups on social media. That, too, was a Very Important Thing.

Now, I'm scrunched in with the boxes in the itty-bitty kitchen of my new townhome in San Francisco, hunting for the necessities of life—spatulas. How can I bake lemon cheesecake blueberry bars for my breakup party tomorrow night without them?

Think, Rachel, think.

I close my eyes, remembering the packing frenzy last week in my Venice Beach home, seeing clothes flying, hearing the screech of packing tape, feeling the skittering of my pulse. The ink was finally dry on my divorce papers, but the news of the birth of my ex's newest child was still fresh in my head. I couldn't spend any more time in Los Angeles with those painful memories chasing me wherever I went.

Ah! I remember now. I jammed the spatulas into the underwear compartment of my carry-on, in between my new Valentina lacy bra-and-panty set and the scorching-hot burgundy bustier, the one I've vowed to wear...*someday.*

Because *someday soon* is a fool's wish.

I rush to the bedroom, unzip the suitcase, and grab the pretty little kitchen darlings from their place of honor next to the pretty little bedroom darlings.

"There you are," I say, relieved, then I return to the kitchen and set the spatulas down on the counter, pushing aside *Badly Labeled Box 2.* I head to the pantry and grab the flour, sugar, and baking soda.

Thank you, Elodie, for stocking the pantry for me. You're the best friend ever.

I'll bake tonight, but I want to make sure I have everything I need ready now. Carter is coming by soon to help me move heavy objects.

Every gal should have a muscular and helpful guy like Carter to call on to lift things, move things, and carry things.

Also, his shoulder is quite nice to cry on. I'd give it a five out of five for sturdiness and absorbency.

As I sort my baking supplies, I review the day ahead. We'll rearrange the living room so I can have a better view of California Street, and after that, I'll spend the afternoon in my jewelry shop. Fable has been handling the shop while I've been absent, and while she's great, business hasn't been smashing while I've been flying up and down the coast of California, managing two shops. This evening, I'll shut myself off from the world and devote the night to baking and, well, wine.

My shrink will be so proud. She's always advocating self-care, and that sounds like baking and merlot to me.

Now that I have a plan for the day, my pulse starts to settle a skosh—then the doorbell rings.

Oh, shit. Is Carter here already? I glance down at my outfit and cringe. Three-day-old yoga pants and a white T-shirt with a red splotch design that says *Of course it's wine, Officer*. The shirt is courtesy of my friend Hazel. But when I sniff myself, I find I'm desperately in need of a shower, and that's courtesy of me.

I race to the window in my slippers, dodging a peace lily to peer from the second story to the stoop below. Oh! It's the delivery guy from the wine shop.

"Coming!" I shout, even though he's already trotting down the steps to the street. But wine gets lonely quickly, so I leave my townhome, rush down the stairs, and hold open the front door of the building to grab the box.

Tucking it under my arm, I spin around, when my feet go out from under me—

Buttplant.

I wince. There must be grease, or powder, or something on the foyer floor. But I make a quick scan and the floor is pristine.

Great. I slipped on my own enthusiasm for discount wine. But hey, I shielded the wine from harm. The box is still safe and sound in my arm, so I get up, precious cargo in hand, and head up the stairs and back to my townhome, ass aching the whole way.

I set down the goods on the kitchen counter and check my phone. Twenty minutes. Just enough time to look presentable.

Note to self: add showers to your to-do list.

As I hightail it to the bathroom, the device vibrates with a text.

> Elodie: Guess what I got for you?

That's such a trick question. I don't even want to play her guessing game, since I'll get it wrong. But I do love gifts from all my friends fiercely. As I strip off my stinky shirt, I reply.

Rachel: A pony?

Elodie: You're close. Think horses.

Hmm. Does my chocolatier bestie know any hot cowboys to set me up with? A gal can dream. With my phone in one hand, I shimmy off my exercise pants, dictate a reply, then hit send.

Rachel: A date with a hot cowboy who'll ride in on a stallion?

Elodie: *writes down idea for next year's Christmas gift.* Anyway, not that, but you can definitely ride this stallion.

I'm simultaneously excited and terrified as I toss my panties into the nearby hamper.

Rachel: Tell me the make and model!

Elodie: I'd better show you. I'll come by later. Gotta go. Customer here.

And I'll have to add *See Elodie* to my to-do list, but she'll be a bright spot for sure, and after a terrible year (or five, but who's counting), I do enjoy my bright spots. I set the phone down on the vanity, then turn on the water in my spacious rainfall shower—another bright spot in my life. As it heats up, I loop my hair into a bun.

Ten minutes later, after a scalding shower that steams up every surface in the bathroom, my butt no longer aches and I'm fresh as a coconut.

With the tropical bodywash scent filling the little room, I grab a towel. While I dry off, my phone buzzes again. I peer at the device, but the glass is steamed up.

Looks like Elodie's texting again.

I'll write back in just a second. Gotta dry my legs first.

The phone rings.

I sigh, but I'm laughing. She's so impatient. I swipe up, answering the call without looking as I dry my back. "I solved your riddle. You got me a ten-speed vibrator. It's called the Cowboy. And yes, I will test it tonight."

Silence.

Nothing but crickets for five long seconds. Then a throat clears.

A masculine throat.

Carter's handsome face looks out at me from the screen. "If that's a hint, I can leave right now and pick that up for you," he says, and when I look closer, I see my street behind him since he's on my front stoop.

I freeze, all my dignity evaporating with the shower steam.

I'm naked, and I just flashed my best friend my boobs.

BE A LOVELY

Want to be the first to know of sales, new releases, special deals and giveaways? Sign up for my newsletter today!

Want to be part of a fun, feel-good place to talk about books and romance, and get sneak peeks of covers and advance copies of my books? Be a Lovely!

MORE BOOKS BY LAUREN

I've written more than 100 books! **All of these titles below
are FREE in Kindle Unlimited!**

Double Pucked

A sexy, outrageous MFM hockey romantic comedy!

Puck Yes

A fake marriage, spicy MFM hockey rom com!

Thoroughly Pucked!

A fake marriage, spicy MFM hockey rom com!

The Virgin Society Series

Meet the Virgin Society – great friends who'd do anything for
each other. Indulge in these forbidden, emotionally-charged,
and wildly sexy age-gap romances!

The RSVP

The Tryst

The Tease

The Dating Games Series

A fun, sexy romantic comedy series about friends in the city
and their dating mishaps!

The Virgin Next Door

Two A Day

The Good Guy Challenge

How To Date Series (New and ongoing)

Four great friends. Four chances to learn how to date again. Four standalone romantic comedies full of love, sex and meet-cute shenanigans.

My So-Called Sex Life

Plays Well With Others

The Almost Romantic

A romantic comedy adventure standalone

A Real Good Bad Thing

Boyfriend Material

Four fabulous heroines. Four outrageous proposals. Four chances at love in this sexy rom-com series!

Asking For a Friend

Sex and Other Shiny Objects

One Night Stand-In

Overnight Service

Big Rock Series

My #1 New York Times Bestselling sexy as sin, irreverent, male-POV romantic comedy!

Big Rock

Mister O

Well Hung

Full Package

Joy Ride

Hard Wood

Happy Endings Series

Romance starts with a bang in this series of standalones following a group of friends seeking and avoiding love!

Come Again

Shut Up and Kiss Me

Kismet

My Single-Versary

Ballers And Babes

Sexy sports romance standalones guaranteed to make you hot!

Most Valuable Playboy

Most Likely to Score

A Wild Card Kiss

Rules of Love Series

Athlete, virgins and weddings!

The Virgin Rule Book

The Virgin Game Plan

The Virgin Replay

The Virgin Scorecard

The Extravagant Series

Bodyguards, billionaires and hoteliers in this sexy, high-stakes series of standalones!

One Night Only

One Exquisite Touch

My One-Week Husband

The Guys Who Got Away Series

Friends in New York City and California fall in love in this fun and hot rom-com series!

Birthday Suit

Dear Sexy Ex-Boyfriend

The What If Guy

Thanks for Last Night

The Dream Guy Next Door

Always Satisfied Series

A group of friends in New York City find love and laughter in this series of sexy standalones!

Satisfaction Guaranteed

Never Have I Ever

Instant Gratification

PS It's Always Been You

The Gift Series

An after dark series of standalones! Explore your fantasies!

The Engagement Gift

The Virgin Gift

The Decadent Gift

The Heartbreakers Series

Three brothers. Three rockers. Three standalone sexy romantic comedies.

Once Upon a Real Good Time

Once Upon a Sure Thing

Once Upon a Wild Fling

Sinful Men

A high-stakes, high-octane, sexy-as-sin romantic suspense series!

My Sinful Nights

My Sinful Desire

My Sinful Longing

My Sinful Love

My Sinful Temptation

From Paris With Love

Swoony, sweeping romances set in Paris!

Wanderlust

Part-Time Lover

One Love Series

A group of friends in New York falls in love one by one in this sexy rom-com series!

The Sexy One

The Hot One

The Knocked Up Plan

Come As You Are

Lucky In Love Series

A small town romance full of heat and blue collar heroes and sexy heroines!

Best Laid Plans

The Feel Good Factor

Nobody Does It Better

Unzipped

No Regrets

An angsty, sexy, emotional, new adult trilogy about one young couple fighting to break free of their pasts!

The Start of Us

The Thrill of It

Every Second With You

The Caught Up in Love Series

A group of friends finds love!

The Pretending Plot

The Dating Proposal

The Second Chance Plan

The Private Rehearsal

Seductive Nights Series

A high heat series full of danger and spice!

Night After Night

After This Night

One More Night

A Wildly Seductive Night

Joy Delivered Duet

A high-heat, wickedly sexy series of standalones that will set your sheets on fire!

Nights With Him

Forbidden Nights

Unbreak My Heart

A standalone second chance emotional roller coaster of a romance

The Muse

A magical realism romance set in Paris

Good Love Series of sexy rom-coms co-written with Lili Valente!

I also write MM romance under the name L. Blakely!

Hopelessly Bromantic Duet (MM)

Roomies to lovers to enemies to fake boyfriends

Hopelessly Bromantic

Here Comes My Man

Men of Summer Series (MM)

Two baseball players on the same team fall in love in a

forbidden romance spanning five epic years

Scoring With Him

Winning With Him

All In With Him

MM Standalone Novels

A Guy Walks Into My Bar

The Bromance Zone

One Time Only

The Best Men (Co-written with Sarina Bowen)

Winner Takes All Series (MM)

A series of emotionally-charged and irresistibly sexy
standalone MM sports romances!

The Boyfriend Comeback

Turn Me On

A Very Filthy Game

Limited Edition Husband

Manhandled

If you want a personalized recommendation, email me at
laurenblakelybooks@gmail.com!

CONTACT

I love hearing from readers! You can find me on TikTok at LaurenBlakelyBooks, Instagram at LaurenBlakely-Books, Facebook at LaurenBlakelyBooks, or online at LaurenBlakely.com. You can also email me at lauren blakelybooks@gmail.com